?

ROTATION
PLAN

DIRTY TRICKS

DIRTY TRICKS

Jo Carnegie

WINDSOR
PARAGON

First published 2011
by Corgi
This Large Print edition published 2011
by AudioGO Ltd
by arrangement with
Transworld Publishers

Hardcover   ISBN: 978 1 445 85800 5
Softcover   ISBN: 978 1 445 85801 2

British Library Cataloguing in Publication Data available

EAST SUSSEX	
03654638	
AudioGO	17.08.11
SEA 5	£19.99
LEW 09/12	1/16/on

Printed and bound in Great Britain by
MPG Books Group Limited

To Joe, my soundboard

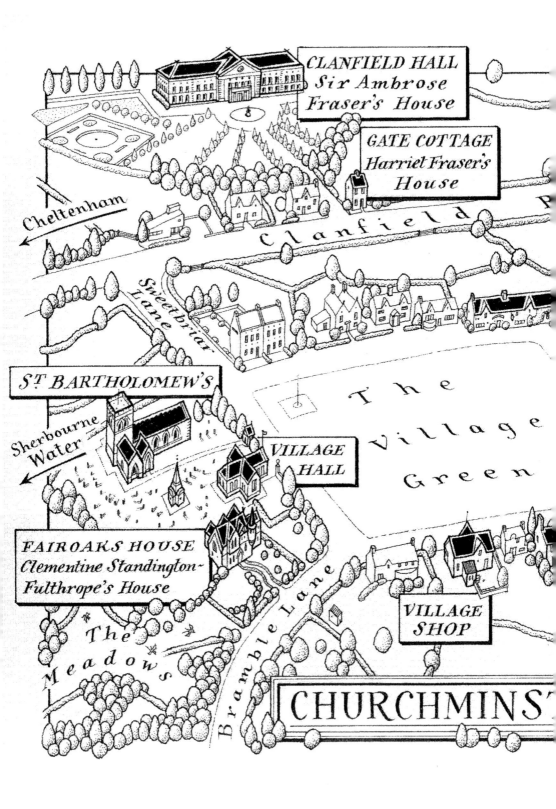

CLANFIELD HALL
Sir Ambrose
Fraser's House

GATE COTTAGE
Harriet Fraser's
House

Cheltenham

Clanfield R

Sweetbriar Lane

St BARTHOLOMEW'S

Sherbourne
Water

VILLAGE
HALL

The Village Green

FAIROAKS HOUSE
Clementine Standington~
Fulthrope's House

The Meadows

Bramble Lane

VILLAGE
SHOP

CHURCHMINST

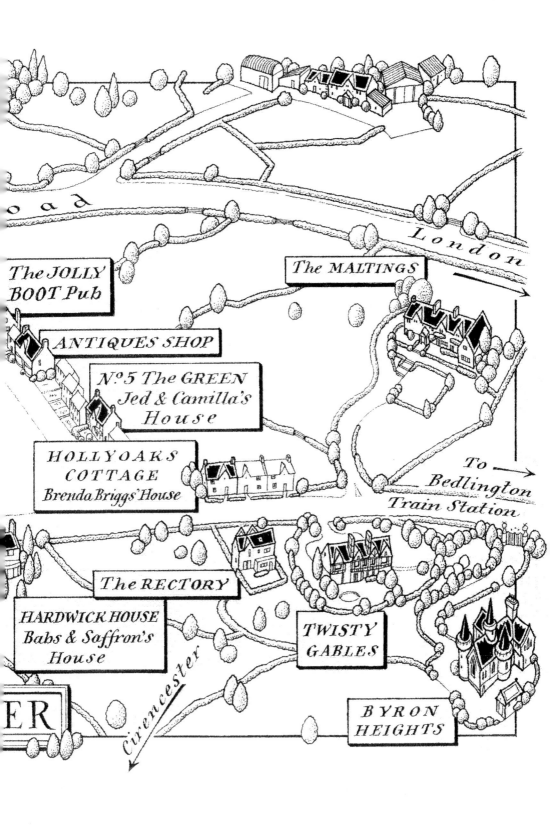

The JOLLY BOOT Pub

The MALTINGS

ANTIQUES SHOP

Nº5 The GREEN
Jed & Camilla's
House

HOLLYOAKS
COTTAGE
Brenda Briggs' House

To →
Bedlington
Train Station

The RECTORY

HARDWICK HOUSE
Babs & Saffron's
House

TWISTY
GABLES

BYRON
HEIGHTS

London

Cirencester

ER

JANUARY

Chapter 1

London

Click. She heard the front door close. Saffron lay back on the bed and waited.

'Saff?' The tread of his footsteps disappeared down the hall. 'Where are you?'

Saffron gave a little smile and adjusted the basque. Bloody thing was so tight she could hardly breathe. Still, no pain, no gain . . .

'I'm in here!'

The footsteps stopped. 'Saff?' There was a note of concern in his voice now. 'Are you OK?'

The bedroom door opened, to reveal the gorgeous sight of her boyfriend, Tom. 'Why are all the lights off . . . ?' He stopped dead. 'Oh.'

Saffron watched his eyes travel up and down her body, which was wearing nothing but Agent Provocateur's finest and her thigh-high, fuck-me boots. The candles placed round the room added a luminous sheen to her alabaster skin. Very slowly, she lifted one long leg and crossed it over the other. 'Have fun?'

His eyes filled up with lust. 'Not as much as I'm about to.' He advanced towards her, pulling off his jacket, then his sweater, whilst unbuttoning his belt buckle. Ten seconds later he was standing in front of her, six foot of pure man. Judging by his erection, her boots were working.

'Come here, big boy.'

Tom climbed on the bed and held her, hands testing the lace and satin.

'Where did this come from? I only went out to get the papers.'

'Does there need to be a reason?'

He grinned, eyes hungry. 'You look incredible.'

As their gaze locked, Saffron felt the ascent into sexual abandon begin.

'I love you, babe.'

'I love you too,' he murmured, covering her face in little kisses. He started to pull at her basque. 'I want to touch you,' he said.

'Let me,' she said, hurriedly unhooking the garment and throwing it across the room. Almost immediately, Tom's mouth was on her pert breasts, her flat white belly. Licking, sucking, his tongue going everywhere . . .

'Keep the boots on. I need you to keep the boots on,' he instructed. Saffron wrapped her legs round his broad back. She could feel his fingers inside her, slipping in and out of the wetness, but Saffron needed more. Sod foreplay, she just wanted to *do* it.

'Fuck me now,' she gasped.

Tom didn't need telling a second time. He nudged her legs open and, as he slid inside her, Saffron gave that little involuntary gasp she always did. Tom was *hung*. She pushed her hips up to accommodate him even more, feeling him fill up every inch of her.

'I want to ride you,' she told him a few minutes later.

In one easy movement, Tom pulled her on top. Saffron looked down at his deep soulful eyes, and strong beautiful face covered with sweat. His hands slid round her hips, grabbing the soft flesh of her buttocks. As she slid up and down his cock

Saffron felt the sensation mounting. 'Oh my God, I'm going to come.'

Underneath her, Tom's breathing had become intense and laboured. 'I've been wanting to for the last five minutes.'

Saffron was ready to let go. She felt the build-up in her groin, those wondrous few seconds before the main event, before it exploded through her body. Gripping with her knees, she arched her back, driving on to him, eking out every last second. An animalistic groan told her Tom had reached his orgasm at the same time. She flopped on to his chest, energy abruptly spent.

'I need to go to the gym more,' she gasped, feeling his heartbeat jump against hers. It was a full minute before Tom could speak.

'This is a very unholy way to spend a Sunday,' he said.

Saffron looked at him. 'It was a toss-up between this and the *Antiques Roadshow*,' she teased. Tom chuckled lazily, adorable dimples appearing in his cheeks. Saffron felt her heart melt. *You are so perfect*, she thought, throwing her arms round his neck.

*   *   *

Half an hour later, they untangled themselves from each other. Saffron's boots lay discarded by the side of the bed, like deflated black bin liners.

'What have we got in the fridge?' she asked. Sex always left her starving. She got up and went to pull on Tom's stripy dressing gown. A quick look in the mirror on the wall revealed a tousled mess of short, white-blonde hair and a rash round her mouth from Tom's weekend stubble. Saffron pulled a face.

'Look at the state of me. Why can't I be one of those girls with long, silky hair that fans out over the pillow?'

Tom put his hands behind his head, showcasing perfect biceps. 'Oh, I don't know. I think the pixie-on-crack look is quite sexy.'

'You cheeky sod!' she laughed, leaping on him.

He gave a mock groan. 'I think you've broken a rib.'

'I'll break more than that in a minute, mate,' she said, snuggling up to him.

Saffron loved their Sundays together in Tom's little flat off the Portobello Road. They both worked in magazines, and weekdays could go past in a blur of deadlines and work things. Weekends were precious, just the two of them. If they could be bothered, they'd get up and go for brunch round the corner, then spend the rest of the afternoon browsing quirky galleries and antique shops. More often than not, they wouldn't step foot outside except for the newspapers, just having lazy sex around the flat. Or fast, furious sex if they wanted it; despite his easy-going demeanour Tom was an animal in bed. Saffron had thought she had a high sex drive until she'd met him. She wasn't complaining, he was the best lover she'd ever had.

'So what do you fancy?' he asked her.

She shot him a saucy look. 'You.'

Tom raised an amused eyebrow. 'I mean, food.'

Saffron stretched out under the duvet. 'I think most things in the fridge have seen better days.'

'Do you want to go out?' he asked.

She pulled a face. 'That would involve showering

and dressing, I don't think I can be arsed.' She reached up and pulled the blind aside to look out the window. 'Anyway, it's minging out there. Let's get a takeaway.'

'My kind of thinking.' He stroked her arm. 'What's it going to be? Thai, Chinese, pizza?'

'I could murder a massaman.'

'That's a bit extreme.'

Saffron smiled. 'Stupid.'

Tom sat up. 'You know I never pass up curry. I think I've got a menu for that new place off Ladbroke Grove.'

'Sounds great.'

He got out of bed and walked across the room. As he picked up a leaflet on the chest of drawers, she propped herself up on her elbow to watch. She never got tired of looking at his body. Tom Fellows had high, sculpted buttocks and long muscled legs, and his stomach was free from the late-twenties spread catching up with most other blokes his age. Tom was a total hottie, but the best thing of all? He didn't even realize. It was one of the many things Saffron loved about her boyfriend. He turned and caught her looking. 'What?'

'Just checking your butt out.'

He shook his head, smiling. 'You want me to go and order?'

'Yes, please. Don't forget coconut rice. Oh, and can you get me some Tom Yum soup as well? And a bag of prawn crackers.'

'I've never met anyone who eats as much as you. Where does it all go?'

Saffron lifted the duvet to look at her flat stomach. 'One day I'll wake up as fat as a house. Will you still love me then?'

'Course I will, beautiful. Besides, I'll probably have a paunch and comb-over.'

Saffron looked at his thick dark hair. 'As if!'

'You never know.'

'I'd still love you if you were a baldie.'

Tom grinned and pulled on the Abercrombie & Fitch tracksuit bottoms Saffron had got him for Christmas. Fit. 'I'll go and call them. Do you want anything else in the meantime?'

'Cup of tea would be wonderful.'

He shot her a humorous look. 'What did your last slave die of?'

'Sex!' Saffron shouted after him, as he left the room. Smiling, she nuzzled back into the warmth of the bed. God, she was being a lazy bitch today. It was great. Her eyes travelled round the room. Tom's taste in decor pretty much matched his personality; laid back and modest. The walls were painted white, there was slightly shabby looking stripped-wood flooring, and the only splash of colour came from his beloved pop art originals on the walls. Aside from Saffron, they were the only things Tom ever really spent money on.

The flat still had the bare, spartan whiff of a bachelor pad, even though they'd been going out for nearly two years. In the beginning Saffron had vowed to put feminine touches round the place: fresh flowers from the market, scented candles. But when they were together, everything else had faded into insignificance. They'd spent hours talking and laughing, in the bath or on the sofa, watching back-to-back box sets of *True Blood* and *Mad Men*. The only thing they could agree on. Saffron thought of that very cosy sofa in the living room, the neat line of Tom's size 13 trainers by the front door. From nowhere, she felt a lump in her throat. She was going to miss it—and him—so much.

Her phone went off, making her jump. Saffron reached down and picked it up from the floor by the bed. When she saw who it was, she felt a mixture of pleasure and irritation. She answered it.

'Hi, Babs. I mean, Mum.'

It was still weird using the term 'mum' after so long.

'Darling!' The wavery voice gushed down the line. 'How are you? How's Tom?'

'We're both fine, thanks.'

'What are you two lovebirds up to? Gambolling like a pair of spring lambs in Hyde Park? Kissing the winter cold away on London Bridge?'

'Mum, have you been at the gin again?'

'Just a little Sunday sharpener! It frees my creative juices, you know.'

Saffron rolled her eyes. Babs Sax made her living as an artist, and from what Saffron had seen of her mother's art, it certainly looked as if it had been painted by someone several sheets to the wind. To say it was bizarre and surreal was an understatement.

'Anyway, I just phoned to see if you wanted me to get you anything special in.'

She stared at the ceiling. Babs was *really* going overboard with the doting mum thing. It was the sixth time she'd called this weekend.

'Nah, don't worry about it.'

'No little treats? How about some Jammy Dodgers? They're your favourite.'

'I went off them when I was twelve.' *If you'd been around then you'd have known that.*

9

Her mother gave an embarrassed laugh. 'Of course! How silly of me.'

Saffron suddenly felt guilty. She knew her mum was trying. 'Actually, Jammy Dodgers sound good.'

'I've got your bedroom all ready, and I've even given my latest painting pride of place over your bed!' Saffron winced; it was bound to give her nightmares. Just then there was a loud crash. 'What's that?' her mother said in alarm.

Saffron called towards the door. 'Everything OK?'

Tom's voice came back down the corridor. 'Dropped a plate. Sorry.' Lovely as he was, he seemed to break something in the kitchen on a regular basis.

'What was that noise?' her mother cried. 'Is someone trying to break in?'

'It's fine, Mum, no one's died. Tom just broke something. Look, I'd better go. We're about to eat.'

Her mother sounded a bit disappointed. 'Oh! Well at least we'll have all the time in the world to catch up when you're home. I am looking forward to it, you know! We'll have such fun, us two girls together.'

'Yay!' Saffron tried to sound chirpy. 'Well, I'll speak to you tomorrow or something? To sort everything out.'

'Wonderful! Bye, darling.'

'Bye, Mum.'

'Goodbye, darling!'

'Bye, Mum,' Saffron said pointedly. Her mother had got into this annoying habit of refusing to put the phone down first. It meant Saffron always cut her off in the end, and subsequently left every phone call they had feeling bad.

'Bye, bye!'

'Mum!' she said in exasperation. 'Will you just put the bloody phone down!'

'Of course, goodbye then!' There was a silence at the other end. Saffron could hear her mother breathing, waiting. She clenched her fists.

'Oh, for God's sake. GOODBYE!' she said and ended the call. She flopped back on the bed. 'Aarrgh!'

Tom came back in. 'What's wrong?'

Saffron sighed. 'Why is it even thirty seconds talking to my mum makes me feel pissed off? Then I feel guilty for acting like a stroppy teenager again!'

Tom gave a wry smile. 'Is this the same mother you are giving up your job to go and live in the country with?'

'Oh, don't!' Saffron wailed. She looked at him, eyes wide with realization at what lay ahead. 'Sweet baby Jesus, what have I done?'

Chapter 2

A few miles away in Chelsea, Saffron's friend Harriet Fraser was lying on her sofa watching a rerun of *Ugly Betty*. She'd meant to get up and go to the gym, but a few too many Chardonnays the night before had put paid to that. Instead Harriet had surfaced at 11 a.m., put her long coat over her pyjamas, and staggered to Tesco Metro for some comfort food. It was only when she'd got home and looked in the hallway mirror that she'd realized the remnants from last night's chilli kebab were still stuck to her chin. No wonder the cashier had looked at her oddly.

Harriet shuffled into the kitchen and dumped the bag on the work surface. A growing mountain of empty wine bottles was stacked by the bin, still waiting to be recycled. Harriet flushed guiltily; she really had to do something about it.

Her New Year's resolution to lose her booze belly wasn't going well. She peered into the fridge at the Waitrose luxury meals for one on the shelf, and the wilting bunch of vegetables in the cooler. As usual they'd slowly rotted away, shrivelling along with her good intentions. She chucked the unopened packets of salad and cabbage in the bin, feeling even more ashamed. How could she be so wasteful?

The only thing that would make her feel half decent was a hot bath and her much-thumbed copy of *Emma*. Despite living in the bright lights of London, Harriet always felt happier in the cosy, chaste romantic world of books, where men were gentlemen, and relationships were lived out through balls in country-houses and stolen kisses in water meadows. She made her way down the fluffy carpeted hallway to the bathroom, the space dominated by the huge, gilt-framed hunting scenes her parents had insisted on giving her when she'd moved to the city.

As she turned on the bathroom light she winced at her reflection. With her sweet, soft face and huge brown eyes Harriet was a pretty, homely girl, her cheeks still rosy from the country air she had grown up in. Today, it had to be said, she wasn't looking her best. As well as still wearing last night's make-up and kebab, she had one dangly earring in. What on earth had she done with the other one? Sleep patterns tracked across her right cheek from where she'd passed out face first on her John Lewis embroidered cushion. *I'm thirty-five years old*, she thought despairingly. *Too old to be doing this.*

She looked at the line of expensive potions lining her bathroom counter. Eve Lom cleanser, Crème de la Mer moisturizer, the latest miracle serum. All courtesy of her job working at *Soirée* magazine, Britain's most famous glossy. In her job as PA and events coordinator, Harriet was sent extravagant gifts on a daily basis. Not that they seemed to be helping at the moment. *I don't even know what half of them are supposed to be for*, she thought, as she picked up some exotically-named cream that promised to get rid of free radicals and enzymes.

An hour and a face mask later, Harriet was feeling marginally more human. Dressed in her fluffy dressing gown and slippers, she walked into the living room. It was gorgeous, with a Victorian fireplace, high ceilings and a bay window looking out on to the tree-lined street. Harriet had worked hard to make it cosy, giving it soft cream carpets and a squidgy three-piece suite from Laura Ashley. She flopped back down on the sofa and stared up at the ceiling. Flashes of the previous night kept coming back to her. She and her friend Cecily had been in a wine bar off Kensington High Street, and Harriet had a vague, unpleasant memory of chatting to a man with extremely large front teeth about the merits of Range Rovers versus all other 4x4s. As far as she could remember, his name had been Guy, he'd had terribly bad breath, and kept

13

trying to shove his tongue down her throat at the bar. Harriet shuddered. She must stop spending all night in pointless conversations with men who weren't her type. It was no way to meet her future husband.

Harriet sighed. For some reason she was dreading work tomorrow. Normally she loved her job, coordinating the editor's diary, running the office and organizing all the *Soirée* parties, but lately she'd started feeling rather empty. Surely there was more to life than work and hangovers?

She wondered if she felt like this because her mother Frances, Lady Fraser of Clanfield Hall, Churchminster, had gone off to do volunteer work in Africa. Harriet still couldn't imagine her mother, an elegant Joanna Lumley lookalike, knee-deep in mud building sanitation blocks for orphans, but from what she'd heard, Lady Fraser was having the time of her life. 'Darling, I only wish I'd done it sooner! It's so good to push one's boundaries in life,' Frances had written on a battered postcard from somewhere in Kenya.

A loud trilling made her sit up. It took several moments before Harriet realized it was the noise of her landline. It was bound to be her father: no one but her parents used it, and her mother was thousands of miles away with no phone reception. Sir Ambrose had also been calling her practically every day since Lady Fraser had left, which was unheard of. Harriet suspected he was feeling rather lonely, not that he'd ever admit it.

'Hello, Daddy.'

'What's that?' her father barked impatiently down the phone. 'How did you know it was me?'

'Just a guess. Oh, that and caller ID.' Harriet

14

settled herself back on the sofa. 'How are you?'

'I'm bloody bored, Harriet! What am I supposed to do when Frances has gone gallivanting off to some godforsaken country and left me?'

Harriet smiled. 'Come on, Daddy, you're just as proud of her as I am.'

'Harrumph!' her father said begrudgingly. 'Well, anyway. What's a man supposed to do round here?'

'You live in one of the most beautiful places in the country!' Harriet pointed out, laughing. Clanfield Hall, the family seat, was a fifty-bedroom stately home that sat on the outskirts of a pretty Cotswolds village. 'There are lots of things to do.'

'Done them all. If I take one more walk round the trout lake I'll turn into a trout myself.' Her father paused. 'The last time I spoke to your mother she told me I should take up an evening class. An evening class! She says I need to "broaden my mind".'

Harriet thought her mum had a point. Her father's world did seem to consist of dogs, horse-racing and tramping the estate grounds with his shotgun. 'Maybe it would be a good idea,' she pointed out tactfully.

'What a load of old rubbish! It's the blasted evenings that get me, though, Harriet. Rattling around this place by oneself. I never thought I'd say this, but I miss the old girl giving me a flea in my ear.'

Harriet felt a pang of homesickness. She hated the thought of her father in the Hall by himself. Even if they did have their band of faithful staff, it wasn't the same thing. 'Why don't you have a cards evening and invite some of your friends over? I haven't heard you talk about Percival Drummond for ages.'

'That's because he's dead.' Her father, at nearly eighty, found that his circle of friends was starting to diminish by the year. Sir Ambrose himself, meanwhile, remained as combative as a terrier with a stick.

'Oh! I'm sorry, I didn't realize.'

'Don't be, old Percy was a dreadful bore. Bad loser as well.' Her father moved on to his favourite subject. 'Got yourself a chap yet?'

'Not since you asked me yesterday.'

Sir Ambrose gave another 'harrumph'. 'You're not getting any younger! Fine sturdy girl from good stock like you, I can't understand why you're not married. I suppose that's London for you.'

Harriet bit her lip. She felt guilty enough being his only child—and a girl at that. If her father couldn't have a handsome, crack-shot son and heir, then the least she could do was marry someone who was handsome and handy with a twelve-bore shotgun. Trouble was, there didn't seem to be that many of them around. It wasn't as if she hadn't been looking.

She changed the subject. 'Guess what? Saffron's coming to Churchminster next week! I'm sure she'll come and visit you at the Hall.'

'Who?'

'*Saffron*, Daddy. She came to stay with us for Christmas that time, remember? Remember—I told you, she's taking a break from work to write a novel, so she's moving back in with her mum, Babs Sax.'

By complete coincidence Saffron's mother lived in the pretty Cotswolds village Harriet had grown

16

up in.

'What? Moving in with that madwoman? She must be off her trolley herself!' Sir Ambrose was being especially irascible today.

'Saffron needs somewhere peaceful to write her book,' Harriet said patiently.

Her father gave a guffaw of laughter. 'Since when has that bloody village been peaceful? From what your mother's told me there's a new scandal every week.' Sir Ambrose rarely went to Churchminster to mix with the locals.

Harriet smiled. 'Daddy, it's not that bad compared to other places! Remember when Wootton-under-Edge had that mystery knicker pincher last year? No washing line was safe.'

'*Knicker pincher?* I've heard it all now. Mark my words. If Saffron's coming to Churchminster in search of peace and quiet, she's in for a nasty shock.'

Chapter 3

Tom kissed Saffron goodbye. He tasted of toothpaste and loveliness, and all the good things in her life. 'I'll be back about 7 p.m. You are going to get up before then, aren't you?'

'Ha ha,' said Saffron, but suddenly staying under the security of the duvet seemed very appealing.

Tom paused by the door and smiled. 'I'll call you at lunch.'

She blew him a kiss. 'I'll have dinner waiting!' Moments later she heard the door bang.

Saffron swung her legs out of bed, shivering.

17

Why did boys never feel the cold? The flat's heating was very temperamental. Pulling a sweater over her head, she put her feet in Tom's enormous slippers and shuffled through to the kitchen. Her heart melted when she saw that he'd laid out breakfast for her, complete with a paper rose lying on her place mat. Origami was one of his many talents.

Saffron walked over to the sink to fill up the kettle. Leroy, the misshapen cactus she and Tom had randomly found on the street outside, was sitting in his usual place on the windowsill. Leroy had flourished under their care, and they joked that the cactus was like their adopted child. As Tom had pointed out, the thing was so ugly only a parent would love it.

Kettle full, she took it back over and switched it on, and the noise of the water heating up was a welcome distraction. It was so *quiet*. Saffron looked at the clock on the wall. Nine o'clock on a Monday morning. This time last week she was walking to work, Starbucks coffee in one hand, her mobile ringing incessantly in the other. Now all she had to think about was packing for her new life—and her leaving party later that week. Suddenly her future felt like a terrifying empty chasm.

The kettle came to the boil, but she didn't notice. She was lost in thought. As features editor at *Soirée*, Saffron Walden had one of the best jobs in the industry. She interviewed A-list celebrities, went on glamorous press trips all over the world and had her name on every VIP list in town. She still couldn't believe she was taking a six-month sabbatical from it all to go and live in the country

18

and write a novel. Saffron was a city girl through and through, who loved late nights and pop-up bars, worshipping at the shrine of Marc Jacobs and Top Shop. Now she was about to move to a place that counted a village shop and postbox amongst its main attractions.

She'd agonized over the plan for ages, talking it through with Tom to make sure she was doing the right thing, working out whether she could live off her savings. More importantly, would she have a job to come back to? But with her late twenties fast approaching, Saffron knew it was now or never. Luckily, when she'd finally plucked up the courage to talk to *Soirée*'s editor, a down-to-earth woman called Fiona MacKenzie, Fiona had been open to the idea, having done a similar thing early in her career. She understood Saffron's desire to go and find out if she had that book in her. 'Just don't become a best-selling author too soon. We need you!' Fiona had joked.

The book, *Gloss*, was something Saffron had been thinking about for a while. The main character was a magazine journalist much like herself, called Serendipity Swift, who falls in love with a rock star she interviews. Not that Saffron had ever done *that*. She was too savvy, and had been in the game long enough to know that business and pleasure just didn't mix, no matter how hot the subject matter. She'd even found a literary agent, Pamela Aston, who was wildly enthusiastic about *Gloss*, and declared it was just what the market was looking for. 'Sex, power and glamour, Saffron, that's what women want to read about!' It was a better beginning than she could ever have imagined.

It had been her Aunt Velda who'd started the ball rolling. Saffron had lived with her since she'd been a teenager, when she and her mother had had their big falling out. When Velda had thought of relocating to Morocco for six months to paint, Saffron had seen it as a sign. This was the perfect time to go off and write her novel! But where? She needed to get away from the distractions of London, but she didn't want to be too far from Tom.

She'd been horrified at first, when her aunt had suggested she move in with her mother. They might be speaking for the first time in years, but Saffron wasn't going to ruin it all by moving in with Babs. Cash funds—and the one-off chance to spend proper time with her mum—had finally swayed her. It would be a good chance for them to reconnect and get to know each other again, and the little country cottage would give Saffron the quiet writing environment she needed. Babs, ecstatically happy since Saffron had let her back into her life, was over the moon. Saffron wasn't quite so excited. She hadn't lived with her mother since she was nine years old and had been sent off to boarding school. Babs hadn't exactly been Mum of the Year back then. What if nothing had changed?

As she started to pour the water into a cup, her thoughts wandered to Tom. Saffron felt a pang at the thought of leaving him. She'd only been living here a few weeks—since Aunt Velda had gone and they'd rented the place out—but already it felt like they'd been in domestic bliss for ever.

She and Tom had met at work, when she'd been the party-mad features writer and he'd been the archetypal office geek. The two had ended up embarking on an unlikely friendship, which eventually blossomed into something more, especially after Tom had undergone a radical makeover. No one could believe what a stunning young man had been lurking under the bottle-top glasses and student baggy clothes.

Tom was still by no means cutting edge—he did his yearly shop at GAP and had his hair cut at the barber's round the corner—but he had an inherent handsomeness that turned heads even in the hard, fast streets of London.

On paper they were polar opposites. Saffron was funky and outgoing, someone who loved kitsch pop music and trashy TV shows like loud *Keeping Up With The Kardashians*. Tom was quieter and more reserved, whose ideal night was spent in front of the television with a BBC4 art programme or *Newsnight*. (Although he did have a secret passion for *X Factor*). But somehow it worked. Tom was different from the pretty, shallow boys Saffron had gone for before. If she admitted it, superficial relationships were all Saffron had ever wanted before. She'd always found it hard to let people in, but there was a strength, a *goodness* about Tom that made her feel calm and happy. Her party pals might take the piss, saying she'd turned into an old married woman now, but for once Saffron didn't care about what she might be missing out on. Tom was so funny and thoughtful, so intelligent and sexy that she'd fallen for him hook, line and sinker. Nearly two years on, Saffron was more madly in love than ever.

Tom had been supportive about her moving away for six months, just as she'd known he would be. It had come at a good stage in their relationship: he'd just landed a promotion as art director on an aspirational new men's magazine called *Dex*, due to launch in September that year. Launches were notorious for their long hours and hard work, and the editor, Jeff Goulding, was known as a brilliant but hard taskmaster. Tom would be pretty much tied to his desk, but he would come out to the country as many weekends as he could. It was going to be tough, but Saffron knew they'd get through it. It was a really important time for both of them.

Saffron took a sip of lukewarm tea and wrinkled her nose. She padded over to the microwave and put the mug in to heat it up. As she watched the cup revolve the excitement started to grow inside her. She was taking the plunge and really doing it! 'Saffron Walden, best-selling novelist!' she said out loud.

Her laughter echoed round the empty room.

Chapter 4

Harriet took a deep breath and dialled the number. It rang and rang, and she was about to put the phone down when a gruff male voice answered.

'Gatsby Road Community Centre.'

'Er, is that the Gatsby Road Community Centre?' she asked.

'That's what I said.' The voice sounded slightly amused. It was a London accent, deep and gravelly round the edges.

'Oh, of course,' Harriet said, feeling flustered.

'Can I help you with anything?' he asked bluntly. 'Only we're pretty busy down here tonight . . .'

'Um, yes, that's what I was phoning about, actually. My name's Harriet Fraser. I'm interested in doing some volunteer work with you . . .'

The man perked up. 'You want to come and join us on the front line, eh?'

'Excuse me?'

'In-joke, sorry. I'm Zack Doyle, I run the centre. To be honest, Harriet . . .' He pronounced her name in a rather unusual formal way. 'Your call couldn't have come at a better time. We're desperate for an extra pair of hands.' He paused. 'How did you hear about us?'

'A friend told me. Well, it was my old boss, actually. She does volunteer work herself.'

Zack sounded pleased. 'Word seems to be spreading, then.' She heard rustling in the background. 'I'll just get a pen . . . Right. Can you tell me a bit about yourself? You know, why you want to volunteer, and all that. We'll need to run some checks on you.' A smile entered his voice. 'You never know who's an axe murderer these days, do you?'

When Harriet put the phone down fifteen minutes later she felt rather sick. Everything was happening so fast and she hadn't had time to think about it properly. The previous editor at *Soirée*, Catherine Connor, now worked for a young person's charity. Harriet had always got on well with her, and when she'd tentatively emailed Catherine about volunteer work Catherine had thought it was a brilliant idea. Harriet had been thinking along the lines of walking old people's

23

dogs or working in a charity shop, but Catherine had had other ideas. The Gatsby Road Community Centre (or GRCC as it was more commonly known) was the first place she had suggested.

'We've done some work with them, I think you'll love it,' Catherine had told her. 'The estate it is on had a bit of a bad rep before, but don't let that put you off. They're doing great things down there.'

When Harriet had Googled it to find out more, she'd had a bit of a shock. Catherine wasn't wrong when she said the estate had a dubious history. The Gatsby Road Estate in Camden, North London, was notorious for its riots against the police in the 1990s. Two decades on, things seemed to have quietened down, although Harriet did feel a bit worried when she read the Met had smashed a major drugs ring there only last year. Her father would have a fit if he knew.

She might not even *make* it there. The talk of background checks had made her nervous. She'd once got a speeding ticket back home when her muddy Hunter welly had slipped on the accelerator, and she'd flown past a police car at 60 mph in a 30-limit zone. What if that was enough to disqualify her?

PMA, she told herself. *Positive mental attitude.* If her past didn't throw up something horrible, and they let her in, she was going to give it a go. What had her mother said about pushing one's boundaries? And Zack had sounded quite friendly. From his voice Harriet imagined a short, cheery man with a pot belly. At the very least, she told herself, volunteer work had to be better than staying in and drunkenly stalking attractive-looking men on Facebook.

* * *

It was Wednesday evening and Saffron and Tom were in their favourite local restaurant, which they called Drama Pizza. Its real name was Marco's, but every time they went there, there seemed to be a major catastrophe going on in the kitchen, the owner Marco running round like a headless chicken. It only added to the atmosphere: the food was excellent, the carafes of wine free-flowing, and every customer was treated like a member of the family. They'd had some of their best times together here, talking and eating into the night. It seemed fitting to choose it for their last meal together before Saffron left London.

Tom poured out two large glasses of the house red. 'Here's to you and your fantastically successful new career.'

Saffron smiled at him over the table. 'Thanks, babe. Now all I have to do is write the thing.' She took a glug, and then gave a little sigh.

He knew her too well by now. 'What's wrong?'

Saffron toyed with her glass. 'Oh, I don't know. Everything's so perfect, you know, with us. I'm worried . . . about how things will change when I move away.'

Tom grinned reassuringly. 'It won't change anything. It's not like Churchminster is a million miles away, and I'll be down as much as I can.'

She glanced up. 'You're being really good about this.'

Tom looked surprised. 'Why shouldn't I be? You've wanted to write a book for ages, and now

25

you're following your dream. I think it's a really amazing thing to do, Saff.'

She gave a mock pout. 'Aren't you going to miss me?'

Tom laughed. 'I'm not sure if I'll miss you turning the bathroom into a boudoir.' In the short space of time she'd been there, Saffron's clothes and make-up had rather taken over the flat.

'Oi! That's my stuff. I need it. Besides, who did I catch using my Origins eye cream the other night?'

He grabbed hold of her hand, smiling. 'Of course I'll miss you. *Really* miss you. But it's only for six months, and you'll be back here before you know it.'

Men were so practical. Saffron grinned, feeling better. 'I've got to stop being so wet. I guess I've just got last-minute nerves.'

'I have complete faith in you. You're one of the most determined people I know.' He changed the subject, dark eyes mischievous. 'Do you think we'll have separate bedrooms at Babs's? I might have to come and pounce on you in the middle of the night.'

'I bloody hope not!' Saffron didn't want to think about it.

Tom started rummaging around in the breadbasket, for his fifth piece of ciabatta. 'H is coming to your party, right? I haven't seen her for ages.'

'Yup, all the *Soirée* lot are coming. Have I told you she's signed up for volunteer work?'

'Doing what?' he said through a mouthful of carbonara.

'Some community centre on an estate in Camden. Guntsby Road or something.'

'You mean the Gatsby Road? I remember watching a doc about that on the riots.'

Saffron looked alarmed. 'Riots?'

'They were years ago.'

'I hope she'll be all right.' Even though Harriet was a good few years older than her, Saffron still felt protective towards her friend. 'H isn't the most streetwise of people, she's barely set foot out of south-west London before!'

'Course she'll be OK. They'll love her. Everyone loves Harriet.' Tom looked down at his pocket. 'My phone, sorry, I forgot to turn it off.'

'No worries.' Saffron watched as he pulled it out. A look of surprise crossed his face. 'It's my brother.'

'Your brother? He never calls.'

It wasn't every day someone had a supermodel twin for a brother, but Tom had been typically low-key about it. Saffron, on the other hand, had nearly fallen off her bar stool when he told her. And not only were they twins, but identical ones at that. Of course, she'd seen the similarity *then*, but Tom generally managed to avoid other people making the connection. Unlike his more famous sibling, he had no desire to be in the spotlight.

The name Rex Sullivan might not mean much to the average punter on the street (even though they might recognize the face and abs), but to someone like Saffron who worked in the industry, he was a big deal. Rex had been just another run-of-the-mill model trying to make it in London, until he'd decamped to the States five years ago to try his luck. There he'd taken his mother's maiden name, hit the gym and never looked back. The Americans had loved the classic, English good looks that

27

fitted in perfectly with the chiselled, clean-cut US market. Ralph Lauren had gone wild for him, Hollister had used him on countless billboards and for the last two years Rex had been the face of the coveted Frontline campaign, America's biggest clothing line. He was also dating Paulina Polansky, who was the face (and body) of the women's range, and the pair could be seen draped erotically across each other in various fashion magazines. In short, Rex Sullivan was an ad man's wet dream.

'He probably wants something,' Tom said. 'Do you mind if I take it?'

Saffron shook her head. 'Course not.'

As Tom left the noisy room, Saffron pulled a piece of bread out of the basket and started chewing thoughtfully. In the whole time she'd been going out with Tom she'd never met Rex. Tom didn't have a bad word to say about his brother. In fact he didn't have much to say about him at all, which Saffron thought was a bit weird seeing as they were twins. Then again they did live totally different lives, three thousand miles apart and everyone knew boys were crap at keeping in touch. From what she'd read in the American gossip mags Rex seemed to be a bit of a playboy, partying hard with the beautiful people and going from one girlfriend to the next. What was that story she'd read once about him being found in a bathful of champagne with one of the girls from *The City*?

To be fair, if Tom did call Rex he always seemed to be out somewhere, or unavailable and would forget to call back. Saffron wasn't sure if she liked the sound of him but Tom typically refused to get worked up about his brother's behaviour, saying it was 'just Rex'. 'Just Rex' sounded like quite a handful.

He returned a few minutes later, bringing a gust of cold air.

'Everything all right?' she asked.

Tom sat down. 'Kind of. He's finished with Paulina. I think he just rang up for a chat.'

'What happened?'

'They had some big argument; he didn't really go into it.' Tom paused. 'Shame, I thought he was quite into this one.'

'He'll bounce back.'

'Yeah, sounds like he was the one who finished it.'

Saffron digested this information. Paulina Polansky had the body of an Amazon, and the face and hair of a blonde angel. 'Blimey, I bet that's the first time she's been dumped!'

'Hmm.' Tom shook his head ironically. 'Who'd date a supermodel, eh?'

He picked up the bottle and began refilling their glasses.

'That's going to be a bit awkward, isn't it?' she asked. 'I mean, them working together.'

His eyes twinkled. 'Never fall for someone you work with, hey?'

Saffron smiled. 'She'll be after you next, wanting sloppy seconds.'

He looked up. 'Who will?'

Saffron grinned. 'Paulina Polansky.'

Tom laughed. 'No chance of that. I'm yours, Saffron Walden.'

She felt her heart melt. 'And I'm yours, Tom Fellows.'

His eyes were full of love and warmth. 'For always.'

Chapter 5

Next day, Saffron was packing up the last of her clothes when there was a commotion outside. As horns blared and angry shouts were heard, Saffron peered out of the living room window to see what was going on. Her stomach dropped when she saw the flame-red hair of her mother in the front of a huge transit van going the wrong way down the one-way street. Saffron stared as Babs attempted to reverse-park into a space clearly destined for a Smart Car. In front of her a line of traffic was building up, one cabbie hanging out of his window shaking his fist.

What is she doing? Saffron cringed as her mother managed to shoehorn the vehicle in, one back tyre hanging off the kerb. Saffron watched as, oblivious to the angry stares of the other drivers as they squeezed past, her mother clambered down from the vehicle and floated across the road. She was wearing a long, tatty fur coat, her dyed red hair wilder than ever. Her spindly legs, encased in thick black tights and what looked like orthopaedic walking shoes, dangled beneath the coat like two pieces of thread.

Babs was now wandering off in the wrong direction, her head fluttering like some kind of manic sparrow as she squinted at the house numbers. Saffron groaned: *Like, how many times had she been here?* She ran to the front door, stuck her head out, and hissed. 'Mum! Over here!'

Babs swirled round, looking confused. When she saw Saffron her face broke into a huge grin. 'Dear heart! I knew it was around here somewhere.' She broke into a tottering jog, arms outstretched. Arriving on the doorstep in a cloud of sickly sweet perfume, she clasped Saffron to her bony breast. 'How are you?'

Despite the upheaval Babs had caused, Saffron was pleased to see her. She eventually managed to wriggle out of her vice-like grip. 'How are you, Mum?'

'All the better for seeing you!' Babs peered down the hallway. 'No Tom?'

'No, he's at work.'

'*Work*,' said Babs, as if going to the office was an alien concept. She looked up and down at Saffron. 'I adore your outfit! Are you wearing it for the party?'

Saffron didn't know whether to be exasperated or amused.

'These are my pyjamas, Mum.' Even though it was 3 p.m. she still hadn't got dressed yet. Saffron watched as Babs peeled off her moth-eaten coat. Underneath she was wearing a lime-green tunic. Even though she was rake thin, her presence seemed to fill the flat. Saffron looked back out of the window at the badly parked van. 'Mum, what on earth is that for?'

Babs followed her gaze. 'It's the van to take all your things home in, darling! I hired it especially, there was no way everything was going to fit in my MG.'

'But I've only got a few suitcases! It's not like I'm moving in with you for ever.'

Babs's smile faltered. 'I just thought that was what parents did, you know, like when they pick their children up from university.'

There it was again, the unintentional guilt trip. Saffron bit her lip. 'Good thinking, Mum. I always have more stuff than I think.'

Babs looked happier. 'Is everything ready for your party later?'

'Nearly. I'm just about to send the guest list over.'

'Trust you to put on a top-notch bash! What time does it start?'

Saffron looked at her watch. 'I want to be there by 6 p.m., so we've got a few hours.' She gazed at her mother quizzically. 'Are you sure you're going to be OK to drive back to Churchminster tonight?'

'Of course! There's no point in paying for a hotel room. Anyway, the weather forecast says it's going to be sunny in the south west tomorrow, and I want to make sure I catch the light.' Babs beamed. 'I'm working on something stunning at the moment.'

Saffron still wasn't convinced, especially as there was going to be free alcohol at the party. 'You're not going to drink, are you?'

Babs looked horrified. 'Darling! With such a precious cargo to take back?'

Saffron couldn't help but smile. Her mother was mad, but she was quite endearing. Sometimes. 'Come on, I'll make you a cup of tea.'

Her mother was right about one thing. Saffron knew how to put on a good party. Her job made sure she was a well-known face on the London scene. Over the years she had built up a bulging contacts book, and a farewell party was the perfect chance to get all her friends together, as well as the *Soirée* crew. Saffron had pulled out all the stops to make sure she left London with a bang.

As the taxi drove her and Babs into Central London the nerves set in. People were only just starting to venture out after the New Year lockdown. What if no one turned up?

The minute she walked into the exclusive bar off Regent Street, she calmed down. Of course people were going to come. Coco's was *the* place to be seen at the moment, and as Saffron knew the owner she'd got it free for the night, in return for filling it full of the beautiful and well-connected. It was a fabulous space: a high vaulted room with glittering chandeliers and a long, sweeping mirrored bar.

The owner, Sammy, had even devised a special 'Sexy Saffron' cocktail: a potent concoction of vodka, apple juice and a Lychee Martini. The tall glasses stood lined up on the bar, waiting for the thirsty punters to come in. In the DJ booth, a short, nondescript man in a T-shirt was busy getting records out of a box. He gave Saffron a nod and she grinned back; DJ Rev was one of London's coolest DJs, and getting him had been a major coup.

Sammy himself, a little man dressed all in black and sporting a goatee, was waiting for them. 'Saffron, darling!' he said, kissing her on both cheeks. He stepped back to admire her Balenciaga rip-off dress and the towering Louboutins on her feet. 'You look fabulous. Just like Agyness Deyn's better-looking sister!'

'Ahh, thanks, Sammy.' Her mother was hovering at her side expectantly. Saffron hesitated. 'This is my, er, Barbara.'

'I'm Saffron's mummy but you *must* call me Babs!' her mother exclaimed, grasping Sammy's

33

hand. She had swapped her green tunic for something lurid and multicoloured, and her hair had been backcombed to within an inch of its life. As she smiled at Sammy, Saffron spotted the red lipstick all over her front teeth. From the look of it, Babs must have reapplied it just as the cabbie took a sharp right turn.

Thankfully, Sammy didn't bat an eyelid. 'Pleased to meet you.'

The front door banged behind them, and all three turned to find a red-faced Harriet. She'd promised to come down with Saffron, but had got held up at work. 'Sorry I'm late,' she said as she rushed up, unwinding her pashmina from round her neck.

'Hey, no worries.' Saffron grinned. 'I know some sad people still have to work.' She added expectantly, 'How is everyone?'

'Dying to see you, they'll be down soon. Fiona sends her apologies, of course, but says she'll be toasting you from the beach.' *Soirée*'s editor had just flown off to Mauritius for two weeks.

'God, I'd like to fly off somewhere this precise moment!'

Harriet smiled. 'The party is going to be great.' She unbuttoned her trench coat and breathed out. 'Phew, that's better!'

'Let me get you ladies a drink,' Sammy said.

As he withdrew Babs threw her arms round Harriet. 'Dearest! How are you?'

'Good, thanks,' Harriet said, suffocating in the tight embrace. Over Babs's shoulder she took in Saffron's outfit properly for the first time. 'And you look amazing, Saff! You must be six foot in those heels!'

34

Saffron looked down at the patent black heels. 'Thanks, H. If I'm going to be living in wellies from now on, I thought I'd better make an effort.'

Harriet looked at her friend fondly. 'Oh, I am going to miss you!'

'Promise me you'll come to Churchminster lots!' Saffron implored her.

'Of course! Daddy is due a visit anyway.'

Sammy reappeared with three tall cocktails. 'Ladies.' Saffron watched to see if her mother would take one, and was pleasantly surprised when she didn't.

'My good man, do you have something soft instead?' Babs said, flashing a proud look at Saffron. 'I'm the designated driver tonight.'

Just then half the *Soirée* team burst through the door, laughing and shouting. The flamboyant fashion director, Alexander Napier, was incongruously carrying a large inflatable penis under his arm, and when he saw Saffron, he waved it enthusiastically. 'Bon soir, darling! Look what I've brought you!

Saffron looked back at Sammy and gave a weak smile. 'They'll behave themselves, honest.'

*   *   *

An hour later the party was in full swing. The question everyone wanted to ask Saffron was what kind of book she was writing. 'Is it like Marian Keyes?' Alexander asked. 'I adore her!'

Saffron shook her head. 'It's a bit more racy than that. Think Jackie Collins mixed with Jilly Cooper.'

Alexander's perfectly groomed eyebrows shot up

in excitement. 'A bonkbuster! You dirty bitch. I love it!'

Even Saffron's party pals had turned up. It was quite a feat, considering most of them wouldn't consider even starting the night before midnight. One of them, a striking black girl called Jasmine, with half her head shaved, came over to chat. 'Hey, girl, great party.'

Saffron grinned. 'Praise indeed!'

Jasmine gave a throaty chuckle, courtesy of hundreds of fun-filled late nights. 'Hey, I had to come and check it out. Saffron Walden, swapping her Manolos for a pair of smelly old wellies!'

'As if, Jas. Besides, it's only for six months.'

Jasmine pulled a face. 'Six months too long, as far as I'm concerned.' She scanned the room. 'Where's that delicious boyfriend of yours?'

'On his way. He had to work late.'

Jasmine licked her fire-engine-red lips. 'If you need anyone to look after him while you're away . . .'

'I'm sure he'll be fine, thanks, Jas,' said Saffron firmly. Her friend might be good company, but she was a full-on maneater.

Jasmine shot her a naughty look. 'Just a friendly gesture. Heaven knows, darling, if I had someone like Tom, I wouldn't let him out of my sight!'

'Yes, well, Tom and I don't have to live in each other's pockets,' Saffron said, feeling slightly annoyed.

Another chuckle. 'I'm only winding you up!' From the glint in her eye, Saffron was sure that she wasn't.

*   *   *

36

Across the room Harriet was talking to Catherine Connor, who had made a surprise appearance. Looking at her relaxed, glowing face, Harriet could hardly connect it to the stressed, rundown *Soirée* editor-in-chief of two years ago. Swapping the power suit for charity work definitely suited her.

Catherine took a sip of her cocktail. 'Have you thought anything more about the Gatsby Road Community Centre?'

Harriet nodded. 'I've spoken with the guy who runs it, someone called Zack. He says they're desperate for people.' She gave a nervous smile. 'I'm a bit worried about all that riot stuff, I must admit.'

'Don't be,' Catherine reassured her. 'It's a different place down there now, and half of it was newspaper hysteria, anyway. You'll be fine.'

There was raucous laughter from the *Soirée* corner, and suddenly the inflatable dildo came sailing across the room towards them. 'Sorry, Catherine!' someone shouted.

Smile twitching, she turned back to Harriet. 'If you can manage to keep that lot in check every day, Gatsby Road is going to be a walk in the park.'

Saffron was just starting to get a bit annoyed and anxious about her missing-in-action boyfriend, when she felt a pair of lips brush her neck. She turned round to face an enormous bunch of flowers. 'I'm really sorry, Saff, I couldn't get away.'

She couldn't be cross with him. 'It doesn't matter, you're here now.'

He held the flowers up. 'These are for you.'

'They're lovely.' As she kissed him, Saffron's heart swelled. Everything was all right with Tom by her side. Out of the corner of her eye she saw Jasmine gliding towards them, predator-like.

Suddenly the music stopped and everyone looked round. A querulous voice crackled through the speakers. 'If I could just have everyone's attention . . .'

Oh God. What was she doing? Saffron's eyes swivelled to the DJ box, where Babs was hovering next to a rather perturbed DJ Rev. Babs peered uncertainly into the microphone as if it were a Venus flytrap, and cleared her throat.

'Do you know about this?' Saffron muttered to Tom. He shook his head vehemently.

'Greetings, friends of Saffron!' Babs cried dramatically. 'My name is Barbara Walden, and I'm Saffron's mother. I'd like to take a few moments to tell you just how proud I am of her.'

Saffron pressed her face into Tom's shoulder. 'Tell me this isn't happening.'

'Saffron has always been a creative person,' Babs carried on. 'Of course, she gets that from my side of the family, rather than her father's.' She looked heavenwards. 'God rest his soul.'

There was an embarrassed cough somewhere in the room. Babs took a deep sigh and carried on. 'Saffron has always had a talent for writing, and I knew she was destined for great things.' Her bony hands gripped the side of the DJ box. 'Of course, there were a few years when Saffron and I were estranged from each other, and I couldn't follow her career as closely . . .'

At this revelation, several people exchanged surprised looks. Saffron cringed and burrowed her

38

face into Tom's chest. 'Somebody kill me. Now,' she mumbled from the depths of his top.

'. . . but that's all in the past, now.' Babs gave a bright smile. 'And I just want to say that I'm determined to make it up to Saffron now, and be the best mother I can.' She scanned the crowd. 'Saffron? Where are you, darling?'

Tom gave a faint grin and pulled Saffron's hand up in the air. 'Over here.'

Babs beamed. 'Saffron, I have complete faith in your book, and I know it's going to be a best-seller!'

Saffron forced herself to grin.

'What's it about?' someone shouted.

'It's a bonkbuster, darling!' Alexander piped up.

'A bonk what?'

'Speaking from personal experience, are we, Saff?' someone else called out.

'Well, this is a bit uncomfortable,' Saffron whispered to Tom. He smiled and gave her a squeeze. Her mother spoke up again, seemingly oblivious to the hecklers.

'To Saffron and her book!'

'Saffron and her book!' everyone chorused. Saffron put on a smile, and faced the room. Despite her acute embarrassment, she was genuinely touched so many people had turned out tonight. 'Thanks, guys,' she smiled.

The music started up again, and people returned to their conversations. Saffron turned to Tom. 'I need a drink.' She couldn't believe her mother had just put out a public-service announcement about their fucked-up family. What a great start!

39

Chapter 6

'Thanks!'

The bored-looking driver watched Harriet climbing off. As the bus trundled away she looked round, trying to get her bearings. The lights from pubs and bars lit up Camden High Street like a string of Christmas decorations. A pink-haired woman floated towards her, wearing what looked like a nightie under her long army jacket. She was drawing on a cigarette, and as she passed Harriet got a whiff of something sweet and heavy. Harriet looked after her. Was that marijuana? She couldn't believe the woman was smoking it so openly!

After a few minutes of negotiating Streetmap (Saffron always told her it was social death to be seen with an A–Z) Harriet finally found what she was looking for. A battered sign scrawled with graffiti told her she'd found the Gatsby Road Estate. Feeling more than a little nervous, Harriet started down the long straight road.

From what she'd read on the internet, she'd been expecting some kind of war-zone, but her first impressions were reassuringly normal. A line of redbrick identikit houses faced each other on either side of the street, the odd England flag in a window or garden ornament marking each out from its neighbours. In the distance Harriet could see a towering high-rise block, lights dotted on intermittently like a giant Connect Four board. Maybe because it was such a cold, dark night, the place was deserted. Harriet was glad of the glow being cast by the orange streetlamps.

She gave a little start; a dark shape was walking towards her. It was a man, the collar of his jacket pulled up against the winter air. Harriet gave him a tentative smile, but he walked past as if she didn't exist.

A few minutes later a long, low-roofed building appeared, standing slightly back from the road. She could just make out the wording of the sign outside: *Gatsby Road Community Centre*. Someone had graffitied something unintelligible over the last word.

Apprehensively, she walked up the concrete steps, and noticed a man by the entrance. He was throwing what looked like bits of furniture into a large yellow skip, which sat on the stubby grass. He was underdressed for the weather in a T-shirt and jeans, his lean frame moving athletically. Even though he had his back to her, Harriet saw a flash of power between his shoulders as he threw an old three-legged chair into the skip.

Aware of her presence, the man swung round. For a moment his face looked guarded, then it relaxed. All Harriet could think was how blue his eyes were, even in the dark. They focused on her like heat-seeking missiles. 'Can I help?' The voice sounded vaguely familiar. Harriet swallowed.

'Y-yes. I'm Harriet Fraser. I'm here for the volunteer work?'

The man stared for a moment. 'I'd totally forgotten. Sorry.' He stepped forward. 'I'm Zack Doyle.'

He definitely did not have the pot belly or Del-Boy-Trotter look she'd been imagining. As she shook his hand, Harriet realized just how good looking Zack was. He had a handsome, yet elegant face, cropped brown hair just starting to curl around his temples. As he smiled, she noticed how his eyes crinkled up in the corners, and a single silver earring glinted in one ear. He had a classic, old-fashioned appeal about him that reminded her of a young Paul Newman. Harriet's stomach did a little flip; *Butch Cassidy and The Sundance Kid* was one of her favourite films ever. She *loved* Paul Newman.

Zack wiped his forehead. 'We're having a bit of a clear-out. The council provides the skip, but unfortunately I'm in charge of the manpower.' He smiled again. 'Come in, you must be freezing.'

She followed him into the foyer, noticing the little dark sweat patch on the back of his T-shirt. Under the strip lighting, Zach's eyes were even more mesmerizing: a faded-blue evocative of sweaty horses and dusty-red plains under the wide skies of Wyoming. She could almost hear the squeak of the saddle, the manly scent of a handsome cowboy . . .

Oh, for goodness' sake. Harriet gave herself a shake. They were in a community centre in Camden, not some 1950s Western!

Zack's gaze flicked over her, taking in the pink cashmere pashmina wrapped around her neck. 'You got here OK, then?'

'Oh yes, I got the bus. I normally take the tube, but I thought I'd take my life in my hands tonight, ha ha ha!'

The laugh sounded midway between a whinny and a snort. Zack blinked. 'Right.' Something about his expression made Harriet feel self-conscious. Keen to move the focus away before she said something *really* stupid, she looked over

42

Zack's shoulder to the set of glass doors into the main hall. Inside, Harriet could see rows of old people sitting in studied concentration. Zack followed her gaze.

'OAP bingo.' He looked down at her, taller by the second. There was a strong smell of industrial bleach. 'Don't interrupt them, they get vicious about their bingo,' Zack said, suddenly looking serious. 'One nearly had a volunteer's hand off last week.'

Harriet wasn't sure how to take it. Zack's face broke into a grin. 'Just kidding.'

She gave a nervous giggle. 'Of course you were.' She tried not to look at his bum, engagingly pert in the dark blue jeans. Her stomach gave another jolt. Oh God, he was sexy *and* funny.

*   *   *

With its peeling paint and blinking overhead lights, there was no escaping the hall's dilapidated state. The atmosphere was one of studied concentration. Elderly people sat at long tables, studiously scribbling away on what looked like giant calendars. A man who didn't look much younger than his geriatric audience stood at the back of the room on a raised podium, dressed in an old-fashioned dinner jacket. He was holding up a large card with a number on it. 'Tickle me, sixty-three!' he called.

Several of the audience shook their heads, grumbling, but one lady with a blue rinse waved her marker pen in the air triumphantly. 'FULL 'OUSE!' She high-fived the woman in the wheelchair next to her.

43

Zack grinned. 'That's Rose. She celebrated her ninety-first birthday last week.'

'Who's this nice young lady, then?' a tremulous voice called out. Harriet looked round to see an old man tottering towards them. He was impeccably dressed in a tie, pressed shirt, tweed trousers and smart brown cardigan, his shoes shining as if on parade.

'Alf, this is Harriet. Our new volunteer,' Zack said.

Alf took Harriet's hand and kissed it. 'Alf Stokes. Delighted to make your acquaintance.'

'Delighted to make yours.' Harriet smiled.

'Alf's a bit of a hero. If you want to know about the Second World War, he's your man,' Zack told her.

Alf looked proud. 'I was there for D-Day and fought all the way to Germany.' He touched her arm. 'I expect a pretty young girl like you doesn't need an old fool like me going on.'

'Oh, I'd love to hear all about it,' Harriet said. 'History was one of my favourite subjects at school.'

Alf's weathered face creased up. 'I can see you and me are going to be chums. You've got a lovely voice by the way, hasn't she, Zack? Sounds like one of the royals.' He winked. 'The Queen Mum was always me favourite. In fact you look a bit like her when she was younger.'

He shuffled off back to his seat. 'What a sweet chap,' Harriet said.

Zack looked after him. 'He lost his wife a few months ago. Puts a brave face on, but it's hit him hard.'

She watched Alf lower himself into his seat, and

44

suddenly felt sad for this brave, spry little man who was now alone in the world.

As the bingo caller started up again, Zack gestured to a door leading off one side of the room. 'Shall we go to my office? We can talk more about the things we do here.'

He led her past a sitting area with squashy sofas, beanbags and a large bookshelf crammed with books. A lone boy with voluminously baggy jeans and Nike trainers was engrossed in a Tom Clancy novel. Zack's office, which was a door off to the right, was more of a broom cupboard with a desk piled high with paper.

He shoved a load of stuff off one of the chairs. 'Take a seat. Sorry it's such a mess.' In the small, airless room Harriet could smell the faint tang of his fresh aftershave. She'd already looked for a wedding ring and been stupidly pleased when he hadn't got one. *Focus on the business in hand*, she told herself. It didn't mean he wasn't going out with someone. Besides, Zack was far too cool and handsome to ever be interested in someone like her.

He handed her a leaflet. 'This is a typical weekly schedule.' Harriet scanned it as Zack gave a running commentary. 'Mondays are socials where people can just drop in, have tea and cake, read, chat, do whatever, really. Tonight is OAP bingo, as you've already seen. Wednesdays we have study club.'

Harriet looked at Thursday's class. 'Salsa looks fun.'

'Dance, do you?'

'Goodness no, I've got two left feet!'

Zack gave a polite smile. 'We've got this dancer

who comes in from the West End. She's pretty good, the oldies love her.'

Friday night was youth club, while each weekend had different activities scheduled in. There was a trip to Thorpe Park, a film club, parenting workshops, and even cooking demonstrations. Harriet was impressed with how much was on. 'Do you work here full-time?'

Zack nodded. 'It's an around-the-clock job. I like to keep the centre open as much as possible, just so people can drop in if they want, have a cup of tea. We've got a lending service with the local library, so people can hire books and DVDs out. Or just stay here and read, like you saw with Ben outside. Some people round here live in pretty chaotic homes, and the centre just gives them a bit of peace and quiet.'

'What do the volunteers do?'

'Come in and help out as much as possible, basically. It's not glamorous work: you might be cleaning the toilets one night and serving out tea the next, but we all muck in together.'

Was it her imagination, or was there a challenging note in Zach's voice?

'I think it sounds like fun,' she said enthusiastically. 'The centre's obviously a real hit with the community.'

Something like pride flashed across his face. 'It's all taken off pretty well. Too well, sometimes. We're bursting at the seams some nights.'

Harriet wondered how they afforded to run the place. 'Do you get funding?'

'Yeah, but not enough. You may have noticed this place isn't quite the Ritz.'

A tall, thin-faced man popped his head round the

46

door. Harriet had noticed him sitting with the OAPs when she'd walked in.

'Sorry to interrupt, Zack.'

'No problem, mate. Harriet, this is Gray, he's one of the volunteers here.'

Gray came into the room and stuck out his hand. 'Nice to meet you.'

She smiled. 'You, too!'

Gray looked at Zack. 'Do we have any more teabags? I can't find 'em.'

'Er . . . try the cupboard on the right. Above the kettle.'

'Cheers.' Gray winked at Harriet. 'Don't listen to what Zack tells you. We're all quite normal, honest.'

'Gray's a star,' Zack said when it was just the two of them. He sat back and chucked his pen on to the desk. 'So that's it about us. Still interested?' he asked. It was obvious he was sceptical.

'Of course.' She felt a bit crushed. Did she really look that hopeless?

He studied her. 'You might find it's not your bag.'

'My bag?'

'I just want to make sure you're in it for the right reasons,' Zack said carefully. 'Lots of people find volunteer work isn't for them.'

Harriet gave a determined smile. 'I'm looking forward to it.'

He shrugged. 'Cool. Let's see how you go, then.'

At that moment Harriet vowed to last.

*   *   *

They'd talked after that about when she could

come in, and by the time he'd added her name to the rota the bingo was finished. Everyone was now chatting, while a plump middle-aged woman called Mary Croft came round and served up steaming cups of tea. She saw Zack and smiled.

'Be a love, Zack, and bring the biccies from the kitchen.'

Harriet jumped up. 'It's OK. I'll get them.' She gave Zack a cheeky nod. 'You've probably got lots to do.'

By the end of the evening Harriet had dished out more Rich Teas than she could shake a stick at, been invited to one couple's golden anniversary party, and promised another lady she'd help her roll up her knitting balls next week. She was buzzing. She hadn't had such a fulfilling evening in ages.

'You seem to have been a bit of a hit,' Zack commented, as they put away the last table together.

'I think they're all fantastic,' she said, not without a glow of satisfaction.

He nodded. 'Yeah, they are.' He brushed his hands together. 'All done. I'll walk you to the bus stop.'

'There's really no need.' Harriet was sure Zack would rather be doing other things.

'It's not a problem. Besides, we can't have someone like you wandering about here late at night.'

Someone like her. He obviously thought she was a dreadful Hooray Henrietta who had fallen straight out of the pages of *Country Life*. Harriet put on a smile and went to get her pashmina.

*   *   *

The estate was still quiet as they left and started heading back towards the main road. Zack walked with the easy confidence of a man who knew how to handle himself. He pointed back down the road, further into the estate. 'I live on the other side. Mostly old folk and families there, but that's the way I like it.'

'Partying days over?' Harriet was impressed with the teasing note in her voice.

Zack laughed, and it was a deep, rich sound. 'Yeah, I'm a boring old fart these days.' He didn't offer any more information.

'Alf's nice,' Harriet said instead, making conversation.

'He's a lovely old boy. Alf, Rose, they were all here when it was a proper community. It's still their home, even if it has changed for the worse.' He kicked a stone out of the way. 'Society doesn't give a shit about old people these days, and that's why the GRCC is so important. Makes them realize they still count.'

A shout from ahead made them both look up. 'Zack!' A tall, thin, blonde girl was walking towards them, a pushchair in front of her. Harriet put her in her early twenties, one of those naturally pretty girls who didn't need a scrap of make-up.

'Hey, you.' Zack grinned at the new arrival. 'What're you doing out? I thought you were going to your mum's.'

'Just popped out to get some cigs,' the girl said, smiling back at him. Up close she looked a lot younger. Her eyes flickered on to Harriet

49

suspiciously.

'This is Harriet, she's a new volunteer at the centre,' Zack said.

'Oh, right,' the girl said without much interest. 'I'm Abby.' Before Harriet had a chance to answer Abby's eyes had swung back to Zack's face. She shot him an intimate smile. 'Kai's missed you.'

Zack looked into the cot. A tiny pink baby swathed in layers gurgled up at him happily. 'How's my little superstar?'

Harriet suddenly felt like a spare part. To her relief she could see a bus coming down the road.

'Ooh, here's my ride.'

Zack looked up from chucking the baby under the chin. 'OK.' He glanced between her and Abby. 'Well, I'll see you next week, then?'

'You most certainly will!' Harriet said, cringing at the fact she probably sounded like an elderly schoolmarm. *What was wrong with her?* Abby linked her arm through Zack's as the bus doors hissed open. Harriet climbed on and swiped her Oyster card. 'That's me off, then!' She turned round to say goodbye, nearly taking out the driver with her handbg, but the happy family were already walking home.

FEBRUARY

Chapter 7

Churchminster

Serendipity ~~tearfully~~ threw the new Rolex on to the bed. It didn't matter how much Jake tried to make it up to her, the fact still remained he had stood her up at her own sister's wedding. Her own sister's wedding! He'd been full of the usual excuses about time running over in the recording studio, and how his manager had pulled him into another ultra-important business meeting afterwards. But that was all a lie, another lie to add to the mountain of bullshit he'd been feeding her lately. Because they both knew that Jake had in fact been ~~fucking~~ ~~screwing~~ ~~banging~~ shagging her best friend, Vanessa.

Saffron stopped typing and pressed 'save'. She did a word count for the tenth time that morning: 5,233 words into her debut novel.

She sat back, feeling very pleased with herself. *Not bad going, Saffo, not bad at all*. It had been nearly a week since she'd arrived in Churchminster with her mother, so drunk she'd tripped over a rogue tree root on the way up the garden path and spent the first twenty-four hours nursing a sore ankle. Once the hangover had subsided, and she had started to acclimatize to her new home, Saffron had been gripped by fear. She had the ideas in her head, but what if she couldn't get the book out? She'd spent the first hour staring in despair at a blank screen, but then something had happened. The words had been flowing ever since, and Saffron was ecstatic. Of course, writer's block was going to rear its blocky little head at some point, but it was a great start.

She leant back in her chair and looked round at her new office. Her mother had given her the little box room at the front of the house to use. There was barely room to swing a cat, but there was a cool, old-fashioned writing desk in there, and a nice view of the village green. Babs had even dug out an old-fashioned ink pot and fountain pen from somewhere, and put them there for her on the first day, just for effect. To the left of her laptop was the pile of writing manuals Tom had bought to help with the book. He was such a sweetie.

Saffron took a mouthful of the tea her mother had brought up, and grimaced. It tasted faintly of turpentine, as if it had been used more for cleaning paintbrushes than dunking a Tetley's teabag. Saffron leaned across and poured the liquid into the pot plant on the windowsill. The rate her mother kept making her tea, the poor plant was going to die any moment.

She clicked on her emails, just to see if Tom had sent her anything.

'Hey my gorgeous little novelist, how's it going?'

Smiling, Saffron hit reply. *'Pretty well so far! I think I might have cracked this writing lark, ha ha. Miss you, babe. Can't wait to see you.'*

Moments later his name popped up again. *'Me too.'*

Saffron's bum was getting sore from the wooden

seat. She got up and made her way down the landing to her bedroom. It looked like a sartorial bombsite, the narrow wardrobe and single chest of drawers barely containing half her stuff. Clothes, bags and shoes were everywhere; the Jimmy Choo peep-toe ankle boots she was still paying off on her credit card, her Luella clutch picked up at a sample sale, the Marc Jacobs leather biker jacket courtesy of a hefty press discount. All mixed in with purchases from Top Shop, Zara, Urban Outfitters and French Connection. Saffron wasn't quite sure when she would have an occasion to wear her new leopard-print backless jumpsuit from Arrogant Cat (another press discount), but just because she was in the countryside didn't mean she had to let standards slip.

The same couldn't be said of her surroundings. Hardwick House may have sounded grand, but it was little more than a quaint, slightly tumbledown cottage. The kind of place an estate agent would describe as having bags of charm, which really translated to temperamental central heating and patches of mildew on the ceiling. Her mum had tried to make her room cosy with a new patchwork bedspread but she was still going to bed with socks and her hoodie on every night. And what was with those creepy dolls on top of the wardrobe? It was like she was stuck in a time warp. Saffron had anticipated being out like a light every night, but she missed the white noise of city life, the constant hum of traffic in the background. Most of all she missed *Tom*, his big warm body curled around her.

Her stomach rumbled. Saffron looked at her Michael Kors watch, a present from Alexander at work. 'I've been inundated with them, darling!' To

55

her surprise it was nearly 1 p.m. She'd been writing for over four hours. *Definitely* time for a break. A cool draught blew through the old windowpane, making her shiver. Pulling her alpaca cape from ASOS out of the wardrobe, she put it on and went downstairs.

She could barely get down the hallway for all the empty canvases and paintings stacked against the walls. Her mother hoarded anything she called 'inspiration' for her art, and the house was filled with weird bits of wood, lurid colour swatches, and even a three-foot-long stuffed pike—which was currently being housed on the table in the dining room. Saffron didn't get the fish thing at all, but her mother had gushed something about the iridescent scales being symbolic of the rise of global warming in the Home Counties.

At the back of Hardwick House was the largest room, an open-plan kitchen-cum-conservatory, with big windows looking out on the long, overgrown garden. At one end were the kitchen units, but the real focus of the room was Babs's easel, which was positioned under a leaf-strewn skylight. It was here she stood, dabbing furiously with her paintbrush. Pots of different-coloured water stood on the floor all around her, while the artist herself was dressed in some sort of shimmery paint-stained smock, a paintbrush twisted through her red mane as an ineffectual hairclip.

'Hi, Mum.'

Babs didn't appear to hear, her eyes darting back and forth over the easel.

'I said, "Hi, Mum!" ' Saffron repeated loudly.

Babs looked up and blinked. It took a few seconds for her to come back to the real world.

'Oh, hello, darling! Is it time for dinner?'

'Try lunch first.' Saffron came over and stood behind her mother. The painting looked like someone had eaten a chicken curry and then thrown up over the easel.

'What do you think?' Babs asked anxiously.

'Brilliant,' Saffron lied. She just didn't get how her mother could make a living out of producing such abstract monstrosities, but there was apparently quite a market for her in Kazakhstan.

Babs looked chuffed. 'Really?'

'Completely.' Saffron walked over to the fridge before her mother could ask her what her interpretation of the regurgitated curry was. 'What have we got in, then? I'm starving.'

'Is it time for supper already?' Babs asked absently.

Saffron shot her mother a look, and went back to inspecting the contents of the fridge. They were pitiful. There was some wilting lettuce, a duck pâté whose sell-by date had expired three weeks ago, and a tube of acrylic paste.

She really had to go food shopping, or they were going to starve to death. A sudden beam of sunlight broke through the clouds, bringing the room alive. It had been raining since she'd got to Churchminster, and Saffron had been pretty much housebound. She had a sudden urge to get out.

'I'm going to treat you to lunch at the pub,' she announced. She'd been looking for an excuse to go back to the Jolly Boot, anyway. The village pub was renowned for its culinary excellence and hospitality.

'That's a very nice offer, darling, but I thought you were meant to be saving your pennies.'

57

'Think of it as a thank you present for having me. Anyway, I'm worried you're not eating enough.' Saffron herself was in serious need of some stodge.

'You don't have to worry about your silly old mum!' Babs said.

'Well, I do,' Saffron said firmly. It already felt like they'd reversed roles. Saffron didn't know how her mother had survived so long by herself.

Babs looked as if she was about to cry with happiness. 'You do look after me! A lunch and a gossip, that's what mothers and daughters do, isn't it?' She clapped her hands in excitement. 'Give me five minutes to get changed.'

As she rushed out of the kitchen Saffron smiled. It was quite sweet how enthusiastic Babs got about things.

Forty minutes later, however, Saffron wasn't feeling so warmly disposed towards her. What the hell was her mother doing? When Babs eventually tottered back into the kitchen it looked like she'd had a fight with a can of hairspray and a combine harvester: her wild hair was sticking out all round. Red lipstick was smeared everywhere but her actual mouth, and she was wearing a cat-sick-yellow jumpsuit with another moth-eaten fur jacket.

Saffron gave her a disbelieving once-over. 'Mum, there is no *way* I am going out with you like that! You've got a massive camel's toe for a start!'

Babs looked down, confused. 'No, darling, the coat is beaver.'

'You can say that again,' muttered Saffron, going over to button her mum's coat up over the offending area. Babs's make-up was so bright Saffron needed sunglasses. 'Can't you at least tone down the purple eye shadow?'

'Don't you like it?' Babs looked crestfallen. 'I thought I'd make an effort, make my beautiful daughter proud of me.'

The inevitable twinge of guilt her mother always managed to provoke. 'You look fine. Let's get a move on before I die of hunger.'

Even the drabness of winter couldn't take away the prettiness of Churchminster. Hardwick House sat on the edge of the village green, a large square patch of grass encircled by enchanting chocolate-box cottages. Grey wisps of smoke curled up from several chimneys, from roaring log fires warming up kitchens and living rooms. The only blot was on the far left of the green, where St Bartholomew's church stood: its ancient stones were still encased in scaffolding after the fire last year.

The Jolly Boot public house was a long, low-roofed building that sat on the far side of the green. Taking her mother's arm, Saffron started to walk along the road, trying to avoid all the muddy puddles. Maybe it hadn't been the best idea to wear wedge heels. A gust of wind came from nowhere, whistling through her Burberry mac. Christ, it was cold! She was going to get her first set of chilblains at this rate.

As they passed a quaint trio of thatched cottages on their right, the front door of one opened, and an impossibly good-looking man came out. It was Jed Bantry, estate manager at Clanfield Hall, and Churchminster born and bred. Saffron had met him before and recognized his handsome face instantly. 'Hey, Jed,' she called.

He looked over and gave an easy smile. 'Saffron, hey. I heard you were back.'

59

'Yeah, I've moved in with Mum for a bit.' As Jed walked over Saffron was again reminded how fit he was. With jet-black hair and green eyes, Jed Bantry looked more like a catwalk model than a country boy. *I could use someone like him in my book*, she thought.

'Hel-lo, Jed!' gushed Babs. 'Don't you look handsome in your overalls?' Saffron shot Jed an apologetic look. Her mother could at least *try* and be subtle.

Jed gave an embarrassed smile. 'So you're writing a book? It's the talk of the village, you know.'

'That's what I'm afraid of!' Saffron wasn't used to having her every move scrutinized, although she had to admit that it hadn't been that bad so far.

'Hey, it's not every day we get a novelist in our midst.'

'Yeah, right.' Saffron laughed, looking past him at the cottage. 'It's a shame the girls aren't about.' Normally, Jed lived with his girlfriend, Camilla Standington-Fulthrope, and her sister Calypso. They were good fun, and firm friends of Harriet's, but they were both away pursuing their different careers at the moment.

'I know. Calypso is away running her events company, and Camilla's travel agency is just starting up. She's in China at the moment, researching an itinerary. Then it's Cambodia, Vietnam . . .'

'You didn't fancy joining her?'

Jed grinned. 'And miss out on all this mud? Unfortunately the Hall won't run itself.'

Babs batted her eyelashes, keen to be back in the conversation. 'Poor boy, all by yourself. You must come and see us!' A slightly leery look entered her eyes. 'We could all have a nice meal together.'

'Come on, Mum,' Saffron said hurriedly, taking her arm. 'We don't want to keep Jed. I'm sure he's busy.'

He shot her a wry look. 'See you around. Let me know if you fancy a pint. Or whatever it is you London lot drink these days.'

'Thanks, Jed,' Saffron said. She knew Jed wasn't much of a socialite, but she appreciated the gesture.

'Maybe I could ask Jed if he would pose for me,' Babs whispered as he walked off. 'A life drawing!'

Seriously, she was too much! 'You'll do no such thing, Mum,' Saffron told her. Reaching the door of the Jolly Boot, she opened it and pushed Babs in before she could say anything else inappropriate.

The pub was warm and cosy, a roaring fire burning in the inglenook fireplace. Freshly polished brass horseshoes and tankards hung above the bar, while behind it, a red-haired man with biceps to rival Popeye's lifted a hand and waved. Jack Turner was the Cockney landlord, and ran the pub with endless generosity and an iron rule.

'Afternoon, ladies! You look nice, young Saffron, how's the book going?'

Saffron laughed. 'Does everyone know about it?'

'It doesn't take long for news to travel round here.'

'It's a bonkbuster, you know,' Babs told him proudly.

Jack's eyebrows shot up. 'A what?'

Babs waved her arms around. 'A bonkbuster!' she

cried. A man standing further down the bar looked up. Babs's voice rose even more. 'You know, with lots of *sex* and gorgeous chaps!'

'Oh, so *I'm* in it then.' Jack winked at Saffron.

'I'm rather hoping for a cameo, too!' Babs said.

'Yuk, Mum!' Saffron watched as her mother tottered off towards the Ladies, like a flamingo in drag. She turned back to the landlord. 'Don't worry, my mother is *not* going to be in it.'

Jack chuckled. 'I'm not saying anything. You girls having lunch, then? We've got Pierre's world-famous meatballs on the menu today.'

The Jolly Boot's chef had been poached from a Michelin-starred restaurant. 'Oh wow, sounds yum,' said Saffron. 'Table for two, please.'

Jack gestured to one over by the fire. 'That one's all yours. The menu's on the blackboard, and I'll be over in a sec to take your drink order.'

Saffron was deliberating on her main course when her mother reappeared. 'Sorry, darling!' she said loudly. 'I've got a touch of cystitis. I'm on the loo every five minutes at the moment.' The couple at the next table glanced at them. Saffron winced. Did her mother really have to make a public-service announcement about the workings of her bladder? Babs sat down. 'What are you going to have?'

Saffron turned back to the blackboard. 'I think I'm going to go for the soup to start, and the rack of lamb for main. With an extra side of chips, because I'm a big fat pig.'

'Super, I'll have the same,' her mother said.

Saffron frowned. 'You haven't even looked at the menu, there's loads of nice stuff here.'

Babs smiled. 'Why should I? I'm sure everything

62

you've chosen is wonderful.'

Jack appeared with the wine list. 'Can I recommend the French Bordeaux? I chose it myself.'

'Great, we're having lamb,' Saffron said.

'How about an aperitif to start?' her mother asked.

Jack grinned. 'We've just got some cracking new bubbly in.'

'Let's have a bottle!' Babs said. 'My treat, of course.'

'I'm not sure . . .' Saffron was meant to be writing some more later.

'But we haven't had the chance to celebrate your new book, yet.'

'I've only just started it!'

'I know, and from what you've told me it's going swimmingly well, so let's celebrate.' Saffron's willpower started to fade. As another gust of wind battered against the window she thought of all her mates in London stuck in their offices, while she was in a lovely country pub about to have a good nosh-up. A glass of champagne would be the perfect start.

'Sod it. Why not?'

*   *   *

'When's Tom arriving?' Babs asked.

They'd had their soup, and drunk most of the bottle, and Saffron was feeling warm and fuzzy. 'Friday. I'm picking him up from the station.'

Babs looked startled. 'I thought he was coming Saturday! Oh dear, I've got a commission to finish, how will I get the house ready in time?'

'Chillski, I'll do it.' Saffron had forgotten how bad her mum was at coping with everyday life.

Her mother looked relieved. 'Will you, really?' She sighed happily. 'It's so nice having you at home. I feel like we've been living together for years already.'

Her words hit a raw nerve. 'Well, we haven't been living together for years, have we?' Saffron retorted shortly. 'You packed me off to boarding school as soon as I became an inconvenience.' There, she'd said it. It was only a matter of time before the topic came up.

Babs looked pained. 'Darling . . .'

Saffron drained her glass. 'Don't . . .'

They eyed each other over the table: Babs imploring, Saffron combative. She'd adored her father, Harry Walden, and been devastated when he'd been killed in a sailing accident when she was eleven. The tragedy had been made even more painful by the fact that Harry had walked out and left them months earlier, something Saffron had always blamed on her ditzy, ineffectual mother. Already of a fragile disposition, Babs had had a nervous breakdown and sent her only child to live with her sister.

It was only two years ago, when they'd started talking again, that Saffron had found out that her father had actually left to live with another woman. It was even more painful to find out that it hadn't been the first time he'd cheated, but Babs had kept quiet about all this, not wanting to shatter Saffron's image of her father. For someone who'd held a candle to him all these years, and seen her mum as the villain, it had been a bittersweet time for Saffron. It still was. She felt guilt for blaming her mum, and the older, more familiar anger at Babs for abandoning her in the first place. Even if Harry had done the dirty on them, they could have made it, the two of them. Why hadn't Babs fought harder to keep her?

'Thank God Aunt Velda was there for me,' she said now. 'At least someone in the family could step up to their parental responsibilities.'

Babs looked like she'd been physically wounded. 'And I'll always be grateful to Velda,' she said. Her eyes brimmed with tears. 'Please, darling, are you never going to forgive me? I know you don't believe me, but I thought I was doing the right thing. I didn't want you to see me like that, and I knew Velda would give you a happier home.' She swallowed. 'It was hard for me too, darling. When I got better I was devastated you didn't want to come home, but I felt I had to respect your decision.' Two tears slid down her cheeks. 'After all, what kind of mother leaves their child?'

Saffron looked at her thin, nervy mum and the resentment disappeared. She'd had too many years of it. 'I know, Mum.' She had to face facts. 'Dad wasn't perfect, I realize that. It must have taken its toll, being married to him.'

Babs sniffed. 'I can never make up those lost years, but I really am trying . . .'

Her voice was rising. The couple on the next table were looking at them again. Saffron sighed and reached across to take her mother's hand. 'Don't cry. Please.'

Mercifully, at that moment Jack appeared with two plates of succulent lamb and a bowl of fat crispy chips. He pretended not to notice Babs's tear-stained cheeks. 'Here you go, ladies.'

'It looks amazing, doesn't it, Mum?' Saffron said, trying to lighten the moment.

'I'll just get your wine,' Jack said.

When he'd walked off, Saffron looked back at Babs. 'Let's not let the past interfere any more. I know you're trying, and I do appreciate it, and I'll try too.' She picked up the last of her champagne. 'OK? To the future.'

Babs's face filled with hope. 'To the future!'

As they clinked glasses, Saffron couldn't help smiling. She'd probably want to murder her mum in a few weeks' time, but at least they'd reached a truce. As Jack returned to slosh out the burgundy, and her mum went into orgasmic raptures about the food, Saffron realized she hadn't felt this close to Babs in years.

Chapter 8

London

London was experiencing a late flurry of snow. It was a bitterly cold night as Harriet made her way to Montague Mews. Nose red and fingers numb, she eventually reached the entrance and buzzed on the intercom. Moments later a disembodied voice spoke. 'Is that you, darling? I'll let you in.'

The entrance gates started to clank open, and Harriet walked into the pretty cobbled mews. It was a world away from the slushy mess outside. A white blanket covered the ground, while the bare boughs from the oak trees next door dripped into the courtyard, bowed under the weight of fresh snow.

At No. 2, behind the mint-green front door, lived Caro and Benedict Towey. Harriet had known Caro for years. As well as being her friend Camilla's older sister, Caro was a kindred spirit because she and Harriet had both grown up in Churchminster. The Toweys had moved to London to be near Benedict's work, and their Chelsea house had become a home from home for Harriet.

A curvaceous blonde with a pretty, open face, Caro was waiting for Harriet on the doorstep. 'Come in before you catch your death!'

Harriet had never been so pleased to get out of the cold. The front room was a sanctuary from the snow, aglow with candles on the low coffee table and mantelpiece. 'You do have a knack for making a place look nice,' Harriet told Caro.

Caro smiled. 'I only get to light them when the children are in bed. Milo is already showing pyromaniac tendencies!' As well as her and Benedict's daughter Rosie, Caro had a five-year-old son called Milo, by her first husband, Sebastian. Thankfully the little boy was every bit as delightful as his father had been horrible.

Harriet dug in her bag and brought out a bottle of M&S Sauvignon Blanc. 'Oh, have I missed them? I bought Rosie some glitter face-paint from work.'

'How thoughtful!' Caro looked apologetic. 'I'm afraid the kids are in bed. We went to the park earlier, and they wore themselves out.'

'Never mind, I'll see them next time.'

'They'll be devastated to know they've missed their Aunty Harriet. Sit down, darling, and make yourself at home. I'll go and put this bottle in the fridge. In the meantime, do you fancy a glass of Moët? We've got tons left over from our New Year party.'

'I'm meant to be detoxing,' Harriet said guiltily. She still hadn't been able to do the top button up on her favourite GAP trousers since Christmas.

'Me too, but isn't it boring? Especially when I keep picking at Rosie and Milo's sweeties.' Caro looked decisive. 'Anyway, it's all about friends and fun tonight. I've made shepherd's pie for supper, by the way, and I know I'm naughty, but I couldn't resist the homemade sticky toffee pudding in the deli round the corner. It really is orgasmic.'

The thought of all that sumptuous food made Harriet's mouth water. She'd only had a measly salad from Boots for lunch, and felt hollow and cold. 'I'd love a glass. You're right, it's far too depressing to diet in this weather.'

As Caro busied herself in the kitchen, Harriet sank back on one of the huge sofas. If—and the chances of it happening were ever-decreasing—she ever had a family home, Harriet would love something like this. Caro had cleverly achieved a relaxed, aspirational look, from the mini-grand piano in one corner to the stunning blown-up picture of the four of them on the far wall. As she reflected what a beautiful family they were, Harriet felt something sticking in her bottom. She shuffled around to find a mini-stethoscope inbetween the sofa cushions. She picked it up and set it on the coffee table.

A minute later Caro came back into the room carrying a tray with the champagne, two glasses, and a bowl of stuffed olives. She set it down on the table and spied the stethoscope. 'Where did you find that?'

'I just sat on it. It was down the back of the sofa.'

'Oh God, sorry.' Caro grabbed the stethoscope and went to put it in a toy box in the corner of the room. 'It's part of Milo's doctor costume. He's very into dressing-up at the moment.' She sighed, looking round for any other errant belongings. 'The kids' things are rather taking over . . . Benedict nearly broke his neck tripping over Rosie's fairy wings yesterday.'

Harriet giggled. 'Is he joining us for supper?'

'Should be home from work any minute,' Caro said. She popped the cork expertly and poured the fizzing liquid into the glasses. 'There you go, darling.' She raised her glass. 'To retoxing.'

'Hear hear!' Harriet said. She'd just taken her first sip when the front door opened, bringing in a fresh gust of freezing air. A tall blond man strode in, cashmere coat in one hand, leather holdall in the other.

'Speak of the devil.' Caro smiled.

Benedict Towey came over to drop a kiss on his wife's head. 'What have I done now? Hello, Harriet.' He bent down to kiss her and Harriet felt a bit gooey. Benedict had that effect on most women he met. At forty-two, Benedict had refined, beautiful looks that gave Brad Pitt a run for his money. But whereas age and fatherhood had started wearing away the film star's looks, they'd only made Benedict more handsome.

He hung his coat on the stand in the corner.

'How was work?' Caro asked.

'Busy. Good, though.'

'They've just been nominated for an industry

69

award, you know,' Caro said proudly. Benedict ran a successful design agency off Sloane Square, called The Glass Ceiling.

'That's fabulous!' Harriet said. 'Congratulations!' Benedict made a modest gesture with his hands.

Caro held the bottle up and smiled at Benedict. 'Can I tempt you?' She turned to Harriet. 'He's in training for the London Marathon.' Harriet was impressed again; she couldn't even do a spin class without wanting to crawl off somewhere and die afterwards.

Benedict grinned. 'Don't want to compromise that personal best.' He looked at his wife. 'What's for dinner, darling?'

'Nigella's shepherd's pie. It's warming in the oven.'

'Uh-oh.' Benedict shot Harriet a look of mock alarm. 'The last lasagne we did from that book went a bit awry. Luckily the patio needed a new paving stone.' A superb cook himself, Benedict enjoyed teasing Caro about her rather limited skills.

Caro stuck her tongue out at him. 'You'll be eating on the patio if you carry on like that, matey!'

Benedict gave her a sexy wink. 'I'm just going to check on the kids.' He strode across the room and up the spiral staircase.

'My husband is frighteningly in love with his daughter.' Caro smiled.

'I'm not surprised. Rosie is adorable. Both of them are adorable.'

'You wouldn't have said that if you'd seen the screaming banshees I had to deal with at bath time!' Caro changed the subject. 'Granny Clem is very impressed they've got an author living back in the village.' Caro's grandmother, Clementine Standington-Fulthrope, lived in a big house set off the green in Churchminster, and was a force to be reckoned with.

'I bet she is! I got an email from Saffron earlier, actually. The book seems to be coming along swimmingly.'

'That's fantastic. I hope she gets time out of her busy writing schedule to go and see Granny Clem. You know how she likes to keep abreast of what everyone's up to in the village.'

Harriet smiled. 'I certainly do. How is she, by the way?'

Caro pulled a face. 'To be honest, I'm a bit worried about her. She hasn't been the same since Errol Flynn died.'

'It's always awful to lose a pet, especially one like Errol Flynn. He and your grandmother were like a double act.'

'I keep trying to get her up here to visit, but she says she's getting too old.'

'That doesn't sound like Clementine.'

'I know.' Caro sounded worried. 'Still, Benedict seems to think we might be able to go back soon, now work has become more stable.'

'Oh, really?' Harriet was dismayed. She'd always known Caro and Benedict's London stay was temporary, and just till he'd built up the business, but she'd got so used, now, to having them around.

'It's not going to happen just yet, don't worry. And we'll still be back and forth lots.' Caro pulled her legs up on the sofa. 'Let's talk about you instead, darling. I'm dying to know what you've been up to. You know how I like to live my life

71

vicariously through you.'

'There's not much there to live!' Harriet laughed. Then she added, 'Actually, I have got some news. I've signed up for volunteering.'

Caro looked interested.

Harriet hesitated. 'It's a bit different from what you'd expect . . .' She told Caro about the Gatsby Road Community Centre. Her friend was impressed.

'It sounds really interesting. Good on you.'

'Good on Harriet for what?' Benedict had come downstairs and caught the tail end of the conversation. He sat down next to his wife and put an arm round her.

'Harriet's volunteering at a community centre,' Caro told him.

Benedict looked at Harriet. 'Fantastic. Whereabouts?'

'The Gatsby Road Estate in Camden? You probably won't have heard of it . . .'

Benedict frowned. 'The Gatsby Road Estate?'

Caro looked surprised, but kept quiet.

'Things are a lot better there, now,' Harriet said hastily.

Benedict didn't look convinced. 'It's still a pretty tough place, by all accounts. We pitched to Camden Council to rebrand it a few years ago, but I think the project was shelved because of money.'

'Since when did you become an expert on London trouble spots?' Caro teased.

'Men know these things, Caro.'

She rolled her eyes. 'Don't let my husband put you off,' she told Harriet. 'I think he has some inbuilt thing where he wants to protect every

72

female on the planet.'

'Honestly, it's fine,' Harriet said. She was touched, if a little unnerved, by Benedict's reaction.

'What are the people like?' Caro asked. 'Have they been welcoming?'

'They've all been lovely so far. Zack, he's the chap who runs it—' Despite her best intentions, Harriet started to blush.

Caro's antennae went up. 'Ooh, is he good-looking? Do you fancy him? Does he fancy you? He must do, you're a dream catch!'

Benedict nudged her. 'I'm sure Harriet doesn't need the Spanish Inquisition about her love life.'

'I'm not!' Caro protested. 'Girls just like to know these things.'

Harriet laughed. 'It's OK. I think he's taken, anyway.'

Caro looked disappointed. 'Darling, do we know anyone we could set Harriet up with?' she asked her husband.

Benedict smiled at Harriet sympathetically.

'I know! How about that chap Jeremy you work with? He's so nice I can't understand why he hasn't got someone.' Caro shot Harriet an encouraging look.

'He's just come out,' Benedict said.

Caro's face fell. 'Oh.'

'Honestly, I don't need setting up with anyone,' said Harriet, trying to sound convincing. 'I'm busy enough as it is, what with work and now the volunteering.'

Caro sighed. 'You don't need a smug married type like me trying to organize your love life, it's too patronizing for words. Sorry, sweetpea.'

'It's fine, really,' said Harriet. She was already quite used to her parents going on about her lack of boyfriends every five minutes.

Caro got up. 'The shepherd's pie should be nearly ready. Do you want a top-up?'

Harriet could almost feel the sugar from the alcohol settling on her spare tyre. She said yes, telling herself she needed a layer of fat in this weather.

*   *   *

After a delicious dinner—'Who can go wrong with shepherd's pie?' Caro had said happily—they retired back through to the living room with a nightcap. Just before midnight they decided to call it a night, and Benedict insisted on calling a company car for Harriet. Caro helped her into her coat, and after kisses all round the Toweys watched Harriet make her way across the snowy cobbles to the waiting limousine.

'I still don't like it,' Benedict said, as he shut the front door afterwards.

'Don't like what?' Caro asked, knowing full well what he meant.

'Harriet going to the Gatsby Road Estate. I played it down earlier, but it's a seriously tough place.'

'Benedict, it's Camden, not war-torn Serbia!'

He sighed. 'Maybe I'm overreacting.'

'No, really?' Caro smiled. Benedict was so protective he wouldn't even let her cross the road without taking her hand. He was even worse about the children.

'Alright, I get it. I shall say no more.' He held her

face and kissed the top of her nose. 'Let's go up.'

'I should really tidy up.'

'Sod tidying, I want you.' He started to pull her towards the stairs. Even though it had been a long day and she had been good for nothing earlier, Caro felt the first stirrings of desire. She still couldn't believe she was married to the most handsome man on the planet.

Benedict squeezed her right breast and leant in to kiss her on the neck. It only took a few moments before Caro was completely overcome with lust.

'Do what you will with me,' she whispered.

'Oh, I intend to, don't worry.' He scooped her up in his arms and made for the bedroom.

Chapter 9

Harriet pushed open the doors of the community centre and walked in. It was study club, and the place had been transformed into a giant classroom. Banks of tables were pushed together, and the students sat round them quietly. They were a mixed bag: from a skinny boy who looked no more than fifteen, to a weathered-looking fifty-something woman, glasses pushed up on her forehead. To Harriet's surprise Abby, Zack's girlfriend, was sitting at a table by herself, surrounded by textbooks.

As if aware of Harriet's gaze, Abby looked up and scowled. Harriet dropped her eyes. She was just wondering where Zack was when the door to his office opened and he walked out. He was wearing a light-blue jumper that matched his eyes, the beginnings of a six o'clock shadow on his chin. She wondered if the matching of jumper to eyes was deliberate, and decided it wasn't. Zack seemed like far too much of a man's man to coordinate things like that.

She raised a hand and grinned awkwardly. Zack walked over, his eyes almost translucent under the strip lighting. 'Harriet! You should have called. I would have come and picked you up from the bus stop.'

'It's no problem, really. You're busy enough with this place.'

He gave a crooked grin. 'I think picking up volunteers falls under my remit.' He looked round. 'So, study club's pretty popular. We've got a mixed bag: NVQs, GCSEs, A-levels, business courses.' Zack pointed to a tall, handsome black teenager who had a huge stud in one ear and an iPod earphone hanging out of the other. He was sitting so far back in his seat he was practically vertical. 'Danny Henderson, our star pupil. Predicted straight As, and wants to go to Cambridge next year. Bio-engineering or something like that.'

'Wow.' Harriet was impressed. Danny looked like he should be in a rap video, shouting about 'hos' and fast cars.

A colourless little man looked up and smiled. He was missing several teeth. Harriet hadn't noticed him before. 'That's Pete, he's a nice bloke,' Zack said. 'Doing his A-levels.' He shot her a glance. 'Come on, I've got someone who wants to meet you.'

As they walked in to the kitchen a Titanic-sized black woman was cutting up a huge cake on the sideboard. By her greying hair Harriet guessed she was in her seventies, but aside from that the woman's smooth, round face and hands were unmarked by the ravages of time. She was wearing some sort of orange turban, and a voluminous yellow dress covered in an orange pineapple pattern. The outfit made Harriet smile; it was like Gatsby Road's very own personal sunbeam.

The old woman looked up, brown eyes as sharp as tacks. 'You must be 'Arriet!' she said in a strong Jamaican accent. 'I've been looking forward to meeting you.'

'Harriet, this is Aunty Win,' Zack said.

The woman came round the table and took Harriet's hand in a strong warm clasp. 'Winsome Johnston, but you must call me Aunty Win,' she said. 'Everyone else does.'

Zack put his arm round her not inconsiderable shoulders. 'Yeah, but you're *my* Aunty Win,' he said fondly. He turned to Harriet. 'Aunty Win near enough brought me up.'

The old lady gave a lovely, treacly chuckle. 'Someone has to keep you on the straight and narrow.'

Harriet smiled. 'It's a pleasure to meet you, Aunty Win.'

Win looked at Zack. 'Hasn't she got lovely manners? That's just what we need around the place, a proper lady.' She held Harriet's arms out, and nodded approvingly. 'Come on now, 'Arriet, let me have a look at you. I like a girl who knows how to dress smartly. You've got a bit of meat on you, too, not like the awful skinny things you see these days.'

Harriet blushed.

'Aunty Win . . .' Zack chided, but she brushed him aside.

'Shush, I'm paying her a compliment. I think you're beautiful, 'Arriet!'

It felt like Harriet was under inspection, but in a nice way.

'Aunty Win helps here as well, sometimes,' Zack said, shooting the old lady a look. 'I don't know where we'd be without her Jamaican fruitcake.'

'Do you want some, 'Arriet?' Aunty Win said.

'Just a sliver,' Harriet said, as she was handed a doorstep-sized piece.

'I might leave you two to it, then,' Zack said. 'When you've finished, Harriet, I'm sure Pete would like to meet you.'

He left, and Aunty Win leant back against the sink, meaty arms folded. 'So what do you make of us, then?'

'Everyone seems really lovely,' Harriet said.

Win looked pleased.

'Do you live near here?' Harriet asked. The cake was as heavy as a brick in her hand. It was going to take hours to finish.

'Since 1963. Before you were born, 'Arriet.' Aunty Win sighed. 'A lot's changed since then . . .'

*   *   *

Pete looked up as Harriet approached half an hour later. His face was drawn, and his blond hair thinning, but Harriet thought he'd probably once been quite good-looking.

'Hello, I'm Harriet Fraser.'

'I know, Zack told me.' Pete flashed pinky-grey gums in a smile. 'Pete Collins.'

78

She looked at the free chair opposite him. 'May I?'

'Be my guest.'

She smiled and sat down. 'So what are you doing?'

He held up a book. *'Jane Eyre.'*

'That's one of my favourite books!'

Pete held up a sheet of paper. 'Maybe you can help me with my essay question, then. *What feminist principles are exhibited by the main characters?* I'm a bloke, how should I know?'

She smiled. 'Let's have a look.'

'Not from round here, then?' Pete asked. 'Chelsea, isn't it?'

She was startled. 'How did you know that?'

'Zack told me. I bet you went to one of those big posh boarding schools, didn't you?' Pete looked wistful. 'I would have loved to have stayed at school. My mum kicked me out at thirteen, though.'

Harriet was horrified. 'You were homeless at thirteen?'

'Yeah.' Pete looked at her. 'She couldn't handle the drugs. I don't really blame her.' He squinted at her. 'How old do you think I am?'

She was put on the spot. 'I really couldn't say.'

'No, go on.'

She scrabbled round for an answer. Pete looked at least ten years older than her, so if she added a year or two to her own age . . .

'Er, thirty-six, thirty-seven?'

He shook his head. 'Twenty-five.'

'Oh.' Harriet felt mortified. 'I'm awful at guessing people's ages.'

Pete smiled. 'Don't worry, I've not exactly looked

after myself.' He sat back in his chair. 'Do you know what turned it all around for me?'

Harriet couldn't imagine.

'I nearly died last year,' he said. 'Stepped out in front of a taxi, off my face. It just missed me, but I was so close, I could *feel* death.' He looked at her. 'It sounds a bit dippy, but I think I had a moment with the bloke upstairs, or something. I'd survived the brown all those years, and there I was, about to be squashed flat by a London cabbie. I went to the rehab centre that day. Got myself clean, and this time stayed clean.' He rubbed his head. 'Touch wood. So here I am.'

Harriet was rather touched. 'It's great you've turned your life round so much.'

'I wouldn't say I'm living the dream yet.' He grinned. 'So how's about you help me with this essay, for a start?'

A few minutes later, Harriet heard a low whistle. She looked up. Aunty Win was standing by the kitchen door. ''Arriet!' she said in a stage whisper. 'Your father's on the phone!'

'My *father*?' Harriet was confused.

'Your mobile started ringing, so I answered it.'

Harriet glanced at Pete. 'Coming!' As she got up her heart started to pound. She hadn't even told her father she was volunteering here. He'd probably read something about Broken Britain in the *Telegraph*, and would go ballistic.

'He sounds a bit grumpy,' Win said.

Harriet tentatively held the phone to her ear. 'Hello, Daddy.'

'Where are you? Who was that obtuse woman who just answered your phone?'

'That was Aunty Win.' Harriet edged away into a

80

corner, and lowered her voice. 'I'm in a community centre.'

'A community what?' She may as well have said she was climbing Mount Everest. Topless.

'A community centre, Daddy. You know . . .'

'I know what one is, Harriet. What the dickens are you doing there?'

Harriet took a deep breath. 'I'm volunteering. On a housing estate in North London. I've just been helping an ex-drug-addict with his English A-level,' she added, almost sadistically.

Astonishingly, the expected tirade didn't happen. Her father grunted. 'Is everyone in my family at it? I'll tell you now, I'm not joining the bloody Samaritans.'

'So you're not cross?' Harriet couldn't quite believe it.

'Cross? About what?'

'About . . .' she trailed off. 'Oh, nothing.'

'Who am I to tell you what to do? You're getting as headstrong as your mother.' Sir Ambrose had never forgiven Harriet for leaving him to go and live with the 'city set'.

Harriet shook her head, smiling. At least she had escaped her father's wrath. 'How *are* you, Daddy?'

'Bloody bored! I'm thinking of getting satellite television, but does that mean I have to have one of those ghastly dish things on the house?'

Aside from the Grand National and the odd *Only Fools and Horses* repeat because he fancied Raquel, she'd never known her father to watch television in his life. 'Um, no, you don't need a satellite dish. You could get Virgin, like me. It's all underground cables.'

'What? Where would they go? I don't want them

messing up the lawns. And will I get the racing channel?'

'Yes, you'll . . .' Harriet stopped. There was no point in getting into this conversation. She had an idea. 'Daddy, why don't you ask Jed? I'm pretty sure he and Camilla have Virgin at the cottage. He can come and explain it to you.' She was sure Jed wouldn't mind helping her father out; he was up at the Hall most of the time, anyway.

'Humph. All right. As long as he doesn't speak all that new-fangled technology gobbledygook.'

People were starting to line up at the kitchen hatch to get their refreshments. 'Daddy, I've got to go. I'll call you tomorrow, OK?'

'I suppose so. So you haven't got yourself a chap yet then?'

'Goodbye, Daddy,' Harriet said firmly and put the phone down.

*　　　*　　　*

Abby was nowhere to be seen as they stacked the chairs back up later. A young, gangly boy was hanging around in the foyer. Zack spotted him and called out through the open door. 'All right, Lewis?'

The boy looked up from under his baseball cap. 'Yeah. She finished yet?'

Zack looked over his shoulder. 'Coming right up.'

Win pushed through the doors, buttoning her coat up. 'Lewis! Have you come to take me home, my knight in shining armour?'

Lewis glanced at Harriet and blushed. 'Dunno about that.'

82

Win waddled over and took his arm. 'Come on, then, before I turn into a pumpkin.' She winked at Harriet. 'I'll see you soon, darlin'.' She looked at Zack. 'You make sure you walk Harriet to the bus stop now, we can't have a young lady like her wandering around in the dark.'

Zack shot her an irritated look. 'I was going to, anyway.'

Ignoring him, Win beamed at Harriet. Lewis opened the door for Win, and Harriet watched as they walked off down the path. Halfway down, Win stopped and turned the young boy's baseball cap round the right way.

Zack did up the last of the padlocks, and turned round. 'Right then, my lady, let's get you home.'

They headed back down the road, walking in silence. Harriet could see Zack's breath in her eyeline, a cloud against the cold night air. 'Who's Lewis?' she asked, trying to start up a conversation.

'Another one Aunty Win has taken under her wing. He was a very troubled lad, but she's brought him right out of himself.'

'She's amazing with young people.'

'She's amazing with everything. I don't know what I'd do without her.'

'Are you related, then?'

'Nah. But Aunty Win's been part of my life for as long as I can remember.' He shoved his hands in his pockets. 'You and Pete seemed to be getting on.'

'He's great.' Harriet decided to strike out into deeper waters instead. 'How long have you been with your girlfriend?' she asked.

The playful look faded from Zack's face.

83

'Girlfriend?'

'Er, yes. Abby . . .' Harriet was regretting going down this road. *She barely knew the guy, and here she was, starting on about his private life.*

Luckily Zack didn't look too offended. 'Abby's not my girlfriend,' he said, sounding more amused than anything.

Harriet was surprised by the relief she felt. 'Sorry, I just thought . . .'

He shot her a funny look. 'She's eighteen. I'm thirty-three. That would be a bit weird.'

'Sorry . . .' Harriet felt like an idiot. 'I just thought, from the way Abby was with me . . .'

'Abby's like that with most people, don't worry. She's had a rough life, finds it hard to trust people. Kai's dad left her in the shit, and now she lives with her mum, who gives her a hard time by all accounts. I feel for the kid.'

He looked up the road. 'Isn't that your bus?'

Relieved by the distraction, Harriet fumbled around in her huge handbag for her Oyster card. 'Thank you for walking me,' she said as the bus pulled up.

Zack stepped back. 'I should be the one thanking you.'

The doors hissed open. 'Well, goodnight, then,' she said, well aware the driver was observing everything with interest.

'Night. You're up next Wednesday, right?'

The driver gave a pointed cough.

'Night, then!' Harriet stepped on the bus.

'Hey, Harriet.'

She turned round expectantly. *Was he going to say how well it had gone tonight?*

Zack gestured with his hand. 'Can I have a

84

word?'

There was a loud sigh behind her. 'This isn't a pick-up joint, you know!'

Harriet flushed. 'I won't be a minute,' she told the driver. She turned back to Zack, smiling. 'Yes?'

He dropped his voice. 'I meant to say something earlier. You've got a bit of currant stuck in your teeth.'

Harriet froze. 'Currant?'

'Yeah.' Zack gestured at his front teeth. 'It's been there all night, I meant to tell you.'

Behind her, the driver snorted with laughter.

The smile dropped off her face. 'Oh!' She stepped back on the bus, and the doors slid shut between them. Zack gave a sympathetic half wave as the bus pulled off. Beetroot red, Harriet shuffled past the laughing driver and sank down in a window seat. *Why did these things always happen to her?*

Chapter 10

Churchminster

Yay! As Saffron manoeuvred her way around another hairpin bend she felt a surge of excitement. She was seeing Tom in a whole five minutes! Even though it had been just over a week since she'd left London, it had felt like a lifetime. Locked away in that study, she'd been counting down the days, hours, and minutes.

Saffron strong-armed the car up into third gear. Her mother's battered old MG had seen better days, and the heater had broken, making it feel like she was driving around in an icebox. Suddenly, a decrepit blue tractor with a geriatric-looking driver pulled out from nowhere in front of her and started trundling down the road. Saffron groaned: getting stuck behind this was all she needed. Sighing, she hauled the car down into first, and hoped the driver would turn off soon.

She spent more tortuous minutes behind the tractor, each one feeling like an hour, as it crawled through the market town of Bedlington, before finally turning off down a side road. The station was just on the other side of the town, and as Saffron pulled in she saw the car park was dark and empty. She cursed aloud. Had Tom got fed up with waiting in the cold and got a cab? She wouldn't blame him if he had. She got her phone out to see if he'd rung, but as usual there was no reception.

A knock on her window nearly made her jump out of her skin. There, muffled up against the cold in a winter jacket and scarf, was Tom. He waved solemnly as Saffron wound the window down.

'Sorry, babe! It sounds a total line but I got stuck behind a tractor.'

Tom grinned. 'S'all right, I made do with the charms of Bedlington station's waiting room.'

Saffron leant across and unlocked the door. 'Get in, you must be freezing. Just chuck your bag in the back.' He walked round and got in beside her. 'Brrr.' His normally pale face was tinged with pink, and his big brown eyes were peeking out from over the scarf. He pulled it down to kiss her properly. Saffron felt his lips, deliciously cold against hers.

'I've been waiting to do that all week,' he murmured.

Saffron was instantly overcome with lust. She didn't care if they died of hypothermia. It was like she had been in a state of inertia all week, and the moment he touched her, she came alive again. Her hand moved down on to his groin and squeezed. 'Oh, hello,' said Tom. Saffron slid a hand inside his pants. His cock felt like an extra-large pocket warmer. Instantly it began to stiffen. 'Are you serious?' he asked. 'I might get a nasty case of frostbite in these temperatures.'

Saffron giggled. 'Might as well get as much use out of it while we can, then.' She kicked off her Ugg boots and wriggled out of her leggings, shivering as her bare flesh touched the cold leather seat. Somehow Tom hauled her over the gear stick to sit on him, her legs scrunched either side of the seat. 'If we can do it in here, we can do it anywhere,' she said, gasping as his hands ran up her back, under her jumper. 'Jesus! Your hands are freezing!'

'It was your idea, don't forget,' he said, kissing her neck. 'And there's no way I'm stopping now.'

Saffron could feel his full erection now, hard and large underneath her. She opened his zip, pulled aside her knickers and slid down easily on him. He felt hot and warm, the perfect antidote to all the coldness. She started to ride him.

'That feels good,' he said, voice thick and low. His hands crept round to her front, his icy fingers making her nipples stand to attention.

The little car started to rock from side to side. Someone might drive in any moment now and see them, but Saffron was beyond the point of being able to stop. As her orgasm started to build she scrunched her toes in ecstatic heaven. 'Aah, aah . . . oh my God, I'm going to COME!' She slumped down on his chest, her heart hammering.

Tom raked his hands through his hair. 'That was some welcome.'

She smiled wickedly. 'Wait until you see my farewell.'

*　　　*　　　*

It was past eight by the time they got back to Hardwick House. The green seemed contented and silent, the impressive outline of St Bartholomew's church watching over the village protectively.

'It's nice to be back,' Tom said, lugging his holdall out of the boot.

'Hello, darlings!' Babs was already waiting on the front doorstep. She cast an anxious look at Saffron. 'I was worried. There's ice on the roads and you've been gone for ages.'

'Sorry, Mum, bad traffic.'

Babs threw her arms round Tom. 'It's my favourite boy-in-law!'

'Thanks, Babs,' Tom said through a mouthful of red hair. 'It's good to be here.'

She took his hand and led him back inside the house. 'We've been so looking forward to seeing you! Saffron's bed is ready. Darling, do you want to take Tom up and show him?'

'Cool, then we'll come and join you for a drink.' Saffron started to say, 'Remember to mind the ceilings . . .' just as Tom banged his head.

He rubbed it ruefully. 'Too late.'

88

'Poor baby, I'll kiss it better for you later.'

In the end Babs had insisted Saffron carried on writing, and had got the bedroom ready for Tom. She had made up the double bed with fresh sheets, and had even put some winter stems from the garden in the little vase on the side table. Saffron was just thinking how sweet it was when she noticed the condom packet on the pillow, with a note next to it in her mum's sprawling handwriting. *It was the last packet in the shop, but Brenda said to let her know if you need any more! Mummy xx*

They looked at each other across the bed. 'Jesus!' Saffron said.

Tom's mouth opened and shut like a goldfish. 'I suppose it's nice the whole village makes sure we practise safe sex?'

'Drinkies are ready!' Babs shouted up the stairs.

'I think I need one,' Saffron said faintly. Suddenly she was pushed on the bed, Tom kissing her. Saffron responded by wrapping her legs round his back.

'Mmm . . .'

'Do you want me to bring them up?' Babs called.

'We're *coming*, Mum!' Saffron sat up. 'If not in the literal sense. Come on, we'd better go. She'll try and climb in with us, next.'

Downstairs, Babs was delighted with the new paints Tom had bought her from the art shop round the corner from where he worked.

'They're just what I wanted, how did you know?'

'You were talking about it last week, on the phone.' Saffron smiled across at him. It was typical of Tom to be so thoughtful.

Babs had found some half-melted candles and stuck them in empty wine bottles. The effect was more student's squat than sophisticated ambience, but the low light did flatter the room. *At least you couldn't see the pile of paintbrushes soaking in the sink*, thought Saffron. She'd already cleaned up once today in here.

Tom had the champagne flute in his big hand. 'Good day writing, Saff?'

She reached out, her fingers brushing the dining room table. 'Touch wood, but it's still flowing! I'm totally into Serendipity.'

'How about the bastard boyfriend, Jake?'

'Still very bastard-like.'

'It's so nice to have a fellow creative in the house,' trilled Babs. 'You know, I think I've produced my best work since you moved in.'

Tom raised an amused eyebrow. 'Oh yes?' His eyes twinkled at Saffron.

Babs's face lit up. 'Actually, you can give me your opinion on my latest masterpiece!' She grabbed Tom's hand and led him round to the easel.

'Yeah, Tom, what do you think?' Saffron said wickedly. 'What's your *interpretation*?'

Babs peered up at him expectantly. 'From one artist to another! What do you think?' Ever since she'd found out that Tom was a designer, Babs had referred to them as 'kindred spirits'.

He cleared his throat. 'It's very atmospheric, Babs. You've done a really good job of capturing, ah, the elements.'

Babs looked chuffed. 'Spot on, as always!' She clasped his hands in her bony fingers. 'I'd like you to have it. Call it a belated Christmas present.'

'Oh, I couldn't possibly,' Tom said hastily.

'Nonsense!' Babs cried. 'It would be a great honour if you would hang it on your wall. Besides,

90

I could do with the space.' A loud beeping went off, making Saffron and Tom jump. Babs beamed. 'Dinner is served.'

They sat down to a dubious dinner made by Babs. She said it was lamb, but it tasted more like old boot. Tom gallantly ate his way through it as he told them about work. After the most edible part of the meal—a shop-bought lemon tart—Saffron was suddenly overcome with tiredness. It had to be all the country air, not that she'd experienced much of it yet.

She put her hand over Tom's. 'Do you fancy going to bed, babe?'

He suppressed a yawn. 'Yeah, I'm pretty whacked. It's been a long week.'

'You'll need to conserve your energy for tomorrow,' Babs told him. 'Saffron's got a big walk planned.' She emptied the rest of the wine bottle into her glass. 'I'm going to stay up for a while and work on a painting, but if you lovebirds need anything just call!'

'*Lovebirds*,' muttered Saffron.

'Can I help with the washing-up?' Tom asked.

Babs shook her head. 'Don't worry. I'll chuck it all in together when I clean my paintbrushes later.'

Saffron took that as their cue to escape. 'Oh my God, what is she like?' she said, flopping down on her bed. 'I swear she embarrasses me on purpose.'

'She loves you.'

Saffron felt a bit guilty. Tom didn't even have a mum. She'd died of cancer eight years ago. He'd been the one who'd persuaded Saffron not to give up on Babs, and to give their relationship another go.

'Yeah, I know that, really.' She sat up and kissed

him. 'I don't mean to sound like a brat.'

'You're not a brat. Mmm, do that again,' he said as Saffron started gently nibbling at his lips.

'What, this?' she said.

'Yeah, that's about right.' He started to pull her jumper up.

'You're insatiable!' she laughed.

'No I'm not, I'm Tom,' he murmured and got down to the task in hand.

Five minutes later Saffron was lying spreadeagled on the bed, having the brains fucked out of her. Tom moaned in pleasure, pinning her down with his strong arms as he pumped away furiously. Saffron lay back and enjoyed the ride; she loved it when he became all masterful. The only thing putting her off was the fact that the bed squeaked furiously every time they moved. Saffron shut her eyes and tried to block it out, but, a minute later, there was a knock at the door. They both froze and looked at each other.

'What the fuck?' Saffron whispered. There was another knock and then the door-handle turned.

'Don't come in!' they yelled in unison.

Babs's voice came from the other side. 'Sorry to interrupt your lovemaking, but I just wanted to say that if the squeaking gets too much, it's much quieter on the left-hand side of the bed. It's mine and your father's old bed, Saffron, and we used to have the same trouble. I think the springs must have gone or something.'

Saffron felt Tom's erection deflate inside her like a burst balloon.

'I'll leave you kids to it!' Babs called out gaily. 'Have fun.'

Tom rolled off Saffron and stared at the ceiling

in shock. 'Tell me that didn't just happen.'

'It did!' Saffron sighed. 'Welcome to my new life.'

Chapter 11

The next morning, Saffron and Tom had barely got down the front path before a voice called out to them.

'Morning, Saffron! Ooh, I suppose this is the lovely Tom?' They both turned to see Brenda Briggs, who ran the village store next door and also cleaned for Clementine Standington-Fulthrope. It was almost as if she'd been waiting for them. 'I saw you go past in your mum's car last night, Saffron, and I guessed you were going to the station.'

Brenda had been at Center Parcs when Tom had visited before, and she'd never forgiven herself for missing out on such a prime bit of village gossip. Her nose quivered inquisitively.

'Tom, this is Brenda. Brenda, Tom,' Saffron said.

The shopkeeper gave Tom an approving once-over. 'You're every bit as handsome as Babs said you were.'

Tom smiled. 'Babs is very complimentary about me.'

Brenda raised her over-plucked eyebrows at Saffron. 'And modest, too! You've got yourself a good one, there.'

Saffron put an affectionate arm round Tom, grinning. 'He'll do, I suppose.'

'How's your bonkbuster going, then?'

Saffron glanced at Tom. 'Fine . . .'

Brenda chuckled. 'Bonkbuster! Whatever will they think of next? I prefer murder mysteries meself. The really grisly stuff.' She dropped her voice. 'Tell you what, if you want some filth, I've got some stories. This place is full of it!'

Saffron thought about the condom debacle from last night. If Brenda brought it up, she would die. 'Anyway, we'd better get on our walk,' she said firmly. 'Looks like rain later.'

Brenda stepped back. 'You kids have fun.'

'Is that the Brenda who, you know?' Tom whispered as they walked off.

'Sure is,' Saffron said. She cast a look back at the shop where Brenda was still watching them, arms folded.

'Bye, then!'

They decided to head for the Meadows, a sprawling woodland site south of the village. Even though winter still had a firm grip, there was a stark beauty about the exposed contours of the landscape and the bare trees. They walked along companionably, arm-in-arm. Saffron looked at Tom in the new waxed jacket she'd encouraged him to buy. They were still big this season, even though Tom didn't really care about trends.

Saffron thought he looked very handsome. He played the country squire to perfection.

'Another of your new village friends?' Tom said.

She looked ahead and saw a figure coming towards them. As they got closer Saffron realized it was Caro's grandmother, Clementine Standington-Fulthrope. The old lady looked stern, her face lost in thought.

'Hi, Clementine!'

She looked up, surprised. 'Oh, Saffron, hello. I

94

was miles away. How's the book going?' Her eyes travelled down to Saffron's bright pink Hunter wellies.

'Good, thanks.' Saffron smiled, but she was inwardly starting to hope she wouldn't have to go through the same question with everyone they met.

Clementine looked at Tom keenly. 'Tom, isn't it?'

He held his hand out. 'Nice to meet you again, Clementine.'

Clementine smiled.

'I was really sorry to hear about Errol Flynn,' Saffron said. Babs had told Saffron Errol Flynn, Clementine's flatulent old Labrador, had died a few months earlier.

Clementine's face hollowed. 'That's very nice of you.' She sighed and looked back behind her, in the direction she'd just come from. 'It doesn't feel the same going round the Meadows without him, but one must keep one's daily exercise up.'

Tom and Saffron both murmured condolences, but Clementine wasn't one to demand sympathy.

'Now then, Saffron, while you're here you must come and see me at Fairoaks,' she said briskly.

'Cool. I'd love to.'

Clementine nodded. 'Well, I won't keep you.'

They said their goodbyes and walked off. 'She seems quite a force to be reckoned with,' Tom remarked.

'I thought she appeared a bit lonely, actually,' Saffron said. 'She must miss all her family being away, especially now Errol Flynn has departed for doggie heaven.'

Tom put his arm round her. 'At least she didn't

95

ask us about our sex life.'

They ended up going on a mammoth three-hour walk, all round the village and into the countryside beyond. Tom hadn't seen Clanfield Hall before, and couldn't quite believe Harriet had grown up there. 'That's H's house?' he said, as they stood at the entrance and gazed up the long straight driveway to the honey-coloured stately home, and its sweeping grounds and landscaped gardens.

'Yup. Pokey, isn't it?'

He laughed, rubbing his hands to keep warm. 'Shall we head back? I don't know about you, but I'm getting pretty hungry.'

On a whim, they decided to go to the pub. Saffron was surprised how packed the place was, but Jack managed to find them a spot by the window.

'I still can't get over the size of Harriet's gaff,' Tom said, taking a sip of his pint. 'I knew she had family money, but Clanfield Hall is something else.'

'You'd never guess, though, would you?' Saffron said. 'H is one of the poshest people I know, but she doesn't go on about it.'

She took a little sip of her drink and fell quiet.

'You OK?' Tom asked.

She looked up. 'Course. You're here, aren't you?'

His gaze was steady, reassuring. 'You've done the right thing, you know.'

'Done what?'

'Moving out here to write your book.'

'I know. It's just so *quiet*. And I miss you. I even miss Leroy. How is our baby cactus, by the way?'

'He's in a bit of a prickly mood at the moment.'

It was such a stupid joke Saffron had to laugh.

Tom smiled. 'That's better.'

The afternoon was already growing dark as they left. The village was settling down for the evening, lights starting to come on in house windows. Saffron had a sudden desire to get back to Hardwick House and light the log fire. Maybe they could even get some crumpets to toast from the shop.

They'd got a few metres down the road when something beeped. 'Excitement!' Saffron said. 'We must have discovered one of Churchminster's rare reception spots.'

Tom pulled his phone out. 'Text message. From Rex.' He read it. 'He's in Sri Lanka.'

'That boy gets about. What does it say?

'You want the full version? *Yo bro . . .*'

'Yo *bro*?'

'He's been in America too long. You have to forgive him. Anyway, *Yo bro, having a few weeks holiday. Need to recharge my batteries and all that. Just want to let you know where I'm at, catch you soon. R*'

'It's all right for some,' Saffron said. 'I could just do with lying on a sandy white beach.'

'I couldn't.' Tom put his arms round her. 'I can't think of anywhere else I'd rather be, even with the mud and freezing temperatures. As long as you're here.' He lifted her off the ground in his bear-like grip. 'I love you, Saff.'

She nuzzled into him. 'I love you too, babe.'

Suddenly, he threw her over his shoulder and swung round.

'What are you doing?' she shrieked. 'Put me down!'

'Who says there's no excitement in the country?' he said, and started for home.

Chapter 12

London

It was Monday evening, and Harriet was just leaving the office, when her phone rang. Scrabbling around in her bag, she pushed through the revolving doors of Valour Publishing and on to the street. The cold dark night was like a slap around the cheeks.

'Hello?'

'Hi, Harriet. It's Zack.'

'Oh, hello!' Automatically her stomach dropped. She'd only just recovered from the dried-fruit disaster.

'Sorry about the short notice, but I was wondering if you'd be able to come in tonight. We've got a kids' party on, and I'm really understaffed.'

'Oh, um . . .' Harriet had been looking forward to swinging past M&S for some gourmet food, and then curling up in her pyjamas on the sofa.

'If it's a problem . . .'

She imagined his blue eyes at the other end. 'It's fine. I'd be happy to come in.'

He sounded relieved. 'You're a star. See you soon.'

*   *   *

'Thanks again for coming in tonight.' Harriet looked up from wiping the kitchen surface. Zack was standing in the doorway. She'd noticed he'd had his hair cut, the close crop accentuating the nice shape of his head.

'No problem, I've had fun.' She laughed. 'I think I may have an admirer, someone called Nathan asked me if I wanted to "get off" with him round the back. At least I think those were the words he used.'

Zack shook his head, smiling. 'Bloody hell. Sorry.'

'I'm rather flattered, actually! It's about the only action I'm getting at the moment.' As soon as she'd said the words she regretted them. 'I don't make a habit of chasing around after fourteen-year-olds,' she added hastily.

Zack laughed. 'Pleased to hear it. Hey, do you fancy a drink after this?'

'A drink?' She felt herself starting to blush.

'Yeah, there's a pub a few minutes' walk off the estate.'

'I'd love to! Thanks for asking me.'

He shot her a quizzical look. 'It was Gray's idea. We were going for a pint, and he asked me to see if you wanted to come along.'

Oh God. This time she went puce. 'Erm, yeah, that's great.'

The three of them were the last to leave. As Zack locked up, Gray was telling Harriet about his middle daughter, Charlie, when the theme tune to *Rocky* started playing from his pocket. 'Uh-oh, that'll be the madhouse.' He pulled his mobile out. 'Hello? What's up?' He listened, face concerned. 'I'll be home in ten, sweetheart.'

He clicked off. 'That was my daughter, she's come down with something. Sue's at work, I'd better go and see if she's OK. Sorry, mate.'

'No problem,' Zack said. 'Hope Charlie gets better.'

'Yeah, sure it's nothing.' Gray waved. 'See you, Harriet.' He unlocked his bike from the railings at the side of the centre, and wheeled off down the path.

Harriet looked at Zack. 'If you want to cancel . . .' She'd only been invited as an afterthought, after all.

He glanced after Gray. 'No, let's go anyway. I need a beer.'

From the little sigh she heard, it was obvious he was only being polite. Rather self-consciously Harriet started to follow him down the path, but Zack suddenly stopped.

'Party's over, guys.'

She looked beyond him, to see a gang of people sitting on bikes at the end of the path. They were wearing hooded tops pulled down over their faces, and even Harriet could feel the hostility radiating off them.

The gang made no attempt to move. Zack started to walk down the path, putting himself between the gang and Harriet. 'I said the centre's closed. If you want to come back, we'll be open tomorrow.'

As he got closer one of them made a guttural 'hoik' sound in the back of his throat, and spat near Zack's feet.

'If you're looking for trouble, you've come to the wrong place.' Zack's voice was studiedly neutral, but Harriet could hear the steel underneath. For a moment nothing happened. One of the gang shifted on their saddle, and Harriet caught a glimpse of the face underneath the hood. She was shocked to see it was a girl, but there was nothing feminine about the aggressive chin and flat, glinting eyes. Another gang member at the front suddenly reared their bike on its back wheels, making Harriet jump. He or she gave an imperceptible nod, and bounced forward, and the others followed, gliding into the night.

Harriet realized she had been digging her fingernails into her palms. Zack turned to her. 'They're just kids with nothing else to do, don't let them scare you,' he said reassuringly.

'I'm fine!' Harriet had been scared, but she wasn't going to admit it. There was a quiet confidence about Zack that made her feel safer, but she was still relieved when they approached the bright lights of the pub. It was a small, old-fashioned place called the Crown, with the definite air of an old-fashioned boozer. Even though it was a Monday, the place was pretty busy, the clientele a mixture of old-school North-London types and new, younger trendies. Zack insisted on buying the drinks, so Harriet went off to find a table. A few minutes later Zack reappeared with a large glass of white wine for her, and a bottle of lager.

'Cheers,' he said. They clinked glasses. Harriet took a sip. Her wine tasted somewhere between dishwater and lighter fuel.

Zack eyed her over his bottle. 'How are you finding things, then?'

'Things?'

'Us. The centre.'

'They're great.'

A flash of humour crossed his face. 'I'll be honest, I didn't think you'd last five minutes.'

'And why's that?' she asked agreeably, knowing

101

perfectly well what he was getting at.

'You know, when you first came in with the Princess Diana thing . . .'

'Princess *Diana*?'

'Yeah.' He smiled, trying to suss her out. 'You know, doing the charity act.'

She felt her face grow unexpectedly hot. 'It's not an *act*, Zack, I just want to help. I thought that's what volunteering was about.'

There was an awkward silence. 'I've offended you. I'm sorry.'

'It's all right,' she muttered. She hated having cross words.

'I mean it. Bad joke, sorry.' He gave a conciliatory smile. 'Let's start again, shall we?' He sat back. 'So tell me a bit about yourself.'

She blinked at the about-turn in the conversation. 'There's nothing to tell really, I work at a magazine called *Soirée*, I come from a little village in the Cotswolds called Churchminster . . . er . . .'

Zack gestured with his bottle. 'Bit different from this place, I imagine.'

She smiled. 'How about you? Have you always lived here?'

'Born and bred.'

'Do you still have family here?'

'There was just me and Mum. I never knew my dad. Mum died when I was fourteen, so I went into a home.'

He didn't volunteer any more information. 'I'm sorry,' Harriet said, thinking how feeble she must sound. He shrugged. 'It happened and I had to deal with it. I had Aunty Win anyway. She's my family.'

'How long were you in the children's home, if you don't mind me asking?'

Zack took another swig. 'Two years. Left when I was sixteen. I went to work on the markets, selling anything and everything. Then a building site, delivering, managing a hardware shop . . . You name it, I've done it.'

'So how did you end up running the centre?'

He rubbed at an old stain on the table. 'I guess I felt like I owed the estate something. You know, growing up here. I'd been away working and stuff, and when I came back loads of places had shut down, including the centre. People had nowhere to go. I just wanted them to feel like they had a community again.'

'I think it's really admirable, what you've done.'

'I don't know about admirable. I'm a sucker for long hours and crap pay, maybe.' He sighed. 'I'm not sure how much longer it's going to last, though.'

'Your job?'

'No, the centre.'

'Really?' Harriet was shocked.

He glanced at her. 'I probably shouldn't be telling you this.'

'I won't say anything,' she said. 'Are things really that bad?' The centre was scruffy and in need of some decent equipment, but it was so vibrant and full of life. Harriet couldn't bear the idea of it being closed down. What would everyone do? Where would they go?

'Things aren't great, put it that way. It was always going to be a battle. I knew that, but we can barely afford to run the place. With all the government cuts it's even worse. Getting money off the council

103

is like getting blood from a stone.'

'What about fundraising? Would that help?'

'We've done little bits and pieces, but it's not enough. We need big money if we've any chance of making the centre a success.' He stood up. 'I brought you down here to say thank you, not bang on about our troubles. Another?'

'Please, I insist.' As Harriet stood at the bar waiting to get served she started thinking. Her trust fund was sitting in Coutts bank, barely touched. She was never going to need all of it . . .

She came back with two bottles of beer and put them down on the table.

'Thank you,' he told her.

'My pleasure.'

They sat there in silence for a few moments. Harriet plucked up the courage. 'Zack, you know what you said before, about needing money. I could help . . .'

He looked at her. 'I don't follow.'

She smiled hesitantly. 'I've got some money, family money. If there's anything I can do to help, I'd love to.'

He gave a short laugh. 'Thanks, Harriet, but you don't have to do that. Save your money for another big house in the country, or something.'

She knew she'd offended him. 'I didn't mean to . . .'

'You haven't, OK?' He grimaced. 'Anyway, I'm sure your family would have something to say about   it.'

'I don't care what they think, Zack, I'm old enough to make my own decisions.'

It was as if she hadn't spoken. Zack drained his bottle. 'I'd better be getting back. Do you want me to book you a cab?'

Harriet bit her lip. 'Yes, please.'

'I'll go and ask the barman.' He got up, body language rigid. Harriet slumped back miserably in her seat. They'd been getting on so well, and then she'd had to go and ruin it.

Chapter 13

Churchminster

Saffron stared out of the window. She was missing London today. Her friends, her job, the hustle and bustle. *Tom.* If it were possible, being apart from him had made her realize she loved him even more than she'd thought. She missed him being part of her day, his presence round the house, the way he touched her if they passed in the corridor.

Saffron looked at the calendar on the desk. It was the first of March tomorrow. She couldn't believe she'd been in Churchminster a whole month. It felt like a lifetime. How would she survive another five without her Tom?

Don't be so wet, she told herself. It wasn't as if they were thousands of miles apart, living in different countries. Willing herself to find it inspiring, she reached for one of the writing books Tom had given her. As she did so, a little white card fell out. Saffron picked it up. Something was written on it in Tom's neat, precise handwriting.

'To my sexy little novelist, don't forget how good you are! I'm very proud of you. All my love, Tom xx'

It was almost as if he'd known. Heart full,

Saffron put the card down and started to write. She knew she could do anything as long as she had Tom.

*   *   *

'Harrumph! How does one move these blasted channels?' Sir Ambrose Fraser stared at the remote control in his hand, as puzzled as if it had just broken off an alien landing craft.

Patiently Jed showed him how to use it again— for the eighth time. 'You press the arrows up and down.' Jed clicked another button. 'And this one shows you what's on all the channels, so you can see what you want to watch.'

Sir Ambrose shook his head. 'Looks like a bloody foreign language to me.'

'You'll get the hang of it, Sir Ambrose, it just takes practice.'

Ambrose grunted. 'I've got plenty of time for that. I hear your other half's left you to go gallivanting off all over the place as well.'

Jed nodded vaguely. It was a bit weird, the boss asking him about his personal life. All the years he'd worked at Clanfield he didn't think they'd discussed any subject more intimate than whether springer or cocker spaniels made better hunting dogs.

Ambrose was shaking his head. 'These bloody women, they think they're Ranulph Fiennes.' The gleam of pride in his eyes indicated he wasn't really that cross. 'I'm having a whale of a time here without the prison gaoler,' he continued. 'One can eat as much Nestlé condensed milk out of the tin as one wants, without fear of getting one's

106

knuckles rapped for it.' A wistful look came over his face. 'Somehow it doesn't taste as good without the threat of discovery.'

'I can imagine, Sir Ambrose,' Jed said tactfully. He really had to get back to work.

Ambrose looked at him. 'Oh, enough of the "sirs". We're compatriots, aren't we?'

Jed took a deep breath. 'Well . . .'

Ambrose's eyes lit up, and he interrupted. 'I know! How about you and I have one of those boys' nights in?'

At this Jed's eyebrows shot up in surprise. 'You, Sir Ambrose? You and me?'

'Yes, yes, why not? We're in the same boat together, after all.' Sir Ambrose peered at him. 'We could have one of those takeout curries or something. Just don't tell Cook, she'll have a blue fit.' He clapped his hands together. 'Ha! I'm looking forward to it already.'

There was no way Jed could turn his boss down. Wondering if Ambrose was losing the plot, Jed gritted his teeth and smiled.

*   *   *

In the kitchen at Fairoaks, Clementine was sitting at the kitchen table with her mid-morning cup of Earl Grey tea. Usually the light, fragrant taste refreshed her, but today she was feeling unusually listless. She looked round the large, stone-flagged kitchen. On the corkboard by the door was a new school photo of Milo that Caro had sent her. Clementine smiled as she looked at it; he was such a handsome little chap. It was frightening how fast her great-grandchildren were growing up. Caro kept suggesting she should get the train up to visit them, but Clementine was getting too old to take on the trials of First Great Western. Besides, she had never been a big fan of London.

She took another sip of tea and looked round the room. It suddenly seemed very big and empty. She'd had such good memories here, setting up home with her husband Bertie, raising children, and then a houseful of her lovely granddaughters. Now Bertie wasn't with her any more, and everyone had their own lives to get on with. Clementine's eyes wandered to the floor in front of the Aga, where Errol Flynn's basket used to be. He would have been sniffing round her ankles now, ever hopeful for a crumb of biscuit . . . Errol, in all his smelly, snuffling glory, was irreplaceable. She would never find another dog like him.

Clementine blinked the tears away. She was turning into a silly, sentimental old woman. She felt so decrepit: without a Labrador by her side her daily walks seemed pointless, her bones seizing up by the day. Her mind felt cloudy, too, as if it was watching what was happening to her body and going the same way. *Is this it?* she wondered in a moment of panic. *Is my life winding down already?*

She got up and took her cup and saucer over to the sink. She washed them and dried up with the National Trust tea towel, then stood looking down at the solitary cup, saucer, and teaspoon on the draining board.

A bird flew past the window, making her look up. Outside, the garden was full of greenery, sunlight glinting off every leaf and tree. Normally Clementine's heart would have lifted at the sight, but she just felt despondent. She couldn't even be bothered to do any gardening, which was normally her favourite activity. Clutching the side of the worktop, she stared off into the distance. Her life had always been so full until now, with family, friends, the village committee. *What had happened?* Something had to change, something new had to come along.

Otherwise, Clementine was frightened that one day she'd sit down and never get up again.

MARCH

Chapter 14

London

It had been over a week since Harriet's ill-fated drink with Zack. Even though she'd been up at the centre since, he'd been locked away in his office and she'd barely seen him. She wondered if he was ignoring her, but told herself not to be so silly. As if Zack hadn't got enough to think about with the centre! He probably just thought she was an idiot. Harriet cringed; she'd been replaying the conversation in her mind for the last ten days. Talk about putting her foot in it! She should have thought before opening her big mouth.

The one person who definitely wasn't ignoring her was Aunty Win. She seemed to have taken a shine to Harriet, and always made a beeline for her. Unless she was a very good actress, Zack hadn't told her about Harriet's ill-fated offer of money.

It was Wednesday study club, Harriet's regular night to come in. She was becoming quite a hit with the study group; well, with everyone except Abby, who was retaking several GCSEs and had rebuffed any offer of help. On the other hand, Pete was coming along beautifully. He was Harriet's star pupil, and it was wonderful to see his confidence grow.

Once again Zack had spent the evening in his office. Harriet was just putting her scarf on, and wondering whether she should go and knock on the door to break the ice, when Aunty Win appeared and grabbed her by the arm.

'Before you go, 'Arriet! What are you doing tomorrow night?'

Harriet was meant to be going to a PR event with some of the girls from work.

'I've got a thing after work, actually.'

The old lady smiled. 'Pff! You can put that off, surely. Come for dinner.'

'Um . . .'

'That's settled then! Seven thirty. I'll write down my address.'

There was no way Harriet could say no now. 'Is it a volunteers' dinner?' Harriet asked, as she watched Win write her address in big swirly writing.

Win looked up. 'No, dear, just you, me and Zachary.'

Harriet's stomach lurched. 'Does Zack know I'm coming?'

'No, dear,' Win said cheerfully. 'But he will.' She waddled off, before Harriet could say another word.

*   *   *

It was nearly home time in the *Soirée* office. Alexander Napier stopped dead in front of Harriet's desk. 'Someone's been shopping!' he said, his trained eye spotting the Jigsaw bag by the side of her chair. 'Let's have a look.'

Harriet reached down and pulled out the heavy burgundy mid-length dress. She'd told herself she needed a new dress anyway, but that wasn't really true. This one had looked rather nice on the rack surrounded by all the other frippery, but now she wasn't sure.

'What do you think?'

Alexander raised an eyebrow. 'Perfect! That's if you're going to a Gothic wedding, or funeral.' He looked down at her. 'I assume it's neither?'

Harriet had to smile. Alexander had a way with words. 'Just dinner at a friend's.'

He perched on the desk. 'A friend you had to buy a new dress for? So, who is he?'

'It's not really him . . .' Harriet had kept her volunteering a secret from work until now. They teased her about having a title as it was, without her letting on she was 'toughing' it out on a bad rep council estate.

'It's some people I've met through this volunteer work I've been doing.'

'How admirable, darling!' To her relief Alexander didn't ask what. He whisked the dress out of her hand. 'Stand up.' He held the dress against her with a critical eye. 'Hmm, yes, I suppose it's not *totally* hideous. Come on.' He pulled her towards the fashion cupboard.

In a glossy magazine like *Soirée*, the fashion cupboard was hallowed ground. Alexander pushed Harriet in, past the rails of Marc Jacobs, Zac Posen and Stella McCartney, while he shouted orders to Jemima, his fashion assistant.

'Jem, darling, can you bring me the gold Alaia belt, the wide one with the stitching—*not* the zip edge—and a selection of earrings. I'm thinking sexy, not slutty.'

Jemima, a size 6 doll with soft pink hair, chewed the top of her fluffy pen. 'The Oscar de la Renta gold leaves?'

'*Perfect,*' Alexander gushed. He turned to

Harriet. 'Right, you, let's see the dress on.'

Harriet looked round. 'Here?'

'I won't look, come on!' As Harriet shuffled over to get changed behind another rail he started looking through a selection of shoes. 'What size are you?'

'Five.' Harriet pulled the dress over her head and came out. Her cleavage positively tumbled out. She hadn't realized the front was quite so low-cut.

Alexander whirled round to look. '*Great* knockers, darling, you should really get them out more.' He started fussing at her dress. 'Belt.' Jem, who was now standing behind him with an armful of offerings, handed it to him.

'It's too tight!' Harriet was horrified as he pulled the wide belt round her. Why on earth would she attract attention to her wobbly stomach?

'No pain, no gain, darling. This will make your waist look positively Victoria Beckham-esque.' He put out his hand again. 'Earrings.' He held them up to her face critically. 'And if you have your hair back . . . Perfect! You know, you are a pretty girl under all that Fat Face clobber.'

Jem shot a smile at Harriet as Alexander reached for a pair of high strappy brown heels done up in ribbons. 'Definitely the Givenchys, show off those thoroughbred ankles.' He propelled her in front of the full-length mirror, looking like a proud uncle. 'There!'

He'd certainly done his magic. Harriet couldn't believe how tall and shapely she looked. Instead of looking like a tree trunk, her waist was waspishly small, emphasizing her full breasts and slim ankles, while the gold accessories brought out the warm tones in her hair and eyes.

116

'We'll just get a bit of make-up on you,' Alexander said, 'and then Cinderella shall go to the ball!'

She may have felt a million dollars leaving the office, but Harriet felt distinctly self-conscious as she tottered up the front path to Win's in a pair of £600 shoes Alexander had told her they had to send back to the PR tomorrow. Harriet was terrified she was going to get a mark on them. The cabbie, who had charged 'danger money' for bringing her there, gave a wolf whistle and went off with a wheelspin.

Turning back to the row of tiny terrace houses, Harriet located Aunty Win's. Pristine net curtains hung at the windows, and the windowsills below were cluttered with china ornaments. *Be cool*, she told herself. Taking a deep breath, she pushed the doorbell. Moments later the door opened. Zack stood there, freshly shaved and smelling of Issey Miyake. His eyes travelled up and down her outfit. Harriet put a hand on her hip, as Alexander had told her to.

'Hello, Zack,' she said casually. 'Fancy seeing you here!'

Chapter 15

Churchminster

She'd been writing for hours, but Saffron was still gripped by inspiration.

'What the hell are you doing here?' Serendipity said. She'd woken to find Jake standing naked in the middle of her hotel room. His clothes were lying where they'd fallen, ~~manhood~~ ~~willy~~ ~~member~~ cock rock-hard and ready.

'The concierge let me in.'

'You followed me all the way out to Italy? What do you want, Jake?'

'I want you.' He smiled, white teeth in a tanned face. '~~It's time to let the tiger out of the cage.~~ I want to make love to you, my little Seren.'

'Like you made love to Vanessa?' she shot back. 'And how about all the others?'

Jake's smile didn't waver. 'Baby, we've been through this. I'm sorry. She's the one who ~~seduced~~ jumped me.'

'Wouldn't surprise me. She's obviously as big a slut as you are.'

He advanced on the bed. 'I miss you. You and me had some good times, didn't we?' He grinned goofily, playing the little-boy-lost act. 'I love you, babe.'

She looked at him, unabashed in his sexuality.

'You love me, do you?' Serendipity asked.

118

'Hey, babe, more than anything in the world!'

She picked up a silk cushion and threw it at his ~~bollocks~~ *nether regions. 'You lying shit. If you loved me, you wouldn't* ~~pork~~ *shag anything that moves. Get out and don't come back!'*

Saffron pressed 'save' and sat back. 'You go, Seren!' she declared. Leaving behind the glossy world of cheating rock stars, she went to phone Tom.

London

'Well now 'Arriet, don't you look beautiful!' Aunty Win pronounced it, 'Bee-yoo-tiful.' She looked at Zach. 'Zachary, don't you agree?'

They were standing in Win's small, immaculate kitchen. A big pot was bubbling on the stove, while a small table in the corner of the room had been laid out beautifully, a vase of cheery flowers placed in the middle.

Zack was looking at Harriet's feet. 'Good shoes.'

'They're by Givenchy, apparently.'

Win cast an impressed look at Zack. 'Ooh, *Givenchy.*'

Zack looked nonplussed. 'Harriet, what can I get you to drink?'

'Oh, here, take these.' She bent down and got two wine bottles out of her bag. 'One's for tonight, and the other one's for you, Aunty Win. Sancerre or a Pouilly-Fumé, which one would you prefer?'

'Lord, I don't care. As long as it's wet I'll drink it.'

Harriet decided to go for the Sancerre. 'You

want a glass of 'Arriet's posh wine, Zack?' Win asked.

He shook his head. 'I'll stick with beer, if you don't mind, wine's not really my thing.' He went over to the fridge and opened some.

'Remember your manners and use a glass, Zachary, I don't like that drinking out of the bottle.'

Zack shot Harriet a wry look. 'She's been extra bossy tonight, hostessing always does this to her.'

Harriet smiled; at least they seemed to be back on good terms again.

'Something smells delicious,' she commented. Aunty Win beamed proudly. 'Goat curry. Secret recipe that has passed down through six generations.'

Goat. Harriet had never eaten it before. They'd actually kept a pet goat called Totty at the Hall once, until it had broken free of its tether and head butted the then-housekeeper. The thought of Totty bubbling away merrily in the big cooking pot made her feel a bit queasy.

'You're not vegetarian, are you?' Zack said.

Aunty Win looked scandalized. ' 'Arriet's not *vegetarian*, look at the colour in those cheeks.' She moved back to the pot. 'Why don't you sit down? Dinner's nearly ready.'

'After you,' Zack said. Harriet chose the chair at the end of the table and sat down, leaving the central seat for Aunty Win, who came over and put two steaming plates of curry down.

Despite her reservations, Harriet's mouth started to water. It smelt gorgeous. Forcing thoughts of Totty aside, Harriet took a tentative mouthful. A mixture of tastes exploded in her mouth, the meat

120

exquisitely tender. 'Mmm,' she said. 'It's really good, Aunty Win.'

Win nodded approvingly. 'Another satisfied customer.'

They ate in silence for a few moments, savouring the food. 'So you live in a nice place in the country,' Win said, wiping her mouth. 'I've been reading all about it.'

'She made me Google Churchminster,' Zack said apologetically.

Harriet laughed in surprise. 'Really?' She couldn't believe he'd even remembered the name.

'It looks beautiful!' Aunty Win declared. 'All those big fields. I expect you lived in a nice house, didn't you?'

'Kind of,' Harriet said, not really wanting to get on to the subject of how she'd been brought up in a stately home.

'Nice big garden, hey? I like to know about people,' Win said. 'And what about your mother and father? They still together?'

'Win, give Harriet a break!'

Harriet smiled; she didn't mind the interrogation. 'Yes, they are. My mother is off travelling at the moment, actually . . .'

'Travelling! You hear that, Zachary.'

'. . . and Daddy's at home by himself. I think he's rather missing her.'

Win nodded approvingly. 'Sounds like a fine marriage.'

Harriet laughed. 'I don't know about that! My father does test my mother's patience sometimes.'

One whole wall of the kitchen was filled with photographs of Win with various children and teenagers. Harriet guessed they were local kids.

Her eyes fell on a black and white photo of a beautiful young black woman, her angular face framed by a turban. The smile and eyes looked familiar.

'Hang on, is that you, Aunty Win?'

Win waved her fork. 'Oh, that.'

'Bit of a stunner, eh?' Zack said.

Win snorted with laughter. 'I had all the men chasing after me! None I wanted to settle down with, though. Besides, I've got Him upstairs.'

As she said this, her eyes strayed to the clock on the wall for the umpteenth time since they'd sat down.

Zack clocked it. 'Are you expecting someone?'

Her eyes widened. 'Of course not.' Just then, the phone on the wall started ringing. Win sprang up with surprising vigour. 'I'll get it.' She picked it up. 'Hello? Oh, it's you, my dear.' Her hand flew to her mouth. 'How could I forget? I'll be round in a few minutes.' She turned back to Zack and Harriet. 'I'm meant to be babysitting for Danielle at number 78 tonight! I completely forgot about it!'

Zack looked at the clock. 'It's nine o'clock. You're normally in bed by now.'

Win was gathering her coat. 'I'd forget my head if it wasn't sitting on my shoulders. You two stay and have fun, now.' She added, 'I'm sure you have lots to talk about.'

Zack frowned. 'How long will you be?'

Win wound her scarf round her neck. 'A long time, probably. Don't wait up!'

The front door slammed before they knew it.

Without Aunty Win's voluminous presence, the room seemed to close in. Harriet was suddenly aware of how close she was to Zack, their legs almost touching under the fold-up table. He grinned awkwardly.

'Subtle, isn't she?'

They fell into silence. Both took a swig of their drink at the same time.

'I'm sorry . . .' They both spoke simultaneously, then stopped, embarrassed.

Zack nodded. 'You first.'

Harriet cleared her throat. 'I'm sorry, Zack, about offering the money. I honestly meant it as a good thing.'

He shook his head. 'No, *I'm* sorry. It just threw me, and I didn't know how to react. It was very generous of you.'

'And probably very inappropriate,' she said ruefully. 'I'm not a Hooray Henry on some kind of mercy mission, I promise.'

He grinned. 'Hooray Henry? Is that what they call them?'

Them. That was better. 'Look, I'm the one with the problem,' he told her. 'I just don't like taking things off people.' He rubbed his left palm. 'I don't want to take anything off you.'

'Even if the money could help?'

His tone was final. 'We'll find another way.' Blue eyes creased into a smile. 'Besides, that place needs so much spent on it we'd probably bankrupt you.'

She laughed. 'Maybe.'

'Do you want to see something?' he suddenly asked.

'OK.'

He stood up and she followed, wondering what it could be. They walked back through the pokey hall into a compact living room, made even smaller by the hundreds of knick-knacks crowding every surface. Harriet didn't know how Win found the time to dust them.

Zack went over to a side table and picked up a framed picture. It showed a young boy with eighties-style gelled hair, and a luminous matching shell-suit. 'Recognize him?'

'Look at you!' She laughed, taking in the picture. 'Our fashion editor would love that get-up.'

She was suddenly aware of how close they were standing to each other. She could see the fine downy hair on his lower arms, the strength in his hands. Suddenly she had a vision of them running all over her body.

Beside her Zack was completely still. Harriet's heart started thumping. She made herself look at him. He was gazing at her, blue eyes intense. 'Can you hear that?'

She was confused. 'Hear what?'

Zack frowned. 'The burglar alarm at the centre. I'm sure it's just gone off.'

*   *   *

The centre was only a five-minute walk from Aunty Win's. In her high heels Harriet had trouble keeping up. Zack was striding on ahead of her, long legs moving easily. Harriet could now hear the alarm herself, clanging out into the cold dark night. She couldn't believe how good Zack's ears were.

'They're tuned into this sort of thing,' he said grimly. They'd reached the centre now, the building standing in darkness. There didn't seem to be anybody around.

'Stay here,' he told her. Harriet stood at the bottom of the path, shivering, as Zack started to walk carefully round the building. A minute later he came back and tugged at the front doors.

'I can't see anything wrong,' he called out. 'There must have been a fault or something.'

Relieved, Harriet started up the path towards him. Her eyes strayed to something on the wall. 'What's that?'

Zack followed her gaze. Someone had graffitied the letters EBZ, the last letter a sharp, jagged outline. His eyes narrowed.

'At least there's no other damage,' Harriet said, trying to be positive. Zack looked *really* pissed off. After a second, he looked up at her.

'Yeah, you're right.' He sighed. 'I'll try and get it off tomorrow.'

He looked at his watch. 'Do you want to come in and call a cab? It's cold out here.'

The easy familiarity they'd had earlier was gone. Zack seemed tired, his normal reserve back. He started to unlock the door.

With a pang of disappointment Harriet looked down at her shoes. How showy and over-the-top they seemed now. What had she been thinking? This wasn't a date; she was only here because Aunty Win had invited her. Zack had given her absolutely no sign that he liked her, and why would he? She had to stop this, viewing every man she met as possible boyfriend material.

Harriet suddenly felt like the biggest fool in the world.

Chapter 16

Churchminster

'Saffron! Tom's on the phone.'

Closing her Facebook page, Saffron got up and went out on to the landing. Her mother was standing at the bottom of the stairs, waving the hands-free set.

Saffron bounded down to get it. 'Ta.' She added, 'You've got paint on your face, by the way.' Her mother looked like she was auditioning for *Braveheart*, a smear of blue streaked across her cheek.

'Have I? Silly me. I'll go and get the turpentine out.'

'Mum, that will strip your skin off! Use my make-up remover.' Saffron watched Babs weave her way back down the corridor. She was sure Babs had been drinking. She sat down on the bottom step. 'Hey, babe! It's so good to hear your voice.'

'We only spoke a few hours ago,' Tom said, sounding amused.

She picked a bit of fluff off her leggings. 'Sorry, I keep forgetting I'm the only one without a life round here.'

Tom laughed. 'Guess where I am?'

'Don't know.'

'The foyer of the Dorchester.'

The Dorchester was one of London's poshest hotels. Saffron looked at her watch. It was nearly 8 p.m. 'What are you doing there?'

'Waiting for Rex while he checks in.'

'*Rex?*' She sat up. 'What do you mean?'

'He just flew in.'

'I didn't know he was coming!'

'Neither did I, until he phoned me.' Tom sounded happy. 'Rex has never been big on giving much notice.'

'Wow!' Saffron couldn't quite believe it. 'How long's he staying?'

'Not sure. He's got an open ticket, so we'll see.' Tom lowered his voice. 'He's asked his agency for an extended break, I think he's suffering from a bit of burnout.'

'The proverbial party boy has calmed down at last?'

'I wouldn't go that far! Knowing my brother, he'll be out clubbing tomorrow.'

Saffron suddenly felt a bit anxious. 'Does this affect our plans this weekend?' Tom was meant to be coming to see her.

'Not at all. In fact, I was wondering, can I bring Rex?'

'Here? To Churchminster?' Saffron looked round the hallway, overflowing with canvases and piles of old books. 'It's hardly the Dorchester!'

'He wants to come. He'll love it.'

'OK. Fine, sure.' Saffron shook her head. 'I still can't believe he's actually here!'

'Larger than life, Saff. It's good to see him.'

'I bet!'

'I'd better go, we're going out for dinner. See you Friday, babe, Rex is really looking forward to meeting you.'

* * *

At last spring was returning. Tentative buds had started to peek out from the trees, and daffodils had popped up on the green and the grassy banks, giving a much-needed injection of colour. At Hardwick House, however, Babs was in no mood to notice the changing season. Ever since Saffron had told her they were having a VIP guest for the weekend she'd been getting into a frenzy. Especially when Saffron had dug out a magazine and showed her one of Rex's Frontline campaign photos. Floors had been swept and polished, and windows cleaned for the first time in years. Even the front porch, which Babs had been using as dumping ground for old paint, had been cleared.

'You didn't put this show on for me,' Saffron said in amusement on the Friday morning, as she watched her mother give the dining table a final rub of beeswax.

Babs's thin face was red with exertion. 'I just don't want to show you up, darling. It's not every day such an important person stays at my house.'

'He's a model, Mum, not the bloody Queen.'

Despite her cool demeanour, Saffron *was* excited. Not only was she meeting the love of her life's brother for the first time, but his identical twin! They might look exactly the same, but what would Rex be like? Would he do that cute crinkled-brow thing like Tom when he laughed? Would Rex have his head stuck up his couture-clad bottom, or would he be just as down-to-earth as his brother? She grinned at her mum. 'It *is* pretty cool. Just try not to faint with excitement when he gets here, OK?'

It was approaching seven o'clock on Friday by the time Saffron heard a car pull up outside. She

128

looked out of her bedroom window to see a black Aston Martin DB7 parked on the verge. Rex clearly had expensive tastes; when Tom had said he'd hired a car, he obviously hadn't meant from Budget.

Saffron stepped back and took a final look in the mirror. Off-the-shoulder oversized black jumper, and skinny leather trousers finished off by her Russell & Bromley pumps. Smart, but not overdone. Saffron smoothed a strand of white-blonde hair. For some reason she was feeling quite nervous.

She ducked back to the window to see two dark heads walking into the porch. The doorbell jangled. 'I'll get it!' she called, but her mother was already at the door. Saffron heard the creak as it was pulled open.

'Tom! How are you? And you must be Rex!' Her mother gasped. 'I can't believe how similar you look. It's *incredible*!'

Saffron started to descend the stairs. 'Mum, calm down . . .' As she reached the front she stopped in her tracks.

It was like having beautiful double vision. Tall and broad, the brothers literally filled the whole door. On the right was Tom, his nose slightly red from the cold. He looked handsome but tired, the beginnings of sleep-deprived shadows under his eyes.

The person next to him looked just the same, but leaner, and in high definition. While Tom had the pallor of someone who had been subjected to a British winter and long hours in the office, Rex was deeply tanned, his complexion glowing. This was one model who clearly didn't need much airbrushing. He was wearing an open black shirt, black trousers and a black blazer—which Saffron recognized as Marc Jacobs new season. The outfit showed off his body, but in an understated way. He was a good stone lighter than Tom, Saffron reckoned, but powerful and supple beneath. Even in the cramped hallway he radiated charisma. His eyes locked on to hers, playful, inviting. For a second, Saffron could see exactly why he was one of the most handsome men in America.

She jumped off the bottom step. 'Hi, you must be Rex.'

'And you must be Saffron.' He had a slight transatlantic twang. 'Tom's told me so much about you.'

'All good, I hope! She laughed as he bent down to kiss her on both cheeks. His skin was as smooth as velvet, and she got a whiff of aftershave, something light and expensive.

He touched her arm, appraising. 'Love the sweater.'

'Thanks.' It was a strangely intimate gesture. Saffron looked over at Tom. 'Hi, babe.' She noticed he was wearing a new cardigan. Fine knit and khaki-coloured, it really suited him.

'Is that new?' Saffron was impressed. 'It looks great.'

'Present from Rex. Nicole Fairly or something.'

'Nicole *Farhi*,' Saffron and Rex said in unison. They grinned at each other.

'I keep telling Tom to invest in some capsule pieces,' Rex said.

Saffron nodded. 'I know! Getting him to go shopping is a nightmare.'

'When you've stopped pulling my wardrobe to

pieces . . .' Tom said mildly.

Babs was looking back and forth between them like a meerkat on heat. 'It's like looking at two peas in a pod!' she exclaimed. 'I can't believe it.'

'Mum,' chided Saffron, but even she couldn't believe how alike they were, from the way their eyes flashed a different brown under the light, to the warm easy smiles across their faces. Rex definitely had a whiff of mischief about him, though. Saffron could imagine getting into all sorts of trouble on a night out with him.

Babs linked her arm through Rex's. 'Come on through, I've got the bubbles waiting.' She pulled him off down towards the kitchen.

Tom watched them go. 'I've been usurped already.'

'Not by me, you haven't,' Saffron laughed. She flung her arms around him. 'Come here, gorgeous.'

Eventually she pulled away from kissing him. 'You look tired, babe,' she said, stroking his cheek. She could feel the start of stubble under her fingertips.

'Work's been pretty full-on this week.'

'A weekend of country air is what you need,' Saffron declared. She glanced down the corridor. 'How's it all going?'

'Fine. I thought he'd be out hooking up with all his old mates, but he's pretty much stayed in his suite as far as I can work out.'

A suite at the Dorchester didn't start at less than fifteen hundred pounds a night. Saffron raised an eyebrow. 'Has he said how long he's staying, yet?'

'He's been pretty vague, but I get the feeling this isn't a flying visit.'

'Saffron! Tom!' Babs called from the kitchen. 'Drinkies are ready!'

Tom's hand rubbed Saffron's thigh. 'These feel nice.'

'You should see what I'm wearing underneath,' she murmured, reaching up to kiss him again.

A cough sounded behind them. Rex was standing there, a wry smile on his face. 'Hey, sorry to interrupt, but can you show me where the bathroom is?'

Saffron flushed slightly and pointed up the stairs. 'First door at the top.'

Rex grinned. 'Thanks.' He clapped Tom on the shoulder as he passed.

Tom normally did most of the cooking at home, being a dab hand in the kitchen, but tonight Saffron had ventured out and made a Nigella Thai curry. Besides, her mother would probably poison them all if she'd been cooking. Babs had been left in charge of doing the table, and had sat herself so close to Rex they could practically have eaten from the same plate. She was now gazing at him as he talked about the reasons for his visit.

'I just fancied a break, you know? I haven't been back for three years.' He looked at Tom. 'I thought I'd see Dad, hang out, and catch up with some old mates, that sort of thing.'

The twins' widowed father, Gerald Fellows, was a lecturer in History of Modern Art at Durham University. He was in his late sixties, a reclusive, bearded intellectual more at home in the company of books than people. Tom inherited his love of art from Gerald so they had some similar interests, but Saffron couldn't possibly imagine what Rex had in common with his father.

132

'How's the Frontline stuff going?' she asked.

'Cool, we're in-between campaigns, so I thought it was a good time to get away.' He forked up a mouthful of curry. 'This is awesome, Saffron.'

'Thanks,' she said, flattered.

Babs was staring at Rex as though he were the ninth wonder of the world. Saffron subtly kicked her under the table. Babs jumped. 'Won't you be bored, Rex, away from your glamorous world of modelling?' she asked.

'Nah,' he said lightly. 'It can get a bit repetitive after a while. And the people can be pretty shallow.' He caught Tom's look. 'All right, I've done my fair share of being shallow.'

Tom grinned. 'Not saying a word, mate.'

Rex turned to Babs and Saffron. 'Tom's always telling me to get a real job.'

'Hey, I'm not knocking it. Wish *I* could get paid for standing in front of a camera,' Tom said.

Rex rolled his eyes good-naturedly. 'You see what I mean?'

'Well, I'd love to get paid to wear my favourite designer clothes,' Saffron said. 'It's the only way I could afford them.'

Rex put his fork down. 'That reminds me, I've got you both a little something.'

Babs looked thrilled. 'You shouldn't have!'

Rex went over to his leather holdall and came back with two beautifully wrapped boxes. 'That's for you.' He gave the bigger one to Saffron. 'And that's for you, Babs.'

Saffron carefully unwrapped hers to find a gorgeous Bottega Veneta silver cuff. Her eyes widened, she'd seen a similar one on Net-a-Porter recently for £600.

'How did you know?' She was a big fan of the Italian fashion house's jewellery line, not that she could afford many of their pieces. 'I love their stuff!'

'I asked Tom what kind of girl you were and kinda guessed,' Rex grinned. 'So did I do well?'

'Amazingly well!' Saffron slipped the cuff over her slender wrist and admired it. 'Thank you, Rex, it's really generous of you.' She was genuinely touched.

Babs was gazing at a chunky turquoise ring as if it were an exotic butterfly.

'Yves Saint Laurent,' Rex told her. 'It's one of their arty diffusion ranges, a bit of fun.'

Babs looked like she was about to give birth with excitement.

The rest of the evening passed merrily, aided by several bottles of wine. Rex was a natural-born entertainer, chatting and amusing them all with modelling stories. He and Saffron traded various bits of celebrity gossip, making her realize how much she missed the same conversations with her *Soirée* colleagues. 'He did *what* with *who*? I can't believe it!'

'I never thought I'd find someone who knew more about celebrities than my girlfriend,' Tom said dryly. 'You're as camp as Christmas, Rex.'

His brother flapped his hand. 'Oh, *don't*,' making Saffron and Babs burst into giggles.

'Oh, Rex! You are funny.' Babs ran a coy finger round her wine glass. 'Saffron was telling me you're recently single again.'

'Mum!'

Rex smiled at Saffron. 'It's cool, don't worry.' He turned to Babs. 'I was dating someone, but it kind of fizzled out. I'm giving girls up for a while, I think.'

'Supermodels too high-maintenance?' Saffron teased.

'Yeah.' Rex smiled wryly. 'Something like that.' He reached over and filled up Babs's wine glass. 'Now then, you must fill me in on all the gossip. I bet a village like this is *full* of it.'

*   *   *

'I really like him,' Saffron said later. They were snuggled up in her bed, Rex in the little spare room down the end of the hallway. Saffron had pointed out it wasn't quite his suite at the Dorchester but he didn't seem to mind.

Tom stroked her back. 'You sound surprised.'

'I suppose I am,' she admitted. 'I mean, obviously he was going to be nice because he's your brother, but I guess I thought he'd have more of an ego. I thought he was quite modest about his modelling, actually. He didn't go on about it.'

'Yeah, he does seem a bit over it. Then again, you never know with Rex.'

She propped herself up on her elbow. 'Do you ever get jealous of him?'

Tom looked genuinely surprised. 'No, why?'

'I don't know.' She shrugged, feeling a bit foolish. 'His charmed life, I guess. As you said, he gets paid shit-loads to just stand in front of a camera.' She thought about her present. 'My cuff is gorgeous.'

'That's Rex, generous to a fault. He's always been pretty good like that.'

Saffron recalled Tom telling her once that Rex

135

had offered to pay off his mortgage. Of course, he wouldn't hear of it.

'How the other half live, eh? His wardrobe alone is probably worth more than my salary.'

Tom was staring at the ceiling. 'I don't know, good on him. He's got money, why not spend it?'

Saffron stared at him affectionately. 'You are so different, aren't you? I mean, even your names are on opposite ends of the spectrum.'

'Are you saying you got the boring one?' Tom smiled.

'Course not!' She craned her neck to kiss him. 'I'm just saying, Rex is quite rock 'n' roll, isn't he?'

'That's because Mum chose his name and Dad chose mine. You can see who we take after,' he added dryly.

Tom's mother had been Sandra Sullivan, a moderately successful model in the sixties. Saffron had never had the chance to meet her, as she'd died of breast cancer when the boys were twenty-one.

'You never really talk about your mum.'

He stared upwards again. 'That's because there's nothing really to talk about. I don't mean that in a horrible way. She was my mum and I loved her, but Rex was always her favourite. I think I reminded her of Dad, and she blamed him in some weird way for the fact that she didn't become the next Twiggy because she got pregnant with us . . .' He paused. 'She wasn't the most maternal of people.'

'Parents, they fuck you up,' she said. 'Didn't some psychologist write a book about it?'

'Oliver James.' He folded his arms around her. 'But don't buy into all that stuff too much, Saff.

Life's for living, not dwelling on the past.'

'My little optimist.'

'Pragmatist,' he told her. 'Someone in this relationship has to be.'

She smiled at his gentle teasing. 'Well, I think tonight went really well!' She rolled on to her back. 'I think Rex is pretty cool. Witty, good fun, great taste in jewellery . . .'

'Here goes another one,' Tom said.

Saffron looked up at him. 'What?'

Tom was smiling. 'The Rex Sullivan fan club swells by another. He's charmed the pants off you, just like he does with everyone.'

'He hasn't *charmed* me. I just think he's nice. You want me to like your brother, don't you?'

Tom ruffled her hair. 'I was just pulling your leg.'

'I'll pull something of yours if you carry on like that.'

He kissed her. 'Yes, please,' he said lazily.

Saffron sat up and climbed astride him. 'I think you'd better remind me exactly why I picked the right brother.'

Chapter 17

'H. It's me.'

'Oh, hello, Saff!'

Saffron stood outside the village shop and put her bag down on the ground in front of her. It was the next day, and she'd just popped out to get some fresh milk and bread for breakfast, taking the opportunity to call Harriet.

'How are you? I feel like we haven't spoken for

ages,' Harriet said.

'I know, I miss you!' Saffron shifted on to her left foot. 'I had to call. Guess who we've got staying at Hardwick House?'

'If you say George Clooney I'm on the next train home!'

Saffron grinned. 'Try Rex Sullivan.'

She heard Harriet gasp. 'As in Tom's supermodel twin?'

'That's the one.'

'What's he doing in Churchminster? Oh shoot, I miss all the fun.'

'He's come over for a holiday. Or should I say *vacation*. He's a bit Americanized.'

'Ooh, what's he like? Is he as gorgeous in real life?' Harriet paused. 'Stupid question, he's Tom's twin!'

Saffron looked across the green, to where Jack Turner was putting the bins out outside the pub. He waved at her and she waved back. 'Actually, I'm pleasantly surprised. I thought he'd be a bit of an arse, but he's really nice.'

'Golly. Is it weird?'

'Is what weird?'

'Having him and Tom together. I'd worry about getting them mixed up!'

Saffron laughed. 'I don't think there's any chance of that. At the very least I can't see Tom ever splashing out a thousand quid for a jacket, can you?'

'A thousand pounds? He sounds very glamorous!'

'Yeah, I suppose. He bought me and Mum amazing presents.' Saffron laughed. 'He had to slum it in the spare room with the damp patch on the wall. I was half expecting him to demand we take him to Babington House or something, but he was pretty cool with it.'

'I bet he was enchanted by the cottage. What are you doing today?'

'Going for a nice long walk, I think, then hitting the pub for lunch.'

Harriet sounded wistful. 'Sounds perfect. I wish I was there.'

'Me too! When are you coming back, hun?'

'Soon, I hope. It's just that work's been a bit hectic, and then I've had the volunteering...' Another reason Harriet was putting off coming home at the moment was that she couldn't face further interrogation from her father over her spinster status.

'Ooh, how's it going? What about that hottie you mentioned?'

Harriet felt a stab of disappointment. 'Zack?'

'That's the one. Any developments?'

'No, no.' Harriet tried to laugh. 'I don't think he's interested in me like that.'

'Why not? You're gorgeous!'

'You are sweet. No, I think this one's definitely a non-starter.'

'Do you think he's gay?' Saffron said, trying to make Harriet feel better.

'Gay?'

'Yeah. You said he's good-looking, hasn't got a girlfriend...'

'At least, I don't think he's got a girlfriend.' Harriet realized she knew next to nothing about Zack's private life. Then again, why would she?

'Well, maybe he's got a boyfriend! I can't imagine why on earth else he wouldn't fancy you,' Saffron said loyally. She knew Harriet wasn't very confident when it came to men.

Harriet thought. There was something reticent about Zack, a level she couldn't connect with him on. She didn't know if finding out he was gay would make her feel better or worse.

'He does dress well, I suppose,' she said, trying to make a joke out of it.

Saffron didn't answer.

'Saff?' Harriet asked. The line was dead. Churchminster's infamous reception had struck again.

                    *   *   *

Some time later Saffron and the two brothers set off for their walk. While Tom was in his old army jacket and wellies, Rex looked the epitome of style in a belted cashmere trench coat and trilby hat, which accentuated his razor-sharp jawline. They set off across the back fields, Saffron walking between the two men. At five foot eight she was no slouch in the height stakes, but the two men still towered over her. It was like walking around being accompanied by two extremely good-looking bouncers . . .

'So is there anything else you have planned for while you're over here, Rex?' Saffron asked. 'Or is this purely a pleasure visit?'

He looked ahead. 'Not sure, yet. I feel like I need a change, y'know? Like I want to do something different while I'm over here.' He glanced at her. 'You're writing a book, right?'

'Thinking about doing an exposé on the modelling world?'

'God, I can't write.' He kicked a stone out of the

way. 'I was thinking about something a bit more meaningful.' He added, 'Not that writing a book isn't.'

'Do I feel a mid-life crisis coming on?' Tom asked.

Rex didn't return the smile. 'I'm serious, bro. It's time for me to move on. Half that stuff they write about me isn't even true, anyway.'

Rex hadn't struck Saffron as a person who'd dwell on things like that. 'How about some sort of charity work?' she suggested. 'One of my friends has just started volunteering. She loves it.'

Rex looked interested. 'Oh yeah, what kind of stuff?'

'I don't think it would be quite up your street,' Saffron said hastily, thinking of Rex turning up at a council estate community centre. 'I don't know, what about something to do with your fashion background? Is there anything you could do with that?'

Rex was thinking. 'That's a really good idea.' He stopped dead, eyes fixed ahead. 'Jeez, that's quite a place, isn't it?'

In the distance the imposing turrets of Byron Heights loomed upwards. A piece of turn-of-the-century Gothic architecture, the sprawling mansion sat on the outskirts of the village, and had once been owned by rock star Devon Cornwall.

Saffron filled the brothers in on the background as they walked towards it. Rex was impressed. 'Devon Cornwall? I saw him in Miami last year.'

'I've been getting the low-down from Brenda Briggs,' Saffron said. 'The people who bought it after Devon went bankrupt before they even moved in. It's been up for rent, but it's empty at the moment.' As they got closer the gargoyles on the roof snarled down at them furiously. 'It gives me the creeps a bit.'

'I think it's awesome,' Rex said. 'Can we go and have a look?'

'Don't see why not,' Saffron said, hoping they weren't going to set off some high-tech security system. Brenda had told her the house had an emergency alarm that went straight through to Bedlington police station.

They skirted round the side of the house into a sprawling garden filled with yew trees and statues. Saffron stopped and looked at a huge stone eagle, wings open in attack. Garden gnomes were clearly not on the agenda in this place.

Tom went over to one of the lead windows and peered in. 'Come and look at this,' he called.

Saffron and Rex followed him and found themselves gazing into a magnificent ballroom with stone pillars and high, soaring arches. 'It's like something out of Harry Potter,' Saffron said.

'It's some room,' Rex agreed. He was so tall he could see over Saffron's head. 'You could throw an awesome party in there.'

'Thought your partying days were over,' Tom reminded him.

'I'm talking in theory.' Rex stepped back to look up at the building. 'It is a pretty amazing place, though.'

A red security light winked at them from one corner of the room. 'Come on, let's get out of here before we set something off,' Saffron said.

Tom looked at his watch. 'Pub o'clock?'

The thought of a glass of red in the Jolly Boot's cosy dining room was very appealing. 'Let's do it,'

Saffron said.

Rex was rather quiet on the way back, leaving Tom and Saffron to stroll on ahead arm-in-arm. By the time they reached the door of the pub he'd perked up.

Jack Turner did a double-take when they walked up to the bar. 'Blimey!' he said, looking between the twins. 'I didn't know you had two of 'em, Saffron!'

She laughed. 'Jack, this is Tom's brother, Rex.'

Rex stuck his hand out and smiled. 'Nice to meet you, Jack.'

'What can I get you to drink?' Jack asked.

Tom went to get his wallet out, but Rex stopped him. 'I'll get these. You two go and find a table.'

A few minutes later he came over with an ice bucket and a bottle of Laurent Perrier champagne.

'Whoa, what's this in aid of?' Tom said.

Rex sat down. 'I thought we needed to celebrate.'

'Celebrate what?' Saffron asked.

He popped the cork, cold air rushing out of the top of the bottle. 'I've just got a feeling. This break is gonna do me the world of good, I know it.' He poured out three flutes and handed one to each of them. 'To new beginnings.'

Tom and Rex clinked glasses, and Tom turned to Saffron. 'Hey, Saff, to new beginnings.'

She looked at her boyfriend and his doppelgänger. 'New beginnings!'

Chapter 18

London

Harriet caught Abby's eye and smiled. She was met with a blank stare. The teenager looked away, face pale under the loose blonde hair. She'd been sitting at her desk motionless for a whole hour now.

Harriet decided to try again. If Abby really didn't want her help she'd leave her be, but she recognized the signs of frustration in the other girl's face.

She got up from her chair. Across the other side of the room Zack's office door was closed. Those few moments alone round the table at Aunty Win's felt like they'd never happened, now. Every time she'd seen him since, he had treated her the same: friendly but detached, as if he was just going through the motions.

Was he really gay? Or was she just trying to ignore the fact that he was yet another unrequited crush?

Forcing thoughts of him out of her mind, Harriet cautiously approached the table. 'Hi, Abby.'

Abby's eyes flickered up. 'Hi.'

Harriet tried not to let the sullen tone put her off. 'What are you up to?'

'What does it look like?'

'Can I help?' She gestured at the empty chair opposite Abby. 'May I?'

'If you want.'

Harriet sat down. 'I just wanted to see if you needed any help.' She looked at the open books on

144

the desk. 'You know, if I can go through anything with you.'

Blue eyes narrowed. 'Are you saying I'm stupid?'

'No! No, of course not.' *This was going well.*

Suddenly Abby's eyes filled with tears. 'I mean, what's the point? I'm going to fail anyway. I should have done these stupid exams years ago.'

Harriet reached and put her hand over Abby's. To her surprise Abby didn't snatch hers away. 'I don't think you're stupid; in fact completely the opposite. There's no way I'd be able to study and bring up a baby. I think you're doing marvellously.'

Abby didn't look convinced. 'I'm not exactly Student of the Year, am I?' Her chin wobbled. 'I'm just so bloody tired. Kai was up all night, and my mum's always on my back, telling me how I've thrown my life away.'

'It must be very hard for you,' Harriet said gently.

'What would you know?' Abby said, but her voice had lost its hostility. 'I wanted to prove them all wrong, you know, make something of myself, but it's just so bloody *hard* . . .'

Harriet squeezed her hand again. 'Don't get yourself in a state. I'll help you, if you want me to. Sometimes you just need a fresh pair of eyes on it all.'

Her words seemed to be having some effect. 'OK.' Abby sniffed.

'What do you want to start with?'

'Maths. I'm *really* shit at it.'

'I was really shit at it, too,' Harriet confided. Abby giggled, suddenly looking younger than her eighteen years. 'Oh, great!'

'We'll muddle through together,' Harriet said.

'Shall I get you a tissue first, before we start?'

Abby wiped her face. 'Yes, please.'

As Harriet stood up she noticed Zack standing by the door to his office, arms folded as if he'd been there some time. His head tilted in the smallest of nods, before he turned and walked back inside.

Churchminster

'Wheee!'

The radio-controlled helicopter soared up high into the ballroom, narrowly missing one of the seventeenth-century crystal chandeliers. Ambrose's faithful black and white sheepdog, Sailor, sat on the floor with his head cocked, watching his master with some bemusement.

'Sir Ambrose?'

He turned to see his butler Hawkins standing in the doorway, Jed Bantry next to him. 'Ah, young Jed! Thank you, Hawkins.' The butler nodded and withdrew. Ambrose glanced about furtively. 'You got the contraband?' he asked.

At least the porn-star moustache had gone. Jed held up the steaming, slightly greasy bag. 'One chicken vindaloo, one prawn madras, two plain rice, poppadoms and a stuffed pakora.'

Ambrose chuckled. 'That's the ticket! Quick, let's make a break for it while Cook's not around. She'll have my guts for garters if she finds out about this little stash.'

Five minutes later they arrived outside a door in the little-used east wing. Ambrose opened it and hurried Jed in. Instead of the elegant antique furniture and priceless watercolours that could be found in every other room of the Hall, it had been converted into a pub-cum-amusement arcade. A flashing fruit machine stood in one corner, a dartboard on one wall, and a huge television screen hung on another, showing horse-racing. There was no furniture, except two black leather La-Z-Boy chairs positioned in front of the television.

Ambrose grinned. 'Impressive, huh? Thought it was about time I had my own lads' pad. Away from Frances's rooms, too, so she can't complain about the noise when she gets back.'

Jed was lost for words.

'This is what you lads have in these pubs, isn't it?' Ambrose said, suddenly anxious. 'I wanted to make it authentic.'

Jed had never been one of the lads, let alone played on a fruit machine, but he wasn't going to say that. 'It's very authentic, Sir Ambrose,' he said sincerely.

Ambrose looked pleased. 'Top-drawer stuff! I'd offer you a glass of claret but you young blades like that lager, don't you? I got Hawkins to go and get some especially.' He went over to the fridge and got a can out. 'Bring the nosh over, then! I don't want my vindaloo cold.'

Jed jumped to attention. Minutes later they were each sat in a La-Z-Boy, plates of curry on their laps. Ambrose chewed on a bit of stuffed pakora thoughtfully. 'Do you think Harriet's one of these lesbians?'

Jed spluttered into his can. 'A lesbian?'

Ambrose eyed him keenly. 'I do know what one is, young man. I watch the racing, remember. That

147

blonde presenter's one.' He picked up his glass of claret and took a reflective sip. 'I'd rather she just came out with it, at least then Frances and I would know where we stand on the matter.'

Jed resisted the urge to smile. 'I really don't think she is, Sir Ambrose.'

Ambrose shuffled round in his chair. 'It's not right, though, is it? Harriet, I mean. A healthy woman of thirty-five with no chap of her own.' He sighed. 'Women are so picky these days. Waiting for some Prince Charming to come along and sweep them off their feet.'

'I suppose it's better that Harriet does wait, rather than just ending up with someone for the sake of it.' Jed was starting to feel like Ambrose's therapist.

Ambrose grunted. 'She's going to end up with no onc at this rate. I tell you what, young Jed, Harriet needs to come home and stop all this gallivanting round London. It's time I put my foot down.' He threw back a lungful of claret. 'Before all the good chaps are gone! The Duke of Roath married the last of his sons off last week. What the hell does Harriet think she's playing at? I need grandsons!'

That was her life planned, then. Jed suddenly felt very sorry for Harriet. Being the daughter of Gloucestershire's most eccentric aristocrat was not a fate he'd wish on anyone.

Chapter 19

It was three days since Tom and Rex had gone back to London. Rex was still staying at the Dorchester, and Saffron had offered to hook him up with some of her socialite friends, including the man-eating Jasmine, but Rex had said he wanted to keep his head down. From what Tom had told her, he was spending most of his time in the spa and gym there, and watching films in his room. Maybe he really was serious about turning over a new leaf.

Saffron stared at her computer screen, but her mind was elsewhere. She'd had a really good time with the brothers. Rex reminded her a bit of the boys she used to go for; fun and frivolous but not much underneath. Not a patch on her lovely Tom anyway—TomLite she was secretly calling him. That wasn't meant in a bad way; Rex was a good laugh and it would be nice for Tom to spend some time with his twin while she was out here, in her self-imposed exile. That's if Tom actually broke free of the office. The hours were stacking up for him already.

Identical twins. *So*, Saffron thought, *did that mean they had identical cocks?* She couldn't pretend the thought hadn't crossed her mind. Well, it was natural, wasn't it? If Rex was as well endowed as Tom he was a very lucky boy indeed. No wonder he had a bit of a reputation.

Saffron shook her head. What was she like? What if Tom rang her at that very moment and asked what she was up to? 'Oh, nothing much,

darling, just thinking about your brother's knob!'
Grinning, she got back to work. It was dark outside
by the time she was close to finishing.

*Serendipity heard a knock at the door. It was
probably nosy Mr Norris from No. 3, so she
didn't bother to change out of the old ~~negligée~~
T-shirt and boxer shorts she was wearing. As she
opened the door, her jaw dropped. Standing in
front of her was the sexiest man she'd ever seen in
her life. Six feet plus, he had ~~white blond~~
jet-black hair and emerald-coloured eyes.*
   *'Hey, I'm Brad, I just moved in next door.' His
smile was as perfect as the rest of him. He held
up a bottle of red wine. 'I was wondering if you
fancied a drink?'*

Saffron smiled. She was so looking forward to
things hotting up between Seren and Brad.
Suddenly, she heard the clanking chime of the
front doorbell. Her mother was going out with an
artist friend tonight.

'Mum, your friend's here,' she called.

No answer. Saffron went up to the door of Babs's
bedroom. 'Mum! Your mate's here!'

'Could you answer it?' Her mum's voice was
muffled behind the bathroom door. 'I'm just
having a tinkle.'

Sighing, Saffron started to trudge down the
stairs. God, she was tired. Dinner and an early
night for her. *My, how exciting my life is*, she
thought.

She could see the shadow of her mum's friend
framed in the door, and wondered if they shared
the same artistic vision. *I bloody hope not.*

Smiling slightly, Saffron pulled the door open, ready to make the introductions. But when she saw who was standing there, her mouth dropped open.

'Hey, Saff,' said Rex Sullivan.

*   *   *

Ten minutes later they were sat at the dining room table with a cup of tea. Babs had gone into raptures when she'd come down and found Rex there, but luckily her friend had turned up and Saffron had pushed her mum out the door without further ado. Now she was looking expectantly at Rex, wondering what the hell he was doing here. *Did Tom know?*

'You're probably wondering what the hell I'm doing here,' he said. His tan showed no sign of fading, and was set off to perfection by the cream cashmere scarf he was wearing. Saffron felt positively drab and ghost-like in comparison.

'It is a bit of a surprise,' she admitted. 'Does Tom know you're here?'

'No, he doesn't, actually. I wanted to check it out first, before I was sure.'

Saffron didn't follow. 'Sure about what?'

Rex grinned and reached down into his bag, getting out some sort of catalogue. Saffron recognized the photo of the house on the front. 'I'm going to rent Byron Heights.'

Saffron's eyes goggled. 'You're *what*?'

'I'm moving into Byron Heights. I've just been with the estate agent now.' He pushed the details towards her. 'Take a look, it's even better inside.'

Saffron looked down at the prospectus. 'OK . . .'

He smiled. 'Bit out of the blue, isn't it?'

151

'Just a bit!'

'I said I wanted to recharge my batteries, didn't I?' His eyes were shining. 'And when I saw Byron Heights, I knew it was perfect!'

She was lost again. 'Perfect for what?'

He paused dramatically. 'I'm gonna put on my own charity fashion show. At Byron Heights.'

This time Saffron actually choked on her tea. 'Now you're winding me up!'

He leant forward, face intense. 'It was you that gave me the idea in the first place! You know when you said about doing something for charity?'

'I didn't mean putting on your own show!'

'C'mon, Saff! Have a little vision here!'

'I take it we're not talking something in the village hall here?' she asked, still reeling from the fact Rex was moving to Churchminster. The local WI would keel over!

He shook his head. 'I want it to be *big*. Elton John big. Something on the scale of the White Tie and Tiara Ball.'

Elton's ball was one of the biggest charity events on the calendar.

'Nothing too ambitious then?' she asked sarcastically.

'OK, so I haven't worked out the finer details yet.' He gave a winning grin. 'But fashion and charity—it's a fail-safe formula.'

'You do know how much time and work these things take, don't you?' she asked him.

'I am a model, remember?' he said wryly. His eyes burnt into hers, a gaze that had looked out from millions of magazines. 'It might sound a little crazy, Saff, but I know I can do it.'

'You're going to need a team of people.'

152

'I kinda want to be as hands-on as possible.' He flashed a cheeky grin. 'You'll help me out, won't you?'

'Rex, I'm really not sure . . .' Getting involved with a fashion show was *definitely* not part of the plan out here. 'A fashion show, seriously?'

'Deadly.'

She ran her hands through her blonde hair. 'You do go into things full-on, don't you?'

He grinned again. 'Always. That's what life's about, isn't it?'

'What does Tom think?'

She saw him hesitate for the first time. 'I haven't actually told him yet; I wanted to come down here first, be sure about it all. Don't say anything, will you? I'm seeing him for lunch tomorrow.'

'I don't know . . .' Saffron felt weird not saying anything. She and Tom didn't have any secrets from each other.

'Just until tomorrow, OK?' Rex pleaded. His right eyebrow rose wryly. 'My brother thinks I'm a loose cannon as it is, this is one idea that needs to be sold properly.'

'I'm sure he doesn't think that, Rex.'

He shrugged. 'It's fine, I deserve it.' The enthusiasm was back in his face. 'I've been selfish for too long, Saff, treated too many people badly. It's time to give something back.'

*   *   *

'He says he wants to give something back,' Tom told her. Saffron was sitting on the landing—the only place with mobile reception at Hardwick House—a cup of tea between her legs, and her

153

iPhone clamped to her ear. It was twenty-four hours since Rex had announced he was moving to Churchminster.

'I know. I feel a bit responsible, giving him the idea in the first place!'

'Don't worry about that, Rex doesn't need any encouragement.'

'Well, what do you think?'

Tom didn't sound as surprised as she had thought. 'This is a new one, even for Rex.'

'Is he talking shit?'

'No, I think he's really into it. But he always is at the start. Rex has these . . . fads. Often. It's like when he got his Harley last year: it was all he could talk about. He had the kit, everything. Six months later, it'd been dumped, forgotten about.'

'You can't really compare a motorbike to a charity show,' Saffron pointed out.

'Maybe.' Tom paused. 'So I guess he told you when he came down yesterday?'

'No. Er, I mean yes. I mean . . .' They'd spoken for an hour on the phone last night and she hadn't said anything.

He sounded slightly amused. 'Either you knew or you didn't, Saff.'

'OK, I did!' she blurted. 'Don't be pissed off at me, babe. Rex wanted to tell you face-to-face.'

'It's no big deal.' He cleared his throat. 'So, what do you think about it?'

'About Rex moving to Churchminster? I suppose it's pretty high on the random stakes. How do *you* feel about it?' she asked slightly anxiously. Tom was the most laid-back man she knew but even this was quite the bombshell.

'Too late to say anything now!' He sounded fine.

154

'If you're cool, I'm cool. Just mind he doesn't rope you in and distract you from the book,' he said. 'I know Rex, he has a habit of sweeping people along with him.'

'No chance. I've got my hands full as it is. I'll help him out with any contacts, but that's it.'

'Famous last words, Saff,' Tom said dryly. 'Famous last words.'

Chapter 20

London

Harriet was being chatted up by 84-year-old Alf Stokes. 'That's a very pretty dress you're wearing.'

'Thank you, Alf, that's really nice of you to say so.'

'Shows off those sexy ankles, cor!'

'Alf!' Harriet laughed.

The music started up again, and Alf wiggled his hips. 'Right, I'd better go and show this lot how it's done. I'll be seeing you.'

Harriet watched him trot off, looking dapper in a bow tie and waistcoat. He did make her laugh.

A moment later Aunty Win appeared at her elbow, garbed in a red, white and blue kaftan. She reminded Harriet of a majestic ocean liner sailing into port.

'Not dancing tonight then, 'Arriet?'

It was salsa night at the centre, and Harriet had taken a break from the kitchen to come out and watch. 'Not me, I'm afraid. I've got two left feet.'

Aunty Win had been shaking her stuff with the

best of them. She produced a handkerchief from somewhere on her person, and wiped her brow. The hanky was red, to match her turban. 'You young people need to move a bit! That's what I tell Zachary, always locked away in that office.'

'He seems pretty snowed under at the moment.' Harriet had barely seen him recently.

'He's getting in a tizz about this place.' Win sighed. 'I keep telling him he's not going to make anything better sitting in there and worrying.'

Just then Alf whirled past, Mary Croft in his arms. He winked at Harriet behind his dance partner's back.

'I haven't seen Alf for a few weeks,' Harriet said, smiling as she watched him twirl Mary off.

'Mmm. He gets this depression, you know. Ever since his wife died. Course, being Alf he doesn't want to bother anyone with it. Locks himself away until he feels better.' Aunty Win sighed. 'I take him food, make sure he eats, but he's lonely, 'Arriet. Him and Enid were married over sixty years.'

Harriet couldn't bear the thought of Alf being so unhappy.

'How's everything going with you, then?' Win asked.

'Good, thanks.'

Win tucked the handkerchief back in the folds of her kaftan. 'So tell me, 'Arriet, do you have a nice young man?'

'No, Aunty Win, it's just me.'

'Thought so!' She nodded. 'I bet your mum and dad are keen to see you settle down, huh?'

Harriet thought of her father. 'You could say that.'

'That's what I keep telling Zachary! He needs to hurry up and find a nice girl, he's not getting any younger.'

So he definitely wasn't gay. At least she wasn't the only one getting stick for daring to be single over the age of thirty. It made Harriet feel slightly better.

'Yup, he needs to get a move on.'

Harriet smiled politely. 'Mmm.'

'He's a nice boy, 'Arriet.' Aunty Win gave her a meaningful look. 'He's just had a tough time. I keep telling him he needs to move on, start afresh.'

Tough time. From Win's face it was clear she wanted Harriet to ask her more. 'Do you mean a relationship?'

'Ay-ay, what's going on here, then?' Harriet nearly jumped out of her skin. Zack had appeared behind them from nowhere. He didn't look very impressed. Harriet cringed. He must have overheard what she'd been saying.

' 'Arriet and I were just chatting,' Win said innocently. Zack shot her a cross look. Harriet felt her face flush. How mortifying that he'd caught her discussing his love life! He obviously guessed what Win had been up to, and wasn't impressed by her matchmaking.

'I'd better get back to the washing-up,' she said, and fled for the sanctuary of the kitchen.

Churchminster

On a bright, spring day in the middle of March, Rex moved into Byron Heights. Tom had taken the afternoon off work to come down and help, and when Saffron drove round in her mum's car later she found him unloading Waitrose bags out of the back of the Aston Martin.

'Hey, lover,' she said, running over.

'Hey, babe.' He swept her up in his arms and kissed her.

'Where's Rex?' she said, as he deposited her on the ground. Tom looked towards the open front door. 'Off in there somewhere.'

'What, and left you to carry the shopping? Cheeky sod.' Saffron picked two bags up. 'I'll take these in. Won't be a sec.'

As first impressions go it was quite something. She was in a vast entrance hall with an expanse of black and white chequered floor. Straight ahead was a wide, arched doorway leading to the back of the house, with two dark wood thrones either side of it. Saffron craned her neck to look up at the Gothic staircase swirling up to the first floor. This place must cost serious money to rent.

'Pretty cool, huh?' a voice said. Rex was standing in front of her, barefoot, in a simple white T-shirt and jeans.

She held up the bags. 'Where's the kitchen?'

'What? Oh, through here.' He turned and went back through a door off to the right. Saffron followed and found herself in a huge square kitchen. Compared to what she'd seen so far, the kitchen was done out in a contemporary style, with black glossy units and chrome work surfaces. In the middle stood an island with four stainless-steel stools tucked underneath it. An iPod with two speakers sat on the top.

'Here, let me take those.' Rex grabbed the bags off Saffron and put them on the island. 'I've just been sorting us out some music.' He leant across and pressed play. A few seconds later the sound of the Scissor Sisters' new track started up.

'I love this one!' Saffron said.

'I've got the album, it's pretty good.'

Tom came in, three bags in each hand. He dumped them down on the floor. 'Shopping's in. Where do you want it?'

'Great, anywhere,' Rex said, looking around. 'There's plenty of places to choose from.' He looked at Saffron. 'Do you fancy a quick tour?'

'Go ahead, I'll do this,' Tom said.

'Cheers, bro!' Rex nodded towards the door. 'Shall we?'

He took her upstairs first, where a grand landing ran the entire back of the house. Six floor-to-ceiling arched windows looked out on the grounds and the countryside beyond. Leading off the landing were eight bedrooms, each with a four-poster bed. Rex had chosen the biggest one, with its own freestanding bath in the corner of the room. That wasn't to mention the en suite next door. It was the size of Saffron's bedroom at Hardwick House.

Rex had started to unpack, and there were clothes and toiletries everywhere. Saffron spotted the labels lying on the bed: Armani, more Marc Jacobs, Ralph Lauren. It looked like a spread out of *GQ*.

'Downstairs is even better. Wait until you see the cinema. *And* the observatory. It's got a telescope the size of the NASA space shuttle.'

The last port of call was the best. It was the ballroom they'd seen the first day, when Rex had decided to have the fashion show. 'So what do you think?' he asked.

Saffron looked round. Rex certainly wouldn't have to worry about space. It was even more impressive inside, with a soaring curved roof that stretched up into the eaves of the building. A massive stone fireplace big enough to hold both brothers dominated the far end of the room.

'So I thought we'd have the catwalk here,' Rex pointed at the other end, 'because it leads out to some other rooms we can use for backstage.' He gestured. 'Which means the seating will go *here*.'

'You've obviously been giving it some thought.' Saffron couldn't knock his enthusiasm.

'Yeah, well, I've got a busy schedule now!'

Tom had put everything away by the time they returned to the kitchen. He was now making coffee with an espresso machine he'd found in a cupboard. It looked brand new, and he'd even located three espresso cups, into which he was pouring the rich black liquid. 'There you go.' He handed the first to Saffron.

She took a sip. 'Lush. Thanks, babe.'

Rex picked his up. 'Guys, come and check this out.'

Next door was a cavernous dining room complete with stag heads on the wall and a twenty-foot dining table in the middle of the room.

'I thought I might use it as my office,' Rex said. He gestured to them to sit down. 'What do you reckon?'

'As far as offices go it's pretty impressive, mate,' Tom said.

Rex looked pleased. 'Saff, you're going to have to come and see me lots. I'll be rattling around in this place.'

'Don't forget, Saff's got her book to write,' Tom reminded him. 'She doesn't need you leading her astray.'

Rex looked affronted. 'Of course I won't.' He glanced between them sheepishly. 'I've been putting a few feelers out. You're right, this show is going to be a lot more work than I thought.'

'Rex!' Tom said warningly. Rex looked at Saffron imploringly. 'If you could spare just a few hours a week, that would be amazing. I've been off the UK scene for a long time.'

Saffron wasn't swayed by the puppy dog expression, but she didn't want to see the man suffer. 'I'll see what I can do.'

'Great!' Rex clapped his hands together. 'We'll need to get a press release out pronto. Then there's a few other things I need to talk to you about . . .'

'Saff said a few *hours* a week, mate, not a few days,' Tom told him. 'You got that?'

Rex did a mock salute. 'Yes, cap'n.'

Saffron looked at her watch. 'I'd better get back. Are you sure you won't join us for dinner, Rex?'

'Honestly, I'm cool. You guys need time to yourselves, and, besides, I've got loads to do here.'

'Well, if you're sure.' Saffron didn't want to abandon Rex on his first night in Churchminster, but she was secretly pleased. She had a surprise for Tom later, involving suspenders, champagne and very little else . . .

God, she loved fucking her boyfriend!

Chapter 21

London

Harriet got out of the shower to find a text from her friend Penny.

'Darling, bloody Benji has given me a bug, and I've been throwing up all night, I feel ghastly, can we resched? x'

Harriet texted back immediately. *'You poor thing, of course! Get well soon, sending a big hug. H x'*

She sat down on the bed, feeling at a bit of a loss. Poor Penny. Their lunch date had been the highlight of her weekend. What would she do now? All the things she normally enjoyed doing, like going to a gallery or watching Channel Five's Saturday matinée, suddenly held no appeal.

This is silly, she told herself. *You're in one of the most vibrant cities on earth*. She sat up decisively. It was such a nice day outside. She would go for a walk. And then stop by M&S on the way home and get something nice for dinner. But even that didn't cheer her up, and Harriet realized she was rather lonely.

A strange noise startled her. It sounded like a muffled voice, as if someone was playing a radio far away.

'Hello? HARRIET!'

She looked down. The noise was coming from under her left buttock. She'd sat on her phone! *Oh God!* Who had she called? Praying it wasn't someone important from work, she picked it up. Her stomach dropped. Somehow, she'd managed to call Zack.

'Er, hi!'

'Are you OK? When you called and didn't answer, I didn't know what was going on. Thought you might have had an accident.'

'God no! I am sorry. You're the last person in my phone memory, I must have called you by accident. Anyway, sorry again. I'm sure you're very busy . . .'

'So you kept my number, then?' Zack said.

'I'm sorry?'

'You saved my number. From when I called you.'

'Er, yes. I just thought, in case of emergencies . . .'

'Or even non ones.' He sounded amused. 'So what are you up to, then?'

She was rather taken aback by his sudden chattiness. 'Nothing, really. A friend just cancelled lunch, so I think I might go for a walk down by the river instead.'

'Mind if I join you?'

Harriet caught sight of her shocked face in the dressing-table mirror. 'I'm sorry?'

'I quite fancy some fresh air. Unless you object . . .'

'Of course!'

'You mean you do object?'

'N-no!' She took a deep breath and started again. 'It would be lovely to have some company.'

'Let's meet at the Tower of London, then. We can walk over the bridge and head south, it's a nice stretch. Say one o'clock?'

'Fabulous!' she said, already wondering if she should change her turtleneck for something a little more daring.

Fifty-four minutes later Harriet arrived at the appointed spot. Zack was there already, leaning on the railings and looking out at the river. Even with his back to her she immediately recognized the wide shoulders and the way he carried his head. She walked up and tentatively touched his arm. 'You beat me to it.'

He whirled round, eyes startling in the March sun. 'Hey. Good to see you.' He stood up. 'Let's do it.'

They started across Tower Bridge, stopping halfway to look down at the river. In the distance Big Ben stood sentry-like on the skyline, flanked by the Houses of Parliament.

'Great view, isn't it?' Zack said. 'That's what I love about this city, you don't need money to enjoy the best bits.'

They continued their way across to the east side of the river. It was an unusually hot day, and the river path was teeming with people.

'So, not working today?' Harriet asked after a few minutes.

'Thought I'd take a few hours off.' His eyes crinkled up at the corners. 'Aunty Win gave me a bit of a talking-to, said I needed to get out more.'

'She did mention it was a bit stressful for you at the moment.'

'Yeah, you could say that.' He looked out over the water. 'But I don't want to think about work now.'

They meandered down the river, past HMS Belfast and Shakespeare's Globe theatre. Zack was on great form, telling her funny stories about

164

Win and some of the other people down the centre. Maybe it was the nice weather, but away from the Gatsby Road he was a different person, as if a hidden weight had been lifted off his shoulders. Harriet was having such a good time she was surprised to see it was nearly 3 p.m. She hadn't even thought about lunch.

'Are you hungry?' Zack asked.

'I'm fine, actually.'

'Me, too.' There was a pub coming up on their left, festooned with hanging baskets.

'Do you fancy a drink instead?' she asked. 'My treat this time, I insist.'

He looked at his watch. 'I should really get back.'

Harriet felt a lurch of disappointment. 'No worries. I'll probably walk on a bit and get a cab home.'

'Thanks for letting me gatecrash your walk.'

'It was nice to have the company.'

Zack looked back, in the direction they'd just come. 'Guess I'll see you down at the centre?'

They'd walked off in different directions, Harriet wondering if he'd really come all the way out here just because he fancied some fresh air, when she heard her name being called.

She turned round. To her surprise Zack was still standing there, looking after her. A sliver of hope sprang up in her chest.

'I forgot to say, Pete said, "Remember the textbook." Whatever that means.'

The hope was swiftly crushed. She nodded and waved awkwardly, then turned to start the long walk home.

Chapter 22

Churchminster

As usual the Aston Martin was parked outside as she drove up to the front of Byron Heights. She parked her mum's MG next to it and got out.

She looked at the huge front door knocker. It was in the shape of a lion's head. With some difficulty she picked it up, hearing it clang away into the house. Nothing. Saffron yelled through the letterbox. 'Rex! Are you there?'

She heard a shout. 'Coming.' A pair of jean-clad legs crossed the hallway and then Rex was there, looking the all-American model in a navy Hollister sweatshirt and matching baseball hat.

She looked him up and down. 'Very preppy.'

Rex laughed. 'It's my at-home look.'

Saffron handed him the pot plant. 'Housewarming present.'

'That's really nice of you, thanks.' He stepped back to let her in. 'I suppose now isn't the time to mentionI haven't had a plant that hasn't died on me yet.'

'Me, neither.' Saffron thought about Leroy the cactus. She hoped Tom was looking after him and brushing his prickles.

Rex's return had got a mention in a gossip column in one of the national newspapers. *The residents of the Cotswolds village of Churchminster must be salivating in their tea cups, after international supermodel Rex Sullivan moved into a nearby property. Rex, 28, who moved to America five*

166

years ago, is renting Byron Heights, the Gothic mansion once owned by rock star Devon Cornwall. Does this mean the model, who made his fortune modelling for US brands like Ralph Lauren and Frontline, is coming back to Blighty for good?

Saffron thought it was funny, and had taken the paper round to show him.

'Man, how embarrassing.' He re-read it, frowning. 'How do they know this shit?'

Saffron grinned. 'Journalists know everything.'

'I forgot you were one of them,' he said wryly. He tossed the paper on the sideboard by the door. 'Coffee?'

'No thanks, I've had about fifty million cups today already.' Saffron had worked long into the night, honing the next batch of chapters for Pamela Aston. She desperately wanted her literary agent to like them.

Rex indicated towards the dining room. 'Come on in.'

He looked like he'd been hard at work. The dining room was covered in piles of printouts, and there were scribbled notepads everywhere. 'I've made a start, as you can see.'

'So you're really going ahead with it?'

Rex looked surprised. 'Yes. Why shouldn't I be?'

She shrugged her shoulders. 'I was just wondering . . .'

'Has Tom been filling your head with ideas?' He didn't sound cross.

'He hasn't, actually . . .'

She was just being cynical. Working in the entertainment industry did that to you.

'I do know what I'm like, you know.' Rex allowed himself a smile. 'Clever, sensible Tom with the

167

career, while silly old Rex is flitting from one clothes fitting to the next, only caring whether he's wearing the right shade of cover-up.'

Saffron felt a bit embarrassed. 'He didn't say that.'

'It's OK, I get it. But I am really passionate about this, Saff.' His gaze was earnest, electric. Saffron could see why he was such a good model: he had the ability to communicate many different feelings in a single look. Fortunately she wasn't impressed that easily.

'I can call you Saff, can't I?'

'Only if I can call you Rexy-Boy.'

'You can call me anything you want.'

'I'll hold you to that!' She laughed. She pulled out a chair and sat down. 'Right then, this is one of my allotted hours for the show. Let's talk.'

'Great.' Rex picked up his iPad and came to sit beside her. She got a whiff of clean skin; he was obviously fresh out of the shower. 'I've had a few ideas I'd like to talk over with you. Have you heard of something called an underground runway?'

'No, but I am out of the loop at the moment.'

'Basically they're getting really big in New York, a kind of rebellion against the big-name fashion-house thing. Any up-and-coming designer, it could be a fashion student, some street kid, a stay-at-home mom . . .'

'*Mum*,' corrected Saffron.

'OK, *mum*, a stay-at-home mum, or just anyone who wants to get their designs seen, only they haven't got the cash or the contacts to do it. They put on these runway shows. I mean, it's really rough and ready, literally taking over a warehouse or park, or some other place. At first it was all quite subversive, word of mouth spread by blogging and so on, but now they're really taking off.'

'And you want to put one on here?'

'Something similar. What do you think?'

'I don't know. It seems a bit of a waste, with all your contacts. You could get some big-name designers.'

Rex shook his head. 'Too complicated, too many egos. Besides, all the favours I can pull are on the American scene. I want this show to be a celebration of all things British. Give up-and-coming talent their big break. I've been doing some research, found some amazing talent.'

'Hmm.' She still wasn't convinced.

Rex grinned, showing Hollywood-white teeth. 'How about I throw Bibi Brown into the mix?'

'Now that *would* be something.' Bibi Brown was the name of the moment. A graduate of the prestigious Central Saint Martins college in London, she was already setting the fashion world alight with her designs. Of course, it helped that she had Kate Moss on her speed-dial, and was best friends with an ultra-famous stylist, but there was no doubting Bibi's talent. She was already getting quite the rep as a diva.

'I want Bibi to open the show.'

'You reckon you can get her?'

'I'm not gonna stop *until* I get her,' Rex said. 'I'm also gonna talk to Browns, see if they'll show one of their collections to sell afterwards.'

Browns Focus was one of Saffron's favourite stores. It was high-end, eclectic and fabulous. 'That is *such* a good idea.'

'Yeah, I thought so. Even though it's for charity,

these designers are gonna need some incentive. It's expensive putting together a collection.'

'Have you thought about the money side?'

'I'm gonna give the designers a bit of a budget, to help buy fabric and stuff.' Rex crossed his arms. 'But we're going to need some help, obviously. Do you think *Soirée* would do something? It would be *great* to get a magazine sponsoring us.'

'I think they're involved with a few things already, but I'll ask. At the very least I'm sure the fashion and beauty team can help with hair and make-up contacts.'

Rex was typing it all in. 'Your Fashion Ed might be able to help with model castings.' He grinned. 'This is *so* coming together.'

'Hang on. There's a lot more to think about. You need caterers, flowers, music, booze, and security. An actual *catwalk*. And all for free.'

'Do you know anyone who could help?'

'Harriet, my friend from work, puts on events for *Soirée*. I'm sure she could give us contacts, especially as her parents live in Churchminster.'

'No way!'

'Way,' Saffron said sardonically. She was finding Rex's enthusiasm a little trying. Did the guy have any idea of the scale of these things?

He was already galloping ahead to the next thing. 'So ticket-wise I'm thinking that ballroom can hold two hundred and fifty. Easily. We should charge £250 per ticket.'

Saffron pulled a face. 'Most celebs live off freebies, why are they going to suddenly dig in their pockets for this one?'

'Because it's for charity and it's gonna be *amazing*,' Rex said confidently. 'Trust me, they'll be clamouring for tickets.'

God, now the pressure was really on.

'Where's the calculator on this thing?' Rex was searching through his BlackBerry. 'Ah, here we go. So 250 times 250 . . .' He looked at the screen. 'Just over sixty-two grand. And that's before we raffle off all the collections!' He put down his phone triumphantly. 'And now, I think my work is done.'

'What about press? This event won't sell itself. You'll need to put something in *Fashion Monitor*, for a start.' It was the industry bible for things going on in the fashion world.

'That's why I need you, Saff.' She watched him type it in, concentrating under the long lashes.

'And how about the guest list? I'd like to see how you're going to get the London fashionistas all the way out here.'

'Ah, I was hoping your fabulous connections could help us.' He looked up. 'We need celebrities. I'm talking A list all the way.'

Saffron raised an eyebrow. That was easier said than done. 'You still haven't mentioned the most important part.'

'Huh?'

'It's a charity show, remember? Who are you going to support?'

'Patience, my dear.' He leant over and typed in a web address. Saffron noticed how nice his nails were. He probably had them done every week when he was back in New York.

An impressive-looking home page flashed up, with the face of a beautiful dark-skinned child smiling out at them. *Handbag Haven*, she read. She was sure she'd heard of it.

'It's a really cool charity, definitely going places.

This business entrepreneur called Saul Barboni founded it.' Rex clicked on a photo of a smart Italian-looking guy with an expensive suit and slicked-back hair. 'One of my model friends from LA, his sister Daisy, works for it. They auction off designer handbags, among other things, to build new housing in the slums of Rio de Janeiro.'

Saffron looked more closely at the site. It had the kind of funky, edgy appeal the fashion crowd would love.

'I don't want to go for one of the more obvious ones, to keep in line with the show,' Rex said. 'You know what the fashion world's like. They love to make out they've found the "next big thing".'

'I agree.' Saffron sat back. Handbag Haven seemed a pretty good choice. 'Have you thought about the name, what you want to call the show?'

'You're the words lady, I thought I'd let you decide.'

Saffron considered this. Something with a fashiony angle that had the charity bit, something that pulled on the heartstrings but wasn't too cheesy . . .

'How about Fashion Cares?'

'Fashion Cares. I *love* it. I knew you'd be good at this stuff.'

'Flattery will get you nowhere,' she retorted, but Rex had such energy and enthusiasm it was impossible not to be affected by it. For the first time Saffron felt a flush of excitement, mixed with queasiness. They had so much to do. But if they pulled it off, Fashion Cares was going to be amazing.

'What date are we thinking, then?' Saffron noticed she was already referring to them as a

172

team. Goddamit, Rex!

He consulted his Blackberry, 'The first of July.'

'That's like, less than four months away!'

He grinned. 'We'd better get cracking then, hey?'

Chapter 23

The first thing Saffron did when she got home was call Harriet. Her friend was thrilled at the prospect of Fashion Cares. 'Churchminster's first fashion show, how exciting!'

'If we ever pull it off! Rex is hell-bent on doing it all by ourselves, but I don't think he realizes how much there is to do.'

'Anything I can help with?'

'That was what I was going to ask, actually, see if we can make use of any of your fabulous contacts.'

'Of course, what do you need?'

Saffron checked her list. 'What don't we need? Food, drink, flowers, music, models, hairdressers, stylists . . . Aargh, I don't know where to start.'

Harriet was thinking. 'The only problem with my contacts is that they're all London-based. It could be a bit tricky.'

'Shit, I didn't think of that.'

'What you need is an events organizer. I know a fab local one, Sue Sylvester. Mummy swears by her. Sue's done all her parties.'

'What? Sue Sylvester! No *way*.'

Harriet sounded confused. 'I don't get it.'

'You really need to watch *Glee* and stop wasting time on all those old costume dramas.' Saffron laughed. 'This is great! Wait until I tell Rex. Have

173

you got the number?'

'It's in my Rolodex, hold on. I'm sure Sue would love to be involved. Sue Sylvester, here we go. Have you got a pen?'

'Ready and waiting.' *Good old H, she could always be counted on in a crisis.* Saffron was feeling much better already. And her darling Tom was coming to visit that Friday, too.

* * *

When Saffron picked Tom up from the station she was in full flow about the show. 'So I've drawn up a guest list for the VIPs. Oh, and guess what? Harriet spoke to Fiona, and *Soirée* are going to cover the cost of printing the tickets and the brochures for the night. How cool is that?'

'Very cool. And what's this you mentioned about an events organizer?'

'It was Harriet's idea, the genius, and I've told Rex we need one. She's called Sue Sylvester.'

Tom raised an eyebrow. 'As in . . . ?'

'Comedy, isn't it? Anyway, I spoke to Sue a few days ago and she sounds great, really on it. Rex is paying her, but it's not loads.' Saffron changed down into third to take a sharp bend. 'You know what, I was pretty sceptical at first, but it's really nice to be part of something like this. Aside from the charity side, you know how I like to put on a good party.'

'It does sound pretty fantastic.' Tom looked out of the window. 'Part of me still can't believe Rex is doing this. Actually, scrub that. This is *so* Rex. Most people take up an evening class if they want a new challenge. My brother has to put on a

174

fashion show and try to save the world.'

Saffron giggled. 'Bless, he is really into it.'

'I know, I'm only teasing.'

'He does really want you to respect him, Tom.'

'I do respect him, what do you mean?'

She shrugged. 'It was just something he said.'

'I do think Fashion Cares is a great idea, Saff.' Tom shot her a knowing grin. 'Just as long as it doesn't interfere with your book.'

'It won't, babe.' It was sweet how he looked out for her. 'To be honest, it's good for me, you know, to keep in the loop, keep talking to all the PRs and managers. I'll make my job a lot easier when I go back to work.'

'Hey, as long as you're happy, I'm happy.' He took her hand and kissed it.

She felt a rush of love. 'I'm always happy round you, babe.'

*   *   *

Tom, Saffron and Babs had dinner that night in Babs's kitchen-cum-conservatory, the French windows open into the jungle-like garden. 'It'll be nice when summer's here,' Saffron said, wondering if she should take her mother round to Clementine's for a gardening lesson.

Babs gave a nervous little laugh. 'Yes, won't it? Hee hee!'

Saffron stared at her. Her mother was acting even more erratically than normal. Come to think of it, Tom had been a bit weird since they'd got back. Like he was on edge about something.

'You OK, babe?' she asked, taking his hand. He looked as if he hadn't been listening.

175

'What's that? Yeah, just a bit tired from work.'

'Well, we'll have a nice day tomorrow. What do you fancy doing? I guess you want to see Rex at some point.'

'Actually, let's do something on our own tomorrow.'

'You sure? OK, cool.'

Across the table Babs started coughing into her wine glass.

*   *   *

The next morning Saffron woke to find herself alone in bed. She sat up and took her watch from the bedside table. Ten past ten. Where was Tom? The clothes he'd been wearing last night were gone from the chair. She listened for the sound of the toilet flushing or something, but the house was deathly quiet. Wondering what was going on, she swung her legs out of bed, grabbed her dressing gown, and went downstairs.

Her mother was in the kitchen, behind her easel as usual.

'What are you painting?' Saffron asked.

'Don't come over! It's a secret.'

'All right, chill your boots.' Saffron looked round. 'I thought Tom would be down here.'

'He's gone for a walk.'

'What? Why didn't he wake me?'

'I think he wanted you to lie in, darling.' There was still something very odd up with her mother. She was all twitchy and nervy.

Saffron was suddenly a bit annoyed. She and Tom hardly saw each other as it was, at the moment. *Why had he gone off like this?* 'Whatever,

176

I'm taking my tea back to bed.'

* * *

It was past eleven by the time she heard the front door go. Moments later she heard the heavy tread of Tom's feet and then he appeared in the doorway.

'Hey, babe.'

'Hey.' She put down her *Glamour* magazine. 'Where have you been? I was starting to think you'd fallen down a ditch or something.'

'You're not cross, are you?' He came and sat down on the edge of the bed. He smelt of fresh air, and his cheeks were pink and healthy.

'No, I just didn't know where you'd gone.'

He leant over and kissed her. 'I'm back now.' The sun was streaming through the windows. It was going to be another lovely day. 'I thought we'd go for a picnic later,' Tom said. 'Do you want to get in the shower?'

Half an hour later, she was washed and dressed. She came down into the kitchen to find Tom waiting.

'Ready?' he said.

'Yup.'

She went to pick up the car keys, but Tom got there first. 'I thought I'd drive today, give you a rest.'

'My driving's not that bad, is it?' She smiled.

'No. It's not *that* bad.'

'Bugger off you, you can make your own way back to the station!' She followed him out of the kitchen, arms wrapped round his waist from behind. 'Bye, Mum!'

Babs's head popped out from the living room door. 'Have a wonderful time!' She smiled manically at them.

'I think Mum's officially gone mad,' Saffron said, as they climbed in the MG. 'All those paint fumes have gone to her head.'

Tom pulled out and turned left. 'Hold on, Bedlington's that way,' she said. 'I thought you wanted to get stuff for a picnic?'

'I want to show you something first.'

'Where are we going?'

'You'll see.'

*   *   *

Fifteen minutes out of the village, they were surrounded by swathes of green fields. A few minutes later Tom took another left into what looked like a private road. 'Where *are* we going?' Saffron tried again. 'You're not taking me somewhere to murder me, are you?'

Tom didn't reply, and Saffron noticed his hands were gripping so tight to the steering wheel that they had gone white. 'Babe, are you OK?' she said, as they turned on to a long grassy avenue, flanked by two straight rows of horse chestnut trees. She could see white banners hanging between the middle ones, as if someone was having a party. In the distance an expanse of water glittered in the sun.

'What's going on, babe?' She looked at him. Tom's whole face was tense. Shit, he was about to tell her some really bad news . . .

Saffron suddenly had a sick feeling in her stomach. He'd been weird, distant even, ever since

178

he'd arrived. Was he about to tell her things weren't working out? A lump rose in her throat. She'd been so wrapped up in the book she hadn't even noticed. Maybe he'd been doing some thinking since she moved out . . .

The car drove slowly onwards, Saffron feeling more distraught by the second. He couldn't be finishing it, what would she do without him?

They were approaching the first banner, now. Saffron suddenly noticed paper lanterns swaying in some of the trees. What sort of party was this? As they got closer she looked up and, to her complete surprise, saw her name printed in big black letters: SAFFRON. She half laughed, nervous and confused. 'Is this some kind of joke?'

Still Tom didn't say anything.

The car continued bumping forwards. She saw another banner coming up. 'WILL', was all it said. She slumped back on her seat, irritated and flummoxed. Who was 'Will'? Tom had clearly gone as mad as her mother.

But then another one came up. 'YOU', it said, in three-foot-high letters.

Now Saffron sat up, a funny feeling creeping through her body. She looked at Tom. He'd gone an odd colour.

They were nearly at the end now. There was another banner coming up. Saffron held her breath, hardly daring to believe . . .

'MARRY' screamed out at her, and then a few trees up, a final one.

'ME?'

'Oh my God!' she screamed. Tom stopped the car and leapt out, running round the side of the car. He pulled her door open and went down on one knee.

'You're the most beautiful, funny, amazing woman to ever walk this planet.' He fumbled in his pocket and brought out a box. Trance-like, Saffron stared down at the vintage diamond ring.

Tom's voice did a little wobble. 'My sun rises and sets with you, babe.' Then, as if by magic, a barbershop quartet stepped out of the trees by the lake and started singing the words to her favourite Elvis Costello song: 'She'.

Saffron looked down dumbly, as he took her hand. 'Saffron Walden, I love you more than anything. Will you do me the honour of becoming my wife?'

Hearing him say the words finally snapped her out of her stupor. 'Yes,' she sobbed, flinging her arms around him. 'I will, I will, I will!'

Chapter 24

They toasted each other with a bottle of champagne Tom had put in the lake to chill earlier. The barbershop quartet, stood under the trees at a discreet distance, serenaded them.

'How did you find this place? Where did you find *them*?' Saffron whispered. This was the most crazy, surreal, romantic thing she'd ever experienced in her life.

'I Googled "barbershop quartet in the Cotswolds" and they came up.' Tom's brown eyes looked anxious. 'It's not too much, is it?'

'I *love* it.' She laughed out loud. 'I still can't believe it! I'm engaged.' She admired the ring again. 'How long had you been planning this?'

'I guess for a while, but then I thought now was a good time. You know, with us being away from each other.' He was only just starting to regain his colour. 'Oh my God, Saff, it was the most nerve-racking thing ever!'

Saffron pulled a wry face. 'You were acting so weirdly I thought you were going to dump me.'

He looked shocked. 'What? No!' He pulled her into a big hug. 'I'm sorry if I was acting weird. I was so nervous you were going to say no, and if we got past that part, that you wouldn't like the ring . . .'

She kissed the ring, and then did the same to him. 'It's all perfect, babe. I couldn't have wished for anything more.'

He shook his head in wonder. 'Wow, we're getting married.'

'I know, Saffron Fellows!' She had been saying the name to herself in wonderment for the last five minutes.

He looked chuffed. 'You're going to change your name, then?'

'Of course, why wouldn't I?'

Tom shrugged. 'I don't know, I thought because of work and stuff. Hey, I'm down with this modern woman stuff.'

'Babe, I'll be proud to have your name. I want everyone to know I'm your wife.'

He leant back on his elbow. 'Saffron Fellows. It's got a good ring to it.'

Mrs Fellows. Saffron lay back and looked out over the lake. Sparkles of sunlight were bouncing across it.

Drunk on love (and Saffron a bit on champagne), they arrived home to find Babs waiting expectantly. She took one look at Saffron's ring and burst into tears. 'My baby!'

'Don't, Mum, you're going to start me off!' Saffron hugged her mother. 'I take it you knew about   this?'

'I had to ask your mum's permission of course,' Tom said, making Babs well up even more.

'It's about time this family had a happy marriage, it's so wonderful!'

'All right, Mum, calm down.' Saffron thought of her aunt. 'I can't wait to tell Velda.' Her aunt Velda loved Tom. Saffron looked down at the ring again, admiring the jewel on her long, slender finger. Saffron didn't care if it cost hundreds or thousands. Tom had bought it with love, and that was all that mattered.

Her mother went over to the kitchen dresser. She came back and pushed something into Saffron's hand.

'What's this?' Saffron looked down at the cheque. 'Oh my God, Mum, fifteen thousand pounds!'

'I had a little nest egg, especially for when you got married, darling. I'm sorry it's not more.'

Saffron felt tears spring into her eyes. 'This is more than generous, thank you!' she said, throwing her arms round her mum again.

*   *   *

They were in full flow about ideas for the wedding

when the front doorbell rang.

'Ooh, I'll get it,' Babs said joyfully. As she disappeared off down the hallway Tom drew Saffron into his arms. 'I'm so happy.'

'Me too, I love you, fiancé.' *Fiancé*. Oh my God, she was engaged!

'Look who it is!' Babs came bustling back into the room with Rex in tow.

He looked surprised to see Tom. 'Hey, bro, didn't think you were down this weekend.'

'It was a bit of a surprise visit,' Tom said, sliding his arm round Saffron's waist.

Rex didn't notice her ring. 'Saff, guess what? I've only gone and got Handbag Haven.'

She stuck her left hand out. 'Guess what? I've only gone and got engaged.'

Rex's face broke into a huge smile. 'Guys, that is great!' He came over and gave them a hug. 'Congratulations.'

Saffron was nearly crushed between them. 'Thanks, mate.'

Rex stepped back. 'So, when's the wedding? And where?'

Saffron looked at her new husband-to-be. 'We're thinking August after next, aren't we, babe? Neither of us is religious, so we'll probably do it in a registry office in London, then have a fuck-off amazing reception.'

'Sounds like my kind of do. I'd better get an invite,' Rex said.

'You're best man, mate.'

Rex stared at his brother. 'You're kidding me?'

'No, why would I be?'

Rex went over and hugged his brother fiercely. 'I won't let you down, bro, it's a real honour.' Saffron watched them, smiling. Both of them seemed quite overcome.

'You must join us for lunch,' Babs said.

'Mum, I think Tom and I are going for our picnic.' Saffron looked out into the garden and noticed the table with a white cloth over it amongst all the weeds. There was an ice bucket standing on it.

'But I've done us a celebration lunch. We've got smoked salmon and everything . . .'

Saffron looked down at the cheque in her hands. 'Sounds great, Mum.' They could do the picnic tomorrow. After all, they had all the time in the world now.

*   *   *

'Let's have a look, then,' Rex said, pushing his Ray-Bans up on his head. The three of them were sitting outside at the table in the sun, while Babs flapped around in the kitchen. Saffron proudly showed Rex her hand, and he inspected the ring closely.

'Gorgeous, isn't it?'

'Sure.' He let go. 'You know, Chanel do *amazing* engagement rings at the moment.'

Saffron raised an eyebrow in disbelief. 'Thanks, Rex! Are you dissing my ring?'

His brown eyes widened. 'No, not at all. It's really cute, Saff.'

'*Cute*,' she muttered. She looked at it again. Maybe it did look a bit on the small side . . .

Rex's phone beeped. He took it out of his pocket and read the message.

'Amazing!' He looked at Saffron. 'We've

confirmed another designer. You know, Julie Friend, that forty-year-old mum I found through the Manchester Fashion Network? She only designs in her spare time but the stuff she does with draping is incredible.'

'Great,' Saffron said, looking at Tom. As if she cared about bloody tailoring on today of all days!

Rex was up, bouncing round like a puppy. 'We've nearly got our ten. I'm gonna call her back straight away.' He strode off down to the bottom of the garden.

Saffron turned back to Tom. 'I can't believe he dissed my ring!'

'He was just being thoughtless. He doesn't mean anything by it.'

'Yeah, but still . . .'

'Don't worry about it.' Tom reached out and stroked her cheek. 'You don't mind it being so far away, do you? The wedding, I mean. I just thought we should wait until you're back in London, so we can do things together.'

'Course not, it makes sense. Looking forward to it is part of the fun.'

He looked relieved. 'I know it's hard for us at the moment, being away from each other. I just wanted you to know how much I love you.'

'I love you too, babe. So much.'

He grinned at her, his forehead doing that sexy crease thing. Saffron suddenly felt incredibly horny.

'Come with me.' She grabbed him by the hand, leading him inside and through the kitchen.

'Where are you going? Lunch is ready,' her mother called.

'Just want to show Tom something!' Saffron

pulled him up the stairs and into the bathroom. She shut the door behind them and pulled up her top, showing off a black lacy bra.

'I wanted to show you *this*.'

Instantly he was rock hard. 'You'll find no objections from me,' he said huskily as Saffron started pulling at his belt buckle. She'd kicked off her ballet pumps and was wriggling out of one leg of her skinny jeans. Nipples erect through the black lace, Saffron pushed him down on the toilet.

His huge erection stood up, beacon-like. Tom spread his legs and pulled her down on to him. Saffron pulled her G-string aside and, positioning herself, slid down on his cock. It felt beautiful, exhilarating.

'I love you,' she said, looking into his eyes. Kissing her passionately, Tom grabbed her hips, driving himself even deeper into her. They got faster and wetter, putting their hands over each other's mouths to stop the moaning.

'God, this is incredible,' he panted. Saffron knew what he meant. They'd made love hundreds of times before, but this was somehow different. It was like they were connecting on a whole new level . . .

As Saffron's orgasm mounted, she gripped her knees tighter, wanting every inch of him.

'Oh God, oh God . . .' They came together in one spine-tingling explosion. Shivers still running through her body, Saffron collapsed on to her fiancé's chest.

Bloody hell. If that's what sex was like when they were engaged, she couldn't wait to be married.

Chapter 25

London

'It's all in the hips, people, so start moving!'

Mariana, the Spanish salsa teacher, was in a particularly strident mood that night at the Gatsby Road Community Centre. She was pacing round the room, correcting couples in her strong accent: 'One, two, three . . . five, six, seven. No, it's *one*, two . . .'

On her way back from the loo, Harriet had stopped to watch the class. Alf Stokes sashayed past, clutching on to an ancient-looking lady who looked like she was about to keel over at any moment. 'I won't have any hips left at this rate,' Alf shouted across to Harriet. 'I only had 'em done last year!'

Harriet smiled. Alf was a lot braver than her. She would rather die than show off her dance moves in public. To say she had no sense of rhythm was an understatement.

It was busy tonight, with people of many shapes and ages. As she watched Abby giggling her way through a turn with one of the more handsome boys from the youth club, Harriet's mind again turned to Saffron. She was so happy for her and Tom. And to be proposed to at Sherbourne Water, the most romantic place in the Cotswolds! A hopeless romantic, Harriet loved a good wedding more than anything. The fact that Saffron had asked her to be chief bridesmaid made it even more special. She was going to have such fun

187

planning the hen . . .

Suddenly the music stopped dead. 'Enough!' Mariana strode into the centre of the room, shaking her head. 'What is happening tonight? Have you forgotten all that I teach you?' Mariana, a muscled strip of a woman in a rah-rah skirt and shiny leggings, started to move back and forth impatiently. 'One, two, three, TURN, five, six, seven! See? Easy.' Her eyes scanned the room, resting on Harriet. 'You! Come over here.'

Forty pairs of eyes swivelled on her.

'Me?'

The dance teacher nodded impatiently. 'Please, come here.'

With a feeling of dread, Harriet peeled herself off the wall and walked over. Mariana pointed to the other side of the room. 'And you! Zack! Over here.'

Zack stopped, mid-walk. Then, with some relief, he held up the folder he was carrying. 'I've got someone waiting on the phone, sorry.'

Mariana tutted and turned away to seek a new victim, but just then Aunty Win stuck her head out of the kitchen hatch. 'I'll get the phone!' Before Zack could get a step further, Win had bustled into the office and shut the door behind her.

Mariana held her hand out to him. 'Come partner this young lady, please.'

Reluctantly he put the folder down on a chair and came over. Harriet was so red her face was actually hurting.

'So!' Mariana pushed them together. Harriet got a waft of Issey Miyake and washing powder. 'Zack, put your right hand on . . . what is your name?'

'Harriet,' Harriet mumbled.

'Put your right hand on Harriet's left shoulder blade. Move closer! Now look at each other.'

Zack was tight-jawed, looking as if he'd rather be anywhere else in the world. 'Sorry about this,' he said through gritted teeth.

'Music!' Mariana shouted and the music started up again. 'Watch me, one, two, three, TURN, five, six, seven! You got that? Go! One, two . . . no, Harriet, wrong way.'

Zack pulled a face as Harriet stepped on his foot. 'I'm frightfully sorry,' Harriet said. The warmth from Zack's hand seemed to have spread through her entire body. She felt like she was about to spontaneously combust.

Mariana clapped her hands together. 'Again!'

Harriet stumbled around, trying to recall what she'd just learnt. She felt even worse because Zack seemed to instantly find the rhythm. Harriet could feel the power of his body as he tried to pull her through the steps with him.

'That's it!' Mariana instructed. 'Put your arm round her waist.'

Harriet instinctively sucked her stomach in as she felt Zack's hands on her spare tyre. She hated anyone touching her there!

'No, Harriet! Move your hips. Like this.' Mariana did an expert wiggle.

Wishing the dance floor would swallow her up, Harriet tried to jerk her hips about. Someone on the sidelines snorted with laughter, and she caught a glimpse of Gray's face, creased with amusement.

'Not like that! It's one long, *sexy* movement!' Mariana shouted. 'Turn! No, that way, Harriet! And smile, you're meant to be enjoying yourself!'

Flustered and red-faced, it was all Harriet could

189

do not to fall flat on her face. Every time she crashed into Zack's body she could feel the hardness, the muscles under his T-shirt. *Just get through this*, she prayed. *Don't break his foot.*

Back and forth they went, until the music finally stopped. Zack let go of her as if she were a hot coal. Gasping for breath, Harriet wiped a wet strand of hair off her forehead, as Mariana looked at her dubiously. 'Yes, well, maybe Harriet wasn't the best person to demonstrate, but I think you got the message. Positions everyone, please! And a one, two . . .'

Harriet felt a complete laughing stock. Even Aunty Win seemed hard-pressed to think of a suitable compliment, and as soon as the class was over Harriet headed for the door.

'Are you not staying for tea and cake, 'Arriet?'

'No, do you mind, Aunty Win? I've got the most awful headache.' Harriet just wanted to get away from there, from the stifled giggles, away from *him*.

Win looked concerned. 'I'll get Zachary to walk you.'

'No!' That was the last thing she wanted. 'I'll be fine, Aunty Win,' she said hastily. 'I just need to go and lie down.'

She'd got a hundred metres down the road when she heard the sound of running footsteps behind her. She moved aside to let whoever it was pass, but suddenly Zack was standing there under the streetlight, face carved in shadow.

'Win said you weren't feeling well.'

'Er, yes.' She couldn't meet his gaze. 'I've just got a bit of a headache.'

He rubbed the back of his neck, his smile rueful.

'Was it from me throwing you around the dance floor?'

'Not at all,' she protested. 'You were great. I was the one lumbering around.'

'You weren't lumbering,' he said. 'You were, you were, er . . .'

'I was lumbering,' she said wryly. 'Sorry for stepping on your foot.'

'It's OK. I think I'll live.'

She suddenly flinched as he reached out and touched her shoulder. He moved his hand away quickly. 'You had a hair on you.'

'Thanks,' she mumbled, unnerved by the crackle of electricity that had just passed between them.

Zack cleared his throat. 'Look, I know now's probably not the time, but the thing is . . .' He took a step closer. 'The thing is, I like you, Harriet.'

She stared at him. 'You like me—as in friends?'

'No, that's not what I meant.' He sighed. 'I'm making a right pig's ear of this.' He tried again. 'I just thought someone like you could never be interested in me.'

'Someone like me?' Harriet could feel the blood rushing to her head.

To her surprise Zack gripped her hands, holding them tightly. 'Yes, you. You're sweet and funny, and lovely, and you have the biggest heart.' He touched her cheek gently. 'And the best smile I've ever seen.'

Up close she could see the faint freckles on his nose, the inky black of the eyelashes framing those mesmerizing eyes. 'You didn't think I fancied you?' Harriet said, thinking of all the times she'd stolen glances at him, all the hours she'd spent dreaming about him.

191

'Harriet?' He was looking at her questioningly. 'Do you like me?' He tried to joke. 'Or have I just made the biggest arse of myself ever?'

She shook her head. 'N-no. I do like you.' She seemed to have lost the power of speech.

Zack's face relaxed. 'In that case, Harriet, I'd really like to kiss you.'

'Y-yes, please...' As if in some kind of wondrous dream, his soft, dry lips crushed down on to hers.

APRIL

Chapter 26

Churchminster

Oh my God, that was it. The one. *Her* wedding dress. Saffron stared at the pictures of Madison Gold enviously. The American socialite had just married Wall Street banker Blane Forster, and *OK!* magazine had published a gushing eight-page spread on the nuptials, which had been held at a luxury hotel in Bel Air. Saffron had to admit she wasn't a fan of Madison, who came across as just another heiress airhead, but damn, the girl knew how to pick a good wedding dress. Ivory silk, with one shoulder, it cascaded down her body like a shimmering waterfall.

She reached for the scissors and cut the picture out. *'The bride's beautiful dress, which has hand-stitched diamonds on the hem and neckline,'* read the caption, *'was by Oscar de la Renta and cost fifty thousand dollars.'*

Ouch. Well, her dress wouldn't be costing *that*. Saffron flicked through the rest of the article, taking in the eight-foot-high wedding cake and cut-crystal tableware. There was only one picture of the father of the bride: the billionaire business magnate, Reuben Gold.

Reuben Gold. Now *there* was a name she remembered. Saffron cast her mind back to the scandal that had engulfed the family last year.

In America, first you had the Obamas, then the Trumps, and the Golds didn't come that much further down the list. Reuben Gold was one of the most powerful, influential men in the country, but his image had been rocked when his youngest daughter Summer had been found wrecked out of her head, in her father's even more wrecked Lamborghini outside their Bel Air mansion. Which happened to be burning to the ground at the time.

The paparazzi had gone wild, from Fox News helicopters swooping over the property watching a hundred million dollars' worth of real estate going up in flames, to the hordes of photographers jostling to get through the police cordon. Despite the media circus the story had suddenly died away, with no charges pressed. Everyone had wondered how many people Reuben Gold had paid off to make *that* happen. The rumours had kept simmering, but the last thing anyone heard was that seventeen-year-old Summer had been packed off to rehab in Arizona, no questions asked. Saffron looked at Gold's unsmiling face. Apparently he'd lost millions on the stock market afterwards. No wonder he looked so pissed off.

But Saffron had better things to think about than some spoilt little rich girl. She gazed at the photo of the wedding dress again. It was so perfect! And she knew just the dressmaker in Notting Hill who could recreate it for her, for a fraction of the price. Smiling, she went over and put it on the mantelpiece for safekeeping. At least it was in no danger of being thrown away; from the dust and piles of junk everywhere, it seemed her mother hadn't been in here to clean this side of the millennium.

Outside the dark little room, the sun was shining. Saffron walked over to the window and threw it open for some much-needed air.

The green was looking almost ridiculously pretty: the honey-gold houses nestled around it, thousands of white daisies studding the deep green grass. A portly bumblebee hummed past, disappearing off into the spring sunshine.

She looked at her watch. Rex had called the first official Fashion Cares meeting today, with Sue Sylvester. Saffron wondered what the events organizer was like. Neither of them had met Sue yet, but Rex had had several conversations on the phone with her, and said she sounded fine. For some reason Saffron imagined a glamorous Jackie Collins type, dressed in black and leopard-print, with a huge pair of designer sunnies clamped to her face. They definitely needed someone flamboyant and fabulous to pull it all together.

*　　　*　　　*

At Byron Heights there was no answer at the front door, so Saffron made her way round to the back. One of the kitchen windows was open, and she could hear a furious whirring noise from within. She made her way over, and standing delicately in the flowerbed, peered inside.

It took a moment for her eyes to adjust before she saw Rex standing with his back to her, topless. In the flesh, he was, of course, leaner than Tom, but their resemblance was still remarkable. Saffron took in the wide shoulders, the torso that narrowed to a tight waist. He even had Tom's bum, the back of his jeans hanging low off his muscled hips. Actually, he had a *really* nice bum . . .

Rex turned round and the whirring stopped.

Saffron averted her eyes, in case he thought she'd been standing there ogling. He raised his hand. 'Hey, how's it going?'

'Good. Your front doorbell not work, or something?'

He looked apologetic. 'This place is so massive I don't hear anything.' He gestured to the French windows leading in from the garden. 'Come on round.'

She stepped back off the flowerbed. Even in the bright sunlight, the gardens of Byron Heights looked like something out of a Tim Burton movie. As she walked in, Rex came over and kissed her on both cheeks. 'Hey,' he said again. The sunlight caught his eyes as he pulled back, making them look like two liquid chocolate pools.

'I'm just making a smoothie, fancy one?' Rex seemed entirely unselfconscious about his semi-nudity, no doubt because, as a model, he was used to taking his clothes off.

Saffron wished he'd go and put some clothes on. For some reason she was finding it rather disconcerting. 'Sounds great.'

She watched as Rex reached up to get two glasses from the cupboard, the muscles flexing across his back. This time Saffron made sure she wasn't still looking when he turned round.

'How're the wedding plans going?' he asked.

'They're not, at the moment. I've promised Tom I'll get the book out of the way first.'

'Aren't you dying to go dress shopping?'

'I've found one actually,' she confessed. 'You know Madison Gold?'

He was busy pouring the liquid out from the smoothie maker. 'I've met her a few times.'

'Show off,' she grinned. 'Anyway, *OK!* covered her wedding and the dress is dress is *amazing*. Oscar de la Renta. I am totally in love with it.'

Rex handed her a smoothie.

'I take my hat off to you guys. What you're doing is huge. I know I couldn't do it.'

She smiled. 'You just haven't met the right person yet.'

'Maybe. But it's still pretty scary, huh? Marriage, I mean. Making that commitment to one person for the rest of your life.' He rolled his eyes upwards and put on a deadly serious voice. 'Till death do us part . . .'

'Don't, Rex, you're freaking me out!' she scolded.

He laughed. 'Hey, I'm only messing. It's a beautiful thing.'

'You arse,' she said, but his words set off something inside her. She was really getting married! Even though she was incredibly happy, it was a pretty overwhelming concept. And it wasn't as if her family had the best track record when it came to marriage . . .

'When's Sue getting here?' she asked, changing the subject. Rex wasn't going to wind her up and give her the heebie-jeebies. Unromantic sod.

He looked at the clock on the wall. 'Shoot, in like five minutes.'

'Hadn't you better go and get dressed then? Standing there half naked is no way to conduct business.'

*　　*　　*

Saffron was taking the opportunity to go through

and delete all her old texts when she heard the gravel crunch out front. She put the iPhone down and walked out into the hall. 'Sue's here!' she called.

Rex's shout was muffled. 'Nearly ready!'

He'd said that fifteen minutes ago. Bloody models. Saffron pulled open the door, but there was only a battered old white pickup there that had seen better days. The driver's side was open, and she could see someone bent over the seat. Saffron frowned. Had Rex called in some builders or something? She was just about to call up to him again when the head of the person in the pickup popped up. Saffron got a glimpse of the sun glinting off a pair of very thick glasses, before a little figure got out and walked round the front of the vehicle.

It was a middle-aged woman with a huge frumpy handbag, an ill-fitting beige trouser suit, and a stash of what looked like magazines clutched to her scrawny chest.

Saffron knew that look. She groaned inwardly, as the woman started towards her. 'I'm sorry,' she said, smiling sweetly. 'We're not really interested.'

The woman stopped in her tracks. 'Oh, aren't you?'

'No, we're not very religious here.' *Bloody Jehovahs!*

'But Mr Sullivan told me . . .'

Saffron blinked. 'You're Sue Sylvester?' What the hell was Harriet playing at? This woman looked like she should be organizing octagenarian coffee mornings, not a major fashion show.

She heard Rex running down the stairs. He'd changed into dark blue trousers and a white shirt, very businesslike.

'Sue! Great to meet you,' he started to say. 'Oh!' He looked confusedly at Saffron. 'Er, hi . . .'

'This is Sue!' Saffron said, her voice falsely bright. 'Sue *Sylvester*.'

Sue stuck out a bony little hand. 'Nice to meet you.' She was so softly spoken it was hard to hear her. Saffron thought she looked like a female version of Penfold, the timid hamster friend of Danger Mouse. She could see Rex was having a hard time trying to make sense of it all.

'Come in, come in,' he said, sounding overly jolly. As Sue shuffled in, Rex shot a slightly desperate look at Saffron. 'Can I get you a tea or coffee?' he asked Sue.

'No, thank you,' Sue said. It was almost a whisper.

Rex pointed in the direction of the dining room. 'Come through.'

As Sue shuffled into the room, Rex grabbed Saffron by the arm. 'This is a nightmare!' he whispered. 'I thought she came highly recommended.'

Saffron felt helpless. 'She did, I don't get it!'

'Let's give her ten minutes, humour her a bit, and get her out.' Rex shook his head. 'Jesus!' Plastering a smile on her face, Saffron followed him in.

*   *   *

An hour later, they were eating a huge piece of humble pie. For all her hamster-like demeanour, Sue Sylvester proved to be a sharp operator. She'd already got a high-end catering company, Bastilles of Bedlington, on board to do the canapés in exchange for a few tickets, and was on the case chasing up everything else. At the end of the meeting she trundled off in her truck (apparently she'd pranged the Merc, and was borrowing one of her husband's work vans), leaving an astonished Saffron and Rex in her wake.

'Sue is something else!' Rex said, going back into the dining room.

'I knew Harriet wouldn't let us down.'

Rex laughed. 'You knew nothing of the sort! I saw your face, you were crapping it.'

'I was not!'

'You so were.' Grinning, he threw himself back down in the chair. 'Although we might have to give her some kind of makeover before the show, that suit looked like something out of a bad 1970s cop series.'

Saffron smiled. 'Don't be mean.'

'Hey, I'm not. Sue puts us to shame. Well, me, anyway.'

'Speaking of fashion, have you had any progress with Bibi Brown?'

'I've spoken to her people. Apparently she's up to her eyeballs with her spring/summer collection for next year, but they said to call in a few weeks.'

'Did they sound interested?'

'Definitely. Apparently Bibi loves the concept. I knew she would. I'm confident we'll get something.' He stretched, putting his hands behind his head. 'How about the guest list?' Between them they had drawn up an illustrious mix of the biggest names from showbiz, fashion and politics. If they even got half of them, it would be amazing.

'Well, as you know, the press release went in

Fashion Monitor, and both *Soirée* and GLAMOUR online have given it a mention. So word is out there. I've sent all the emails out and I'll start chasing people up next week.'

'Great! This is going even better than I thought.'

Saffron knew from experience it could take months of wrangling with a PR or manager to get one celebrity to commit to a single interview, let alone getting a load of them to agree to be in one room together.

'Yeah, well, don't get too carried away. We need them all to say yes first.'

'I have compete faith in you.' Rex looked down at the steel Rolex adorning his left wrist. 'You hungry? Let me treat you to lunch at the pub.'

Saffron thought of her laptop, waiting for her patiently at home. 'I should really get back to work.'

'Come on, it's the least I can do. I really do appreciate your help with all this.'

It was a tempting offer. There was only a mouldy piece of cheese and some bread in the kitchen at Hardwick House.

'I promise not to keep you out late. Come on, lunch in the sun with my scintillating company to amuse you. What could be better?'

*   *   *

The Jolly Boot was busy with people having a leisurely Friday lunch. Rex attracted several looks as they walked in, but it was Saffron who got the star treatment.

'Young Saffron!' Jack Turner said. 'We'd been wondering when you'd be coming in.

203

Congratulations on the engagement!' He gestured at the buxom middle-aged woman standing next to him. 'You know my wife, Beryl, don't you?'

'Congratulations!' Beryl said. 'Jack, give 'em a bottle of bubbly on the house.'

'That's too kind, really,' Saffron said, but Jack had already pulled a bottle of house champagne out of the fridge. Bang went her afternoon of writing. Jack stuck a meaty hand over the bar towards Rex.

'Well done, Tom, my son, you got yourself a good 'un there.'

There was a silence. 'Er, this is Rex, actually, Tom's brother,' Saffron said.

Rex smiled easily, not in the slightest bit embarrassed by the mix-up. 'We've met before, hi, Jack.'

The landlord looked confused for a moment. 'Blow me down! You had me fooled then. Aren't they alike, Beryl?'

'Peas in a pod!'

Jack winked at his wife. 'Cor love, lucky Rex didn't find us salivating in our tea cups.'

Rex had the grace to blush, as the other three started to laugh. 'Jeez, I'm sorry about that.'

'What you got to be sorry about?' Beryl declared. 'It's nice to put Churchminster on the map. Even if we do sound like a bunch of perverts.'

'How are you finding Byron Heights?' Jack asked.

'Pretty cool, actually.'

'I find it a bit creepy,' Beryl said. 'All those goggly-eyed statues.'

'I know what you mean,' Saffron told her.

'There was talk of ghosts up there and

204

everything!' Beryl went on.

Jack rolled his eyes. 'What are you going on about, woman?' He turned to Rex. 'Don't let her put you off.'

Rex laughed. 'No chance of that. I've rather fallen in love with the place.'

Saffron nudged him. 'Rex is putting on a charity fashion show there, aren't you?'

'*We* are,' he corrected, grinning.

Beryl's eyes were out on stalks. 'A fashion show? Here, in Churchminster?'

Rex nodded. 'Yep. It's called Fashion Cares.'

'Fashion Cares! What a great name.' Beryl looked like she was about to faint with excitement. 'When is it?'

'The first of July.'

Beryl looked at her husband. 'Blimey, how exciting! Will there be any celebrities there? Like Cindy Crawford? She's still my favourite model, you know. Classy, she is.'

'I can think of another word for her,' Jack said. 'Cor!'

'I'm not sure about Cindy, but we're hoping for some VIP guests,' Rex said.

'Did you hear that, Jack, VIPs!' Beryl said. She looked hopefully at Rex.

'If you or anyone else would like to come from the village, I'll save some complimentary tickets,' Rex said, playing the generosity card perfectly.

Beryl clutched her ample chest. 'Would we! Tell you what, Rex, you should get my Stacey on-board. She's doing a hair and beauty course at college, and she'd love to come and help out.' She winked at Rex. 'Now she *is* one who's been salivating at your arrival!'

Rex deflected the compliment. 'She sounds great.'

Saffron, who remembered the Turners' daughter as a walking, talking Jordan lookalike, thought Rex had no idea what he was letting himself in for.

'If you need anyone to stick up posters, or sell tickets, we'd be happy to help,' Beryl said. 'Ooh, a fashion show! I've got a bit of a sixth sense, you know, about things happening . . .'

'Don't get her started.' Jack groaned.

'Shut it, you,' Beryl told him. 'You mark my words: this Fashion Cares is going to be a success. I can feel it in my waters.'

It was busy in the beer garden, but they managed to bag the one remaining free table. Saffron was aware of every pair of female eyes flickering on Rex, now wearing a white Tom Ford shirt with his jeans. A fifty-something cougar in a tight dress, licking her lips in his direction, nearly spontaneously combusted.

They sat down and Rex poured them both a glass. 'I propose a toast. To Super Sue and Fashion Cares.'

They clinked glasses. 'And Tom,' Saffron added. That was why they had the champagne, after all.

'To you both, the happy lovebirds.' Their eyes met. Rex grinned. 'And to Churchminster's fabulous first show!'

Chapter 27

London

It had been seven days, twelve hours and fourteen minutes since Zack had kissed her, and Harriet's world had shifted into some kind of delicious, romantic dream. After he'd taken her in his arms under the gloom of the streetlamp it had been on her mind constantly. The way his lips had moved across hers, how he'd gently caressed the back of her hair. Now Harriet was going to see him that evening, and could barely contain her excitement.

She was sitting, staring dreamily at her desk when Alexander, *Soirée*'s fashion director, walked past.

'I know that look! Someone's getting a good seeing-to.'

Harriet looked up and flushed scarlet. 'No! Alexander!'

He winked and raised an eyebrow. 'Don't worry, darling, I won't say anything. You dirty little minx!'

He sashayed off, swinging his hips. Harriet looked at the pile of invoices she'd meant to file that morning. It was very unlike her to be so unproductive, but she was finding it impossible to concentrate today. Her desk phone rang.

'Hello, *Soirée*!'

'Darling, it's me. Caro.'

'What ho, Mrs Belmont!'

'I know you must be sooper dooper busy, but I just wondered if you fancied coming over for supper tonight. Benedict's out, and it's just me and the kids. Well, it's just me, actually, the kids will be in bed.'

Harriet pulled an apologetic face. 'I would have loved to, but I've got plans.'

'I thought you probably would, darling. Off to some fabulously glamorous party, are we?'

'Not quite . . .' Harriet was about to tell Caro about Zack, but she detected something amiss in her voice. 'Is everything all right?'

'Oh, I'm just tired, darling.' Caro sighed. ' Sebastian's been on the phone causing trouble. Benedict and I had a bit of a ding dong about it.'

Sebastian Belmont was the ex-husband from hell. After ruining their marriage by cheating on Caro with a succession of mistresses, Sebastian now hardly ever made the effort to see his son Milo, even though he only lived on the other side of London.

'Oh dear, what's happened?'

'Nothing huge. He just rang up out of the blue and demanded to see Milo, which I wouldn't mind normally of course. But Milo was meant to be going to a birthday party and Sebastian accused me of being difficult. Then Benedict waded in . . .'

Ex-husband versus current one! To say there was no love lost between the two men was a bit of an understatement.

'Poor you, you must feel stuck in the middle.'

'It is rather trying! Never mind, I'm sure it will iron itself out.'

Harriet checked her diary. 'I'm free tomorrow if you still want to do supper.'

'That would be lovely. Now then, don't let me keep you. See you then, bye.'

Thirty seconds later the phone went again. 'H,

208

it's me.' Saffron sounded upbeat.

'Hi, hon.' Harriet shot a guilty look through the glass wall into the editor's office. Luckily Fiona hadn't seemed to notice she'd done virtually no work today.

'I just had to phone and say, Sue Sylvester is amazing. She's practically running the thing for us.'

'Glad to be of help!'

Saffron laughed. 'You're in a good mood today.'

Harriet flushed happily. 'Actually,' she lowered her voice. 'Zack and I kissed the other night.'

'That's brilliant! I knew he wouldn't be able to resist you. Didn't I tell you your Prince Charming was out there somewhere?'

'I don't know about that, he'll probably have gone off me by the time I see him again.' Even though he'd sent her a really sweet text afterwards, Harriet was still worried it was all too good to be true.

'Oh, stop that, course he won't.' There was a thud in the background. 'Shit!'

'Everything all right?'

'Just tripped over a hideous Art Deco doorstop Mum bought. Honestly, this place is like a bloody junk shop.'

Harriet smiled, imagining the chaos. 'How's Tom?'

'Putting in twelve-hour days, poor thing. I feel like I haven't seen him for ages.'

'He'll be down to see you soon.'

'I know, I know. Hey, I popped in to see your dad the other day. I got a right bollocking for not going to see him earlier!'

'Don't mind him, he doesn't mean it.'

'I think it's funny. I love the go-karting track he's built out the back.'

Harriet's eyes widened. 'A *go-karting* track?'

'Didn't you know? Ooh, I think the postman is at the door. I'd better go. Thanks for all this, speak soon, yeah?'

Harriet put the phone down, for once not thinking about Zack. Her father had built a go-karting track? At the Hall?

She *really* had to go back and see him.

* * *

As soon as she walked into the centre that night, Win was over like a shot. ' 'Arriet! So good to see you. Are you well?'

'Hi, Aunty Win, yes, thanks.' She surreptitiously looked round for Zack, but there was no sign of him. *Oh God!* She suddenly felt sick with nerves.

'Good, good.' Aunty Win's brown eyes twinkled knowingly, and Harriet felt herself start to redden. Did Win know something?

'Harriet, hi.' She whirled round at the familiar gravelly voice. Zack was standing there, eyes bluer than ever. He was wearing a striped polo shirt she hadn't seen before, that showed off his broad chest perfectly. God, he was lovely.

'Have you got a minute?' he asked, looking rather serious. Harriet felt her stomach lurch as she followed him across the hall to the office.

'It won't take a minute, it's just a few admin questions.'

As soon as he'd shut the door behind them he was kissing her. 'I haven't been able to stop thinking about you.'

210

'M-me neither,' she said, feeling dazed and delirious. He still liked her! Zack rested his arms on her shoulders, looking into her eyes.

'Win's dying to know what's going on, it's very funny.'

What *was* going on? All Harriet knew was that she was here, in Zack's arms. She still couldn't quite believe it.

'Hey, listen.' He stroked her right cheek with his hand. 'Do you fancy going to an "open mic" night after this? Danny Henderson—study night's star pupil—is performing.'

'A what?'

Zack grinned. 'An open mic night. It's kind of hard to explain, I guess, but it's where people get up on stage and take turns to rap.'

'Like karaoke?'

He laughed. 'I suppose you could say that, in a very loose sense.'

Harriet was finding it hard to breathe. 'Sounds like fun.'

'Great.' He released her. 'As much as I'd like to stand here and kiss you all evening, I need to get on with some work.'

Harriet floated out of the office on cloud nine. The study club was deep in concentration, oblivious to her orgasmic happiness.

She was about to go and see Pete when Abby waved her over. 'Can you come and help?'

Rearming, Harriet walked over and sat down. 'What are you studying tonight, then?'

'It's this play. *Romeo and Juliet*?'

Harriet was puzzled. 'But that's not on your reading list, is it?'

There was a definite smirk on Abby's face.

Harriet went pink as she cottoned on. She picked up the textbook and pretended to be engrossed. 'So, where were we?'

*   *   *

Study club went on for ever that night. Harriet found herself sneaking little glances at Zack's door, but he didn't come out until the end. When he did appear, she noticed he looked a bit tense.

'Are you all right?' she asked, as they walked through the estate afterwards. Zack took her hand in his, sending hot little flushes through her body.

'I think I'm going to have to cancel the Thorpe Park trip for the oldies.'

'Oh no, really?' She knew Alf was really looking forward to riding the Nemesis Inferno, declaring he'd love it even if it gave him a heart attack.

'We just can't afford it.' Zack sighed. 'Anyway.' He pulled her closer. 'How was your night?'

Harriet was finding it hard to walk and talk at the same time. Just the feel of Zack was doing funny things to her. 'Good,' she managed. 'You know, I think Pete could seriously get an A in all his exams. He's super-bright.'

'And did Aunty Win try and interrogate you again?' he asked.

Harriet smiled. 'No, but I did get quite a few meaningful looks.'

'That woman has all the subtlety of a bull in a china shop.'

'I think Abby has guessed something, too.'

Zack laughed. 'Of course she has. She's already told me I'd better treat you right.'

Harriet was taken aback, but in a nice way. 'Abby

212

said that?'

'Yeah, you've made quite an impression.' He squeezed her hand. 'Abby's not the only one.'

'Zack, can I ask you something?' It had been bugging her all night.

'Shoot.'

'What made you change your mind?' She blushed. 'I mean, I had no idea . . .'

'How I felt?' He looked at the road ahead. 'I guess I'm just rubbish at things like this, Harriet. I find it hard to let anyone close to me. I wasn't sure how you felt, either, but when we danced at the salsa together you just looked so sweet and flustered . . .' His eyes were intense again. 'I knew I had to say something. Even if it did make it awkward if you weren't interested. Besides,' he added dryly, 'I think Win was about to out me.'

'She knew all along?'

'She knew something, Win doesn't miss a trick.' Zack stopped. 'I meant to say, you look really pretty tonight . . .'

As he turned to her, Harriet's phone suddenly started ringing in her bag. *Bugger!* She didn't want to answer it and spoil the moment, but it might be her mother ringing from some remote landline in Africa.

'Excuse me . . .' Reluctantly she opened her bag and started digging around for her phone. She pulled it out and looked at the screen. It wasn't her mother, it was her father. Harriet was about to press the 'silence' button when she felt guilty. She looked at Zack. 'Do you mind if I take this call quickly? It's my father.'

He shook his head. 'Course not.'

Self-conscious, Harriet answered it. 'Hello,

213

Daddy.'

'What's that?' Ambrose's voice boomed out of the other end. 'How did you know it was me?'

'I've told you, your number flashes up.' She smiled at Zack and gestured for them to keep walking. 'How are you, anyway?' she asked her father.

'Oh, keeping myself occupied,' he said.

'Daddy, what's this I hear about a go-karting track? You haven't really, have you?'

Ambrose chuckled. 'Great, isn't it? Your friend Saffron was quite impressed when she came round. I've challenged her to a bit of a derby.'

Harriet couldn't believe it. 'What will Mummy say?'

'She won't say anything, she's in bloody Africa! Anyway, it's only gone through a few of her flowerbeds.'

Harriet thought of the almighty row there'd be when her mother returned to find the historic gardens ruined. They'd reached the entrance of the estate now, and a police car went wailing by on the road in front of them.

'What's that dreadful racket?' Ambrose asked.

'Just background noise. I'm in Camden.'

'Why are you in Camden?'

'I'm just going to the pub with someone.'

'Is this *someone* a chap?'

'Hmm,' Harriet said neutrally. 'Anyway, I'd better be going.'

Her father hadn't finished yet, however. 'What does he do, then? Banker, hmm? Lawyer?'

'I'll call you tomorrow.'

'Am I going to meet him or what?'

Harriet was sure Zack must be able to hear the

booming voice. 'Bye, Daddy!'

Ambrose grunted. 'I can tell when I'm being got rid of. All I can say is keep your hand on your ha'penny.'

Harriet hastily ended the call and stuffed her phone back in her bag. Zack looked at her curiously. 'What was that about a ha'penny?'

*   *   *

The open mic night was in a basement club, off the back of a fairly rough-looking pub. There were two intimidating men on the door, but they smiled and nodded at Zack as he led Harriet down the stairs. Loud music was blasting out, making the walls reverberate. Harriet clutched her handbag tightly. 'Are you OK?' Zack asked.

She nodded. 'Yup!'

He smiled. 'Come on, then.' Opening the swing doors at the bottom of the stairs, he steered her in.

It was like walking into one giant, crowded speaker. The music was so loud she could barely think, and the sea of bodies pushing and jostling made her lose her footing. But Zack was there at her elbow, keeping a firm grip on her. At the front of the room was a stage, on which young people were taking it in turns to rap into a microphone. From what she could make out, a person rapped until he or she stumbled over their lyrics, or the crowd booed them. As she watched, Harriet became transfixed. The whole place had such power and energy. Beside her Zack was casually moving to the beat, blending in.

'What do you think?' he shouted above the music.

'It's actually really good! Ooh, look, there's Danny.' The teenager bounded on to the stage and started rapping furiously, working the crowd. Looking at him up there, Harriet could hardly connect him with the bright young man who was predicted to go to Cambridge. Those stuffy old dons were going to have the shock of their life when Danny turned up. Harriet shook her fist in the air. 'Go, Danny!'

It was so loud that it was hard to make conversation, they could only smile and nod at each other. Half an hour later, just as Harriet thought she was about to go deaf, Zack turned to her. 'Shall we make a move?' She nodded, suddenly wanting to get out of that packed sweaty space. Her new shoes, two inches higher than she'd normally wear, were killing her.

By the time they were back on Camden High Street, she could just about hear normally again. Harriet noticed the pub across the road. 'Do you fancy a drink?'

'Actually, it's getting on a bit. Do you mind if we take a rain check?'

'Oh, OK.' She felt rather flat that the evening was ending so abruptly. She just wanted to stay with Zack, talk to him, look at him, *kiss* him.

He took her hand again. 'I'll walk you to the tube.'

Suddenly Harriet was overcome by a wild recklessness. She didn't want Zack to walk her to the station, she wanted him to take her home and make wild, passionate love to her. As their bodies brushed together she imagined Zack's naked flesh, pressed down on top of her . . .

All too soon they reached the station. 'You got

your Oyster card?' he asked.

She nodded. 'I've had a really nice time tonight, Zack.'

'Me, too.' He kissed her again, and Harriet could feel a surge of white heat between her legs.

'You're a real lady, Harriet,' he murmured. 'I like that.'

But I don't want to be a lady, she thought. *I want you to ravish me!*

Zack squeezed her tightly, and let her go. 'Text me when you're home, OK?'

Normally she would have loved the way he was being so gentlemanly, but her requirements had been sharply revised. She didn't care if she was being a floozy . . . Harriet Fraser was a woman in need of sex!

Chapter 28

Churchminster

Meanwhile at Fairoaks, Clementine was getting distinctly twitchy. She'd known about Fashion Cares for some time now, and neither Saffron nor Rex had been round to see her. It was especially grating, since Brenda had told her they'd enlisted the services of Sylvester Events in Bedlington. Clementine was rather old school when it came to things like this, and she didn't believe in hiring someone to do your dirty work for you. Or maybe it was that, as various members of her family had teased her, she was a complete control freak.

She hadn't even met Churchminster's temporary

resident yet, aside from a few glimpses of his sleek black car flashing up and down the drive to Byron Heights. It was most perturbing, and if she were frank, rude. By the next afternoon she could stand it no longer, and marched straight over there.

Rex answered the door, looking very suave in a fitted dark-blue suit. Not that Clementine noticed. She had far more pressing things on her mind.

'I'm Clementine Standington-Fulthrope, I live at Fairoaks,' she announced briskly. 'May I come in?'

Rex blinked, then his face spread into a polite smile. 'Oh, course. Sorry, you've caught me on the hop a bit. I've just got back from London.'

He stepped aside and she swept in. Clementine had been to Byron Heights a number of times over the years and knew it quite well. 'Shall we go through to the drawing room?'

Rex blinked again. 'Er, yeah. It's just through there on the left . . .' She was already off, leaving him standing in her wake.

The drawing room was a rather gloomy black and red creation dominated by a new painting of Ozzy Osbourne as Jesus. Clementine's lips pursed. She certainly didn't approve of *that*. Since she made no attempt to sit down, Rex remained standing.

'Uh, can I get you anything?'

'No, thank you.' Clementine looked over her spectacles at him. 'I gather you are putting on a fashion show.'

Rex relaxed slightly. 'Yeah, that's right. It's a charity catwalk show called Fashion Cares. To raise money for street kids in Brazil.'

'Very admirable,' she said in a crisp tone.

Rex smiled winningly. 'There will be plenty of

218

tickets to go around. I'll make sure I personally reserve . . .'

'I assume you've got your licence?'

Rex's eyebrows shot up. 'We need a licence?'

'Of course you do. One can't have a gin and tonic in one's own garden these days without the pen-pushers at the council sticking their nose in.'

'Oh, shoot,' Rex said.

'Shoot, indeed,' Clementine said wryly. 'I have a rather high-up friend at the council, do you want me to talk to him? I am sure we can get something organized.'

Rex looked relieved. 'That would be great!'

'You'll also need to do something about traffic. I suggest getting some of the villagers on board to direct people through so they don't get lost, or even worse, *churn up the verges.*' At this, her eyes glinted dangerously. 'And what about the car park?'

'Car park?'

Clementine was getting rather tired of his goggle-eyed expression. 'Where is everyone going to *park*? You'll need attendants, cordons, designated parking areas. Wootton-under-Barley's summer fête was dreadfully disorganized last year. Some people didn't get out until 11 p.m!'

Rex ran a hand through his hair. 'I hadn't even thought about car parking.'

'Of course you hadn't, young man. No one does think of these things at events like this. It's easy to get carried away with the fun, glamorous side, all the who's sitting next to who and wearing what, but one needs to think about *practicalities.*'

She'd given him quite a wake-up call. From the sound of things he and Saffron were out of their depth. They needed someone to oversee them, someone who *knew how these things worked*. Rex cleared his throat. 'Would you be able to help, Clementine? I'd be really grateful.'

She smiled pleasantly. 'Of course, my dear! You only had to ask.'

*   *   *

As she walked home Clementine felt more invigorated than she had in a long time. Her approach might have been forceful, but it had worked. At least she now had some control again over what was happening in her beloved village.

She walked round to the kitchen and let herself in. Clementine never locked her back door, even though there had been a spate of burglaries in Bedlington recently. Errol Flynn had always been a most reliable guard dog, and even though he wasn't around any more, old habits died hard. To change the way she lived would be an admission that the halcyon days of country life were finally over. Clementine had too much faith in dear old Churchminster to accept that.

The flashing red light on the answering machine indicated a message. She played it back. It was Caro, checking in and seeing how she was. Milo had had his school play that day. Clementine smiled, thinking of her great-grandson. She did miss them all. They still had a house in Churchminster, a converted watermill on the other side of the green, but it was a huge undertaking getting the family back just for a weekend, so they spent most of their time in London these days. Clementine understood; she knew Benedict's job was important, and that the children had things on at weekends. But she still lived in hope that they would come back one day soon. Before she got too old to enjoy them all.

She moved busily round the kitchen, humming along to Classic FM as she prepared a light supper. Suddenly there was a loud knock on the back door, making her jump. In the darkening gloom, Ambrose Fraser loomed, in his green checked jacket and plus fours.

She went to let him in. 'Ambrose, you startled me.'

He looked over her shoulder into the cosy, warm kitchen. 'Not interrupting anything, am I?'

'Not at all.' To be honest, Clementine was surprised to see him. Ambrose never came down to the village.

He seemed to read her thoughts. 'I was a bit bored up at the Hall, thought I'd come down and see young Jed. He seems to be out, though.'

'Oh, I see.' She was rather at a loss, as Ambrose didn't appear to be in a hurry to go anywhere. 'Well, would you like to stay for supper? I'm afraid it's not much, just homemade soup, and salad from the garden.'

Ambrose's face lit up. 'That would be splendid! It's Cook's night off, and, besides, the dining hall at Clanfield does feel like a bit of a waste for one at the moment.'

'I can only offer you my kitchen table.' She smiled apologetically, but Ambrose looked delighted.

'Two old friends having supper together! That's what it's all about, isn't it?'

Since Ambrose had shunned the company of

anyone apart from Frances and his dogs for years, Clementine suspected she wasn't the only lonely person in Churchminster.

Chapter 29

Being engaged had taken Saffron and Tom's relationship to a whole new level. Saffron had never thought of herself as the marrying type (not with her parents' track record) but it was such a lovely, comforting feeling that they were building a future together. She'd started imagining things like their kids running round the forty-foot garden of her dream house in Notting Hill. Their daughter would have eyes just like hers, and their son would be tall and dark, just like Tom. She'd taken to twisting her ring round her engagement finger, a new, comforting habit. Just looking at it made her feel closer to Tom.

Today, her brain was all worded-out. A quick look on Facebook wouldn't do any harm. At the moment, it was virtually her only contact with the outside world. She logged on to see what people were up to.

Jasmine, her maneating friend, was clearly still living it up. *'Jasmine is hungover, but having breakfast with someone very sexy . . . :)'* informed her status update. Jasmine had only just stopped teasing Saffron about getting engaged at the grand old age of twenty-six. *'What next, baby girl: tomato-growing competitions in the country?'* Jas had written when she'd heard the news. *'Swear you won't get up the duff yet and abandon me completely.'*

Saffron shook her head, smiling. Jas was such a minx. She read through her messages and wall posts, and was about to log off when she thought she'd have a quick look on Tom's page, see if anyone had said anything nice about their engagement.

The profile pic was still the same as last time: him wearing a funny hat at Christmas two years ago. She didn't know why Tom was even signed up to Facebook, he never went on it. Sure enough, there was virtually no activity, apart from some arty-farty design group he'd joined. Saffron was about to click off when she saw a new post from someone called 'Bondy' on his wall.

'Tommo, heard about the engagement. Better luck second time around mate!'

She went numb. *Second* time? Who the hell was this Bondy? She clicked on his profile and saw he'd gone to Warwick University, same time as Tom. WTF?

Her mind was spinning, throwing out questions. Tom had been engaged before? To who? This had to be some kind of wind-up. It wasn't bloody funny.

Snatching up her mobile, Saffron went out to the reception spot on the landing. Tom answered after three rings. 'I'm in a meeting,' he said in a low voice. 'Can I call you back?'

'What the hell is this about you being engaged before?' she demanded. 'Some mate called Bondy just posted something on your wall!' She really expected him to laugh and tell her it was some kind of infantile wind-up.

Tom hesitated. 'I'll call you back in a moment.'

Five minutes passed, and Saffron was getting more wound up by the second. Tom had been engaged before? Why the hell hadn't he told her? A minute later her phone went. She let it ring four times before picking up. 'I think you've got some explaining to do,' she said coldly.

'Look, I didn't know Bondy had written anything. I would have taken it down if I'd known.'

'Why, have you got something to hide?'

Tom sighed. 'Of course not!'

'So who's fiancée number one then?'

'Oh, God.' He stopped. 'Look, I can explain.'

So now he was giving her the clichés. 'Well?'

'Her name was Cassie.'

Saffron felt physically sick. She'd honestly thought it was some kind of sick joke. 'So you *were* engaged then?'

'Yes. No. I mean, it wasn't meant to be like that.'

'Either you were or you weren't, Tom,' she said acidly.

He was quiet, too quiet. 'Cassie was someone I met at university. We went out for two years.'

Her throat closed over. 'Why haven't you mentioned her before?'

'Because she's my ex, Saff. To be honest, the whole thing didn't end that well and I haven't thought about her for years, and that's the God's honest truth.'

'You were *engaged*, Tom!'

'It wasn't like that!' He sounded frustrated.

'Oh, so you go around getting engaged to people for fun?'

'Of course I bloody don't!' He lowered his voice. 'The whole thing was blown out of proportion. Cassie was kind of . . . intense. We'd been going

224

out for a while when she got really drunk in this bar and proposed to me in front of a whole load of people.' He sighed. 'Bondy being one of them. When he found out about you and I, he obviously thought he was being funny posting something on my wall.'

Very funny. Like, hysterical!

'Saff, are you still there?'

'Yes,' she said quietly.

'Look, I can imagine this is a bit of a shock for you . . .'

'A bit of a *shock*, Tom? Fucking hell!'

'Please. Hear me out. I didn't want to embarrass her, but there was no way I wanted to get *married*. Then everyone started cheering and congratulating us and I just stood there . . .'

'So technically you *were* engaged?'

'For three days,' he said reluctantly. 'I knew I couldn't go along with it so I called it off.'

'Did you love her?' Might as well hear it all, add another kick to the stomach.

'Yes, at the time,' he said simply. 'Or at least I thought I knew what love was, until I met you.'

'Oh please!' she spat bitterly.

'I mean it.' For the first time his voice broke. 'I should have told you, but I didn't because it didn't matter. You matter to me, Saff, that's all.'

'Then I shouldn't have found out from Facebook.'

'It was a bad call. I'm sorry.'

She heard another voice in the background. Tom gave a muffled reply; 'Yeah, I'll be there.' He came back to her. 'I've got to go into a meeting. I'll call you later, OK? Please, babe, don't be cross with me.'

Cross was exactly what she was. After they'd said a stilted goodbye, Saffron started pacing up and down the landing. Why the hell hadn't he told her? He'd given her an explanation, but even so, the thought of this girl proposing to him made her feel sick. Still fuming, she rang Harriet.

'I don't believe this! Tom's been engaged before! I just found out from some twat friend of his on Facebook!'

'Tom?' Harriet sounded shocked. 'Are you sure?'

'OK, so he reckons it was all a big mistake. This girl Cassie proposed to him in front of like, loads of people, and he didn't have the heart to turn her down. Apparently he ended it a few days later, but how do I know if that's true? I don't know what the fuck to believe.'

Harriet tried to calm Saffron down. 'Hon, I'm sure that's what happened. You know what a nice chap Tom is, he probably didn't want to upset this girl.'

'What, so he let her walk around thinking she was engaged? Don't you think it's weird he didn't mention it? I didn't even know he'd had a long-term relationship before me!'

'Tom loves you. I'm sure he had his reasons.'

Saffron kicked the skirting board unhappily. 'He should at least have *told* me.' If Tom hadn't said something about this, what else wasn't he telling her?

Chapter 30

By 8 p.m. Saffron had managed to calm down. Maybe she was overreacting a tiny bit; after all, Tom couldn't stop his dick mates putting messages on his wall. But as the minutes ticked by and he still hadn't called, her good intentions started to dissolve. It was so unlike him, especially as their last phone call had ended on such a bad note. Left alone with her own thoughts, Saffron started to wind herself up again. *She* wasn't going to call. Sod him. Sod it all! She wasn't going to sit here and be made to feel like this.

Her mother had taken over the kitchen with a new art 'installation', and the whole house reeked of paint. Saffron needed fresh air before her head exploded, both metaphorically and physically. She grabbed the car keys and yelled to her mum.

'Going out, see you later!'

She got in the MG and started for Rex's.

*　　　*　　　*

She found him in the hot tub at the back of the house. It looked like a scene out of *Miami Vice*. He had a glass of champagne on the go, sunglasses pushed up on his head, his BlackBerry lying by his side. All that was missing was a big cigar hanging out of his mouth.

'Hey, Saff! How's it going?'

'Fine.' She dumped her bag and went over. Rex had obviously been out sunbathing, his face and chest were more tanned than ever. He nodded

227

towards his BlackBerry. 'I've had a great call from Handbag Haven today. They love the logo. And Super Sue is going great guns. We've got our champagne sponsorship.'

'Great.'

He studied her. 'You don't seem very happy.'

'Did you know about Tom and this Cassie?'

Rex paused for a fraction of a second. 'You know about Cassie?'

'Sure. How Tom was with her for two whole years and she proposed to him, and he didn't bother bloody telling me!'

'Saff, don't sweat it. All that stuff was so long ago.'

'I *am* sweating it. Why didn't he tell me, Rex?'

'Why would he? It was dead in the water, done. From what I can tell she proposed, then he had a hell of a time trying to let her down gently.'

'Bully for him,' she said grudgingly. 'What a great guy.'

'Come on, Saff, Tom adores you,' Rex said. 'You must know that.'

She sighed heavily. 'I know, I know, I just wish he'd said something earlier.'

'He didn't, because it doesn't mean anything,' Rex said. 'You're his life now.'

That's what Tom had told her. 'Looking out for your brother, eh?' she said, feeling marginally better.

'Looking out for *both* of you,' he corrected. 'After all, I am giving advice to my future sister-in-law.'

Saffron gave a small smile. 'Thank you, Rex.'

'Don't mention it. Hey, I'm gonna get another bottle. Fancy a glass of the fizzy?'

Christ, she needed something after the last few

hours. 'Go on, then.' He pulled himself up, bronzed body covered in bubbles. Saffron caught a glimpse of a large packet in his Daniel-Craig-style swimming trunks. Maybe she was right, after all . . . The thought made her unexpectedly smile, and she quickly looked out over the garden, taking in the view. Even her gloomy mood couldn't take away the glory of a perfect April evening. She kicked off her pumps and sat on the edge of the hot tub, feet dangling in the water.

Rex came back with a bottle of Cristal and a glass and sat beside her. 'I found a whole load in the wine cellar, I'm sure no one will mind.' Saffron indicated the tub. 'Not pouring it in there, then?'

He looked confused. 'Eh?'

'Hotel room. Bath tub?' she said, trying to lighten up.

He caught on and groaned. 'Don't, the bad old days.' He filled the glass. 'This stuff is strictly for drinking now.'

She emptied a huge mouthful down her throat. 'That's better.'

'You know, has anyone ever told you you look a bit like Agyness Deyn?' Rex was looking over her with a practised eye. 'You could be a model, you know, you've definitely got the figure.'

'Is that what you say to all the girls?' She needed to move, the sun was in her eyes. Saffron got up to walk over to the other side of the hot tub, but as she took a step she felt her foot slide from under her. 'Ah, shit!' she shrieked, toppling sideways.

'Whoa!' Rex tried to catch her but she was out of his reach. Crashing into the water, she went in right up to her neck. Somehow, she managed to keep her champagne glass out, holding it aloft like a prize trophy.

Rex clapped his hand over his mouth. 'You OK?'

'Oh my God! I'm *soaked.*' She started to struggle up, her Kate Moss tea dress clinging to her like a second skin. Rex stood up, holding a strong arm out to help her. Saffron could see he was struggling to keep a straight face. 'It's all right, you're allowed to laugh,' she said.

His mouth twitched. 'I'm sorry, that was seriously funny.'

'At least I managed to keep the champagne dry,' she dead-panned.

'Dry! That's really funny...' Rex started laughing, his whole body shaking. 'Keep the champagne dry...'

He started Saffron off, and they held on to each other, giggling. 'I've got to drive home soaking wet!' she said.

'I'll give you some dry clothes.' Rex put on a falsetto voice. 'Ooh, whatever will the neighbours say!'

Saffron started laughing wildly, all the pent-up emotion of the last few hours coming out. 'Stop, I'm seriously going to wet myself...'

'Yes, what will the neighbours say?' They both spun round. Tom was standing there, an overnight bag in his hand. He didn't look happy.

Chapter 31

'I just didn't expect to see you there looking as happy as Larry,' Tom said. They were back in Saffron's bedroom, sitting cross-legged opposite each other on the bed.

'It wasn't how it looked,' she said, uncomfortably aware Tom had said the same thing about Cassie hours earlier. 'I slipped and Rex was helping me.'

He looked at her reproachfully. 'Why didn't you answer your phone?'

'I didn't realize my battery had died!' she flared back, guilt making her even angrier.

'Don't shout.'

'I'm not shouting.' She took a deep breath. 'Is that why you came all the way out here?'

'Yeah. I got worried, so I got the train straight from Paddington.'

'I'm sorry.' She bit her lip. She *was* sorry, but Tom was the one who'd bloody lied about Cassie! OK, not exactly lied, but whatever.

'I thought you were upset,' he said.

She looked at him disbelievingly. 'I am upset! That's why I went round to Rex's. I needed to talk. He stuck up for you actually,' she added. 'Although I guess I should have known blood is thicker than water.'

Tom gave her a weird look. 'You should have talked to me, not him.'

'I didn't know you were trying to call!' She rubbed her eyes. 'We're going round in circles here.' There was another pause. 'I'm sorry for dragging you out here,' she said, unable to resist the slight. 'I know you're very busy.'

'You didn't *drag* me out here.' Tom rubbed the bridge of his nose, something he always did when he was tired. 'Can we start again, please?' He put his hands on her shoulders and the familiar warmth made her feel like weeping.

'I'm sorry I didn't tell you about Cassie,' he repeated. 'Just because it doesn't matter to me doesn't mean the same for you. I get that now.'

Her bottom lip wobbled. 'I just feel like this, *us*,' she looked down at her engagement ring, 'it all feels tainted.'

'Don't say that!' She was taken aback by the force of his words. His hands gripped her. 'What happened with me and Cassie, it was a stupid, drunken thing that got out of hand. Can't you see that?' He stroked her face. 'From the moment I set eyes on you, Saff, I knew I wanted to marry you.'

Her eyes filled up. 'Don't . . .'

'What we've got is so special.' He stared into her eyes, trying to see every inch of her soul. 'Why would I want to bring up something that happened so long ago? Something that has nothing to do with us now?' He looked genuinely upset. 'Saff, if I could go back and change it, I would.'

She just had to know one thing. 'What was her surname?'

'Saff, don't do this.'

'I want to know.'

'Williams. Cassie Williams.' He gave a great shuddering breath. 'I don't know how this has happened, I just want things to get back to how they were.'

He looked so crestfallen. Despite the exhausting range of emotions she'd been through, Saffron was

232

starting to weaken. She did believe him, and she hated arguing with him. When he put his arms out, she didn't resist. They stayed there for a moment, reconnecting with each other.

'There aren't any more ex-fiancées I should know about?' she asked. It was a crap attempt at humour, but she needed some relief from this situation right now.

He didn't need to even answer. 'Can we just move on? Babe, we've got so much to look forward to.'

She managed a small smile. 'No more secrets?'

'No more secrets.' His arms enclosed her tightly again, making her breathless with his love.

London

It was Friday night, and Harriet was out with Alexander and some of the girls from work. They were in a little wine bar just off Oxford Street, and she and the fashion director were sat together, discussing Saffron's wedding.

'I'd better get an invite, or I'm never speaking to her again!' he said.

'Of course you will, Al. Saffron loves you.'

Alexander adjusted his bow tie. 'She'll love me even more when she finds out I've just got Lee Greene to do the hair at that show of hers!'

Lee Greene was an in-demand hairdresser, favoured by the celeb set. He tended to only the coolest famous tresses.

'That's fab! She'll be so chuffed.'

Alexander winked. 'Lee and I have a bit of history, naughty boy.' He took a sip of his Campari and soda. 'Talking of naughty boys, what is Rex Sullivan doing living out in the sticks? I thought he'd die away from the liquor fumes of NYC.'

Harriet smiled. 'Have you ever worked with him?'

'Once, years ago. Before he went to the States. He turned up late, with a hangover, bad Rex, but he still looked *annoyingly* gorgeous.' He raised a questioning eyebrow. 'Talking of men, how is your Mr Wonderful? Moved things up a level yet?'

Harriet blushed. 'No, we haven't. It's only been a few weeks . . .'

The eyebrow arched even higher. 'Harriet, you need to start thinking like a sexy, empowered modern woman, and close this deal. After all, what if he's rubbish in bed, or got a small knob? You'd've been wasting all this time when you could have been out getting it from someone else.'

'It's just a bit difficult. Zack works such long hours, you see, that we only really end up going for drinks locally.' As she said it, she did wonder why she'd never been back to Zack's flat. Maybe it was really messy . . .

The fashion director was looking distinctly unimpressed. 'Do you want sex or not?'

'I suppose it would be nice,' she admitted, face crimson. Why did Alexander always make her have these conversations?

He nodded, satisfied, and held out his hand. 'Give me your phone.'

'What? Why?'

'I'm going to call him.'

Harriet shook her head violently. 'No, you are not.'

'One of you kids needs to make the move! You

234

call him, then. Ask him over for dinner tomorrow.'

'I don't think we're really at that stage yet.'

'Well, you *need* to get to that stage.' He nudged her leg gently with his lemon-yellow boat shoe. 'Go on. Ring him now. I'm not saying another word until you do.'

Buoyed up by a large glass of white wine, Harriet stood up. 'I'm doing it. I'm going to ask him over tomorrow.'

Alexander nodded. 'That's my girl.'

She stood outside the bar, and was just about to type in Zack's number when her phone started ringing. *Zack mobile.* She answered. 'You must be psychic, I was just about to ring you.'

He laughed. 'Maybe I am. How are you doing?'

'Good. I'm in a bar with some friends from work.'

'Sounds fun. I should be doing something like that.'

'Why don't you come and join us?' she asked spontaneously.

'Can't really. I'm tied up here.'

Harriet took a deep breath. 'How about tomorrow? I was wondering if you'd like to come to mine for dinner?'

'Actually, I was going to ask you over to mine.'

'Really?' Harriet could hardly believe it.

'Yeah. What do you reckon?'

'I'd love to. What time do you want me?'

There was a loaded pause. 'I mean . . .' she said, getting flustered.

'Say seven thirty? I'll text you my address.'

'Great. Do you want me to bring anything?'

'Just yourself.'

'See you, then.' His tone was distinctly flirty.

With a sudden feel of sick excitement, Harriet went back in to report mission accomplished.

Chapter 32

Zack lived down a quiet cul-de-sac a few minutes' walk from the community centre. As the cab pulled up outside the three-storey block of flats Harriet tried to get out without flashing too much leg. She was wearing this dress, a short flowery number she'd bought in Top Shop with Saffron. Saffron had talked her into buying it, but Harriet had just spent the whole journey pulling the skirt anxiously down over her knees. Still, it was too late to do anything now.

Giving the dress one final tug, she crossed the road. No. 11, he'd told her. She pressed the buzzer.

A few minutes later Zack's voice crackled out. 'Door's open, I'm on the first floor.'

She stepped into a municipal-looking hallway and started to climb the stairs. He was there already, leaning against the door frame. Harriet thought he'd never looked so gorgeous. His outfit was nothing extraordinary—just dark blue jeans and a black shirt—but they both fitted him perfectly, hinting at what lay underneath.

'Come in.' His gaze lingered on her legs appreciatively. As she walked in, he leant over and kissed her.

He tasted of toothpaste and freshly applied Issey Miyake. The mix made her heady. She got a bottle of wine and a four-pack of lager out of her bag.

'For you.'

'You know me too well.' He gestured through a doorway. 'Go on through.'

It wasn't messy at all. It was small but tidy, with an open-plan kitchen and living room, and what looked like doors to the bedroom and bathroom off to the right. The light-wood floors and fresh white walls made it feel light and airy. A large, vintage-looking leather sofa stood in the living room, several shelves of books above it. On one wall was a massive framed poster of Jimi Hendrix.

'You've got a good eye, Zack. This place is really nice.'

'Thanks.' He walked through into the kitchen. 'Make yourself at home, I'll get us drinks.'

He started moving round the kitchen. In contrast to Win's, Harriet noticed there were no photographs, save one on top of the television, of a young woman with a little boy in her arms. She walked over to get a better look. The woman was wearing what looked like eighties-style clothes, and both she and the child were laughing into the camera.

Zack came over and handed her a large glass of wine. 'My mum, Suzanne.'

'You can tell.' Harriet smiled. 'You've got the same blue eyes.' She hesitated. 'You can tell me if it's none of my business, but I just wondered how she died.'

'Hit and run in Camden High Street. They never caught the person who did it.'

Harriet was shocked. 'Zack, how terrible.'

He stroked the picture, tracing over his mum's face with his finger. 'It was years ago, now. Sometimes feels like it happened to a different

237

person.'

'Is that why you ended up in care?'

'Yep. No one left to look after me.'

It was said very matter-of-factly. Once again Harriet thought what an admirable person he was. He'd had so much bad luck in his life, but he'd still made something of himself.

Zack checked his watch. 'I don't know about you, Harriet, but I'm starving. Shall we begin?'

Harriet hadn't known what food to expect, but Zack turned out to be a pretty good cook. For starters they had a selection of antipasti, followed by a delicious carbonara, and a homemade tiramisu for pudding. Despite her intention to eat bird-like portions Harriet attacked everything with gusto. Zack was the perfect host throughout, repeatedly filling up her glass. Aside from the kiss at the door, he also hadn't laid a finger on her. Harriet was starting to wonder if anything was ever going to happen. Maybe Zack just wasn't *like that*.

She looked down at her empty pudding plate. 'That was delicious,' she said regretfully. Her stomach was already sticking out through her dress.

'Good. I like a girl who can eat.' Zack added another splash of wine to her glass. 'You can tell I spend too much time at Win's house. She sends her love, by the way. It was all I could do to stop her coming in here to cook.'

Harriet laughed. 'Did you always live on the estate?'

'On and off.'

'Where else have you lived?'

'Around a bit. I was in Liverpool for a while.'

'I've never been to Liverpool, it sounds like a fun

place.'

'Hmm. It's a long way away.' He grinned, but it was slightly forced. 'I missed this place too much.'

Harriet wondered how he'd ended up there. 'Why Liverpool? Did you have a job there?'

Zack suddenly seemed to find his beer glass fascinating. 'I met this girl up there,' he said finally. He glanced up. 'We were together for a while.'

This must be the relationship Win had alluded to! Harriet wondered what Zack's ex had done to make him react like this.

'I know you said you find it hard to get close to people,' she said.

He was still staring at his beer. 'Yeah, well. That's all in the past now.'

'Do you still speak to your ex?' If there was a ghost of girlfriend past she had to try and be all right about it.

'No. Look, can we stop talking about this?'

She looked down at her plate. 'I'm sorry. I didn't mean to go on.'

'I can just think of better things to talk about.' At least he was smiling again.

They looked at each other across the table. The tension that had been building up all evening suddenly came to a head.

'Actually, screw that. I'm done with talking,' Zack said. Before she knew it, he had pulled her across the table and was kissing her. 'This is getting in the way,' he murmured, pulling her out of the seat. She melted into him, as he ran his hands over her breasts, her back, her bottom. Instinctively Harriet tightened her buttocks.

'You have such a lovely body,' he murmured. He

239

started to gently push her out towards the hallway. Zack was lean and muscled, his hardness pressing against her soft flesh. Harriet could most definitely feel something pushing into her groin area. *Oh God! This was really happening!*

As they reached the bedroom, Zack pulled back, his breathing heavy. 'Is this OK? Do you want this? Only I don't think I can keep my hands off you much longer.' She responded by kissing him even harder, her hands moving to squeeze his taut, strong bottom. It was a sexy, hard one, the kind grown women would commit murder just to touch, and Harriet just couldn't get enough of it.

They fumbled their way over to the bed, and Zack gently laid her down. He slipped her high heels off, carefully putting them on the floor by the bed. Then off came the dress, pulled roughly over her head. Down came the tights, peeled off in one. His hands moved down the groove of her cleavage, pulling her bra off to expose full rosy-nippled breasts.

It was still light outside, making Harriet feel rather exposed. Her hands moved over her tummy, but Zack pushed them away. 'Stop that, you're beautiful.'

'I want to see you,' she whispered, her hands fumbling at his shirt buttons. Her eyes widened. It wasn't just his body, which was like some beautiful anatomical drawing, with every muscle and sinew defined. On his left pectoral was a large tattoo of a grinning skull surrounded by a ring of barbed wire. It was crudely done, a blot on an otherwise perfect canvas, but as Zack's fingers found their way into her knickers Harriet's attention moved. Slowly and deftly he started to rub against her clitoris. The more he played, the wetter she got.

He pulled at his belt with his free hand and kicked away his jeans. His erection was large in his Calvin Klein underpants. 'If you don't mind, Harriet, I'd very much like to make love to you.'

Harriet had imagined this moment so many times in her head. In her fantasy she was sexy and come-hither, but here, now, all she could do was lie there as Zack reached to get a condom out of the bedside drawer. He peeled his pants off, and there his cock was, big and hard and perfect. As he rolled the condom on Harriet wriggled out of her knickers and lay back, feeling both excited and self-conscious.

Zack pushed her legs open wider and pulled her hips up toward him. As he positioned his cock their eyes met, ready for what was about to happen. Harriet felt a little stab of pain, then pure joy as Zack pushed himself into her. The light-blue eyes were even more intense in their passion. 'Harriet, you've no idea how many times I've thought about this.'

It soon became apparent he was a very good lover. Moving in and out of her, changing positions, asking if she liked it this way or that, kissing and caressing her body. For Harriet, who'd only really experienced missionary and the occasional ill-fated doggy, it was like being taken on a wonderfully erotic fairground ride. As he lay back on top of her, his pumping more intense now, Harriet started to feel something funny happening.

'Oh!'

Zack looked down, his face concerned. 'Are you all right?'

'More than,' she gasped, as delicious little thrills

241

started to dance through her body. Her fingers and toes seemed to have gone numb. 'Don't stop!'

'I'm not.' As he got faster and faster, Zack groaned. 'I think I'm going to come.'

'So am I!' she gasped. As a glorious spasm gripped her body, it felt like she'd entered heaven for the first time. Zack fell on top of her, his heart hammering against hers, and Harriet stared in wonderment at the ceiling. At the grand old age of thirty-five, she'd finally had her first orgasm.

'When did you get your tattoo?' she asked later, as they lay entwined in each other's arms.

'Call it a mistake from my youth. I was going through an Iron Maiden stage.'

She smiled, tracing it with her fingers. 'You're still gorgeous.'

'*You're* gorgeous.' Zack took her hand and held it in his. 'I knew as soon as I met you, Harriet, that you were something special.' He touched her nose with his finger. 'And here we are.'

She laid her head against his chest, searching out the sound of his heartbeat. 'I thought you were never going to seduce me,' she said, a cheeky smile on her face.

He chuckled softly and raised his head a fraction. 'Did you, now?' She felt his strong arms squeeze her. 'You were worth waiting for.'

They lay there entwined in each other, watching the night shadows fill the room. Just as her eyes were getting heavy, Zack spoke. 'I think I've fallen for you, Harriet.'

She grinned into the darkness, feeling as happy as she could ever remember.

Chapter 33

Churchminster

Clementine had been as good as her word. Not only had she organized the parking and strong-armed the village committee into stewarding, their application for an alcohol licence had been fast-tracked by the council, no questions asked.

Fashion Cares was coming along in leaps and bounds. As well as a confirmed piece in *Soirée*; *Marie Claire*, *Cosmopolitan* and *The Sunday Times Style* had all promised to try and do something. It was never a certainty as so much changed on a weekly basis in the magazine world, but at least word was getting out and people were talking about it.

Unfortunately, Saffron wasn't having quite the same response with the guest list. She'd had quite a few B-list confirmations from TV presenters, socialites and the like, but none of the A-listers they'd been hoping for. That was the problem with celebrities; no one would commit until they knew someone of worth was going and at the moment, they didn't have that person of worth. Saffron was holding out for one in particular; Savannah Sexton. The British actress had taken Hollywood by storm and Saffron had got on really well with her when she'd interviewed Savannah for *Soirée*. From experience, Saffron knew she had to be tenacious and keep plugging away. Savannah had just the type of glamour and talent they needed.

Rex was just as busy with the designers. They had

ten, some of the brightest up-and-coming talent in the country. Rex hadn't set a theme for the show as he wanted to give them creative free rein, but each designer had to do ten outfits for their three-minute slot on the runway. It was a big call and Rex seemed to be forever on the phone giving advice or calming someone down. He was thriving off it though, and according to him they were making good progress with Bibi Brown. It was just a matter of finding a window in her schedule. Saffron would have preferred a 'yes' at this stage—Bibi was a guaranteed crowd puller—but she trusted Rex. It was his area of expertise, after all.

Saffron was actually surprised how low-key Rex was still being about it all. She would have thought he'd have wanted to be involved in the VIP list, especially as there were a lot of ex-models on there, and people from his 'world', but he seemed happy to let her get on with it. It was a lot more work than she'd anticipated, but Rex had such an easy way about him that she couldn't say no. Plus it was a good cause, and she was used to juggling fifty million things at once from her days at *Soirée*.

It was good she was keeping busy. She and Tom hadn't spoken about Cassie again, but she hadn't been able to stop thinking about this ex-girlfriend/fiancée. As soon as Tom had left the next day she'd Googled *Cassie Williams*, but only come up with some tarty-looking blonde from Wisconsin on Facebook and a sixty-four-year-old gardener who lived in New Zealand. Saffron kept imagining what this Cassie might look like. Tom had said she was 'intense', and to Saffron's mind that meant a raven-haired intellectual, with legs up to her armpits.

She knew there was no point in obsessing about it, but she couldn't stop herself. She somehow felt more vulnerable out here, less confident, away from her busy life full of work and friends in London. She'd never been one to dwell on the past before—and this relationship had finished like, six years ago!—but it had shaken Saffron. She understood now why Tom hadn't told her but she still felt like a bit of a tit. How could she not have known he'd been engaged? She had been too embarrassed to mention it to anyone except Harriet and Rex, but Tom's uni mates must have had a right laugh about it. At least bloody Cassie hadn't posted something on his wall, now that *would* have sent her over the edge.

It didn't help that since Tom's mercy mission, she felt like they'd hardly spoken. He was working harder than ever, and had been in the office late virtually every night. Saffron knew all they really needed to get back on track was some proper time with each other, but by a cruel irony their weekend together had been cancelled, as Tom was being sent on a last-minute photo shoot to Berlin. Saffron understood—she worked in the magazine industry after all—but it was still a bummer. As far as Tom was concerned it was water under the bridge, but it didn't stop Saffron feeling a bit insecure. *She* just wanted to see him, feel his lovely warm body against hers, and know they were cool again.

On Friday lunchtime she was sitting in front of her computer, trying to write. Only, for some reason, the words weren't coming today. She stopped typing and sighed. The weekend stretched in front of her like a yawning chasm. Tom would

245

be off having fun—OK, working—while she was stuck here. Saffron was gloomily contemplating a night in front of the telly when the front doorbell rang.

'I'll get it!' she yelled, springing up. Answering the door to the postman had become the highlight of her day, along with her 4 p.m. trip to the shop to buy a packet of Minstrels and get the daily village gossip from Brenda.

But when she opened the door it wasn't Royal Mail, but a man from Interflora clutching a huge bouquet of flowers. 'Saffron Walden?'

'That's me,' she said in surprise. She signed for the flowers and shut the door. The note was short but sweet. *I'm really sorry about this weekend. Can't wait to make it up to you. I miss you, babe. All my love, Tom xxx'*

As she inhaled the scent, Saffron's heart softened. *Poor Tom. It wasn't his fault he had to work.* She ran into the kitchen to show her mum. 'Look what Tom sent me!'

Babs looked up from her easel. She had a smudge of something purple smeared across her right cheek. 'Darling! How romantic!'

'I'd still rather have him here for the weekend.' Saffron sighed.

Her mother looked sympathetic. 'I know. We can still have lots of girlie fun together, though!'

'Hmm,' Saffron said diplomatically, thinking her mother's idea of girlie fun was a whimsical discussion of the effects of astrology on avant-garde art, aided by several bottles of Pinot Grigio.

'I'm going to phone Tom, to say thank you.'

'Say hello from me!'

When Saffron went to her usual spot on the

landing to get reception, there was a voicemail from Rex. *'Hi Saff, it's me. Do you fancy coming over for dinner later? No shop talk, I promise.'*

She needed time with someone born in the same decade as her. Saffron typed out a quick reply. *'Love to,'* she texted back. *'CU about 7.30?'*

The answer came back almost immediately. *'Great. CU then.'*

She tried Tom. Voicemail. Saffron left a message and went to have some lunch instead.

*   *   *

Her mother was in the conservatory spray-painting a garden gnome when she went down later. The late-evening sunlight was flooding into the room.

'I'm going out.' God, how long was it since she'd last said those words?

Babs got up, her hands covered in silver paint. 'You look beautiful, darling!'

'I wouldn't go that far.' Saffron glanced down at her animal-print maxi-dress, accessorized with a long silver chain that fell down her cleavage. Probably OTT for Churchminster's social scene, but she didn't care. 'I'm off to Rex's for dinner.'

'Ooh! I wouldn't mind a one-on-one with him!'

'You're sick.' Saffron went over to get her bag from the table. 'Will you be OK here by yourself?'

'I'm going to make the most of this gorgeous light! I feel another painting coming on.'

Uh-oh. Saffron went over to the fridge to get the bottle of champagne she'd bought for her and Tom. No point letting it go to waste.

'See you later then, Mum, I might be late.'

'You kids have fun!'

Rex turned out to be a pretty good—if basic—cook. They had two delectable steaks, both medium rare, washed down with a nice bottle of red. After dinner he got the iPad out and showed her some photographs from the designers' collections. There were some incredible pieces so far; from metallic jumpsuits with huge shoulder pads to a stunning white evening dress with an oversized corsage.

'I love that,' Saffron said, spotting an asymmetric chiffon dress that cascaded down like silk.

'That's one of Julie Friend's. I told you she was incredible with draping.' Rex studied the picture. 'Look at it; innovative, but incredibly wearable. I can totally see this in the shops next year.'

'You're really into this, aren't you?' she smiled. She was standing over him at the breakfast bar, so close she could smell the wax he'd put in his hair.

'I love it. It's been so inspiring working with such new, fresh talent. Made me realize why I got into the industry in the first place.' He closed the last picture down and stood up. 'I promised I wouldn't talk shop. Come on, let's have a little nightcap on the terrace.'

It was still warm enough to sit outside, listening to the creaks and calls of the wildlife as the countryside settled down for the night.

'It is pretty here.' Rex was staring out over the dark outline of the fields.

'Not missing the bright lights of NYC, then, yet?'

He shrugged. 'Not really. You miss London?'

'Some days more than others.' They fell silent, listening to a fox barking. 'It's a bummer Tom can't come down this weekend,' Rex said.

'*Total* bummer.'

He glanced at her. 'You guys work things out?'

'Yeah, we're cool.'

'Good.'

She shot him a look. 'Did he talk to you about it?'

'Hell, no, Tom doesn't talk to me about stuff like that. He's his own man.' Rex ran a hand over his face, as if he were tired. The exuberance of only a few minutes earlier had drained away.

'You OK?'

'Me? Yeah. Why?'

'You seem a bit down.'

He stared out into the blackness. 'Guess I'm just tired. I drove up to see Dad last night.'

'Did you?' Saffron thought he would have mentioned it.

'Yeah. I took him out to dinner, we had our normal conversation. "Why can't you get a proper job, Rex? Do you really need that car? Why can't you be more like your brother?" '

'He didn't say that!' Saffron was shocked.

'Not exactly.' He shot her a wry look. 'Might as well have, though.' A slight smile entered his face. 'Makes a change from being told I'm the dog's bollocks all the time, I suppose. Dad's very good at keeping my feet on the ground.'

'What did he say about Fashion Cares? He must be pretty impressed.'

Rex shrugged. 'Dad doesn't really see much outside his lectures and books.'

He lifted his glass, emptying the remaining dregs into his mouth. 'What a week, eh? I'm knackered.'

'I did warn you!'

He picked up the bottle and refilled their drinks. Saffron waited until he'd finished. 'What really

249

happened between you and your ex?' she asked.

'Paulina?' He drank from his glass. 'We broke up.'

'Why, though? You can tell me to butt out if you want.'

He glanced at her. 'If you really want the truth, I fucked up.'

'Really? I thought you finished it, though?'

'Ah, that's what *I want* people to think,' he said, a wry note in his voice. 'Male pride, and all that. But no, I behaved like a selfish dickhead, always thinking about myself. She got fed up and kicked me out.'

Saffron studied his handsome profile. 'Why don't you talk to her, try and win her back?'

'Paulina might look like a gorgeous waif, but she is one strong woman. As far as she's concerned, we're history.' He nursed his drink. 'I don't know, maybe it's for the best.'

'Must make work tricky.'

'You could say that.'

She could tell it wasn't a prospect he relished.

Rex jumped up, making Saffron start. 'Come on, I want to show you something.'

'What?'

'You'll see.'

*   *   *

Forget big, the wine cellar was massive. From where they stood, Saffron could see rooms leading off rooms, into an underground labyrinth. Bottles glinted out of the darkness like jewels studded into the walls. 'Oh my God, we could have some lock-in down here!'

'Pretty cool, huh? I found it when I was having an explore of the house earlier.' Rex pulled a dusty bottle of red out of the nearest rack, and looked at the label. 'There's some serious wine here.'

Saffron walked over to another rack and pulled out a 1959 Dom Perignon. This was vintage stuff all right. 'This whole collection must be worth thousands. Hundreds of thousands.'

Rex had a wicked glint in his eye. 'Fancy a little tasting session?'

*   *   *

By midnight Saffron was so drunk she'd already fallen over twice—and spilt a very expensive merlot down the front of her dress. They were now dancing barefoot in the garden, Chesney Hawkes's 'I Am The One And Only' blasting into the night air. Rex had even more random cheesy pop tunes on his iPod than she did.

Saffron threw out her arms and twirled around, feeling free and loose. 'Woo!' She stood on the hem of her maxi-dress and stumbled on to her knees. 'I'm all right, don't panic!'

Up the garden Rex was calling something.

'What?' she yelled back.

'Your phone's going.' He walked down towards her with it in his hand. 'Here, it's Tom.'

She pressed the phone right into her ear. 'Tom? Is that you?'

'Yeah, we've just finished dinner.' His voice sounded far away. 'How are you, babe?'

'I'm drunk!' she said happily. 'Me and Rex are dancing round the garden to cheesy pop music. All the stuff you hate!'

'Riiiight.'

'How's Brighton?'

'Berlin.'

'That's the one!' She knew she had something to tell him. 'I'm really drunk.'

'You sound it.'

'So how's Brighton?'

'Berlin,' he repeated patiently. 'Look, Saff, shall I call back . . .'

'Oh my God, Rex is doing the running man. It's hilarious! Rex. REX, do that again. Babe, you have to see this, I'll video it,' she said into the phone. Tom didn't answer. 'Babe?' She looked down at the screen. It had cut out again. 'Ah, bollocks!' As she stood there swaying slightly, it suddenly came to her. She'd meant to thank him for the flowers.

Half an hour later, she was fading. As she felt her way up the steps to the terrace she stood on the hem of her dress again, and nearly went flying. This time Rex was there to catch her. 'I got you.' Saffron squinted up through one eye. His face was swimming in and out of focus, the features melting into each other.

'I'm really pished.' She swayed. 'I think I need my bed.'

She heard Rex chuckle. 'Come on, pish-head, let's get you home.'

*   *   *

Even with Rex's helping hand, the walk from Byron Heights to Hardwick House was taking twice as long as usual. Saffron was finding it hard to put one foot in front of the other. 'So what's this

252

Cassie like? Is she prettier than me?'

'What? Oh, Saff, you're not still hung up about that, are you?'

'I'm pished off!' she announced. 'I'm gonna call Tom and tell him . . .' She fished her phone out of her bag, but Rex took it off her.

'Not a good idea.'

Her mind was all over the place. 'Why's Tom not here?' she slurred.

'He had to work, didn't he?'

'Work schmurk! Boring.' As her ankle went over Rex tightened his grip.

'Not long now.'

By the time they'd reached Babs's front door, Saffron could hardly stand up. 'Can you find my key?' The thought of rifling around in her bag seemed like an insurmountable challenge. She held it out. 'Key, please.'

'Give it here.' She watched, swaying, as Rex located the key and unlocked the door. The house was dark and quiet, the lingering scent of paint in the air.

Saffron managed to locate Rex's shoulder and clapped a hand on it. 'Great stuff. Super.'

'Are you going to be all right?'

She flapped a drunken hand. 'Course I am!'

'Remember to drink lots of water.'

'Water?' Saffron's mind was wandering. Where was she again? She blinked and looked at the face in front of her. Suddenly Tom's features swam into focus. But wasn't he meant to be in Bristol or something?

'Tom, you made it . . .' she slurred. She wrapped her arms around him and planted a big kiss on his lips.

He was wearing a different aftershave from normal. But his mouth felt really, really *nice . . .*

'Er, Saff . . .' She suddenly realized what she was doing.

'Oh shit!' Saffron tried to focus through one eye. She let out a horrified giggle. 'Oh my God! Rex, I'm so sorry.'

'Don't worry about it.'

'Tom's going to kill me! I just snogged his *brother.*' She started to fumble for the door-handle. She was suddenly feeling really sick. 'I need to lie down . . .'

The last thing she remembered was the floor coming up at her face.

Chapter 34

Clementine stood up from her gardening mat and massaged her aching knees. It was ironic, she reflected, that ever since Errol Flynn had died and she'd stopped walking as much, she had started suffering all kinds of ailments. It was almost as if her body were protesting against the absence of its normal energetic routine.

She stood back and looked over her garden with a critical eye. One of the finest in the county, it was a well-organized riot of colour. Clementine didn't like her garden to look too manicured; there was something of the dreaded suburbia and Saturday morning car-washing about neat, plastic-looking lawns.

As she squinted through the mid-morning sun Clementine spotted something lurid and green

254

lurking under the apple blossom. What was that? She went over to investigate and found it was a stuffed green frog. One of the great-grandchildren must have left it last time they were here. Clementine smiled at the thought. Churchminster's spring fair was coming up soon and Caro was bringing Milo and Rosie down for it. Clementine was aching to see them all.

She picked up the soft toy, dangling it aloft from one froggy leg. She'd better go and wash it through and put it in the Aga to dry. Aside from doing her own laundry, Clementine didn't have much else planned today. She could always drop in on one of her friends, and the Reverend always needed his tail chasing about church business, but Clementine didn't feel much like socializing. Besides, she told herself, she had some Fashion Cares business to attend to. She hoped that Saffron and Rex realized how pressing time was. Clementine knew that one couldn't afford to take one's eyes off these things for a minute.

As she looked up at her huge, empty house a feeling of loneliness washed over her. Was such a big place really necessary for one person? Fairoaks had been in the Standington-Fulthropes for generations, but suddenly it seemed self-indulgent, extravagant. Clementine's heart clenched at the thought of giving it up, though. She raised her eyes to the upper windows, and the mauve wisteria blanketing the exterior wall.

'What to do, old friend?' she murmured. The house looked back stoically, as if it knew her thoughts. *We're one and the same*, it seemed to be saying. Clementine allowed herself a wry smile. People really would think she was going senile if they knew she was talking to her house.

Clementine's plans to spend the day alone, however, were not to be. She was in the conservatory hanging up her gloves when there was a fearsome rattling on the kitchen door.

'What the . . . ?' Clementine rushed out to look.

Ambrose Fraser was outside, knocking impatiently. He saw her through the glass and flapped a driving glove. 'Clementine!

She went over and pulled the door open. 'Ambrose, are you all right?'

He was wearing some sort of old-fashioned racing cap, a pair of goggles pushed up on his head. 'Perfectly! Are you busy?'

'Well . . .' Clementine was at a loss for words.

Ambrose grinned broadly. 'Fancy feeling the wind in your hair?'

'I beg your pardon?' Now she was really confused.

Ambrose grinned impishly. 'Let's not hang about, then, your carriage awaits.'

*　　　*　　　*

Clementine opened her mouth to say something, and then shut it again. 'Does Frances know about this?' she said eventually.

Ambrose barked with laughter. 'Ha! She soon will when she gets back.'

She'll throw a fit, Clementine thought, as she stared at the go-karting track stretching across the back of Clanfield Hall. It was huge, cutting straight across the lawn and several of Lady Fraser's prize-winning flowerbeds. One of the gardeners walked past, looking slightly peaky. He glanced at the track and shook his head. Clementine knew how he felt.

What looked like two mini racing cars, one red and the other yellow, were parked on the track. Clementine thought they looked awfully flimsy. Even if she was paid all the money in the world she wouldn't get into one of those death traps.

Ambrose handed her a pair of goggles. She looked down at them. 'Why are you giving me these?'

He rolled his eyes. 'You've got to wear them, woman!'

Normally Clementine would have taken exception to being called 'woman' but she was still rather in shock.

'We're going to race each other,' Ambrose explained.

'Race?'

'Yes, of course. I've already beaten everyone here, I need some fresh blood.' Ambrose's eyes glinted competitively.

Ambrose was being ridiculous, and Clementine told him so. 'I've never driven one of those before in my life, and I don't intend to start now!'

Ambrose frowned, shaking his head. 'Where's the Clementine Standington-Fulthrope I used to know? She would have grabbed this with both hands.'

Clementine's voice was bleak. 'I'm afraid that woman's not here any more.'

He put one hand on his hip, the other pointing at her. 'You know, I've always admired your spirit, Clemmie. Aside from Nanny, you're the only woman I've ever really been frightened of.'

If Clementine didn't know him better, she would

have said Ambrose was looking positively empathetic.

'Come on, old girl, don't give up yet,' he said.

'I'm not giving up!' she snapped.

He eyed her. 'Do you think I don't know what they're saying about me down in the village? That I've lost the plot?'

'I'm sure I don't know what you mean,' she said, knowing perfectly well what he was talking about.

Ambrose let out a snort of laughter. 'Let them think I'm a few sandwiches short of a picnic! The point is, I'm having fun.' He looked surprisingly vulnerable for a moment. 'People leave, Clementine. They've got their own lives to live. That doesn't mean we should stop living ours.'

For some reason his words produced a most unexpected reaction in Clementine. She was mortified to feel her lip wobble.

In the nick of time, there was a shout behind them and she turned round, grateful Ambrose couldn't see her blink away the tears. A young, round-faced boy dressed in jodhpurs was hurrying across the grass. He was carrying a chequered black and white flag.

'You're late!'

'Sorry, Sir Ambrose,' the boy puffed. 'One of the mares was playing up.'

'Justin is going to start us,' Ambrose told Clementine. He clapped the stable boy on the back. 'Justin time, what? Ha ha ha!'

He looked back at Clementine. 'So, Clemmie, what do you say? Twenty quid to win?'

She stared back for a long moment. This was a farce. There was no way she was doing this.

'Fifty.'

He guffawed. 'That's the spirit!' He strode off towards the go-karts. Not really knowing why, Clementine followed. Ambrose pointed out the yellow one. 'That's yours.' Justin helped her in and put on her seatbelt. 'The accelerator is there, brake's that one. She's got a hell of a start on her, so hold on. Oh, and keep her tight round corners.'

The machine felt awfully cramped, the pedals very rudimentary. Tentatively Clementine started it up. The engine roared into life. *Goodness, it was loud!*

Justin shouted something. Clementine held a hand to her ear. 'I can't hear you!'

'I said, go easy on the clutch . . .' He watched as Clementine bunny-hopped her go-kart towards the start line.

Ambrose was there already, waiting impatiently. 'Bloody woman drivers, ha ha ha!'

In spite of herself, Clementine stifled a smile. With his goggles and fizzing boyish energy, Ambrose reminded her of Toad from *Wind in The Willows*. Except Toad had stolen a racing car and promptly crashed it. Clementine's expression quickly became worried. But she had no time for last-minute nerves. Ambrose was revving up his engine. The track stretched ahead, winding and perilous. Standing by the side of it, Justin raised the flag high in the air.

'Three, two, one, GO!' he said.

Clementine felt her innards curdle as the machine leapt forward. Then, nothing. She looked down in confusion: she'd stalled the blasted thing. In front of her, Ambrose was already zooming off, taking the first corner at alarming speed.

'Restart her!' Justin shouted. 'You've still got a

chance!' Repositioning her goggles, Clementine turned the ignition key again, and the engine roared into life. She flew down the first straight, rather more out of control than she would have liked. The first corner loomed on her right. Slowing down slightly, she rounded it, heart in mouth. There was a hairy moment when she bounced over a stone or something, but somehow she made it.

First obstacle cleared, Clementine was spurred on. She pressed her walking shoe flat down on the accelerator. Ambrose was still out in front, but his lead was shortening. As Clementine made it through the first lap without any major mishaps, her nerves vanished. *This was fun!* Adrenalin coursed through her, carrying her round corners at high speed. The Hall, the grounds, Justin; they all passed in a blur. All she could do was concentrate on the red car in front of her. By golly, she was getting close!

'Final lap!' Justin yelled as they zoomed past, but Clementine barely heard. Eyes watering, she blinked furiously and focused as Ambrose came into her sights. They were coming to the last corner now . . . Clementine flew round it on two wheels, bumping back down to earth. Foot jammed against the accelerator, she leant forward, willing the machine on. Slowly but surely, she crept up behind him. Ambrose glanced back, his face alive with excitement, shoulders tensed.

They were shoulder to shoulder now, as they hurtled towards the finishing line. Clementine could see Justin waving the flag. Somehow, her machine started to pull away. Inch by inch, she crept past Ambrose. She could almost taste the victory . . .

As she shot past the flag, Clementine whooped in excitement. She'd won! 'Fifty pounds to me!' she shouted.

She was so euphoric that she veered off the track, failing to notice the ramp Ambrose had been working on, right ahead in her path. She was suddenly aware of frantic yelling behind her. But it was too late. Clementine watched, in some kind of horrified wonder, as the go-kart flew up the ramp and four foot into the air. For a second she seemed to hang, suspended, before hurtling outwards into the blue beyond.

Chapter 35

London

Harriet and Zack were on their way to Caro and Benedict's for Sunday lunch. 'Are you sure they don't mind me coming?' Zack asked, as they walked through the pretty network of back streets to Montague Mews.

'Of course not, they're dying to meet you.' Harriet was still in post-coital bliss from their steamy shag in Zack's bed that morning. It felt like they'd had sex more times that week than she'd had in her entire life.

A young woman was coming the other way, the Sunday papers under her arm. She looked like she'd just got out of bed after a heavy night.

'Afternoon!' Harriet said brightly. 'Isn't it a lovely day?'

The young woman glanced up at the rain clouds and frowned. Harriet gave her a huge grin. *I've just been bonked stupid, you know.* She kept expecting to wake up any minute, find herself alone in her bed with only her Marian Keyes novel for company. But Zack was really here, smelling of Issey Miyake and gorgeousness, his warm hand holding hers.

Forget lovely, today was a *great* day.

'I'm looking forward to meeting them, too,' Zack said, as they reached the entrance to Montague Mews. He winked at her. Joyfully, Harriet pressed the buzzer for Caro and Benedict's.

'Hello?'

'Caro, it's me. Us,' she added, starting slightly as Zack's hand squeezed her bottom.

'Fab! Come on in, guys.'

The gates swung open to reveal the mews at its prettiest. Wisteria climbed the walls, and an apple blossom tree stood in the far corner, its white flowers covering the cobbled tiles like spring confetti. As a slight breeze blew through, it brought a fresh wave of blossom floating towards them. 'What a great little place,' Zack said. 'You could be in the middle of the countryside.'

'Heavenly, isn't it?' Harriet said, as the front door to No. 2 opened and an adorable little blond boy came flying out.

'Harry-at!'

'Hello, Milo!' She almost lost her balance as Milo ran full pelt into her. Milo's eyes wandered to Zack. 'Who are you?'

Zack knelt down on one knee and stuck his hand out. 'Hello, Milo, I'm Harriet's friend, Zack.'

Milo stared suspiciously, then he touched Zack's

hand and ran off again. 'Mummy! Harriet and Sack are here!'

'Well, Sack, I think you've made a friend in Milo,' Harriet laughed. Benedict appeared in the doorway, looking tall and impossibly handsome. He had a curly-haired blonde moppet in his arms, wearing some sort of princess dress. She was wriggling madly.

'Rosie, calm down.' Benedict smiled at Harriet and Zack. 'They get a bit excited when we have visitors. Anyone would think we usually leave them chained to the staircase.'

They followed him into the living room, where he deposited his daughter on the floor. 'Rosie, this is Zack, Harriet's new friend,' Benedict told her. 'What do you say?'

The little girl blinked huge blue eyes, the same colour as her dad's. Suddenly shy, she wrapped her arm round Benedict's leg.

Zack bent down. 'Hello, Rosie, what a beautiful dress you're wearing. I think I'd like one for myself,' he said.

She giggled at him.

'You'll have opened a can of worms there,' Benedict told him. 'She'll have you in the dressing-up box before you know it.' He held his hand out. 'Benedict Towey.'

'Zack Doyle.' The two men shook hands heartily, subtly sizing each other up.

Caro appeared from the kitchen, wiping her hands on a tea towel. 'Hello, darlings!' She came over to Zack, and kissed him on both cheeks. 'Hello, Zack, it's lovely to meet you.'

Her friends were so good at putting people at ease. Harriet flashed Caro a grateful smile.

'Come through and have a glass of champagne,' Caro told them. 'Benedict's just cracked open the Laurent Perrier.' They followed her through to the kitchen, where a smell of roast beef filled the air. Harriet dug in her bag and produced a good burgundy. 'This is for you.'

'Ooh, looks very nice,' Caro said. 'I'll put it by the Aga and we can have it with lunch.'

Benedict was busy pouring the champagne out. He handed one to each of them, before pouring a flute for himself. 'I think a toast is in order. To friends.'

'To friends,' they chorused. Benedict took a sip of his drink and looked at Zack. 'So, you run the community centre Harriet's volunteering at?'

'Yeah, my official title is "Community Action Leader".' He grinned. 'What that really means is glorified caretaker-cum-PA-cum-general-dogsbody. I like it, though.'

'Oh, nonsense, you do much more than that.' Harriet smiled. 'He *is* the centre,' she told the others. 'I don't know what they'd do without him.'

Their conversation was interrupted by the reappearance of Milo, who was now dressed in a pirate's outfit. 'Sack!' he bellowed. 'Come and sail the high seas with me!'

'Good luck,' grinned Benedict, as his stepson pulled on Zack's leg.

Zack put on a funny face. 'A-ha, me hearties,' he growled, making the little boy laugh.

'Let's play!' Milo grasped Zack's hand.

'I guess I'll see you later,' Zack said, as he was pulled off down the hallway, Rosie following behind.

Caro grinned at Harriet. 'He's lovely!' she

whispered. 'Is it going well?'

Harriet nodded delightedly.

Benedict rolled his eyes. 'Poor chap doesn't need you two standing here whispering like a pair of fishwives.'

'Can I do anything?' Caro asked.

'No, you girls carry on gossiping. Or rescue Zack from Milo and Rosie.'

The living room was a scene of chaos. Zack was on all fours, Milo on his back waving a plastic sword in the air, while Rosie was hanging off one of Zack's legs.

'A-ha, me hearties!' Milo shouted. 'I'm Captain Bluebird.' He brandished his sword again, nearly sending a vase flying.

'Welcome to the madhouse,' Caro said. 'Oh,' she went on, turning to Harriet. 'Did you hear about Granny Clem? She was riding in a go-kart at Clanfield Hall and came flying off it!'

Harriet was horrified. 'Is she OK?'

'She's fine. She just has to wear a neck brace for the next month.'

Harriet shook her head. 'I don't know what's happened to Daddy.'

Things had settled somewhat by the time they sat down to lunch in the dining room. Zack was the easiest of guests, chatting happily with Caro and Benedict, and even helping to cut up Milo's roast potato when the little boy asked him to. Milo had taken quite a shine to him.

'Are you Harriet's boyfriend?' Milo suddenly asked Zack.

'Milo, that's a very personal question,' Caro reprimanded.

Harriet wasn't sure what to say, but Zack looked

at her and dropped a quick wink. 'Yes, I am,' he told Milo. 'I'm Harriet's boyfriend. She's my girlfriend.'

Harriet felt a rush of happiness. He'd called her his girlfriend! They really were in a proper relationship. Like Saffron, maybe she'd get that fairy tale ending after all.

Chapter 36

Churchminster

The headboard was banging furiously against the wall. Mrs ~~Wallace~~ Norris from next door was going to be round complaining soon, but Serendipity didn't care. Above her, Brad's suntanned body was soaked in sweat, his sexy face ~~contorted~~ full of lust. 'You are something else,' he told her, as his huge ~~dick~~ ~~penis~~ cock drove into her. She smiled, wrapping her legs round his muscular back. Brad was so gorgeous, all she wanted to do when she saw him now was have hot, sticky, rampant rex.

Saffron reread the last sentence. 'Have *rex?' What was wrong with her? Guilty conscience*, piped up an annoying little voice in her head. She ferociously hit the delete button, putting SEX instead, in big capital letters. Just so there was no doubt.

Since that drunken night when she'd kissed Rex, Saffron had been doing her best to avoid him. She was so embarrassed. What on earth must he think of her? Rex had sounded perfectly normal when

266

he'd sent her a text the next morning to see if she was OK, but Saffron had been plagued by The Fear ever since. When she'd eventually crawled out of bed and checked her phone, she had found four voicemails from Tom. She was sure she'd sounded guilty as hell when she'd called him back. God, she was the world's worst girlfriend. Scrub that, fiancée!

She couldn't put off seeing Rex any longer. He'd called a Fashion Cares meeting, and Saffron was supposed to have been there five minutes ago. Grabbing her bag and the MG car keys, she rushed out of the house.

By the time she got to Byron Heights Sue's pick-up truck was there, along with Clementine's Volvo estate. The sight of the cars made her feel better; at least with other people around she could act like nothing had happened. *Stay cool*, she told herself. *It had been a drunken mistake. Rex would know that.*

She lifted the lion's head and knocked on the door. As she waited, the forbidding grandeur of the Heights looked down on her. For a moment Saffron forgot her worries, envisaging the place full of beautiful, glamorous people, champagne waiters wafting around to cater to their every need. If it all went to plan, Fashion Cares was going to be one hell of a party.

She heard footsteps across the hall and the door opened.

'Hi!' she trilled, hoping she wasn't going to start going red.

Rex's brown eyes held a hint of amusement.

'We were just waiting for you.'

'Sorry,' she said, breezing past him to escape any

267

kisses. 'I was kind of in book land.'

'Going well, is it?'

A fuzzy memory of their kiss flashed before her eyes. 'Yes, yes!' she said brightly. He nodded, seemingly finding something funny. 'Cool. Well, come on through. Sue and Clementine are already here.'

Sue was still going great guns and had managed to secure the services of a firm to come in and assemble a catwalk. The catwalk people had suggested another firm to do the lighting for the event, and so it had gone on. Even Clementine, who had strangely turned up in a plastic neck brace looked impressed by Sue's efforts.

Now Sue and Clementine turned to Rex and Saffron. 'I'm afraid I don't know much about this,' Clementine said, as Sue chewed her pen thoughtfully.

'We've got our ten designers, and they're producing the most amazing collection,' Rex said. 'I reckon this show could make stars of quite a few of them.'

'How about the hair and make-up?' Sue asked. Rex tried to hide his surprise that she knew about such things. 'Uh, yeah. Through Saffron's contacts at *Soirée* we've got Lee Greene. He's like this amazing hairdresser . . .'

'I know him,' Sue chipped in. 'I did a burlesque-themed party for him and his boyfriend down here last year.'

Saffron saw Rex's face and stifled a laugh. Was this woman the bloody oracle or what?

Rex blinked. 'Right. Anyway, I'm speaking to Alexander Napier—he's the fashion director at *Soirée*—about make-up artists and models. I'm going to start doing castings in the next few weeks, hopefully.' He looked at Saffron, signalling her turn.

'Well, we've had a pretty good response so far from the industry. Lots of people want to come.'

'Is Dame Helen Mirren attending?' Clementine enquired, turning her neck stiffly. 'I do admire her, especially after her marvellous portrayal in *The Queen*.'

'Er, I haven't tried her actually.' Clementine looked mildly disappointed. She hadn't heard of most of the names on the VIP list and hoped the show wouldn't be full of those ghastly Reality TV type people.

After she and Sue had left, Saffron helped Rex carry the empty coffee cups through to the kitchen. 'Just put them anywhere,' he said. 'The cleaner's coming in later.'

She dumped them on the draining board. 'Rex?'

'Yeah?' He was fiddling with the iPod dock. She took a deep breath. 'Look, I'm really sorry about what happened the other night. You know, when I . . . it was a total mistake. I'm really sorry.'

He looked up. 'Hey, don't sweat it.' He grinned. 'I quite liked it.'

She blushed, refusing to enter his playful banter. 'You—you haven't told Tom, have you?'

'Of course I haven't.' He looked at her. 'There's nothing to tell, is there?'

Relief. 'No, of course not!' Honestly, I don't know what came over me. I don't make a habit of that sort of thing.'

'You were pissed, that's what came over you. It was funny, Saff, especially when you flashed your boobs on the way home.'

269

Saffron looked at him in horror. 'I didn't!'

He chuckled. 'No, you didn't.'

'You bastard.' Grinning, she threw the nearest thing at him, which was a tea towel. He dodged, and it missed him. 'Your face was a picture, that was hilarious.'

'Ha ha. For you, maybe.'

Jesus! She was never drinking again.

MAY

Chapter 37

Even though she was meant to be concentrating on the book, Saffron was doing some sneaky wedding planning. It was just so hard not to! She'd been looking at various West London venues for receptions, and had fallen in love with Belvedere House, a wildly romantic seventeenth-century mansion-turned-restaurant, right in the middle of Holland Park. Prices weren't cheap, she had to admit. But it wasn't as though she wanted a big flouncy wedding with a horse-drawn carriage or anything. Besides, with the money her mum had given her, she could afford it. They could afford it.

When she rang Tom's mobile she was surprised to hear him answer. He normally had it switched off at work.

'Hey!'

'Hey, Saff.'

'Where are you? I can hear traffic.'

'Taking a walk round the block. I had to get out—Jeff's doing my head in.'

She'd never heard him sound stressed before. 'Bloody editors, what's he done now?'

'Well, you know that new section for the first issue I was working on all weekend?'

Only too well. He'd been meant to be coming to see her on the Friday evening and, in the end, hadn't come down until Sunday lunchtime. 'Yeah?'

'Jeff's dropped it. Doesn't like it.'

'No! What an arsehole. And he made you stay and do it.'

'I know, I know.' Tom sighed. 'The annoying

273

thing is, he's right. It's not good enough.'

'I'm sure it is, babe,' she said loyally.

'It's not, trust me. I guess my mind was elsewhere, I was pissed off about not seeing you, and probably rushing to finish it . . .'

'He's working you too hard.'

'He's a perfectionist, Saff. He can be difficult, but I am learning loads from him.'

'Well, I think he sounds like an arsehole!'

'Fighting my corner, eh?' She could hear the smile. 'How're you doing? Just hearing your voice makes me feel better.'

'I'm good. Look, I was wondering if we could talk about venues for the reception. I've found this amazing place in . . .'

He interrupted her. 'Babe, we've talked about this. I thought we were putting it on hold for a while.'

'Yeah, I know, but places do get booked up, Tom!'

He sighed. 'OK.'

'OK what?'

'Go ahead and book it.'

'I haven't even told you where it is!'

'As long as you're happy, I'm happy. It could be a hole in the ground as long as you're there.'

'That's not funny.'

'I'm not trying to be funny . . . I'm sorry, Saff, my head's not in the right place to discuss this at the moment. Can we talk later? I promise you when you come back to London I'll give it my undivided attention. I can't wait to plan it with you.'

'Doesn't sound like it,' she muttered.

There was a long pause. Then Tom spoke. 'Hey, guess what?'

'What?'

'I've been put up for the Magazine Periodical Awards. Art Designer of the Year.'

Damn. Why did he have to spring this when she was feeling moody with him? 'That's great.'

'You don't sound very happy.'

'Of course I am!' She forced herself to sound more cheerful. 'That's wicked, clever old you.'

'Yeah, it is pretty cool. The ceremony's the week after next, and I've got a plus one. Do you fancy it?'

'In London?'

'Yeah, where else would it be?'

'Count me in.'

*   *   *

After she'd hung up Saffron wandered down the hallway to the loo. Tom could have sounded a bit happier about the reception venue. She knew he was having a bad day at work, but Saffron still felt a bit stung by his reaction. This was their wedding they were talking about, not some knees-up in a bar. Saffron was sure part of it was because Tom didn't like big parties, but she wanted everyone who was special to them there. *I'll go ahead and book it anyway.* She just wouldn't tell him.

Saffron reached for the loo roll, only to realize it was nearly empty. For God's sake, was she the only person in this house who stocked up on things? They'd run out of milk again as well, and spread. She'd better pop next door to the shop before the whole house went under.

Clementine was talking to Brenda as she walked in.

'Hello there, Saffron,' the shopkeeper called out. 'Mrs S-F was just telling me all about the fashion show! It sounds very exciting. What's the charity again, Horsebag Heaven?'

'Handbag *Haven*,' Clementine corrected dryly, smiling at Saffron.

'Well, I can't wait! I'll have to buy a new frock, of course.' Brenda glanced up at the poster on the wall. 'Still, we've got the summer fête to get through first. You coming along?'

'Summer fête?' Saffron said, knowing full well what Brenda was talking about. There were posters plastered all over the village, but coconut shies and apple bobbing weren't really her thing.

'I was thinking you and Rex could run a Fashion Cares stall, to publicize the event,' Clementine said. 'It would certainly get local interest going.'

Brenda nodded enthusiastically. 'A supermodel stall! That would be something. We get lots of these showbiz types coming along, you know. Last year we had Simon Cowell's brother or something. He's got a weekend place round here. And then the other time we had SamCam.'

'SamCam?' Clementine said.

'You know, David Cameron's wife! And Beryl Turner was convinced she saw Prince Harry once.' Brenda paused, thinking. 'I wouldn't know him, though, those gingers all look the same to me.'

'Brenda, please . . .' Clementine looked at Saffron. 'So you'll do it?' It was an order, not a question.

'Great, we'd love to.' *Rex, please don't hate me.*

Brenda clapped her hands together. 'That's that, then!' She stood up. 'Now, Saffron love, how did you find those condoms? You'll probably want to

276

stock up for the next time Tom's down. I've got the . . .' She leant back to look at the shelf behind the counter. '. . . ribbed Trojans, or some flavoured things called Penis Colada. I'd go with the Trojans if I were you. Maureen from *Slimming World* said the Penis Colada ones gave her an awful itch.'

Saffron's mouth opened and closed like a goldfish. 'Honestly, I just need some magarine and loo roll.' She added redundantly, 'I'm on the pill.'

Brenda winked again. 'I'll put 'em aside just in case, eh? I know what you young folks are like, at it like rabbits!'

There was a brief silence, when all that could be heard was the hum from the ice cream freezer. *Oh my God*, Saffron thought. *That did not just happen.*

'Flora or Olivio?' Brenda asked breezily.

Chapter 38

London

Zack looked up from between Harriet's legs. 'I take it you enjoyed that.'

'Amazing,' she gasped, flopping back on the pillow. She'd never known oral sex could be so incredible. Until now, her limited experiences had been rather sloppy, like the time after a Young Farmer's Ball when Marcus Feeley-Bevington had tried to *bite* her down there. Harriet thought she'd been put off for life. Thank God for Zack. His tongue did things she had scarcely thought possible.

He moved up the bed to lie back down next to

her. He was so manly and muscled, a six o'clock shadow starting on his chin. Harriet couldn't help but smile. The combination looked incongruous against her flowery Laura Ashley duvet.

Zack looked at her quizzically. 'Private joke?'

She stroked the stubble. 'I was just thinking how pink suited you.'

'You won't find it so funny when you find me with your pearl earrings on.'

'Oh, I don't know. I think you'd carry them off with aplomb.'

'Aplomb, eh? I'll have to remember that word, use it down the pub with the lads. They'll be blown away.'

Harriet smiled, but his comment did make her think. Apart from the odd night playing pool, Zack didn't seem to really go out with any mates. But then again, he hardly ever had a free night off. She snuggled into his chest, her fingers tracing the lines of his tattoo. Zack stiffened.

'Don't . . .' He grinned, mouth awkward. 'I don't like being reminded of it. The tattoo, I mean. Talk about a stupid thing to do.'

She had to admit it wasn't the best tattoo she'd ever seen. Zack sighed. 'Still, it could be worse. A mate of mine had Meat Loaf's mug on his back. Gave us all a fright in the summer when he took his top off.'

His delivery was so deadpan it made her laugh. 'I think the most rebellious thing I did was getting my ears pierced. I fear I was rather boring.'

'Better than being stupid.'

'Is there any reason you had that tattoo?' she asked.

'Yeah, not the most inspired choice, was it? It

was probably the first thing I thought up.' Zack propped himself up, and looked into her eyes. 'I've never really told you about my mum, have I?'

Harriet had got the impression Zack didn't like talking about her. 'I'd love it if you did.'

'Before she met my dad she was training to be a PE teacher. She was quite the athlete at school, you ask Aunty Win.'

'Win knew her?'

Zack chuckled. 'Everyone knew my mum, she was the local stunner. Pity she ended up with my dad, but Win said he had a way with the ladies.'

'Do you remember him?'

'Not really, left when I was two. Said he "couldn't hack it".' Zack laughed humourlessly. 'Real man, eh? My mum had more guts than ten of him.'

'She must have been devastated.'

'I think she saw it coming. In her heart of hearts she knew what a wrong 'un he was, but she loved him.'

'And she had you.'

'Yeah.' Zack smiled. 'She used to call me her little prince. Except when I came tramping in with my muddy football kit on. Then she'd let me have it. You could hear her three streets away!'

Harriet laughed. 'She sounds great.'

'She was.' He squeezed her hand. 'Can I tell you something?'

'Of course.' She propped herself up to look at him. Zack was staring at the wall, eyes faraway.

'The day she died, I'd been playing her up. Nothing major, just being a little shit the way teenage boys can be. You know?' He glanced at her. 'We'd been shopping, to get me some new trainers, and it wasn't going well. She wanted the

279

twenty-pound sensible ones that would last, I wanted the fifty-pound Nike high-tops all my mates were wearing. Mum didn't have the money, I was just being difficult. We'd been in loads of places, and we were in a sports shop arguing about this pair—I can still see them on the shelf now—when Mum says, "You know what, Zack? You want those trainers, you can save up and buy them your bloody self."

'Course I gave her a bit of lip back, said something about her being a crap mum, and she looked at me and said, "I've had enough of this." She picked up her handbag and stormed out. Next thing I heard was the sound of a car hitting her.'

Harriet went cold. She just didn't know what to say. 'Oh, Zack, I didn't know. You should have told me.'

He shrugged his shoulders, and she could see the heaviness. 'If I hadn't been playing her up, it wouldn't have happened.'

'Zack, you can't blame yourself . . . it was an accident.'

'I've never told anyone this, not even Win. That we were arguing, and that was why she rushed out of the shop, and wasn't looking where she was going.'

Harriet held him tightly. What a terrible burden for a young boy to carry around with him! 'You poor, poor thing. It must have been horrible for you.'

He gave a resigned smile. 'It's all right, I've kind of come to terms with it, now.'

Harriet couldn't believe it. 'To get through all that, Zack, and be the person you are! I'm so proud of you.'

He stared at her, eyes white-hot in their intensity. 'Harriet . . .'

'Yes?'

'Nothing.' He wrapped his arms tightly round her.

Chapter 39

Churchminster

It was the day of Tom's award ceremony. Saffron had her outfit planned—the glamorous strapless black Paul & Joe dress she'd got in a sample sale—and had bought her ticket for the 5 p.m. train out of Bedlington. Hopefully she'd have enough time to meet Tom for a quick drink, before they went on to the awards. They were being held in the ballroom of a five-star hotel nearby. There'd be a champagne reception at 7 p.m., followed by a sit-down dinner and the main event.

Even though Tom was being typically modest, Saffron knew he was excited. The Magazine Periodical Awards were a massive deal, and this nomination was just the boost he needed. He'd been working even harder than ever, because one of the design team had announced she was leaving, and had left them in the lurch. They were trying to recruit someone to replace her, but the editor, Jeff, didn't like any of the interviewees he'd seen so far.

Saffron and Tom were on the same table as his boss tonight. She thought she'd better stay off the white wine, in case she told Jeff exactly what she thought of him. 'Slave' and 'driver' were the two words that sprang to mind.

At one o'clock Saffron finished writing. Her train wasn't for a few hours yet, but she wanted to give herself enough time to get ready. Saffron felt a flash of nervous excitement at the thought of going back to London. It was weird: she'd lived and breathed the city all her adult life, but suddenly it seemed big, fast-paced, terrifying.

She was just deciding between Chanel Black Satin or glittery gold NARS nail polish, when she heard her mobile ringing on the landing. Kicking a dirty pair of leggings out of the way, she ran out to get it.

It was Rex. Saffron snatched it up just as it was about to go to voicemail. 'Lo!'

'Have you got a minute?'

'Yeah, sure.' She sat down on the windowsill. 'What's up?'

Rex's voice was serious. 'We have a situation. Can you come over?'

*   *   *

In total shock she stared at him. 'Please tell me you're joking!'

'I wish I was.' Rex had just given her the news that Saul Barboni, Handbag Haven's founder, had been arrested for embezzling charity funds. Daisy, Rex's contact there, had rung that morning to tell him.

'There's no way we can be associated with them now,' Saffron said.

'I know, I know.' Rex ran his hands through his hair. 'This is a nightmare!' He started pacing up

282

and down the dining room. 'Right Rex, think . . .' He looked at her. 'At least the papers haven't got hold of it. Daisy says their lawyers are trying to keep it hush-hush.'

'They're bound to find out at some point.' The press loved scandal like this.

'Let's hope it's not before we find a new charity that makes an even better story.' He stopped pacing, and stared out of one of the huge windows. It was a full minute before he turned back to her. 'OK, this is what we do. We're gonna keep this down low, and still let people think Handbag Haven is on board. We won't lie to them, we just won't go out of our way to tell them otherwise. Then we find a new uber-cool charity, announce we're changing, and Bob's your uncle. What do you think?'

Saffron had a bad feeling. 'I don't know, Rex, the show is, like, six weeks away!'

He gazed at her. 'What else are we going to do, Saff? Cancel it? After all the hard work we've put in? I've got ten designers working their socks off, and halfway through their collections. Do you want me to call them and say "Sorry, guys, the whole thing's off?" '

'Of course not!' It wasn't a great option but it was their only one. 'Shit!'

They spent a nerve-racking few hours drawing up a new list of charities. There were a few good alternatives, but it was still going to be a sensitive situation to deal with. The last thing either of them wanted was word to get out in the fashion world that they were in trouble, and that the whole show was in danger of collapsing. That's if the press didn't get hold of the story first. Saffron hoped this

283

Barboni bloke's lawyers were as good as Rex said they were. What a bloody crook!

The only reason she noticed the time was because the sun glinted off her watch, drawing her eyes to it. 3.30 p.m.

'Shit!' she said again. 'I've got to go!' She leapt up and started gathering her things together. 'My train's in like, forty-five minutes.'

'Where are you going?'

She looked up for a moment. 'Tom's award thing, of course.'

'Shoot, yeah, you better go. Say good luck from me.'

*   *   *

Babs was hovering by the bottom of the staircase. 'Darling, we'd better be going,' she called for the second time.

'I *know*, Mum!' Saffron shouted crossly, as she staggered across the landing, trying to put on a shoe and an earring at the same time. This was a bloody disaster! She hadn't had time to wash her hair, let alone give herself a manicure and pedicure.

'I'll start the engine . . .'

'Aargh! I'm just coming.' Saffron chucked a few things in her overnight bag and grabbed her mobile. There was a new text from Tom. She read it as she was running down the stairs. '*Hey beautiful. Finished work, in the pub. Can't wait to see my gorgeous wife-to-be and show her off. Give me a call when you get to Paddington. xx*'

Saffron stopped and smiled. She couldn't wait to see him, either. She was staying at the flat tonight, and it was going to be just like old times. She was even excited about seeing Leroy. Taking the stairs two at a time, she ran out the front door.

Ten minutes later her excitement was quickly waning. 'Can't you get past it?' she said for the umpteenth time, as the horribly familiar blue tractor in front of them trundled along maddeningly slowly. Babs nudged the bonnet of the MG out a fraction. 'Darling, I can't, the road's too narrow.'

Bollocks. Saffron looked at her watch. Her train was in five minutes and twelve seconds exactly.

'Don't worry, we'll make it,' Babs said. Saffron glared at the tractor, its elderly driver blissfully oblivious to the drama behind him. After what seemed like an hour, but was actually two minutes, he finally turned off down a farm track.

'Right, Mum, floor it!' They were on the outskirts of Bedlington now, only a few minutes away. Saffron started to relax, she was going to make it.

Up ahead there was a line of traffic in the road. 'What the . . . ?' Saffron started to say, until the 'road works' sign appeared on the side up ahead. A man in a bright yellow jacket was standing by a set of temporary traffic lights, looking bored while he held a big red sign saying STOP.

'Aargh!' she shouted, throwing herself back against the seat. Of all the bloody days to have road works. She *had* to get this train. It was the last fast one to London, the next one would get her there miles too late, and she would have missed half the ceremony. She stared at the sign, willing the man to turn it. Come on . . .

Eventually the traffic lights started to change.

'Move, people!' Saffron shouted, as the cars in front started to pull off. She checked her watch again; they had less than two minutes. As the MG flew down the 30 m.p.h. High Street at 50 m.p.h., Saffron put her bag on her lap, hand on the seatbelt buckle. She could still just about make it . . .

The car screeched into the station. Even before they'd stopped Saffron had her door open. 'Thanks Mum, bye!' Kicking off her heels, she picked them up and flew across the car park.

There was a station guard standing in the little entrance hall. 'Which platform is the train to London?' she gasped.

He pointed. 'Platform One. But you'd better hurry . . .' Saffron barely heard him as she ran towards the stairs, and flew up them. She rounded the corner, lungs on fire, her legs feeling on the verge of collapse.

'No, wait! WAIT!' As the train pulled away from the platform, she locked eyes with a little girl in a window seat, holding a teddy. Saffron came to a shuddering halt and the girl gave her a curious look, before the train carried her away towards London.

Chapter 40

London

The Gatsby Road study club were having an evening picnic on Hampstead Heath. It was exam time for the GCSE and A-level students, and they'd had their heads down for weeks now, revising. Harriet had suggested a night off would do them a world of good, and looking at them all sprawled out on the grass, talking, laughing and helping themselves to Win's delectable offerings, she knew it had been a good call.

'Danny, no, shut up! Don't you dare!'

Danny Henderson, A-level whiz and rapper extraordinaire, grinned and aimed the water bottle at Abby. 'Like, what are you going to do if I do?'

'I'll kill you!' she shrieked, clearly loving every minute of it. Danny took a step closer. 'I'm warning you, Danny!' As he started running towards her, Abby screamed and took off, long blonde hair flying behind her.

Harriet smiled. It was so nice to see Abby just acting her age and having fun.

'I reckon those two have got the hots for each other,' Pete said, as Danny squirted some water and Abby dodged out of the way.

'I think you're right.'

Pete took a huge bite of treacle flapjack. 'These things are pukka. They'd rot my teeth away if I had any left.'

Harriet looked at the impressive spread laid out in front of them. 'I think Win's made enough to feed an army!'

'I'm not complaining,' Pete said through a mouthful. 'I won't have to eat for weeks now.'

Win had been playing frisbee with Zack and Gray, but now she was waddling towards them breathing heavily. Pete, will you go and take my place now? Someone needs to show those two how it's done.'

'Might burn off a few calories.' Pete jumped up, and Aunty Win lowered her huge bulk into the deckchair he'd just been sitting in.

'Lovely evening, 'Arriet.'

So it was. Even though it was nearly 8 p.m., the sky was still blue above them, a salmon-pink sunset spreading on the horizon like ink on blotting paper. The heath was full of picnickers, while a rowdy game of mixed rounders was taking place in the distance.

Win sighed in contentment and sat back. ' 'Ow are things going with you and Zachary?'

Harriet still couldn't help but blush a little. 'Good, thanks.'

Win shot her an observant look. 'You think I'm a nosy old woman asking all these questions, but Zachary tells me nothing!'

Harriet laughed at the comical look on her face. 'I don't think you're nosy.'

'Zachary does! Ah well, as long as you're happy.' She placed her hands in her lap. 'You and Zachary have good talks, then?'

'Talks?'

'Talks, 'Arriet! Good, open communication. That's what I'm talking about, a-huh.'

'Er, yes, we do.'

'Good, good. That's all you need. I keep telling

288

him: trust and honesty.'

A little bubble of worry floated into Harriet's mind. *Trust and honesty*. It seemed like an odd thing to say. Win gave her an encouraging smile. 'I just tell Zachary he needs to be open about his feelings. These men, they're never good at opening up, are they?'

Harriet wondered if Win was referring to the ex again. The one from Liverpool. Was there something Zack should be telling her? Aunty Win leant down and patted her arm. 'He likes you a lot, you know, 'Arriet. You're very special to him.'

'Right then, you lot!' Zack was striding towards them, frisbee in hand, and looking tall, sweaty and gorgeous. 'Who's up for a game of group rounders?' His laser-blue eyes settled on her, playful and knowing. 'Ah, Miss Fraser. Care to join in?'

*   *   *

'Are you going to be OK, Gray?' Harriet peered anxiously at his swollen eye. The picnic had come to a rather premature end when she'd lost control of the rounders bat and hit Gray, who was fielding behind her, straight in the eye. Luckily there had been a medical student nearby having a barbeque, and after a quick examination he'd said Gray would probably live. It didn't make Harriet feel any better, especially as she'd almost hit Zack in the groin with a stray ball moments earlier.

Gray touched his face gently. 'I'll be fine, don't you worry. Professional sportsman like me, injuries are part and parcel.'

Harriet smiled. 'I'm dreadfully sorry! Your poor

289

wife will wonder what's happened to you.'

'Listen, this is nothing compared to the shiner she gave me when I came back after a two-day bender when we first got married. In fact I'd better be getting off home before she gives me another one. I'll see you later, Harriet.'

'See you, Gray,' she said, watching him walk out of the double doors. Thank goodness he'd been so understanding. Harriet was still mortified. What a klutz.

She and Zack were walking Win home from the centre, and then going back to his. In between the teasing, he'd been shooting her sly little looks, making it clear what he wanted to do when they got home. Zack clearly had one thing on his mind. Harriet shivered with anticipation, hoping he'd like the sexy new underwear she was wearing. Even if the thong had spent most of the evening halfway up her bottom.

*   *   *

As Zack locked the outside door of the community centre, Win was in full flow about the evening, but she suddenly stopped dead. Harriet glanced up to see what she was looking at, and a shiver ran down her spine. The gang of hooded kids were back, blocking their path with their bikes, clearly with no intention of moving.

'Haven't you got homes to go to?' Win called out sharply.

'Aunty Win, leave it,' Zack told her. 'You two stay here.' As he walked down the path towards them, Harriet's heart started thudding.

'What do you want, lads?' he said.

He's so brave, Harriet thought. She would never be able to confront them like that. Beside her, Win was very still.

'I said, what do you want?' This time there was a very definite warning in Zack's voice.

To Harriet's surprise, one of them spoke.

'Ain't no law to say we can't be here.'

Zack had almost reached the end of the path now, and there were just a few feet between him and the eight black-clad menaces. 'Surely there's more interesting places to hang out?' he said.

'What, you think you own this place?' A taller youth, his hood pulled up tight round his thin, ratty face, stepped forward. 'You think you're some kind of fucking hard man?'

'Zack!' Win's voice was tight, fearful.

'Just trying to do my job,' Zack said pleasantly. The taller kid edged nearer and Zack took a very deliberate step off the pavement. Harriet's heart was in her mouth. She instinctively went into her handbag for her phone.

The youth and Zack were close now, the rest of the gang sitting on their bicycles behind their mate like a pack of hyenas, watching. 'If you lot don't bugger off, I'm going to call the police,' Zack said. 'You don't want that, do you?'

His aggressor spat on the ground at Zack's feet. 'I wouldn't do that, blud.'

Zack's voice was unnervingly pleasant. 'And why's that?'

'Zack!' Win broke the tension.

The youth looked back at his gang and laughed. It wasn't a nice sound. A few cackles and obscenities echoed back and he tilted his chin at Zack arrogantly. 'You better go, gay boy. Don't want to keep your bitches waiting.'

There were more cackles from behind him. Harriet saw the tension ripple through Zack's shoulders, and for one terrifying moment she thought he was going to explode. Then Zack shook his head.

'Go home, lads.'

As Zack turned back towards them Harriet saw the kid reach into his jacket.

She saw something glint under the glow of the streetlight.

'Zack!' she screamed. 'He's got a knife!'

Chapter 41

Quick as a flash, Zack whirled round. There was a glint of silver, the moment punctured by someone screaming. With a shock, Harriet realized it was her.

The youth gripped the handle, his thin, pale face contorted with hate. 'Scum!'

He jabbed the knife wildly, but Zack stepped back in time. Harriet heard Win moan almost inaudibly.

'I'll fucking shank you!' the youth spat, but he seemed uncertain what to do with the knife. As he came towards Zack again, Harriet was gripped by terror. On the other side of the road the gang seemed to have swelled, bristling with expectation . . .

'Cut him, blud,' one of them ordered.

'Get the cunt!' another jeered. Buoyed by the taunts, the kid's lips peeled back into a ghastly grin.

'Hear that? I'm going to cut you, scumbag.' As if she were in the middle of a terrible nightmare, Harriet watched as the knife came down in a terrifying arc.

'Zack!' she screamed helplessly, as they locked into a tussle. Oh God, any second now that knife was going to pierce his flesh . . .

There was some kind of muffled shout and she saw Zack put his hand up, as if to protect himself. Someone cried out, the sound piercing her very soul. *Oh no. Please. Not Zack.*

Instead the kid staggered back, cradling his arm. His face twisted in surprise and pain.

'You've fucking broken it!'

Harriet could see Zack's shoulders heaving from the exertion. His attacker started to back away, his gang sitting up straighter on their seats as they sensed the off. Once he had the road between him and Zack, the kid regained some of his swagger. He locked eyes with Zack and, even though he was clearly in pain, he managed to slowly cock two fingers of his other hand, imitating a gun.

'I'll get you, fucking scumbag.' Clambering back on to his bike, he wheeled off, his injured arm held tight to his body. The gang followed, their whooping and catcalling fading into the night.

Harriet had been paralysed with fear throughout, but suddenly her legs were working again. 'Zack!' She raced down the path towards him. 'Oh God, are you hurt?'

As he turned to face her Harriet almost stopped dead in her tracks. His face was deathly pale, two red spots burning high on his cheeks. He looked at her, but it was almost as if he didn't see her, his eyes were so preternaturally bright.

'Zack?' she said uncertainly. They both looked down at the knife in his hand. He suddenly dropped it, as if it were red hot. The knife clattered down on to the tarmac.

Harriet looked up at him. 'How did you get . . .' The shock kicked in. 'You could have been hurt!' *Or worse.* She swallowed.

Zack wasn't listening, he was still staring at the knife in disbelief.

'Zack!'

His eyes snapped up. 'I'm fine, don't worry.' He saw the fear in her face, and reached out to touch her arm. 'Are you all right? I'm so sorry you had to see that.'

'Zachary?' Win hurried over, breathing heavily. She looked down at the knife. 'Oh Lord!'

'Win, it's OK,' he said. 'Please don't get yourself in a state.' Harriet noticed a vein pulsing in his forehead. He was obviously more shaken than he was letting on.

Win's eyes darted past Zack, in the direction the gang had gone. 'We should call the police.'

'Why? What can they do?' Zack said. 'Those kids are long gone.' He sighed. 'We don't even know what they look like.'

'But we have to!' Harriet said. 'They had a knife.'

'And I have that knife now. Win, do you have a handkerchief?' Win looked confused, but duly pulled out a bright yellow one from her handbag. It had a monogrammed W on one corner. She handed it to Zack, who bent down and gingerly picked the knife up in it.

Win gripped his arm. 'Promise me, Zachary, if they turn up again you'll call the police.

294

Straightaway. None of this heroic stuff, all right?'

Zack nodded. 'I promise, Aunty Win.' He smiled. 'Hopefully we've seen the last of them.'

They'd all heard what the youth had said. *I'll get you.* Harriet felt sick. 'We should call the police anyway, tell them you were threatened.'

He shook his head. 'I'm not going to be scared by a load of jumped-up little idiots trying to put the frighteners on us.'

Win wasn't reassured. 'He had a knife, Zachary.'

Harriet looked at the weapon, lying in the middle of the open handkerchief. Not that she had any experience of things like this, but it didn't look like your average kitchen knife. Large and curved, it looked antique, with a kind of criss-cross pattern snaking down the handle.

'Seems old,' Win said. She shivered. 'Where would they get something like that? You should take it to the police.'

'I'll take it in tomorrow, Aunty Win, OK?' Zack sounded so calm and rational that it made Harriet feel better.

'Do you really think you broke his arm?'

Zack gave a dry smile. 'No, but I gave it a pretty good twist. He wasn't such a big man then.'

'Oh, Zack,' Harriet said weakly. He put an arm round her, and the other round Win.

'Everything's all right now. C'mon, girls, let's go home.'

*   *   *

'Were you really not scared?'

Harriet and Zack were standing in his kitchen, drinking a cup of tea. For some reason, she couldn't get the chill out of her bones. She put her hands round her cup, trying to warm herself on it.

He paused. 'A little.'

Harriet looked at him with concern. 'You don't have to pretend.'

Zack put his cup down. 'Yes, I was scared. But more for you and Win. If they'd got past me to you . . .' He held his arms out. 'Come here.' He nuzzled his face into her hair. 'That's better.'

'You are going to take the knife in to the police, aren't you?'

He sighed. 'Yes. I just don't want to make a big deal of it, you know? Give those little creeps any leverage. We're working so hard to make this estate better, and I don't want people to think they've got to start looking over their shoulders. Fear spreads in places like this, believe me.'

He did have a point. Harriet squeezed her eyes shut. 'I was so scared. If anything happened to you . . .' She stopped, not able to think about it.

He hugged her fiercely. 'It didn't. I'm not going anywhere. OK?'

Chapter 42

Churchminster

Tom sounded hoarse when he eventually answered the phone the next morning.

'Tom, it's me.'

'Hi, Saff.' She could still detect a hint of reproach in his voice. That made her feel even worse, she'd been up half the night thinking about it.

'I've been trying to get hold of you.'

'I know, sorry. I had a bit of a late one and I've only just got up.'

'So, how did you do?'

'I won.'

'What? That's amazing, babe! Well done!'

'Thanks.'

She felt gutted she hadn't been there to share it with him. 'You're still in a mood with me, aren't you?'

'I'm not in a mood, Saff. I'm just disappointed you couldn't make it.'

'Tom . . .' How many more times could she say sorry? 'I wanted to be there more than anything in the world, babe, I really did.'

'Yeah, me too.'

Saffron read the undertone. 'It wasn't like I did it on purpose,' she said irritably. 'I had things going on too, Tom, Handbag Haven dropping out is like a major head-fuck for us. If we don't find someone we're going to have to call the whole thing off!' She knew the excuse sounded feeble.

He didn't comment. 'I'd better go, I'm late for work.'

'Tom!' There was a silence. 'I am really proud of you. You do know that, don't you?'

'Yeah, Saff.' He didn't sound convinced.

She spent the rest of the morning brooding. She had tried to get there, she really had. If it hadn't been for that bloody tractor . . .

Her mum popped her head round the study door mid-morning. 'Can I get you a glass of wine, darling?'

'Mum, it's eleven o'clock!'

'Is it? Better wait an hour, then. Have you spoken to Tom?'

'Yeah, he hates me.'

'Of course he doesn't! You've explained what happened, haven't you?'

'Yes.' Saffron sighed. 'I should have been there, Mum.'

Babs looked sympathetic. 'Oh, darling, it was just bad luck. I'm sure Tom will understand.'

'Maybe. Thanks, Mum.'

After Babs had fluttered out again, Saffron turned back to her laptop. There was no point trying to write today, her head was filled with too much other stuff. Out of habit she went onto PerezHilton, the Hollywood gossip website. There was another story about Summer Gold being caught drunk, falling out of a nightclub. She was fast becoming the new Lindsay Lohan, Saffron thought. Still feeling restless, she logged on to her Facebook page. Her friend Jas had just put up new photos and Saffron clicked on to see what she'd been up to. She recognized the location as Place 58, a cool bar in East London she and Jas used to hang out at in Saffron's previous life as an envied journalist with a half-decent social life. Only half concentrating, Saffron started flicking through them: Jas looking stunning in hot pants and thigh-high boots; Jas downing shots at the bar with some girl Saffron vaguely recognized; Jas pulling a stupid face . . .

Hold on, she did recognize *that* person. In growing disbelief Saffron stared at the next picture of Jas with her arm around someone who, if she wasn't very much mistaken, was Tom. They were both laughing into the camera, Tom looking

298

dishevelled and sexy, his tie loose around his neck. She looked closer, there was even a bloody lipstick-mark on his cheek!

* * *

'You didn't tell me you went to Place 58.' Saffron had sat on her hands for an hour, then phoned Tom at work. She was doing her best to sound pleasant, even though her stomach was in knots. Jas might be a friend, but Saffron wouldn't trust her as far as she could throw her. She could just imagine her draped all over Tom. *Bloody slut!*

'So I've just been told.' Tom sounded even rougher. 'I don't remember anything past midnight. I think we took the celebrating a bit too far.'

'Do you remember seeing Jas?'

'Jas? Isn't she one of your friends?'

'Yes, the stunning six-foot one with the morals of an alley cat. She's just put up some Facebook pics from last night with her draped all over you.'

'I don't remember any of that!'

'Oh, great,' Saffron retorted.

'Oh, great what?'

'If you were that out of it, she could have been doing anything to you!'

He dropped his voice. 'What are you trying to say? Don't be ridiculous.'

Guilt, mixed with sleep deprivation and sudden paranoia, was not having the best effect on her. 'I'm not the one being ridiculous,' she shot back. 'From the state of you last night it sounds like you were!'

Tom paused. 'I'm not going down this road

299

again.'

'And why's that? Was your ex-fiancée Cassie there as well?' As soon as she'd said the words she regretted them.

'His voice was like ice. 'Don't take it out on me just because you feel bad about last night, OK? If you're honest, you weren't really that excited about coming in the first place.'

She felt sucker-punched. 'That's not fair! I was just . . . frustrated about the wedding planning.'

'Right. Now I've got the worst hangover ever, and a pile of work to get through. So let's speak later, when you've calmed down a bit.'

'Don't patronize me!' Saffron was left listening to the dialling tone. For the first time in their relationship, Tom had hung up on her.

Chapter 43

London

Harriet was deep in thought as she made her way to the centre that night. Things between her and Zack were getting serious enough now that she was going to have to say something to her father. Harriet was *dreading* it. For as long as she could remember, it had been drilled into her that she was expected to marry into another aristocratic family, and keep the dynasty going. If Ambrose had had his way, she would have been married off years ago and marooned on a thousand-acre country estate with four sturdy sons and heirs-in-waiting. Ambrose thought her moving to London and getting a fluffy job in the media was just a 'phase' she was going through.

Although she loved her father, Harriet was still rather terrified of him. Ambrose was Clanfield born and bred, but Harriet had always felt ill at ease growing up in a huge stately home with all the responsibilities and expectations that went with it. She wished her mother were here to talk to. Even though Frances took her role as the wife of Sir Ambrose Fraser very seriously, she knew the world had changed.

And what did her father hate more than 'pinky liberals' (as he called politicians and feminists), but 'townies' (his words)—and you couldn't get more city than Zack. He didn't hunt, shoot, fish or do any of the other activities her father measured a man by. Harriet couldn't think of two people who had less in common.

She was so busy imagining the horror of them meeting her dad—and noticing Zack's earring—that at first she didn't notice the little old man to her left wobbling up a path to a block of flats. As the shopping bag he was carrying suddenly split open, he gave a cry. Harriet looked at the frail figure bent over, and the tins rolling across the path, and hurried to help him. The man was trying to pick his groceries up, but his stiff hands were clumsy and uncoordinated. Despite the warm May evening he was wearing a heavy overcoat.

'Here, let me,' she said. The man whirled round, looking startled. Harriet saw watery blue eyes and a sad, wrinkled face. She bent down and gathered up two tins of tuna, a packet of Rich Tea biscuits, and a discounted bag of potatoes past their sell-by date. It didn't seem very much.

'Very kind of you,' the man said in a quivery voice.

Harriet smiled. 'Not at all. Your bag looks a bit broken, though.'

The old man looked down at the well-worn tartan bag, now split right across the bottom.

'Can I carry these in for you?' she asked, the food still in her arms.

The old man looked at the entrance to the flats and back to her. 'Yes, please, if you don't mind.' His voice was tired, hesitant. Harriet smiled and followed him, as he started shuffling back down the path.

'Lovely evening,' she remarked cheerfully.

He turned his head slightly. 'Yes, isn't it?' He had a polite, slightly formal manner. Harriet watched as his fingers fumbled on the keypad. It took several attempts before he got the right one and the door buzzed open.

He made an apologetic gesture. 'I miss door keys . . .'

'Me, too,' she said, thinking of the over-the-top security system at work. 'These things are a pain, aren't they?'

He smiled, as if surprised. 'Over here . . .' He started towards a door on the right.

'This all looks very smart,' Harriet said, trying to make conversation. In truth the lobby was small and dark, with frayed holes in the carpet.

'They moved me here three months ago.' The old man got his key out of his pocket carefully and unlocked the door. 'If you could just bring it all through to the kitchen.'

'No problem.'

The flat smelt stale and fusty as she followed him

down the narrow corridor into a little square kitchen. Although spotlessly clean, it was drab, and barely furnished.

Harriet put the groceries down on a cracked yellow Formica table. 'Here we are.'

The old man started fumbling through his pockets. 'I'm afraid I haven't got any money to thank you with.'

'Oh no,' she said quickly, 'it's not necessary. Really, I was just passing . . .'

He beamed at her, and she saw a glimpse of what he might have looked like many years ago, full of vigour and hope. 'Thank you so very much,' he said. But Harriet was horrified to see his eyes filling up with tears. 'I'm sorry,' he croaked, covering his face with his hands. 'It's just that it's been a while. Oh dear . . .'

As he looked for a handkerchief, Harriet took out the packet of tissues she always carried around in her bag. 'There you go,' she said gently. She pulled out a chair and helped the old man sit down.

He blew his nose loudly and looked at her. 'I'm sorry. I didn't mean to embarrass you. An old codger like me gets a bit lonely, you know.'

She sat down opposite him and took his liver-spotted hands in hers. 'You haven't embarrassed me, please don't think that.' She smiled again. 'I'm Harriet.'

He gave a little nod. 'Bert Cooper, delighted to make your acquaintance.'

She looked at him in concern. 'Now, Bert, are you all right?'

'Not really, my dear.'

'I'm a good listener,' she offered.

He looked at her, as if weighing her up, before his face relaxed. And with that, Bert Cooper started to talk. Talked as if he hadn't had a proper conversation for months.

What got Harriet the most wasn't the fact that, like Alf, Bert had lost his wife. Or that, despite having four children, none of them seemed to visit much. He had his own social worker, since the council had moved him onto the estate a few months earlier, but from what Harriet could make out, aside from a cheery comment to the checkout girl that went ignored at his weekly shop, Bert Cooper spoke to literally no one.

He'd previously lived with his wife in Kilburn, where they knew the area and had friends. 'I was in a nice terraced house you see, but when I lost Irene they wanted to give it to a family. Quite right, it was too big for one person.' Harriet listened as he talked and talked, ecstatic to have some human contact.

'Oh, Bert,' she said finally. She felt dreadful that all the time she'd been here, he'd been existing by himself in this cold, lonely little flat.

He smiled. 'I'm sorry. You don't need a silly old man going on about his problems.'

She squeezed his hand again. 'There's nothing to be sorry about.' She just wished she could do something. She looked at Bert, his frail frame under his big coat, his hands clasped round hers, savouring the touch of another person. Suddenly it came to her. 'Ooh, I can think of something that might help,' she told him.

'Oh yes?' His expression was confused but hopeful.

She grinned. 'Are you any good at bingo?'

Chapter 44

Churchminster

Her parents loved Brad, just as she'd known they would. As they sat on the terrace of the exclusive restaurant in Knightsbridge toasting each other with champagne, Serendipity felt on top of the world. Just for once—and she could hardly dare believe it—things were going right in her love life.

'Well, doesn't this look cosy?' drawled a familiar voice. Serendipity looked up. To her total shock Jake was standing there, looking more like a rock star than ever, in a crumpled white shirt undone to the waist. From the stink smell of him, he'd been dining on pure whisky.

'J-Jake,' she stuttered. 'What are you doing here?'

'Actually, I should ask what you're doing with him.' Jake looked across the table, green eyes dangerous. 'I thought you were dead, loser!'
'Hello, Brad.'

Saffron stretched her arms above her head, anticipating the Brad-Jake run-in. Sparks were going to fly then! She went back and checked her word count: 2,431 words this morning alone. If she carried on like this, she was going to have *Gloss* finished in no time at all.

At least the book was going well. The same couldn't be said for Fashion Cares. With only five weeks to go they still didn't have a new charity, Bibi Brown or any celebrity guests of note to make it into the A-list event they so desperately wanted. To make matters worse, she'd gone and committed the cardinal sin and texted Savannah Sexton's private mobile. They'd had such a rapport when they'd met that the star had taken the unusual step of giving Saffron her number, just in case she wanted to check anything. There had been an unspoken agreement that Saffron wouldn't take advantage but now she'd done exactly that and gone behind her management's back to ask Saffron to the show. Unsurprisingly, the actress hadn't replied and every time Saffron's phone went she expected it to be Savannah's manager, going ballistic. Saffron's stress levels had reached new heights.

At least she and Tom seemed to have moved on from their argument, but something was niggling her. Tom was acting perfectly normally, so why was she still feeling like a hysterical girlfriend? Then again, why bloody shouldn't she? You couldn't drop a clanger like Cassie, and carry on as if nothing had happened. They needed to talk about these sorts of things—especially as Saffron was locked away in her study for twelve hours a day, with only her own thoughts for company. All this introspection was starting to drive her mad.

Long-term relationships rule number 48: long periods of time away from your other half will lead to wild delusions and unjustified feelings of insecurity.

Saffron allowed herself a wry smile. At least there was a good magazine piece in this when she got back to work.

*   *   *

Rex was in a particularly exuberant mood when she arrived at Byron Heights later that day.

'Guess what? We've got Bibi!'

'Oh my God!' Saffron slung her handbag on the kitchen counter. 'Rex, that's amazing!'

'I know.' He was grinning broadly, his face looking even more handsome. 'There's a couple of loose ends to tie up, and I don't think we're gonna get a full collection like the others, but it's still awesome.' He came over and high-fived her.

Saffron mischievously mimicked his voice. *'Awesome!'*

'Ha ha. There is one thing, though.'

'Oh, what?'

'We can't tell anyone Bibi's taking part, yet.'

She stared at him. 'Why not?'

'Apparently she's been commissioned for this big bespoke collection for a really demanding client, and Bibi's manager doesn't want *them* to get the wrong idea, and think Bibi's doing something else on their time.'

'But that's stupid!'

'I know, but you know how precious the fashion world is. They just don't want to ruffle any feathers unnecessarily. Once Bibi gets this collection out of the way, we can tell the world.'

It wasn't ideal, but she'd have to go along with it. Rex rubbed his hands together. 'I was thinking, do you fancy a barbecue? Make the most of this weather.'

Saffron blinked. She still hadn't got her head around Rex's ability to leapfrog from one topic to another. 'Uh, yeah.' She realized she hadn't eaten since breakfast. 'What do you want to do about food? We can go to the shop.'

'Cool, let's go in my car.'

They sped down the Bedlington Road towards the village, the wind whipping through Saffron's hair. The leather car seats felt luxuriantly cool against her bare legs, the expensive smell filling her nostrils. Rex leant across and turned on the stereo, Mt Eden Dubstep's latest track blasting out.

'I love this!' she shouted above the roar of the engine. Rex grinned under his Ray-Ban aviators. 'Me, too.'

They were just approaching the village green when Rex suddenly slammed on the brakes.

'Jesus, what are you doing?' she gasped.

'Did you see that?' Putting one arm behind her seat, he started to reverse back up the road.

Saffron tried to ignore the curve of his bicep, flexing beautifully inches from her face. 'What?'

'I think I just saw something . . .' The Aston Martin came to a gentle halt, and as she looked round Saffron could see a little pale brown deer, huddled in the undergrowth at the side of the road.

'Maybe it's been hit,' Rex said, unbuckling his seat belt.

Saffron suddenly remembered something they'd been taught about wild animals at school. 'Rex, I don't know if you should go near it. It might die of fright.'

'Well, we can't leave it here, cars come flying round this corner . . .' he pointed out. Unfolding long legs he got out of the car to investigate, with Saffron following.

'Here, little fella . . .' Rex approached cautiously. The deer pressed itself back in the undergrowth, eyes darting in terror.

'I think it's a baby,' he called back, without taking his eyes off it. 'There's a little bit of blood on its leg, but it doesn't look as if anything is broken.' He stuck his hand out. 'There's a jumper on the back seat. Grab it, will you?'

Wondering what he was doing, Saffron hurried back to the car. There was a coffee-coloured jumper lying behind the passenger side. Saffron picked it up, instinctively reading the label. Armani, and cashmere too, by the feel of it.

'Got it.' She took it back over to Rex, who was now bending on one knee beside the little deer, talking to it.

'Can you give it me?' She watched as Rex laid the jumper over the animal and carefully scooped it up. Very slowly he got up.

'Right, you're going to have to drive us to the vet's, Saff.'

'The vet's? I don't know where it is.'

Rex looked down the road, towards the direction of the green. 'Won't that shop lady, Brenda, know? You did say she was the village oracle, didn't you?'

Two minutes later, with Rex cradling the deer in his arms in the passenger seat, Saffron nervously started the ignition of the £80,000 sports car and slowly pulled away.

*   *   *

'I'm going to have to start calling you Doctor Doolittle.' Even at five o'clock the sun still felt hot enough to burn. Saffron was sitting on the edge of the hot tub, legs in the water as Rex leant over the super-sized barbecue on the terrace.

309

He looked up and smiled. 'I hope the little fella's going to be all right.' Brenda had pointed them in the direction of a vet's practice a few miles outsidethe village. Miraculously, the baby fallow deer was only heavily bruised—probably from being hit by a car—and didn't have any serious injuries. The vet was going to give it to Bedlington Wildlife Rescue.

Saffron watched as Rex turned over a pair of salmon steaks, squinting slightly as the smoke came sizzling upwards. He'd taken off his shirt, and his bronzed body was looking even more ripped than usual. Her eyes lingered over the line of his shoulders, the board-shorts hanging off the narrow waist. Rex caught her looking, and smiled quizzically. 'What?'

'I was just thinking.' She smiled, and took a swig of her ice-cold beer. 'I never had you down as the animal type.' There was something in the way Rex had handled the baby deer that had rather touched her. She'd never seen that tender side of him before.

Rex reached across to take a taste of his own beer. 'I love them. I used to have the most amazing cat called Tiger when I was little. He was a rescue: ginger and built like a friggin' quarterback.' He smiled at the memory. 'Me and Mum took on the animal side of things in our house, Dad and Tom were more into books and stuff.'

Saffron imagined an eight-year-old Rex with his cat. 'The animal lovers versus the intellectuals, eh?'

'Something like that.' He turned the sausages over. 'Nearly ready.'

'Have you spoken to Tom recently?' Saffron

asked, watching him.

'Yeah, the other night. He's working like a bastard, from the sound of it.' He glanced up. 'We didn't really talk about you guys. Did you explain why you missed the train?'

'Yeah.' Saffron didn't really want to go into the details.

Rex busied himself back with the meat. 'Tom's cool about stuff like that. Guy's the most forgiving man I know.'

'I still feel pretty shitty, though,' she admitted.

'Hey, don't sweat it. He'll be down soon, and you can polish his trophy or whatever he's got, to your heart's content.'

Saffron flicked a bit of water in his direction. 'Sod off, you!'

Rex chuckled, his broad shoulders bent over in concentration. Saffron finished her beer and set it down on the side. 'I suppose we should have a charity chat at some point . . .'

'Not today, eh?' His brown eyes looked chocolatey in the sunlight. 'We've got Bibi, so let's take a load off for the moment. Just eat, drink and take in this beautiful British countryside.'

'Do you *ever* worry about stuff?' she asked him.

His brow furrowed. 'Stuff?'

'You know, the show. Pulling it off. Or anything, I guess. It seems like nothing bothers you.'

'Ah, I don't know.' He started transferring the sausages on to a plate. 'C'mon, we're good to go.'

She noticed he didn't answer her question. Maybe there was nothing to answer. Rex picked up one of the sausages and held it aloft. 'Who does this remind you of?' He started talking in a hilarious rip-off of Brenda Briggs's voice.

'Ooh, hello, Saffron! What do you want for your barbecue then? Ow about that sausage over there? That's a nice big one!'

She started to giggle. 'Oh God, don't!' Saffron didn't know if it was intentional, but Brenda had somehow managed to make every comment she'd made about food sound like a commentary from a porn film.

Rex put his hands on his hips, camp style. 'Ow about that baguette instead? Something to get your mouth round. Now that *is* a big one!'

'Rex . . .' Saffron was getting a serious case of the giggles.

'I do like a nice bit of pork, me!'

'She did not say that! You're such a dick!'

They both stared at each other. 'Ooooh!' he retorted, in an even better Kenneth Williams impression.

That was it: Saffron was off. It took five minutes before she could draw breath again. 'Oh my God, oh dear . . .' She wiped her finger under her eyes, hoping her mascara hadn't run. She exhaled, breath still shaky. 'Thanks, Rex.'

His face was warm, delightful. 'For what?'

'You've no idea how much I needed that.' Smiling, Saffron got up and went to help him.

Chapter 45

'Rex, we can't do this.' Saffron knew her protestation sounded half hearted.

His dark brown eyes looked into hers, hungry, penetrating. She could feel the heat from his naked torso flooding into hers. A drop of sweat ran down her back into her knickers.

'I should go . . .' It was the last thing she wanted.

He grabbed her arms, pinning her against the car. 'I can't hold myself back any longer, Saff. It's no use pretending.'

As he started kissing her passionately, Saffron's head began to swim. His lips and tongue were so like Tom's, yet even wilder, unrestrained. As he hitched her mini-skirt up and lifted her against the side of the Aston Martin, she was weak with desire. She couldn't stop him now even if she wanted to.

'Shit!' Saffron sat bolt upright. It took a few seconds for it to sink in that she wasn't being ravished by Rex, but was in fact in her bedroom at Hardwick House. The porcelain dolls looked down from the top of the wardrobe, their painted faces suddenly accusing. Saffron reached for the Chanel watch on the bedside table. It was just past nine, eight hours after driving home from Rex's—where she had certainly not been seduced on the bonnet of his Aston Martin. Where had *that* come from? She closed her eyes again, but all she could see was his brown torso, his tanned, ripped arms as he pushed her back against the side of the car . . .

She needed to get *up*, forget about this. Forcing

313

the image from her mind, Saffron headed for the bathroom.

Despite her resolve, she spent the rest of the morning feeling slightly freaked out. It had been one of those dreams that seemed so *real*, leaving her with the same emotions and feelings as if it had really happened. What disturbed her most was that she'd been so turned on. The wetness between her legs when she'd sat down on the toilet had told her that. *It's just because you're missing Tom*, she kept telling herself. It could have been anyone. She'd once had a horribly erotic dream about shagging the spotty youth who'd given her an upgrade in Carphone Warehouse. It didn't mean anything.

Except somehow, this was different. Saffron knew what Rex's lips felt like, after drunkenly snogging him in the front porch of Hardwick House. Saffron had managed to put the memory out of her mind since, but the dream had brought it all back. Those few seconds she'd spent pressed against Rex's hard body, his mouth on hers. Was there a little part of her that had known all along that it hadn't been Tom?

Shit. She was steering into dangerous territory here. Was it her imagination or had she caught Rex's eyes lingering on her a few times at the barbecue when he'd thought she wasn't looking?

You're imagining it, she told herself firmly, and got up to put the kettle on.

'You seem rather quiet today, darling.' Babs popped her head out from behind the easel, and Saffron looked up from where she'd been standing against the counter, nursing a cup of tea.

'Am I? Sorry. I guess my head's all full up with

314

the book.'

'Did you have fun last night? I didn't hear you get in.'

'Yeah, it was cool.'

Babs put her brush down and reached for a splattered rag to wipe her hands on. 'How's Tom, darling?'

For some reason Saffron felt her hackles rise. 'Why do you ask?'

Babs fluttered a hand. 'No reason, I just haven't heard you talk much about him lately.'

Saffron put her cup on the counter. 'That's because there isn't much to tell,' she said gloomily. 'He works, I write, we speak for about ten minutes at night, and then we both go to bed.' She looked down at her engagement ring, as if aware of its presence for the first time in weeks. 'I dunno, when Tom proposed . . . I thought it would all be angels and butterflies. But if anything, it's the opposite. I feel like he's almost forgotten we're engaged!'

'Darling, of course he hasn't. He's just a little bit swamped with work. You know how bad men are at multitasking, he just wants to get through this and then give you and the wedding his undivided attention.'

'Maybe.'

Babs smiled reassuringly. 'Talk to him, tell him how you feel!'

For once, her mother was talking sense. 'You're right, I'll talk to him when he comes down for the summer fête.' She paused, debating whether to tell Babs about the Cassie thing and that, rightly or wrongly, she'd been a little bit shaky since. She decided she couldn't cope with her mum's reaction. Besides, as far as Tom was concerned, it was dead and buried. Saffron leant on the counter, scrunching her hands through her hair. 'To be honest, Mum, I'm just a bit stressed about things at the moment.'

'Not the book?' Babs asked anxiously. 'I thought it was going so well!'

'It still is,' Saffron assured her. 'But it's this bloody show.' She shot her mum a look. 'Can you keep a secret?'

'Of course, cross my heart and hope to die.'

'You don't have to go that far.' Saffron sighed. 'At this moment in time, we haven't got a charity. Handbag Haven messed up, big time.'

Babs's eyes widened. 'No charity? What are you going to do?'

'Find a new one. We have to.'

Babs looked at the Picasso calendar on the wall. 'But isn't it only . . .'

'Five weeks away, yes.' Saffron finished it for her. She pressed her face down on the counter and groaned. No charity, no VIPs, a fiancé she never saw. Not to mention the totally inappropriate dreams she was having about his twin brother . . . 'Aargh, someone take me away from it all!'

London

One person having a lot of hot sex was Harriet. Zack was dynamite in bed, and his love of her body—wobbly bits and all—had given her more confidence in the bedroom than she'd ever thought possible. Which was why, spurred on by Alexander, she'd just had her first ever Brazilian bikini-wax at the place all the beauty girls from work went.

She hadn't realized quite how painful it would be, and was now hobbling down the streets with her private parts on fire. The waxer had been a sadistic South African woman, who'd seemed to take pleasure in making Harriet yelp. Harriet was just wondering whether to pop into Boots to buy some kind of cream—but what on earth would she ask for?—when someone called her name.

'Harriet!'

She turned to see her old boss Catherine striding across the road towards her. Even though it was rush hour and mad with traffic, the taxis and buses stopped for her without the usual angry cacophony of horns. Catherine Connor had that kind of effect everywhere she went.

She kissed Harriet on both cheeks in a cloud of Jo Malone nutmeg and ginger. 'You look fabulous! Have you lost weight?'

If she had, it was from all the sexual gymnastics Zack had been putting her through. 'Maybe a little. How are you, Catherine? It's great to see you.'

'Really good! Busy. I've just been at a meeting round the corner.' Her blue eyes sparkled. 'Actually, it's a bit of luck I've run into you.' She grinned. 'I just heard something that is possibly very exciting for you.'

'For me? Really?'

Catherine glanced around. 'Have you got time for a quick coffee? I shouldn't really be talking about it like this.'

Now that sounded intriguing. Ignoring the world of pain going on in her pants, Harriet suggested the café just down the street.

317

Chapter 46

Churchminster

It was the day before the village fête, and Tom's
first visit for weeks. As Saffron drove into the
station that Friday evening he was already there,
holding the biggest bunch of flowers she'd ever
seen. As she pulled up, he looked out from behind
the bouquet and gave her a grin. Despite
everything going on in her head, Saffron melted.
He *was* gorgeous.

She undid her seatbelt and got out. Tom picked
her up in his arms, bouquet and all. 'I've missed
you, beautiful.'

He'd lost weight, and as she stepped back she
noticed the dark circles under his eyes. 'You look
really tired, babe.' She gave him a motherly look.
'I'm worried you're working yourself into the
ground.'

He brushed the back of his hand against her
cheek. 'Don't you worry about me. It'll all calm
down soon.'

They drove back towards the village, through the
green and yellow landscape. 'You seem a bit quiet,'
Tom commented.

'Do I?' She couldn't get the bloody image of Rex
out of her head. 'I'm just a bit tired, too.'

He reached across and squeezed her knee. 'I'm
really pleased the book's going well.'

'Just call me Barbara Cartland!'

Tom laughed. 'So I've been looking at the
website for Belvedere House . . .'

Saffron raised her eyebrows. She hadn't been expecting that. 'Oh, really?'

'Yeah. I think it looks great. Let's book it for the reception.'

'Really?' she repeated. 'Oh, wow.' For some reason she didn't feel that excited.

Tom squeezed her knee. 'I know I've been a bit preoccupied at the moment, Saff, with work and stuff. I'm sorry.'

How could she ever have doubted him? 'There's nothing to be sorry about, babe. I know I got a bit ahead of myself . . .'

'And your enthusiasm about everything is one of the many reasons I love you.'

'Don't you mean bossiness, and totally wanting to take over?' she said.

Tom nodded. 'Yup, that too.'

They reached the outskirts of Churchminster, the spire of St Bartholomew's reaching up in the distance. 'Can we drop in and see Rex?' Tom asked. 'I haven't spoken to him for a while.'

Saffron felt that unpleasant lurch again. 'Sure,' she said, as Byron Heights loomed up on the left. She indicated and pulled in down the long straight track. Amidst the harmonious surroundings, the house looked almost unreal, all spiky spires and turrets jutting out.

'Any word back on the charity?' Tom asked.

'We've got the go-ahead from a Tibetan eco one, but Rex doesn't think it's "relevant" enough.' She sighed. 'We'd better find something relevant soon, or we're going to end up with "Save the Croc Shoe", or something.'

'Ouch,' he said. 'I suppose at this stage beggars can't be choosers.'

319

'I know.' Saffron suddenly felt a jolt of nerves. 'And this VIP list is doing my head in! We've still got no one really worth getting excited about.' She sighed. 'I just wish we could let people know we've got Bibi. She's still fannying around with this other collection.'

'Can I do anything?'

'Don't worry, babe, you're busy enough as it is.'

Tom gave his best solid, reassuring face. 'It'll be fine, Saff, don't worry. You've still got a month.'

His well-meant words had the wrong effect. *A month*. The thought made her stomach turn over. They were running out of time, big style.

The Aston Martin was parked out the front, and Rex was opening the boot on a load of shopping. He looked up as their car crunched over the gravel.

'Howdy,' Saffron called, as she got out. As she said it, her voice did a funny wobble thing. Tom gave her an amused look, as Rex walked over and gave him a hug.

Rex stood back and surveyed Tom. 'You look tired, bro.'

Tom raised an eyebrow. 'Saff said the same thing. Do I really look that bad?'

'Of course not, babe,' she said brightly. She was trying to blank out that persistent image of being ravaged by Rex against the car door. 'You just need a good night's sleep.'

'They working you like a bastard?' Rex asked sympathetically. By contrast, he looked tanned and rested, his eyes sparking with vitality and good health.

Tom pulled his jeans up, which were hanging low on his hips. 'Yeah, it's pretty intense.'

'Doesn't help that the editor sounds like a total twat who keeps changing his mind every five minutes,' Saffron interjected.

Tom laughed. 'I think the expression more widely used is that Jeff is a bit of a perfectionist.'

'That's an understatement,' Saffron said.

Tom gave her a wink, before looking back at the house. 'Still enjoying the country life then, Rex?'

'It's been the remaking of me, I tell you. I haven't felt so rested in years.'

Tom grinned. 'Well, well.' He play-punched Rex on the arm. 'At least I know what to get you now for your birthday. A pipe and slippers.'

'Fuck off.' Rex shoved him back, grinning. 'You can talk, you've been an old fart for years.'

'Come on now, children,' Saffron said. She peered into the boot at the bags. 'Been shopping?'

'Yup, I was getting a bit low on supplies.'

Saffron thought of Rex strolling down the aisles at Budgens in Bedlington. The female customers were probably still having to be revived.

Rex pulled the last of the bags out. 'You want to come in for a drink?'

Saffron looked at Tom. 'Maybe we'll take a rain check tonight. Tom's knackered.'

'No worries. We can have a few bevvies in the pub tomorrow.' Rex glanced at Tom. 'Looking forward to the village fête, bro?'

'Rock and roll.'

Rex grinned. 'See you both tomorrow, then.' As they started back towards the car, he called out. 'Saff!'

Her stomach did an annoying little jerk again. 'Yeah?'

'I've sent you an email, just some Fashion Cares

admin. Can you have a look at it, and we'll talk tomorrow?'

She nodded neutrally. 'Cool. See you then.'

As they pulled up outside Hardwick House Saffron cut the ignition. But instead of getting out, Tom sat there. 'I wish it was just us this weekend,' he said.

Saffron touched his face. 'I'm sorry I've been roped into the fête. It'll be fun, I promise.'

After a moment he nodded. 'Cool. Whatever.'

Something in his tone annoyed her a bit. 'Tom, I'd like the weekend off as well, you know. It's not just you working hard.'

He unbuckled his seatbelt. 'I'm sure you are.'

'You could sound like you mean it! What, do you think Rex and I are just sitting around on our arses?'

He looked at her. 'Of course I'm not saying that.'

'I'm pleased to hear it,' she retorted hotly. All of a sudden, the sun drained from the day.

*   *   *

Clementine, her neck collar accessorized with a National Trust green ribbon, was sitting at the kitchen table with Milo on her knee. He'd just been telling her all about a school trip he'd been on, while on the other side Caro held a sleeping Rosie in her arms.

'Keep your voice down, Milo,' Caro said, as her son's excited descriptions got louder. 'You'll wake Rosie.'

Clementine looked over at her blonde great-granddaughter fondly. 'I can't believe how much she's growing. She's a proper little girl now.'

Caro looked down at her daughter. 'More like a proper little madam!' Rosie did a little hiccup and threw her arm out.

Milo was getting restless. 'Can I go and play?'

'Yes, but stay where Mummy can see you, please.' They'd had a hullabaloo last time they'd been home, when Milo had gone wandering off round Fairoaks and got his head stuck in the old cat-flap.

Caro reached over and touched her grandmother's wrinkled hand. It was good to see her again. 'How are you, Granny Clem?'

'The collar is a bit annoying, but it'll soon be off, so no complaints really.' Clementine had only just got her composure back after the whole debacle.

'I mean, how are you in yourself?'

'I'm fine, dear, really,' Clementine smiled. 'You don't have to worry about me.'

Caro did worry, though. She knew how her grandmother hated to be a burden to anyone, but she had been shocked at how much Clementine had aged since she'd last been home.

'Are you all ready for tomorrow?' she asked brightly. If anything would put colour back into her grandmother's cheeks, it was Churchminster's summer fête.

Clementine nodded. 'Jack is kindly opening up his car park, so at least we won't have cars parked all over the place like last time. Rex and Saffron are doing a stall, to promote Fashion Cares.'

'Oh, wow.' Caro was looking forward to bumping into their resident supermodel. She'd reserved her and Benedict's tickets for the fashion show already.

'Wow, indeed.' Clementine permitted herself a

dry smile. 'Have you heard of the charity?'

'Handbag Haven, isn't it? Sounds very cool.'

'I've been researching it on the internet. It's one of these flashy new outfits.' Clementine sighed. 'I wish Saffron and Rex had let me have a little more *say* in matters, but they do insist on doing it all by themselves.'

Caro stifled a smile. She knew how involved her grandmother liked to get when it came to charity. 'I'm sure Saffron knows what she's doing.'

'I certainly hope so.' Clementine picked up her glass of dry sherry. 'So Benedict is heading down tomorrow?'

'Yup. It's a shame he couldn't get out of his client dinner tonight. I must admit, I'm rather dreading going back to Mill House. There's bound to be a foot of dust everywhere!'

'Actually, I hope you don't mind but I took the liberty of letting Brenda in there to give it a quick clean for you. I thought it would be the last thing you'd feel like after your journey.'

Caro smiled appreciatively. 'Granny Clem, you complete angel! That's really nice of you.'

'Don't thank me, darling, it was Brenda.' Clementine took a small sip of her drink. 'Any more news from Sebastian?' Her tone made it clear what she thought of her former grandson-in-law.

'It's all gone quiet again.' Caro stroked her daughter's hair. 'This sounds awful, but I don't know if I'm pleased about it or not. At least it makes for a more peaceful life.'

Clementine had quite a few choice words to say about her former grandson-in-law but she was far too respectful of Caro and Milo to say them.

'I suppose I should be grateful,' Caro offered. 'At least he has made some sort of effort.'

Clementine didn't answer. That awful man had nearly destroyed her granddaughter, striking at the very core of the Standington-Fulthropes. It would be a cold day in hell before he'd win any 'Father of the Year' prizes from her.

Chapter 47

The next morning dawned cool and misty, with a hint of good things to come. By the time Saffron and Tom walked out on to the village green with a box full of stuff to decorate the Fashion Cares stall, the place was already humming with activity. Stalls and tents were being set up, and, in the far corner by the church, a large bouncy castle was being pumped up. A man dressed in football kit hammering in a 'Beat The Goalie' sign wished them a cheery good morning as they walked past.

'I'll have to show off my Wayne Rooney skills later,' Tom said. Saffron didn't say anything. Their spat had died down as quickly as it had flared up last night, but for some reason she was feeling distracted, edgy. It was as if the usual comfy intimacy that existed between them suddenly felt weird and strained. *We just need some time together*, she told herself. It was hard to just pick up from where they had left off.

Clementine was walking towards them looking officious, clipboard in hand. 'There you are, Saffron! Hello, Tom. Your pitch is over there.' She pointed. 'In-between the Bedlington cheese stall and the organic microbrewery.'

They made their way over to the stall and Tom dumped the box down. 'Shall I get this stuff out, then?'

Saffron nodded and looked around distractedly. 'Where's Rex? He should be here by now.'

'He'll turn up eventually,' Tom said, dropping a string of brightly coloured silk bunting festooned with sequins. 'This is pretty cool.'

'Mum and me made it out of some of her old nightgowns.'

'Very fashion, darling.' His eyes twinkled. He was clearly trying.

'Thanks.' Normally Saffron would have shot back a witty reply, but she couldn't engage for some reason. She bent down. 'Here, I've made up some posters. If you could pin them up I'll get out the information packs . . .'

*   *   *

By one o'clock the fête was in full swing. The sun had come out in force, and a throng of people wandered round, tasting cheese, meats and bread from local suppliers, or enjoying a pint of homemade cider. The biggest draw so far was the face-painting, which had a long line of children snaking out of the tent.

As yet another excited child emerged with a face full of fluorescent paint, Clementine grew slightly concerned the face-painting team weren't exactly what she'd hoped for. Ghastly 'boink boink' music was being blasted out of a stereo, while the face-painters themselves were young, suntanned, and mostly sporting those sheepdog-looking dreadlocks. As she watched, one wide-eyed tangle-haired woman started dancing crazily on the spot with some kind of glowing stick in her hand. Clementine frowned. They were taking the carnival atmosphere a little too far. She'd have to keep her eye on them.

On the Fashion Cares stall they had been getting a good response, despite Rex still not showing. Saffron was getting distinctly twitchy. 'Do you think he's OK?' she asked Tom for the umpteenth time. 'Maybe I should go up there.'

Tom shook his head. 'He's probably having some sort of wardrobe drama. Hello, madam, would you like one of our leaflets?' he said, as a woman walked past. His dark good looks didn't go unnoticed, and the woman took one and smiled flirtily.

Saffron felt an unexpected glow of fondness. Bless Tom for making an effort. As for the other brother . . . She looked round for Rex again, but instead saw someone who looked like the spitting image of Harriet's dad. Except this man had pink and blue stripes painted on his face, and was waving a plastic pint glass.

'Hello there, young Saffron!' Her mouth fell open as she realized it *was* Sir Ambrose.

'Hi there! Nice face-paint.'

Ambrose chuckled. 'Pretty natty, huh? It's meant to make me feel all "tribal" or something, at least that's what the chap in the tent said.' He took a healthy swig of cider. 'This is all right, isn't it? I've never bothered with these fairs before, damned silly I thought, but I'm having rather a good time.' He stood back and surveyed her stall. 'What's all this, then?'

Saffron was still getting over the fact that this genial man covered in rave paint was Harriet's father. 'Uh, it's for Fashion Cares? The charity catwalk show we're putting on at Byron Heights.'

Ambrose nodded vaguely. 'Yes, yes, I think Harriet mentioned it. Put me down for fifty pounds either way.'

He wandered off to a nearby pottery stall.

Saffron laughed out loud. 'Did you see that?' she said to Tom, but he was over getting another pint from the microbrewery. She hoped he wouldn't get too pissed. If Rex was a no-show she needed Tom to keep a clear head.

'Speak of the devil,' she muttered. Striding towards her, as if in the climactic scene of a movie, was Rex. Compared to Saffron, who had been up since the crack of dawn and felt knackered, he was glowing. He was freshly shaved, and his handsome face drew glances from swooning onlookers. The expensive linen suit looked like it should be gracing a Milan catwalk, not a local village fête.

Rex's brown eyes were apologetic. 'Guys, I am so sorry.'

'Where have you been?' Saffron asked crossly. 'We've been here for hours!'

'I know, I had a nightmare. The pipe burst in my en suite and I woke up to two foot of water. I had to wait ages for a plumber.'

Tom held up his pint. 'Want one?'

'Maybe later.' Rex looked at the stall. 'I am *loving* the bunting.'

Saffron smiled at him. A burst water-pipe was hardly Rex's fault.

He grinned back. 'What do you want me to do?'

328

*　　*　　*

Half an hour later, their stall was more like the stage at a pop concert. Word had spread that they had a supermodel in their midst, and the mainly female audience were clustered round, trying to get a look at Rex. For his part, he was working his charm, and already one rather enamoured farmer's wife had offered to lend them her husband's tractor for the show.

'What will we do with that?' Saffron smiled through clenched teeth.

'I have no idea,' he said as he waved the farmer's wife off.

A teenage girl with ruddy cheeks and braces held out a notepad. 'Can I get your autograph?' she asked shyly.

Rex smiled. 'Of course. What's your name, sweetheart?' The girl looked like she was about to faint with excitement.

Saffron was watching it all in amused disbelief. 'He's good,' she remarked to Tom.

He took the top off his new pint. 'Uh-huh. I might go for a wander, if I'm not needed.'

'Oh, OK.' They looked at each other. There was that awkwardness again.

Tom gave a tight grin. 'See you later.'

Saffron watched him walk off, his head and shoulders clearly visible above the rest of the crowd.

'This all looks fabulous!' Caro stepped out of the crowd in front of the stall, holding Milo's hand.

Saffron's face lit up. 'Hey, guys!' She came round and hugged Caro, before bending down to Milo's level. 'How are you, superstar?' She'd built up a bond with the little boy when they'd lived next door to each other in Montague Mews.

Milo smiled. 'Hiya!'

'He still recognizes me!' Saffron ruffled his hair. 'Benedict not here?'

'He's literally just got down. Rosie's dragged him off to the face-painting.' Caro's eyes strayed to Rex, who was still busy signing autographs at the other end of the stall. 'Oh my goodness,' she whispered. 'It's Tom's doppelgänger!'

'Except I can't quite see Tom in an Armani suit, can you?' Saffron asked wryly.

'Oh, I don't know, I think Tom's got a style all of his own.' Caro smoothed Milo's hair down, still casting glances in Rex's direction. 'We're all very excited about the show. Granny Clem was telling me about it last night.'

Saffron forced a smile. If only they knew!

'How's the book going?' Caro said.

Saffron perked up. 'Really well, actually. It's nearly finished. Well, *I* think it's gone well. Whether any publishers agree is a different matter.'

'You'll be fighting them off,' Caro declared. 'I can't wait to read it, I just know you're going to be my new favourite novelist!'

'Darlings!' Now Babs popped up in front of them, her hair even more red and Fraggle-like than ever. She was wearing a long, chiffon cape, the midnight-blue colour clashing with the summery day.

She made a big show of air-kissing Caro. 'How are you? Down from the Big Smoke?'

'Are you a witch?' Milo said, looking at this

330

strange newcomer.

'Darling, don't be rude,' Caro told him. 'Yes, we're here for the weekend, Babs. It's lovely to see you.'

Rex was signing autographs. 'Nice cape, Mrs Sax,' he called over. 'Vintage Ozzy Clarke, isn't it?'

Babs's eyes widened. 'I bought it in 1979, on the King's Road. Oh, Rex, you are clever.'

'I'm a big fan of some of his stuff.'

Saffron laughed. 'Rex is probably the only straight man I have ever met who gets more excited about clothes than I do.'

Tom wandered back up. 'Hi, Babs. Do you fancy a pint of this cider? It's pretty good.'

'Ooh! I'm not sure I could manage a whole one. Can you get me a half?'

'Coming right up.'

'Don't worry, I'll come with you. It does wonders for one's ego to be seen on the arm of such a *handsome* young man.'

'I'll leave you guys to it,' Caro said, laughing. 'Come and find us later.'

As they wandered off, an ample-breasted young woman who had been poured into a skin-tight minidress sashayed up to the stall. Her skin-tone was bright orange, her long dark mane backcombed to within an inch of its life. She ignored Saffron and zoomed in on Rex. 'Hiya,' she pouted, holding out a hand with Stars and Stripes talons. 'I'm Stacey Turner. My parents own the Jolly Boot.'

'Ah yes,' Rex said, shaking it. 'Your dad's mentioned you.'

A look of delight spread across Stacey's face. 'Ohmigod! What did he say?' She stopped and composed herself, shaking her hair haughtily. 'Yeah, well, since I've started this beauty course I'm not in the pub much.' She batted false eyelashes. 'Mum tells me you're putting on this fashion show. I suppose you'll be looking for make-up artists . . .'

Rex looked at Saffron for help. 'Er, will we?'

'It's a *fashion* show,' Stacey said patronizingly. 'Here.' She rifled through her rip-off Jimmy Choo shoulder bag. 'Take one of my cards. Give me a call nearer the time and we can discuss looks.' And with that, she waltzed off, giving her bum a final shake for good measure.

Rex seemed to have lost the power of speech. 'That reminds me,' he eventually managed. 'I need to finalize things with your man at *Soirée* about make-up.'

'All sorted, don't worry.'

'Really?' He looked relieved. 'What would I do without you?'

'Have a Jordan lookalike doing the make-up?'

As they grinned, there was an unexpected crackle of something between them. Embarrassed, Saffron turned away and pounced on a passing woman.

'Hello, there! Have you got two minutes so I can tell you all about the fabulous fashion show we're putting on here in Churchminster?'

*   *   *

By six o'clock things had started winding down. Rex had been on and off his phone all day making work calls, so Saffron called Tom over from the beer tent to help pack things up. He looked in the first stages of drunken contentment, eyes

332

beginning to droop at the corners. Saffron on the other hand was tired, thirsty, and had burnt the end of her nose.

'At least someone's having fun,' she said sarcastically.

Tom's face was flushed. 'Don't be like that, Saff.'

'I didn't mean it like that,' she said tartly, knowing perfectly well how it had sounded. She watched as he went to lift a box up. 'Watch it!' she said, as a pile of leaflets went flying.

He shrugged helplessly. 'Sorry.'

'Here, I'll do it,' she said, bending down and pushing his hands aside. She ignored the reproachful look. 'By the way, Rex has invited us to dinner at the Jolly Boot.'

'I'm not hungry,' he said abruptly. It was so out of character Saffron was shocked.

'Tom!'

There was a long pause. He sighed. 'We need to spend some time together, Saff. Alone. I mean, I thought you wanted to talk about the wedding . . .'

'Of course I do,' she said. 'Look, Rex asked me and Mum, and you know how excited she gets . . . I didn't want to be rude.' *You could have said no*, a little voice said at the back of her head. 'Don't you want to spend time with your brother?' she asked, her guilt coming out as aggression.

He stared at her, then shook his head. 'I'll take this back.' He grabbed the box and walked off.

Ambrose Fraser chose this moment to wobble past their stall, supported by Jed and Benedict. He was clutching a glow stick, which he waggled at the sky.

'Ayia Napa! Ayia Napa!'

Benedict looked as gorgeous and collected as

333

ever, in an immaculate pale-blue shirt. 'Hi, Saffron.'

'Having fun, gents?' She tried to smile.

'Loads,' Jed said wryly. 'No, Sir Ambrose, this way!'

* * *

Caro and Benedict joined them for dinner in the end, and they all sat round one of the circular tables in the Jolly Boot's dining room. Rex was on terrific form, bantering with Benedict and making the girls laugh. By contrast Tom was rather quiet, sitting back and observing the conversation rather than taking part in it. He'd swapped his beer for a pint of orange juice and lemonade.

'Is Tom OK?' Caro whispered to Saffron.

'He's just a bit tired at the moment,' Saffron said.

Caro looked sympathetic. 'Work?'

'Something like that,' Saffron agreed, feeling a bit shitty for pointing the finger of blame away from herself. She didn't want to tell Caro they'd been bickering all day. Not here, anyway.

She caught up with Tom at the bar after the main course. 'Are you all right?'

'Yeah, fine. A bit of a headache.'

'Your hangover's probably kicking in,' she said, sounding far more sanctimonious than she'd meant to.

'Actually, I've had a headache all week, eye strain probably.'

'Sorry,' she mumbled, feeling like a complete bitch.

He eyed her curiously. 'You're acting really weirdly.'

334

'No, I'm not,' she said defensively.

'Hey, guys!' Rex came up and put his arms round their shoulders. 'I'm just getting a round in, what do you fancy?'

'Actually, I might take a rain check,' Tom said.

'You sure?' Rex asked.

'I'm pretty whacked.' He looked at Saffron. 'Do you mind?'

'Um, no, babe. I think there's some paracetamol in the bathroom cupboard,' she said, trying to make amends.

'Thanks.' He got his wallet out. 'What do I owe?'

'I've got it,' Rex said.

Tom chucked two twenties down on the bar as if he hadn't heard. 'Can you make my excuses?'

Rex frowned. 'Are you all right, bro?'

Tom straightened up and looked him squarely in the face. Saffron was suddenly aware of just how big and powerful the brothers were.

'Actually, I was wondering the same thing about you,' Tom said.

Saffron looked between them. There was some kind of weird tension.

'Tom, what do you mean?' she asked.

He glanced back at her. 'Nothing.'

Putting his wallet back in his jeans pocket he leant over and gave her a dry peck on the cheek. 'See you later.'

'What's up with him?' Rex asked, as they watched him walk off.

Saffron laughed uncomfortably. 'I have no idea.'

Chapter 48

London

Harriet was having a rare night in by herself. After she'd finished work that night, she'd popped to Tesco Metro to replenish supplies. She'd been staying at Zack's so much her flat was beginning to grow cobwebs.

She was just about to sit down with her dinner and a glass of wine when Zack called.

'How's my favourite girl?'

'Good.' She put the plate down. 'How are you?'

He sounded upbeat. 'We've had some good news.'

'Oh yes, and what's that?' She smiled.

'Seems like all our hard work isn't going unnoticed. The centre's being put up for an award: "Community Project of the Year". You know, the one sponsored by the *Daily Standard*.'

'Zack, that's just brilliant!' Harriet had a slight confession to make. 'Actually, I did have an idea. You know Catherine, my old boss? She caught something about it on the grapevine.'

He sounded astonished. 'Really? Why didn't you say anything before?'

'Because I didn't want to get your hopes up if it wasn't true.' Harriet suddenly felt anxious. 'You're not cross, are you?'

'Cross? I'm over the bloody moon!' It was a great thing just to get shortlisted; the winners were given a substantial cash prize and access to all the right sorts of people. Last year Prince Charles had been guest of honour at the ceremony.

'I don't want to get too carried away yet,' he continued. 'But I was wondering if I could ask you a favour.'

'Ask away.'

'They're sending down a journalist and photographer, to get the info on the place and take a few pictures.'

'You'll be famous!'

He didn't sound thrilled at the prospect. 'God, who wants to see my ugly mug plastered across the papers?'

She smiled. 'There's nothing ugly about your mug.'

'Yeah, well. It's short notice, but do you think you'd be able to come down tomorrow morning, while they're here? You know how these things work, and I don't want to put my foot in it.'

'Worried they'll get your bad side?' she teased.

'Yeah, something like that.'

Harriet thought quickly. She could get the work-experience girl to cover the phone for a few hours, and she was sure Fiona, her editor, wouldn't mind, as it was for such a good cause.

'I'd love to.'

'Great! See you about 10 a.m. ?'

'See you then.'

Chapter 49

Churchminster

'Tom, it's me.'

'I know it's you, Saff. I'd never forget your dulcet tones.'

'Yeah, of course.' She was still feeling a bit on edge.

'Got much writing done today?'

'Yeah, loads. Listen, Tom . . .' She stopped, wondering how to phrase it. Tom had seemed tired but OK on Sunday morning, but they hadn't really had any time alone to talk properly since.

'What was that thing between you and Rex? You know, in the pub on Saturday?'

'I don't follow.'

'By the bar. When you kind of faced up to him.'

'I wasn't facing up to anything.'

He was lying, she was sure. Saffron had a flash of guilt as she remembered that weird electric moment between her and Rex on the green. There was no way Tom could have seen anything, was there?

'So it, er, wasn't about me?' she asked nervously.

There was a pause. 'What makes you say that?'

Saffron swallowed. 'Maybe the fact that Rex and I have been spending quite a bit of time together because of the show . . . I mean, you do know there's nothing to worry about, don't you?'

'Of course I do,' he said shortly.

Well, this was awkward. 'I didn't mean anything by it,' she mumbled.

338

He didn't say anything.

'Tom?'

'Yeah.' He sighed. 'Look, babe. I know things aren't great at the moment between us.'

There, he'd said it. Saffron felt her throat close over.

His voice softened. 'I know it's been hard, with both of us doing our own thing.'

'Mmm,' she mumbled, suddenly pathetically close to tears.

'You OK?'

'Yes,' she whispered. 'I don't know, it just suddenly feels a bit *weird* . . .'

He took a moment to answer. 'I know.'

'I don't like it. I miss you.'

'Me too. It isn't for ever, babe. We've just got to make more of an effort, look to the future. We've got so many amazing things to look forward to.'

'Yeah.' Saffron knew she should say something reassuring back, but nothing was coming.

'OK, then,' Tom said eventually. He sounded a bit uncertain. 'So tell me about your day. Did you get much writing done?'

He'd already asked that. Saffron blinked. 'Uh, a couple more thousand words.'

'Great! You must be pleased.'

'Yeah, it should be finished soon.'

'Good timing for the show!'

Saffron stared unhappily out of the window. It all felt horribly cautious and polite, like two strangers dancing round each other.

Chapter 50

London

Aunty Win was vigorously mopping the floor when Harriet arrived the next morning. She beamed when she saw her.

' 'Arriet! Zachary told me you were coming for our big day.'

Win was wearing a green and yellow patterned creation, her head encased by a bright orange turban. The photographer was going to have a field day with such a flamboyant subject.

'Here, let me finish that,' Harriet told her. 'You don't want to get your outfit dirty.'

Win handed her the mop. 'You're a good girl, 'Arriet. The cleaner's been in, but, between you, me and the gatepost, she's not good. Too slapdash! We need this place looking as shiny as a new button for our newspaper friends.'

It was a relief to see Win back to her normal self after the knife drama. Zack had studiously avoided the subject ever since, but they all knew this nomination couldn't have come at a better time. A door slammed behind them, and Harriet turned to see him striding in. He'd had his hair cut again, and was wearing her favourite light-blue shirt, the one that matched his eyes. As usual Harriet's heart did a little leap. *I can't believe he's mine!*

He came over and planted a soft kiss on her cheek. 'Thanks for coming.'

'I wouldn't miss it for the world! What time are they getting here?'

'Half an hour.' Zack pulled a face. 'I must admit, I'm not really looking forward to this bit.'

'Zachary's getting all camera shy,' Win told Harriet.

'It's not that, I'm just not comfortable being in the spotlight. I don't do this job to get recognition.'

Harriet smiled at him. Zack's modesty was just one of the many nice things about him. 'Why don't you ask if they'll take pictures of Aunty Win instead? They'd love her.'

He looked thoughtful. 'Do you think?'

Harriet smiled at Win, whose face had lit up like a circus sideshow. 'I don't see why not, Aunty Win's as much a part of this place as you are.'

Zack nodded. 'That's a great idea. What do you reckon, Aunty Win? Ready for worldwide fame?'

Win's face split into a huge grin. 'I thought you'd never ask!'

The *Daily Standard* people took one look at Win and fell in love with her. Once Harriet had explained that Zack didn't want to be the main focus of the piece, they were more than happy to concentrate on Win, with a brief mention of Zack and how the centre had started. After the photo shoot, in which she posed in a variety of flamboyant attitudes—and even suggested ideas to the photographer—Win dragged the female journalist off on a tour of the centre.

'Did you really not fancy it?' Harriet asked Zack, as they watched Win throw back her head and cackle with laughter at something. She certainly was providing sparkle for the story.

'Fancy what?'

'Being a bigger part of the whole thing. You've worked so hard, Zack, it's a shame people don't

341

know about it.'

He smiled, watching Win work her magic on the journalist. 'How could I deny Win her big moment? She's loving it.'

'Zachary!' Aunty Win bellowed across the hall. 'Come and have some cake with Helen and me. You too, 'Arriet.' She hooted with laugher. 'All this modelling has left me starving.'

Chapter 51

Churchminster

The next day Win was the main picture on the front of the newspaper, with a big double-page spread inside. The story got picked up on immediately, and *BBC News at Six* even featured it that evening, as a feel-good piece after a bulletin about the increase in knife crime.

Rex was reading the *Daily Standard* when Saffron went round that evening. 'Have you seen this?' He waved the paper at Saffron as soon as she walked in. 'I saw it when I was up in London today. Full story page five.'

Saffron looked at the headline. 'THE SAVIOUR OF GATSBY' stretched over the two pages, accompanied by a fantastic picture of a large, smiling black woman. 'The Gatsby Road Estate was once the most notorious place in London,' she started reading aloud, 'but now a run-down little community centre has breathed new life back into the area.' She looked up at Rex. 'This is the place Harriet's volunteering at! I must call her.' Her eyes scanned the page. 'Any mention of Harriet's bloke?'

'I don't know, who is he? There's a bit about someone called Zack, how he started the centre.'

'I wish there was a picture, I'm dying to know what he looks like.'

Rex had gone quiet. She realized he was looking at her. 'What are you thinking?' she asked. She hadn't seen him look so excited in ages.

'I'm thinking we should have this as our charity.'

'What?'

'I think we should go with this instead. It's perfect.'

'What?' She tried to take it in. 'It's not very "fashion", is it?'

'True,' he conceded, 'but there's a really good buzz about this story. Everyone was reading it on the way home. It's even been all over the news.'

'Has it?' Saffron had been sitting at her laptop all day.

He fixed her with those charismatic eyes and Saffron felt a funny thrill she couldn't explain. 'Think about it, Saff!' he said. 'This one little community centre has become a beacon of hope for society. Think of it like good triumphing over evil.'

'OK, now you're going too far.' Saffron tried to get her business head on. This was certainly a lot more relevant than the Tibetan eco-warriors, though. 'Do you really think it would work?'

He nodded confidently. 'This is the zeitgeist we've been waiting for. The London lot will *love* it.'

He started striding up and down the kitchen, fizzing with enthusiasm. 'We need to get Harriet and this Zack down. Can you see if they can come this weekend?'

'Hold on, we don't know if they're interested yet!'

Rex stopped pacing and looked at her. 'Saff. This is an amazing opportunity for them. It even said in the article how the centre is struggling with funding.' He knew he had her. 'So you'll call, right?'

'OK! Rex, you'd better be right about this.'

'I am, trust me.'

She stood, looking at that handsome, confident face. He didn't seem to have a care in the world, despite what Tom thought. Had Tom got it wrong, after all?

'Rex, is everything all right at the moment?'

'It is now we've got our charity!'

'No, I mean with you.' She looked at him, trying to fathom it out. 'You can talk to me if you want to, you know, about anything.'

He stared at her. 'Course I'm all right, Saff, why wouldn't I be?' His lips curled up wryly. 'Unless you count a minor breakdown from putting on this show.'

'You and me both!' she laughed.

He came over and put an arm round her, the weight of his muscles heavy against her shoulders. 'We're gonna get through this, Saff, you'd better believe it.'

All she could focus on was his heartbeat, high above hers. It was as if she had been walking round in a daze, and suddenly her whole body had come alive.

Chapter 52

London

Harriet and Zack were walking to Win's for supper. Saffron had rung her that morning with the potentially life-changing offer. It was all either of them had thought of since.

'So, what are your thoughts?' she asked.

'About this fashion show?' Zack looked at Harriet. 'It sounds incredible. Are you sure they're serious?'

'Completely. Saffron is really excited about it.'

'Wow!' Zack blew out his cheeks, considering.

Harriet tucked her arm into his, feeling the hard muscles against her skin. 'I think it's brilliant.'

Zack was quiet for a moment. 'But what's in it for them?'

'What do you mean?'

'Come on, Harriet,' he said, smiling wryly. 'Nothing in this life comes for free.'

Saffron had confided in her about the Handbag Haven disaster, but she didn't want Zack to think he was the last resort. 'Rex wants to,' she made quote marks with her fingers, ' "Give something back". He's had some sort of epiphany.'

Zack raised an eyebrow. 'Well, if that's the case I take my hat off to the bloke.'

'So is that a yes?' Harriet was really excited at the prospect of Fashion Cares; it could do such good things for the centre. With the added bonus of being held in her home village.

'Yeah, I suppose so.'

'You don't sound very pleased.'

'I am. It's just that whole limelight thing again.' He sighed. 'I guess I'm just being a grumpy old git.'

She slid her hands round his waist. 'You're not being grumpy, I'd feel a bit self-conscious, too, if it was me.'

'Lucky Win's there to lap up the attention, eh?'

She smiled. 'Exactly. Think of yourself as the silent partner.'

Zack looked down at her, face expectant. 'It could be bloody good for us, couldn't it?'

'It could be amazing!'

He smiled and kissed her.

*   *   *

Win wasn't in when they got there, so Zack let himself in with his key. A few minutes later she came bustling into the kitchen and dumped two full shopping bags down on the table. 'Gita at No. 43 has got her gallstones back again, and she asked me to pick up her lottery ticket.'

'You should take a load off sometimes,' Zack chided.

Win made a 'pff' sound. 'What am I going to achieve, sitting around all day with my feet up? You fuss worse than an old woman, Zachary.' She winked at Harriet.

They started to help her unpack. 'I popped round to see Alf earlier,' Win said, as she put a can of tinned tomatoes in the cupboard. 'Seems like he's taken Bert under his wing. They're off to play bowls tomorrow.'

'I'm so pleased.' Harriet knew taking Bert down to the centre had been a good idea. He'd been welcomed with open arms; especially when Alf had found out they'd both served in the same places in the army.

Win was frowning. 'I still can't believe I didn't know. About Bert, I mean.'

'Win, you can't be expected to know everyone on the estate.' Zack smiled. 'It's a big place, and from what it sounds like, the poor old guy hardly ever left his flat.'

Win folded away the shopping bag purposefully. 'At least we've got him now.' She shot a sly look at them and patted her hair. 'I had another person ask for my autograph in the minimart. My, I'm getting good at this fame lark.'

'I knew all this attention would go to her head,' Zack told Harriet.

'What are you talking about? There's not much excitement an old woman like me gets in her dwindling years.'

Zack laughed. 'I think you do all right, Aunty Win.' He glanced at Harriet. 'Actually, there was something we wanted to discuss with you.'

Win raised an eyebrow. 'Well, let's start on dinner and we can talk about it.' She handed Zack a red pepper. 'You can chop that. 'Arriet, you do the mushrooms, please.'

They worked away in silence for a few moments. 'So?' Aunty Win said. 'Out with it!'

'Well,' Zack put down his knife, 'Harriet's friend is putting on a fashion charity show, and they want to do it with us. You know, raise money for the centre.'

'Uh-huh.'

'It's going to be called Fashion Cares, and it's being held in Churchminster, the village Harriet comes from.'

'Uh-huh.'

'Well, what do you think? They'd like you to be the poster-girl for it, seeing as you're such a celebrity now.' He grinned cheekily.

Win carried on chopping. 'And when is this show?'

'The first of July,' Zack told her.

'Five weeks,' Harriet added.

Win whistled. 'What, you going to magic it out of the air?'

'We don't have to worry about that side of things, Aunty Win, it's all been taken care of,' Harriet told her. She watched as the old lady carried on her methodical chopping.

'Well?' Zack repeated. 'What do you think?'

Eventually Win put the knife down. 'What I *tink*, is that it's a brilliant idea! So why are you standing gassing when you've got a fashion show to be getting on with?'

Chapter 53

Churchminster

On Wednesday lunchtime a press release announced that Fashion Cares would now be supporting the Gatsby Road Community Centre as their chosen charity. It was still a massive risk, making the change so late in the day. But all they could do was sit back and wait, and pray no one would back out on them.

On top of it all Saffron was getting seriously

348

stressed about the VIP list. They still hadn't got enough big names, and people weren't getting back to her. It didn't help that Rex kept asking her about Savannah Sexton every five minutes.

Even though she'd only been out of the showbiz world a few months, it had started to dawn on Saffron that it was long enough to lose her cachet. It had been different when she'd been working in the hustle and bustle of *Soirée*, taking agents out for lunch and building up contacts. But now she was out in the sticks, miles from the action—and trying to organize a fashion show to boot. It was hopeless. Anyone who lived outside the M25 was *dead* to these people. Plus everybody knew celebrities took off on months-long holidays in the summer. She sighed loudly, cursing herself for ever getting involved in the first place.

Across the dining room table Rex looked up. 'What's up?'

'Nothing. Aside from the fact I seem to have lost my powers of persuasion for our celebrity guests. I doubt I could get Timmy Mallet at the moment.'

Rex looked alarmed. 'Are things really that bad? I thought we'd confirmed some names.'

'I'm waiting to hear back from their people, which is an entirely different thing.'

Rex tried to look on the bright side. 'At least we haven't had any straight nos.'

'Oh, we have, don't worry,' she said darkly. 'I just haven't told you about them.'

Rex pulled a face. 'You're making me a bit nervous!'

'*You're* nervous! Can't we say we've got Bibi yet? It would make such a difference.'

He sat back in his seat. 'They still don't want us

349

to.'

'Rex, this is killing me!'

'I know, Saff.' He looked apologetic. 'What can I do? My hands are tied.'

The bad feeling came from nowhere. 'Rex, are you bullshitting me?'

'Bullshitting you?'

'About Bibi Brown. We have got her, haven't we?'

He looked insulted. 'Of course we have! Look, trust me. I know how these things work.'

'Trust is about all I can do at the moment,' she grumbled. 'I thought celebs were bad, but they're nothing to these bloody designers!' She stood up.

'Where are you going?' he asked.

'To the loo. That's OK, isn't it?'

Rex's eyes followed her. 'Aren't you going to take your phone with you?'

She looked at him in disbelief. 'I'm not exactly going to take a call from Cheryl Cole's agent sitting on the toilet, am I?'

He grinned sheepishly. 'Sorry.'

She threw him a sardonic smile over her shoulder. 'You can set the stopwatch if it makes you feel better.'

Byron Heights had five downstairs cloakrooms, each the size of a double bedroom. She chose the farthest one away, the one with the wooden throne in the corner. She locked the door and sank down on the seat.

She felt a sick lurch again at everything they still had to do. This bloody show was going to give her gallstones! Or whatever it was you got when you were stressed out of your head. So much for moving to the country for a quiet life. Saffron couldn't remember ever feeling this bad at *Soirée*, even when she'd had a million things on her plate.

But then again, she hadn't had a book to finish back then. Or been battling ever more confused thoughts about the state of her relationship.

Not wanting to go there, *refusing* to go there, Saffron stood up and stared hard at herself in the mirror. Maybe it was a good thing she was miles away in the Cotswolds. Her hair had never looked so bad. The dark roots she could just about get away with, in a rock-chick Courtney-Love way, but the rest of it was all split ends, and sprouting off in different directions. She was starting to resemble one of the weird half dead plants her mother kept dotted about her conservatory.

As she walked out, Saffron suddenly felt overwhelmed by gloom. She went back into the dining room and slumped down in her chair.

'Has something happened?' Rex asked, looking concerned.

'My hair, among other things.'

'Oh.' His lips twitched. 'I did wonder what look you were channelling.'

'Try that scarecrow in the field down the road.'

'It's not that bad. Let's have a look.' He stood up and came round to stand behind her.

'Whoa, what are you doing?' she asked, as Rex's fingers started to move expertly through her hair.

'Do you want me to give you a trim?'

'I didn't know hairdressing was one of your many skills.'

'Come on, I've worked with enough hairdressers.'

'That doesn't make you an expert.' He put his hands on her shoulders, their warmth pushing down through her body. Saffron felt a funny little

351

frisson where she least expected it.

'We need a break. Let's go and sort you out, Worzel Gummidge.'

*   *   *

They sat in the kitchen, in front of the antique mirror that hung on one wall. The mirror was at odds with the kitchen—the only modern room in the house—but somehow it worked. That was Byron Heights for you, Saffron thought, throwing up quirks and contradictions everywhere you looked.

Like having Rex Sullivan, supermodel, cut her hair with a pair of kitchen scissors. As she watched him in the mirror, his long fingers dextrously moving over her head, she had to admit he at least looked as if he knew what he was doing.

'Who taught you to cut hair?' she asked, very aware that his crotch was inches from her face.

'Oh, Ken Paves gave me the odd lesson when I worked with him.'

Saffron raised an eyebrow. Ken Paves was, like, the hottest hairstylist in Hollywood. The man had practically *made* Jessica Simpson.

'Show-off.'

He laughed. 'You asked!'

'I know.' Saffron smiled. She fell silent, watching him again. It was relaxing, sitting there. She had no sense of time passing, and there was also something in the way he ran his hands through her hair that made her feel slightly breathless. Her scalp tingled every time he touched her.

'Easy, tiger!' she said in alarm, as a chunk of hair fell to the floor.

352

'Sorry, that bit has been annoying me for ages.'

She eyed him in the mirror. 'Have you been doing a silent critique of my hair or something?'

He smiled. 'I think you've got cool hair, Saff.'

'Humph,' she said, trying to ignore the little rush of pleasure as he brushed a few stray clippings off her neck.

'There, finished.' He blew on her skin, starting off a wave of uncontrollable little thrills through her body. It finished under her vest top, her nipples stiff and aroused. *For Christ's sake!* she told herself angrily.

Rex held her head, and looked into the mirror. 'What do you think?'

Saffron turned to one side, then the other. It actually looked pretty good. Rex was an instinctive hairdresser, only cutting where it was needed.

'I think I'll have to come back here next time I need a trim.'

He looked pleased at the compliment, eyes roving over his work. 'You see, I've just cut in a bit, here. To show off your lovely long neck.'

Was he trying to pull? Saffron started to blush before she knew it. 'Thanks,' she mumbled, getting up. Why did he make her feel like this?

'Here.' He leant over and touched her cheek. 'Another hair.'

Saffron's skin burnt at his touch. Embarrassed, she stepped back and looked round for her bag. 'Anyway, I'd better be getting back.'

'OK, sure.' For the first time she saw a flicker of uncertainty cross his face. But he immediately got down to business. 'We've made the right choice haven't we? I mean supporting the Gatsby Road?'

Saffron met his gaze. 'Let's hope so.'

Chapter 54

On Friday evening, Harriet turned her Golf into the drive of Clanfield Hall. As the huge building rose out of the landscape, she waited for the inevitable reaction. Beside her, Zack gave a low whistle. 'Bloody hell!'

'It's my parents' home, really. That's mine, Gate Cottage,' she said as the car went past a sweet little gatehouse set back from the entrance.

'Quite an upbringing though, eh?'

Harriet didn't smile back. She hated this part: when she brought people home, and they suddenly started treating her like she was different. Zack glanced at her, and went back to looking out of the window.

'Course, it's nothing compared to the children's home. We had bigger windows, for a start.'

She shot him a grateful smile. Zack got her so perfectly.

'I've never turned up unannounced before. I hope Daddy's not off somewhere.' As she pulled up in the huge gravel turning circle in front of the house, she saw the light in her father's study was on. Her stomach turned. *Please behave yourself, Daddy.* If he got the shotgun out, even as a joke, she honestly didn't know if she could cope.

The Hall was still and quiet as they let themselves in. Harriet could see Zack taking in the corridors framed with family portraits of her ancestors, and the suit of armour that stood guard at the bottom of the sweeping staircase. Somewhere a clock chimed, the noise fading into the vastness of the building.

'Miss Harriet?'

'Jesus!' Zack jumped a foot in the air as a tall, suited figure appeared from nowhere.

'Oh, hello, Hawkins.' Harriet was used to their butler's noiseless, genie-like arrival.

He nodded, deferential yet regal. 'Miss Harriet. I wasn't aware we were expecting you?'

She smiled brightly. 'I thought I'd surprise Daddy!'

The butler's eyes strayed imperceptibly to her left for a second.

'Hawkins, this is Zack,' she said.

The butler gave a little bow. 'Delighted to have you staying with us, Zack.'

'Thanks, Hawkins,' Zack said easily.

Harriet looked around. 'Is Daddy about? I saw his study light on.'

For perhaps the first time in her life, she saw wariness on Hawkins's implacable face. 'Ah, yes. Sir Ambrose is in the public house.'

Harriet didn't follow. 'The public house? You mean Daddy's gone to the Jolly Boot?'

A muscle in Hawkins's cheek twitched. 'If you'd like to follow me.'

'What's going on?' Zack whispered, as the butler led them down a labyrinth of corridors towards the east wing.

Harriet shook her head. 'I have no idea.'

The butler eventually drew up in front of a closed door. Behind it could be heard the muffled beat of what sounded like pop music. Harriet blinked. What was going on?

Hawkins knocked on the door. No answer. He tried the handle and they were hit by a blast of

355

music. As he pushed the door open, Harriet couldn't believe her eyes. The pink drawing room had gone, replaced by what looked like a real-life pub. A bar stood in one corner, complete with beer pumps and stools and bottles of spirits lined up on the shelves behind. All the priceless rugs had disappeared, replaced by a selection of wooden chairs and tables. As Harriet stepped into the room, the wooden floor felt sticky underfoot.

The music was coming from a jukebox by the wall, and at the other end of the room her father was playing snooker with Jed round a full-size snooker table. He was tie-less and wearing what looked like a felt skullcap on his head.

Hawkins cleared his throat discreetly, and when that didn't work, he went over and turned the jukebox down. Ambrose looked up from potting a red ball.

'Yes, man, what is it?'

'Miss Harriet is here to see you,' Hawkins said solemnly. 'And her friend, Zack.'

Ambrose looked across at the door and his whole face lit up. 'Harriet! What the dickens are you doing here? Did I know you were coming?'

She smiled tentatively. 'Er, I thought I'd surprise you.'

Ambrose opened his arms. 'Well, come here then, girl, and give me a hug!'

She ran over and flung her arms round him. He squeezed her tightly. 'There you are, then, don't strangle me.'

Over his shoulder, Harriet raised an eyebrow at Jed, and he gave her rather a sheepish smile.

She pulled back and looked more closely at her father. 'Daddy, what are you wearing on your

356

head?'

Ambrose chuckled. 'Jed, do the honours.'

Jed looked rather pained. 'Sir Ambrose . . .'

'Come on, man, don't shilly-shally! He's got a crack aim,' he told Harriet.

Looking like he'd rather be anywhere but there, Jed picked up some sort of foam ball and took aim. He hesitated, as if throwing an object at his boss's head went against the very grain of his nature. Then his arm came back and the ball flew across the room. It landed on the side of Ambrose's head, and stuck there like a bizarre antenna.

Ambrose chortled with laughter. 'It's one of those drinking games I bought off the Internet. It really is a capital way to pass the time. We've been having no end of fun, eh, young Jed?'

There was a flash of humour in Jed's green eyes. 'Yes, Sir Ambrose.' He put his cue down. 'I'd better be getting back, though, there's still work to be done.'

'Yes, yes, very good.'

'Maybe we'll catch up tomorrow?' Harriet said to Jed pointedly. She and Jed went way back, and she knew he'd give her the full story. Had her father gone completely mad? *Oh God, she should have come back sooner and seen him . . .*

Jed smiled neutrally. 'Sure.' He nodded at her and Sir Ambrose. 'Have a good night.' He walked down the long room and, with an acknowledgement to Zack, swiftly left.

Harriet looked back at her father. 'Daddy, why don't you have a little sit-down?'

Ambrose grunted. 'What do I want to do that for? I was about to trounce young Jed three games in a row!' Suddenly, his eyes landed on the stranger standing by the door.

Harriet's stomach lurched. 'Daddy, I'd like you to meet my friend, Zack.'

Zack smiled and took a step forward, but all the cordiality had vanished from Ambrose's face. He stared at Zack, taking in the cropped hair and trainers, the casual, trendy clothes. The hawk-like eyes settled on the earring.

'Well, well, well. What have we got here, then?'

*   *   *

They ate dinner that night in the formal dining room, a space so huge and echoing it took five minutes just to get up and pass the salt and pepper. It wasn't the most comfortable of environments, and Harriet suspected her father had chosen it deliberately. He'd smartened up for dinner and put his tie back on, his snow-white hair brushed back on his head.

Cook had prepared three plump roast wood pigeons, which Ambrose informed Zack had been winging happily around the estate only hours earlier. If he'd been trying to unsettle Zack it wasn't working. He had cheerfully digested the information and was now eating his food with gusto.

Harriet had been filling her father in about Fashion Cares, but he wasn't really listening. Sitting at the far end of the table, Ambrose was methodically chewing—and checking Zack out with the lazy menace of a hawk circling its prey.

'So what is it you do, again?'

'Zack's a community action leader,' Harriet said.

358

'You know, at the centre I'm volunteering at.'

'Community action leader.' Ambrose grunted. 'What, fancy yourself as a bit of a superhero, then?'

'Daddy,' Harriet chided, but Zack smiled.

'I agree it's a bit of a silly title, Sir Ambrose. Unfortunately I didn't get to think it up.'

'Someone was probably paid silly money to do that.'

'Knowing the council, most probably.'

'Bloody councils. We have a hell of a time with our local one.'

Zack grinned. 'I'm with you there.'

Ambrose stared back, not altogether unfriendly. 'So, Harriet, is this your boyfriend or what?'

'Dad-dy!'

Ambrose's mouth twitched. 'Harriet blushes at anything,' he told Zack. He turned to her. 'Remember that time you started crying when our old lurcher got locked on the blacksmith's bitch and we had to get the vet out to pull them apart? You shut yourself away in your room and Cook had to entice you out with her homemade shortbread.'

Harriet blushed beetroot. 'I did not!'

Ambrose winked at Zack. 'It wouldn't have been so bad if she'd been a young whippersnapper, but she was twenty-one at the time.'

'That is a lie,' Harriet said hotly. 'I was eighteen, actually.'

'A sensitive type, eh?' Zack smiled.

'You can say that again!' Ambrose gave a short bark of laughter. 'Now, then, young man, can I interest you in a glug of port?'

Harriet nearly dropped her fork. Her father was

very particular about who he took port with. This was quite a breakthrough.

Several minutes later Zack excused himself to go to the loo. Ambrose eyed his daughter down the table. 'Is it love with this Zack, then?'

'Daddy! You can't ask me that.'

'Why not? It's a perfectly reasonable question, isn't it?'

'So you do like him?' she said, steering Ambrose off the subject.

'He's all right, I suppose, apart from that damned silly thing in his ear. Some sort of new-fangled hearing aid, is it?'

Harriet couldn't believe this was going so well. 'I was a bit nervous about bringing him back to meet you,' she admitted.

Sir Ambrose shot her a perceptive look. 'What, thought I'd get the shotgun out, did you?'

'Something like that.' She smiled.

'Ha!' He leant back in his chair. 'I know I can be an awkward sod, Harriet.'

'Daddy, I didn't say that.'

'You don't have to.' He steepled his fingers, looking thoughtful. 'I've been doing a lot of thinking since your mother's been away, you know, about what makes a person happy.' He shook his head. 'Who would have thought I'd end up with a bloody wife gallivanting off over the world on some mercy mission?'

'You're as proud of her as I am,' she told him fondly.

'You're right, I won't deny it. What I'm saying here, Harriet, is that a chap has to let a woman be herself, no matter what tomfoolery she's got in her head.' He nodded. 'So if this Zack chap makes you

360

happy, that's good enough for me.'

She was nearly moved to tears. 'Thank you, Daddy.'

*   *   *

'I can't believe your dad's a "Sir".' They were lying together on Harriet's bed, Zack's arms wrapped around Harriet.

'Don't tell anyone at the centre, will you?'

'Why not? I think it's pretty cool.'

'I just don't want people to get the wrong impression of me, think I'm some kind of stuck-up snob.'

'No one thinks that, because you're not. In fact you're the least snobbish person I've met in my life.' Zack sighed. 'Aunty Win would have loved to roll out the red carpet for you.'

'Oh, stop it!'

He was on a roll. 'I've got it! Why don't we have a prize-giving ceremony for our new coat hooks next week, and you can cut the ribbon?'

'Now you are pushing it!' Harriet pretended to put a cushion over his face.

'All right, I'm sorry,' Zack said, voice muffled. 'Please don't hurt me.'

'Cheeky sod,' Harriet said.

Zack kissed her and put one hand behind his head, looking round the room. Her selection of cuddly toys was still on the armchair in the corner, a somewhat faded poster of Take That looking incongruous next to the polished walnut wardrobe. On the wall above the writing desk were old photographs, one of a young, frizzy-haired Harriet with her best friend Camilla in their school blazers and boaters, another of Harriet at pony club camp aged eleven, looking very smart on her grey mare, Dizzy.

'Mummy likes to keep my room the same,' Harriet said apologetically. 'It makes her feel close to me, like I haven't grown up and moved out.'

'Your mum sounds nice, I'd like to meet her.'

Harriet snuggled into him. 'I know she'll love you. I can tell Daddy likes you already.'

He stroked her hair. 'I like him, too.'

Harriet sighed contentedly. This was all going brilliantly!

After a few minutes Zack looked down regretfully at the hard bulge forming under his trousers. 'I should go, look what you've done to me.'

Ambrose hadn't gone as far as letting Zack sharea bedroom with Harriet. He'd been put in the Turner bedroom, so called because there was a real-life one hanging on the wall.

Harriet rubbed Zack's crotch. 'Please don't.'

He groaned. 'Stop tempting me.'

'I want to tempt you.'

'What about your dad?'

'Shush about my father.' It was too weird. Zack gave a little sigh as she pulled his cock out of the front of his shorts and started caressing it. His hands moved over her skirt and down the front of her knickers, feeling the smooth skin of her Brazilian.

'It's no good, I have to be inside you.' She barely had time to look up, before he had pulled her on top of him. She wriggled out of her knickers and felt the familiar rush of pleasure as he entered her, then manoeuvred her hips to start riding him.

'Oh God . . .' He was so far gone it wasn't going to take long. Harriet started to go faster, her thighs gripping hard.

'Oh God . . . aah . . . Jesus!'

Harriet could literally feel him explode inside her. He put his arms around her and held her, his heart hammering against hers.

'You didn't come,' he gasped.

'Don't worry about that!'

Zack was the most amazingly considerate lover, and always made sure he brought her to orgasm first. She was happy to return the favour.

They lay there in the dark, their bodies slowly returning to normal. '*That* was amazing,' he said, when he'd eventually got his breath back.

'You're amazing.' She looked up and kissed him on the nose. As she lay back down, he held her so tightly it was almost hard to breathe.

'Harriet?'

'Yes?'

'I love you.'

Harriet lay still, letting the words sink in. Thinking that she wanted this moment to last for ever.

'Did you hear what I said?'

'Yes.' She sat up and looked into his eyes. 'Oh, Zack, I love you, too.'

Chapter 55

Rex had called a lunchtime summit at the Jolly Boot, which gave Harriet the chance to show Zack round the estate in the morning.

It was just before 1 p.m. as they set off down the driveway towards the village. As Zack's hand gently caressed her thigh, Harriet found it hard to concentrate. She had woken up literally giddy with love, and hadn't floated down since.

'What are you smiling at?' he asked. He looked more handsome than ever in dark jeans and a white T-shirt, cool new sunglasses propped up on his head.

'Oh, you know.'

He gave a cute little wink. Harriet literally wanted to honk the horn with happiness. They were really in love!

'So let me get this straight,' Zack said, as they reached the main road. 'Rex is the brother of Saffron's boyfriend Tom? And he's renting a house in the village?'

Harriet nodded. 'Yup. I must say, I'm quite excited about meeting him. It's not every day Churchminster has a supermodel in its midst.'

The pub car park was already filling up with people. Harriet reversed the Golf into a narrow space between two Range Rovers and they got out. Zack looked up at the wisteria creeping down the far wall, the long, golden building with its sage-green painted window frames. 'This is a bit more salubrious than the Crown.'

She smiled at the memory of the first pub he'd

taken her to, before anything had happened between them. How long ago that seemed now. 'Yes, but the Crown does have its own special charm.'

'That's one way of putting it.'

Saffron was already standing at the bar, looking as stunning as ever in an indecently short pair of shorts that only her long legs could get away with. Harriet's eyes swung to the man beside her and did a double take. He might be a bit more groomed than his brother, but Rex Sullivan really was the spitting image of Tom. It could be Tom, from the dark chocolate-brown eyes and manly chin to the wide shoulders. Saffron's face lit up when she saw Harriet.

'Yay, it's you!' she said, throwing her arms around her.

'Hullo, sweetpea!' Over Saffron's shoulder Harriet was unable to take her eyes off Rex. Up close, the resemblance was even more remarkable. There was an aura and glamour about Rex, from his flawless skin and dark, not-too-styled haircut, to the beautifully cut shirt and trousers. She stepped back and managed to wrench her gaze away, before Rex could think she was some kind of mad stalker.

Saffron did the introductions. 'Harriet, this is Rex, Tom's brother.'

Rex gave a relaxed smile. 'Hey there, Harriet. I've heard lots about you.'

Even though she was madly in love with Zack, Harriet's heart did a little flutter. Rex was so good-looking!

'All good things, I hope!' She turned to Zack. 'Zack, this is Rex Sullivan and my very dear friend,

Saffron Walden.'

The two men shook hands. Saffron kissed Zack on the cheek. 'I hear you're a fellow Londoner like me. We've got to stick together in these parts, you know.'

'So I've heard.' Zack smiled.

'Do you want a drink, Zack?' Rex asked.

'I'll have a lager, please, mate.'

*   *   *

Out in the beer garden, the conversation went straight to the show. 'Congratulations on the nomination,' Rex said. 'I've been reading up about the centre, all the work you've done. To do what you do—day in, day out—it's really inspiring.'

Zack looked rather flattered. 'We try our best,' he said, glancing at Harriet.

'I have to admit, I was slightly shitting myself about changing charities so late,' Saffron said. 'But fingers crossed, no one has pulled out.' She grinned weakly. 'Yet.'

'If they were going to pull out, they would have by now.' Rex put his hand round the back of her chair. 'I knew we'd be OK.'

Saffron rolled her eyes. 'It's quite annoying, working with an eternal optimist.'

'Harriet's been telling me about the show,' Zack told them. 'It sounds pretty cool.'

'You like what you're hearing? Great,' Saffron said.

'We're really grateful to you both,' Zack said. 'I can't tell you how much it means to the centre.'

'Hey, we're really happy to be involved with something so worthwhile,' Rex said. 'I'm actually loving it, you know, working with these designers who are going to be at the top of their game in a few years.'

'Let's talk business,' Saffron said. She dug in her bag and brought out four printouts, one for each of them. 'This is where we are so far.'

'Wow,' Harriet said, her eyes scanning down the list.

'Half of this is thanks to you, H.' Saffron grinned. Zack gave Harriet's knee a little squeeze under the table.

Rex was talking about his part in the show. 'Normally there'd be a compere, but I'm going to front it. I thought it would be good to give a speech at the beginning about the charity and what you do.'

Zack nodded. 'I can give you the full low-down.'

'What I was actually hoping,' Rex said, 'was that Win would do it with me. We could walk out together, I could welcome everyone and say a bit about the designers taking part, then pass the mike over to her.'

'Oh God.' Zack and Harriet started laughing.

'Is there something wrong?' Rex looked anxious. 'Do you think it'd be too much for her?'

'Quite the opposite,' Zack said. 'But you lot won't have to live with her ego afterwards.'

*   *   *

After a sociable lunch, which Rex insisted on paying for, they decided to walk back to Byron Heights. Zack and Rex were deep in conversation in front while Saffron and Harriet walked behind, arms linked.

'Everything sounds great,' Harriet told Saffron.

'I hope so.' Saffron sighed. 'I just want to tell people we've got Bibi.' She'd filled Harriet in on the Bibi situation over lunch.

'Honestly, darling, I wouldn't worry. Rex works in the industry, he knows how these things work.'

'And I know how things work in *my* industry. Oh well, I suppose it will be worth the wait. Apparently she's doing something amazing.' Saffron squeezed Harriet's hand. 'God, it is so good to have you back! I've been dying for some company.'

'Rex seems like fun.'

'Yeah, he is.' Saffron grinned at her. 'So, Zack's pretty gorgeous!'

Harriet glowed. 'You think so?'

'Totally! Sexy eyes.' She squeezed her friend's arm. 'And he's so completely into you.'

Harriet couldn't stop herself beaming. 'He told me he loved me last night.'

'Oh my God! I take it from the gooey look you feel the same way.'

Harriet laughed. 'He's just perfect. Funny, kind, caring . . .'

'Good shag?' Saffron was straight to the point as normal.

Harriet nodded vigorously, only just stopping her cheeks from blushing. 'Uh-huh!'

'Don't worry, I won't go on about it. But I'm so pleased it's all working out for you.'

'Thanks, darling.' Harriet looked out happily over the green countryside. It was good to be home. Up in front of them, Rex was waving his arms around animatedly, saying something to Zack.

'How's Tom?' Harriet asked.

Saffron was quiet. 'Actually, it's not that great at the moment,' she said slowly.

'Oh no, hun. Why?'

'I don't know.' Saffron grabbed the head of a passing cow parsley, crumbling it in her hand. 'I would never say this to anyone else, but it all seems to have gone pear-shaped since we got engaged. Since I found out about this bloody Cassie, and then I missed the award ceremony . . .'

'Have you mentioned it to him?'

'No point, is there? As far as Tom's concerned, it's done.' Saffron sighed. 'I don't even know if it *is* that.' Saffron watched the little white flowers fall from her palm into the road. 'This should be the happiest time of our lives, but it's like we've got nothing in common any more.'

'Darling, it is hard being apart from each other. Even the most perfect couples would struggle.'

'That's what Tom says. That's what I always thought . . .' she trailed off.

'What is it?' Harriet said gently.

'If it's like this now, what's it going to be like in ten years? When we've got a mortgage, kids and stuff. Maybe we've rushed into this.'

'You're just having a little wobble, it's perfectly normal.' Something drew Harriet's eyes up the road, towards Rex. 'There's nothing else, is there?'

Saffron looked at her sharply. 'What do you mean?'

When she'd walked into the pub, Harriet had definitely picked up on an intimacy between Rex and Saffron. She decided to take the jokey approach. 'I don't know, having a supermodel around must be very tempting.'

'Are you being serious?'

'No!' she said hastily. 'It was just a joke, ignore me.'

'Yeah well, bad joke,' Saffron said shortly. Harriet coloured, sure she'd hit a raw nerve. There was an uncomfortable silence for a few moments, then Saffron sighed.

'Sorry, H, I didn't mean to bite your head off. I'm just tired, trying to finish the book and all this show stuff.'

'It's fine. You must be exhausted, poor thing.' They smiled at each other, relieved to be back on an equal footing. Harriet tried again.

'But if there is anything . . .'

'There's nothing, babe.' Saffron flashed her a smile. 'Now, you must tell me all about the wild sex you're having.'

* * *

'I've never seen anything like it.' Zack was standing in the middle of the ballroom, gazing round. Rex had just taken him on a tour of the place, and had spent the last five minutes explaining how the fashion show was going to work.

'Pretty cool, huh?' Rex said.

'Pretty cool. Win is going to *love* this place.'

'Shoot, that reminds me.' Rex looked at Saffron. 'We haven't mentioned the photographer yet, have we?'

'I was going to, don't worry. We don't want to overwhelm poor Zack.' Saffron smiled at the other two. 'By some random piece of luck, this photographer I know is in the area next week.

Shooting some It girl at her stately home. But he's only free Tuesday afternoon. Zack, do you think your Aunty Win could come here then?'

'To Churchminster?' he said uncertainly.

'Yeah, we need to update all our PR stuff, get some pics. I'll look after her, don't worry,' Saffron assured him. 'H, maybe she could stay at the Hall? Your dad won't mind, will he?'

Harriet had a sudden image of her father and Win running into each other in their pyjamas. It was extremely unsettling.

'So is that sorted?' Rex asked. 'Guys?'

Harriet looked helplessly at Zack. 'Well, er . . .'

'I don't want to push you,' Rex said, 'but we've got just over four weeks left. We *have* to get going.'

Her father would have a blue fit. 'Sounds good to me.' Harriet smiled weakly.

JUNE

Chapter 56

It was mid-afternoon at Fairoaks, and outside the skies were heavy and thunderous. It was still warm enough to have the back door open, though, and as Clementine went to stick her head out, she could smell rain on the way. Another day stuck inside with only Radio 4 and her book for company. She decided to have a slice of the fruitcake she'd made, to cheer herself up.

As the kettle boiled, Clementine thought back to the show. She'd been most perturbed to hear the charity was changing so late, but luckily for Saffron and Rex they seemed to have got away with it. The Gatsby Road Centre was a cause closer to her heart, especially with Harriet volunteering there, but Clementine did not approve of the way it all had been handled. Young people seemed to fly by the seat of their pants these days.

Normally she would set her afternoon tea up on a tray and take it through to the drawing room, but she didn't bother today. All that pomp and ceremony; there was no one to see it anyway. She made herself a cup of tea, before getting the cake tin out and cutting a modest slice. Her cakes seemed to last a lot longer these days. Clementine sat down at the kitchen table, but even the plump, moist cake couldn't lift her spirits today. Maybe it was the weather, but she was feeling rather low again.

'Oh, for goodness' sake,' she chided herself aloud. What on earth did she have to feel sorry about? She had a wonderful family, good friends and a

beautiful house to live in. They'd all had a lovely time when Caro and the family had visited, and now she had Fashion Cares to look forward to. Normally Clementine would be bristling with anticipation at such a prestigious event in Churchminster, so why did she feel such overwhelming weariness?

There were a few stray crumbs left on the plate and automatically she picked it up and bent down to offer it to Errol Flynn.

The empty space under her chair hit her like a physical blow. Clementine put her head in her hands as a tear slid down her cheek.

'Oh, Errol,' she said. *'What's happening to me?'*

*　　　*　　　*

That day Aunty Win arrived on the 12.28 from Paddington. Saffron was waiting for her on the platform, and as soon as she saw Win, she knew who she was. Who else would arrive in Bedlington wearing a floor-length dress festooned with pink flamingos?

Win spotted her first. 'You must be Saffron!'

'Lovely to meet you, Win,' Saffron said. 'Here, let me take your bag.'

'You're a good girl, thank you.' The gold holdall, with the slogan 'Love Las Vegas' emblazoned across it, looked light enough, but Saffron's knees nearly buckled under the weight. It was packed full of what looked like more kaftans and, rather oddly, a pineapple.

Squeezing Win into the MG was like trying to push a tub of Play Doh into a pen top, but somehow Saffron managed it. As they left

376

Bedlington and sped back towards Churchminster, Win kept up a running commentary. 'What beautiful houses! Everything looks so fresh. I can see why 'Arriet loves it here.'

Before long, they reached the green. Win leant forward over the dashboard to get a better look. 'Oh my. This is pretty as a picture!'

'Sweet, isn't it?' Saffron pointed out the house on the left. 'That's my mum's house, where I'm staying at the moment.'

'Very charming. Am I going to meet your mother?'

'Of course. But let me take you up to the Hall to get settled first.'

As Saffron drove towards Clanfield Hall, she had a slight feeling of trepidation. Harriet had assured her it was OK, but Saffron knew from experience how unpredictable a host Ambrose could be. *Oh well, it was too late now* . . . She turned left into the long sweeping drive and let Win suck up the sight that greeted them.

'Welcome to your hotel,' she told her.

*　　　*　　　*

' 'Ello, Sir Ambrose.'

The three of them were standing in the drawing room. Saffron had made the introductions and Sir Ambrose was looking at Aunty Win like she'd just landed off some alien spacecraft. He frowned. 'Winston. Damned silly name for a woman.'

Saffron cleared her throat. 'Actually Winsome, Sir Ambrose.'

He frowned. 'Well, Mrs Winsome . . .'

'Call me Win,' she interrupted. 'And I'll call you

Brosie. We had a parrot called Ambrose when I was a little girl. Brosie for short, that's what we called him.' She shot him a wry look. 'He was grumpy, but it was only puff. Deep down he was a real softie.'

Ambrose looked rather shocked. 'I beg your pardon?'

Oh shit. Saffron waited for the explosion, but none came. Ambrose turned to her rather uncertainly. 'Well now, Saffron, Hawkins will be along for Mrs Winsome's bag in a minute. So if you'd like to wait with her . . .'

Win sucked her teeth. 'What you chatting about, Brosie? I want you to give me a tour of the place.'

Ambrose's cheeks were starting to go red. 'I'm not your personal guide, woman.'

Win ignored his outraged expression. 'And who else is going to be able to tell me about your beautiful home?'

She'd hit a soft spot. Ambrose was inordinately proud of Clanfield Hall.

'Well, er . . .'

Win held out a ham-sized forearm. 'Come on, stop your noise now.' Saffron held her breath, but, to her surprise Ambrose went over and took it meekly.

He looked back, like a man who had had all the wind knocked out of him. 'Ah, yes. Saffron. Er, can you tell Hawkins Mrs Winsome is in the green bedroom?'

Win patted her bun. 'I've told you, call me Win.' She fastened her grip on him. 'Onwards, Brosie!'

It was all Saffron could do to hold it together until they left.

Win was an instant hit: cooing over the flowerbeds, flirting with the gamekeeper, and even giving Cook her fiercely guarded recipe for Jamaican gingerbread. Although Ambrose had initially been railroaded by this colossal, exuberant woman, he amazingly started to thaw. By the afternoon Saffron found them chortling over tea and ginger thins, and Ambrose even offered the use of the Hall for their photo shoot. It was an excellent idea. They'd originally planned to use the Heights, but the stately backdrop of Clanfield was much more fitting for the subject's larger-than-life personality.

The photographer turned up with an hour to spare. After a whistle-stop look round, he decided they would use the drawing room of the west wing. On a whim he had the idea of shooting Win like the Queen: in all her finery on a Louis XIV armchair, hands poised demurely in her lap, wicked twinkle in her eye. It was risky, but the shots looked killer. As she viewed them on his camera, Saffron felt excited for the first time in ages. Maybe things were going to go right for them, after all.

The shoot finished just as the light was beginning to fade, and shadows were lengthening down the long terraces of the Hall. 'Care to stay for supper, Saffron?' asked Ambrose, who'd somehow harassed the photographer into taking a couple of shots of Sailor before he'd left.

Saffron looked at her watch. Rex was meant to have turned up for the shoot, but there had been no sign of him. *Surely he hadn't forgotten?* Luckily everything had gone smoothly, but she had still wanted Rex there. Photo shoots were his forte, after all.

'Could you give me half an hour? I just need to go home and check something.'

'Certainly!' Ambrose said. 'I can show Mrs Winsome the portrait gallery.' He rocked on his heels and chortled. 'I must admit, young Saffron, I do like a strong woman!'

Leaving the pair to their love-in, Saffron hopped in the MG and zoomed back up the driveway.

*   *   *

When she got to Byron Heights, Rex was leaning against the bonnet of his car on the phone. From the way he was gesticulating it looked like he was having a heated conversation. He glanced up and saw her, raising his hand to say: *Give me one minute.*

Saffron waited discreetly in the car until she saw him walking over. She climbed out.

'Hey, you're wearing my present.' He touched the Bottega Veneta cuff lightly, making her arms unexpectedly goose-pimple. 'How you doing?' He was wearing a gorgeous camel V-neck that brought out the rich brown of his eyes.

'Forgotten something?' she asked.

'What?'

'The photo shoot!'

Rex hit his forehead with his hand. 'I am *so* sorry. I've kind of had a hectic afternoon with calls from America.'

He did look a bit stressed. 'Was that one of them just now?' she asked.

'Yeah. My agency are getting a bit antsy, want to

380

know when I'm coming back.'

'What did you tell them?' She was annoyed at how disappointed she felt.

'Nothing definite.' He ran a hand over his face. 'It feels kinda weird thinking about it. I've got used to being here.'

She smiled. 'I've got used to you being here.'

They stared at one another. 'You want to come in for a drink?' he said, suddenly.

'I've told Ambrose I'd go for dinner . . .'

He shrugged. 'Oh well, maybe next time.'

For a moment neither of them spoke. Rex shuffled his feet on the gravel. 'Thanks, Saff,' he said.

'Thanks for what?'

'For doing all this. I couldn't do it without you. You do know how much I appreciate it, don't you?'

The intensity of his gaze was electrifying. 'You'd better,' she said, trying to cover over the fact that she was suddenly feeling rather breathless.

Out of nowhere, he lifted his hand and touched her cheek. 'You and me, we make a good team, don't we?'

Her heart leapt into her mouth, body on red alert. 'Uh, yeah . . . you mean with . . .' She stopped, not knowing which direction to go.

He was still looking at her with those charismatic pools.

'You mean with the show . . .' she said.

Something shifted behind his eyes. 'Yeah, that's what I mean.' He gave a grin. 'What did you think I meant?'

She felt her cheeks flare up. 'Nothing, nothing!' *Oh my God, how embarrassing!*

'OK, cool.' He nodded and stepped back. 'I'll

ring you tomorrow.'

'See you,' she said, as his eyes strayed down to the denim shorts she was wearing.

He looked back up, and met her gaze. 'See you, Saff.'

Her legs were suddenly not working for some reason. Clumsily she started the engine, bunny-hopping away in first gear. The car stalled twice before she finally managed to get off down the drive. Saffron wiped her sweaty hands on her shorts, and saw her flushed face in the rear-view mirror. *Will you hold it together?* She couldn't believe she was acting like this, Rex would think she was a total dick.

She was nearly at the main road before she dared look in the rear-view mirror. Her heart leapt back into her mouth.

He was still standing there in the distance, watching.

Chapter 57

London

When Harriet got to the community centre Thursday evening, she had a nasty shock. All the windows at the front had been smashed, and unintelligible red graffiti was scrawled across the brickwork. Someone had already put cardboard up to replace the broken glass.

Harriet rushed up the path and found Zack in his office, hunched over a pile of paperwork.

'What's happened?'

He looked up, his face weary. 'Someone decided it would be a good idea to smash all our windows.'

'But why would they do that?'

'Why would someone do anything? It's probably kids, thinking it's a laugh.'

Harriet's stomach dropped. 'Do you think it could be that gang on the bikes?'

Zack grimaced. 'God knows. Whoever they were, they'd done a good job on it by the time I'd got here.'

'Have you told the police?'

'They came down this morning, but there's not much they can do. We've got someone coming out to fix it, and we should be able to claim on insurance.'

It was so mindless. 'Does Win know?' Win had hit it off with Ambrose so well she was staying in Churchminster until tomorrow.

'No, and I don't want to spoil her little holiday.' He managed a smile. 'Sounds like she's gone down a storm in the country.'

'I know! She's got Daddy wrapped round her little finger, by the sound of it.'

'Now that I would like to see.'

She smiled sadly at him. 'Oh, Zack,' she said, 'what a horrible thing to happen.'

He stood up and came over to plant a kiss on her forehead. 'Don't let those bastards get you down, not when we've got the show coming up. Everyone here's really looking forward to it.'

There was a tap at the door. They turned to see Alf and Bert standing there, the former with some sort of bizarre paper hat on his head.

'I say, Harriet,' Alf put on a faux-posh accent, 'do you think the fashion folk will like my hat? It's very in style, don't you know.'

'I made it out of the serviettes from the kitchen.' Bert smiled. Alf stuck his nose in the air and did a little twirl.

Harriet giggled. 'Alf, they'll adore you.'

'It's darling to you from now on,' Alf said, and sauntered out.

Bert looked at the other two. 'He's crackers.'

It was wonderful to see him looking so happy. 'How are you, Bert?' Harriet asked.

'Apart from the arthritis in my left knee and my cataracts? Blooming marvellous, thank you.'

The desk phone started ringing. 'We'll leave you to it,' Harriet told Zack. Bert held the door open for her and they stood outside, watching the salsa couples twirl round. One of the ladies from OAP bingo shimmied by and gave Bert a vampish smile.

'I think she likes you!' Harriet teased.

He shuddered. 'Alf told me she's a bit of a maneater. Makes me want to run a mile.'

'So you and Alf have hit it off, then?'

'He's a nice chap. Talks far too much, but I just turn my hearing aid down.' He smiled, and touched her arm. 'Thank you.'

She was surprised. 'Thank you for what?'

'For helping me.'

'I didn't do anything, Bert.'

'You cared, that was enough.'

Harriet was surprised at the sudden lump in her throat. She reached out and put her hand over his.

Five minutes later Zack came and found her in the kitchen. He was frowning. 'You haven't seen my wallet, have you?' he said, patting his pockets.

'No, is it in your office?' she asked.

'Nope, looked everywhere.' He sighed heavily.

'This is all I need.'

'Do you think you might have left it at home?'

'I don't know. I suppose I did take off in a bit of a rush.'

'Do you want me to go and have a look?'

'Do you mind? I can't really leave.'

She put down the plate she'd been drying. 'Of course not.'

He smiled for the first time that evening. 'You're an angel, I'll go and get my keys.'

*   *   *

The night air was warm as she made her way to Zack's flat. The estate was still busy, little kids playing in their gardens, watched from the front door by a parent or elder sibling. She didn't know if it was just because it was summer, but the place seemed more lively these days. Harriet could hardly recognize it as the silent, brooding estate she had first encountered back in January.

As Harriet let herself into the flat she realized it was the first time she'd been there alone. She could still feel Zack's presence, the scent of his Issey Miyake hanging in the air of the hallway.

Now where could his wallet be? She didn't have to look hard. As soon as she walked in the kitchen she saw it lying by the microwave. Zack must have had his mind on other things as he'd left. She picked it up, and was about to leave, when she remembered she'd left her favourite bracelet in the bedroom. It was a silver Wright & Teague one her mother had bought her for Christmas a few years ago, and she felt a bit naked without it.

She walked through into the bedroom and

385

looked on the bedside table. No bracelet. Harriet frowned. Where would Zack have put it? She didn't want to start going through his drawers. Then she remembered the pot inside the bedside cabinet where he kept his bits and bobs. He could have placed it in there, for safekeeping.

She struck lucky. The bracelet was lying next to some spare coins and an Oyster card jacket. She picked it up, and was about to shut the door, when she stopped.

Something—half hidden in a yellow cloth—was glinting at her from the back of the cabinet. Harriet pulled the cloth aside. Then she snatched her hand back quickly, as the knife that the hooded kid had threatened Zack with looked malevolently back. She was *sure* it was the same one. It looked even more horrible close up, with its weird curving blade and engraved criss-cross handle. Harriet shivered. Why on earth hadn't Zack taken it to the police? Surely he hadn't forgotten about it? It was horrible to think she'd been sleeping in the bed, with that thing inches away. Harriet didn't want to look at it any more. Gingerly pulling the handkerchief back over it, she shut the door and sat back on her heels, thinking.

Was the real reason he'd kept it for protection? Zack had played the whole incident down, but was that because he was secretly worried they'd come back for him? It was understandable he'd be on his guard, but surely this was making things worse? Harriet swallowed, deliberating nervously. She could hardly tell him she'd been going through his bedside cabinet. He'd never trust her in the flat again.

She stood up, feeling deeply unsettled. Zack was

playing with fire by keeping this knife, she was sure of it. She could feel its presence in the room, violent, hateful. It didn't belong in Zack's world. *Please don't do anything stupid*, she prayed. Grabbing the bracelet, she ran out.

Chapter 58

Churchminster

'So, Serendipity, is this really it?' Brad's eyes were sad.

'Why didn't you tell me you and Jake ~~were long-lost brothers~~ knew each other?' Serendipity said.

'We fell out years ago! After he stole my songs and tried to pass them off as his own . . .' Brad ~~cried sighed~~ shrugged. 'I knew it was no use trying to fight it. Jake was desperate for fame and fortune.'

'Jake's a talented musician, why would he do that?' Serendipity couldn't bear to believe what Brad was saying.

Brad's face plummeted ~~changed dropped~~. 'Oh my God, you still love him, don't you?'

Saffron sat back from her laptop and looked out of the window. The village was in full bloom, from the swathes of daisies sprinkled across the green to the multicoloured hanging baskets outside the Jolly Boot. Beryl Turner was out there every day at five o'clock, watering them. You could set your watch by her.

Flowers, however, were not the focus of Saffron's

mind at the moment. It was a miracle she'd nearly finished the book with all the shit going on in her life right now. It was three weeks until the show, and a third of the tickets were still unsold.

But the thing was, Saffron was used to working in this kind of high-pressure environment. She knew what the real cause of her anxiety was. Tom.

Over the last two weeks they seemed to have drifted even further apart. He was trying to reach out to her, she knew that, but Saffron just felt so *confused*. All the things she used to associate with Tom—the in-jokes, the hanging out together, telling each other about their days—she was now doing with Rex instead. She tried to tell herself it was entirely natural, what with Tom in London and she and Rex practically neighbours. Of course they were going to spend time together. That's what friends did, didn't they?

But it was more than that. The frisson of electricity she was sure she wasn't imagining; the times she had caught Rex's eyes on her body when he didn't think she was looking. Saffron knew she should stay away, keep things on a professional level, but she couldn't. Rex had become like a drug to her, and just being around him made her happy. When had she last felt that way about Tom?

Saffron took off her engagement ring and studied it. It somehow seemed smaller, reduced, as if mirroring what was happening with their relationship. She stared at the diamond. Was she really such a cliché that she was falling for her fiancé's twin brother? Or was Rex just a symptom, and had there been something fundamentally wrong with her and Tom's relationship even before he came along?

Oh God. She never used to be this introspective. Feeling like she had the weight of the world on her shoulders, Saffron dragged herself out of the chair. She needed something to take her away, and out of herself, even for a couple of minutes. Picking her way past all her mother's clutter in the hallway, she headed downstairs.

As soon as she walked into the kitchen Babs's head popped out from behind the easel. 'Hello, darling! Can I get you anything?'

Her eager words made Saffron bristle. 'For God's sake, can you get off my back?'

Babs's face dropped. 'Sorry, darling,' she said in a small voice.

Saffron felt like she'd run over a kitten. 'I didn't mean to snap.'

'Don't worry, that's what mothers are here for.'

Saffron gave her the smallest of smiles. 'No, you're not.' She walked over to the kettle. 'Cuppa?'

'Please.'

The kitchen fell silent except for the whistle of the kettle coming to the boil. Saffron could feel her mother looking at her. Babs wasn't stupid.

Please don't ask me about Tom, Saffron thought. She just couldn't handle it at the moment.

Instead, her mother stood up. 'I've got something to show you.'

Saffron looked over, teaspoon in her hand. 'Oh?'

Babs picked up a crumpled photograph from the kitchen counter. 'I found it when I was looking for something in one of the cupboards.' She came over and held it out to Saffron. 'Here, I thought you'd like it.'

Saffron took it, and her heart skipped a beat.

It was a picture of her dad, standing on a beach, looking young and rakishly handsome. He had a little girl on his shoulders, and the two of them were laughing.

'Is that me?' she said, brushing her finger over the picture. She had so few photos of her dad, and hardly any of her and him together.

'Yes, darling, that was at Cowes week. Gosh, it must have been the mid-eighties.' Babs looked at the photo again. 'You look adorable, but of course you always did. I remember those red wellies. Even though it was scorching hot all week, you refused to take them off. You even wore them to bed one night.'

'Did I really?' Saffron felt a lump in her throat. She and her dad had looked so happy. Now, here she was twenty-three years later, with just a few measly photos to remember him by.

She thought how Tom had never seen it, how she'd like to show him. Then she remembered and her eyes welled up.

'Oh, Mum, I'm in such a mess!'

Chapter 59

Aunty Win turned out to be the best thing that could have happened to Fashion Cares. The press, desperate for a feel-good summer story, had given the new publicity shots a good response. Several newspapers had expressed interest in doing something with her nearer the time of Fashion Cares, and she'd even been invited on Capital Radio's breakfast show. Saffron had been a bit nervous she might put her foot in it, but Win had been brilliant. They'd ended up keeping her on for the entire programme, and there'd been a hilarious moment when she'd berated the DJ live on air for not combing his hair. A few hours later, someone had started a 'Vote Win for PM' campaign on the internet.

It was having a ripple effect in the celebrity world, too. The managers and agents Saffron had been chasing were finally starting to return her calls. There were still no definite 'big' names confirmed, but they were tantalizingly close on a few. All they needed was a yes from Savannah Sexton to start the ball rolling.

That morning Saffron, Rex and Clementine were sitting round the dining table at Byron Heights. Sue had sent her apologies, having another event to work on that day. Clementine was taking notes as Rex went through everything: the castings, which stylists he'd secured, the dressers on the day. As Saffron listened, she realized it was finally starting to sound like a real fashion show.

'So I've been liaising with Alexander Napier, and hair and make-up are all completely sorted,' Rex told them. 'And the designers' final fittings are next week.' He grinned. 'You wait until you see the collections, they're awesome.'

Clementine had to give him his due, Rex had certainly been busy. 'What about this Bobo Brown person?' she enquired. She saw Rex glance at Saffron with a smile.

'We can put it out there that she's involved next week.'

'That's cutting it rather fine, isn't it?'

For the first time Rex looked rather pained. 'Best

I can do, I'm afraid.'

'How about the dress rehearsal,' Saffron said hastily as she noticed the disapproving look on Clementine's face. 'When are we thinking, again?'

'It's going to have to be Wednesday the thirtieth,' Rex said, 'and, yes, I know it's the day before the show, but that's the earliest I can get people here.' He looked at Clementine. 'Normally we'd have weeks to rehearse for something like this. But then again, this isn't your average fashion show. We're going to have to wing it a bit, I'm afraid.'

Clementine raised an eyebrow. '*Wing* it?'

'Yeah.' Rex grinned sheepishly. 'Put it this way, we're going to be flying by the seat of our pants.'

'Oh dear,' she said faintly.

*   *   *

Saffron was staring out the window when he came back from seeing Clementine out. 'Jeez, she doesn't take any prisoners, does she?'

She looked up. 'What was that?'

'Clementine. Talk about the dragon headmistress. I thought she was going to lock me up for detention just then.'

'Mmm,' she said.

Rex looked at her from under his long dark eyelashes. 'Hey, you OK?'

Saffron couldn't be bothered pretending any more. 'Not really.'

He came over and pulled the chair out next to her. He was so close that she could feel the heat of his gaze, the now familiar scent of expensive aftershave. Overwhelmed, she went back to staring out of the window.

'Is it Tom?' he said gently. 'I know you guys have been having a few problems.'

Her stomach dropped. 'Has he said something to you?'

Rex shrugged wide shoulders. 'Not as such. I just had an inkling.'

'Well, your inkling was right.'

'Do you want to talk about it?'

She looked at him curiously. Could he really not see what was going on? It was as if they were dancing around the subject, not wanting to vocalize the frisson between them. *Because talking about it would make it real.*

'We aren't getting on well,' she admitted. 'I don't know if it's to do with never seeing each other or . . .' She trailed off.

'Or what?' he said quietly.

She picked at the ring binder on her notepad. 'Nothing.'

Out of nowhere her chin wobbled. Embarrassed, she put her face in her hands. 'Everything is just so fucked up.'

Rex put his arms round her. 'Hey, hey. No tears.'

The feel of his embrace was overwhelming. *Tom used to hold me like this. Used to. Oh God.* To her total embarrassment she started sobbing. 'Sorry, it's just doing my head in . . .'

He was stroking her hair. 'You've got nothing to be sorry about. I'm sure you can work it out.'

Even through her tears, Saffron could feel the warmth flooding from the contours of his body. *Everything about Rex was so beautiful, vibrant.* Saffron pulled away violently, furious with herself. *Why was she thinking like this when she was upset about Tom?*

There was an awkward pause. 'I'm OK, just ignore me.' She sniffed.

A strange look passed over his face. 'Saff . . .'

'Can you get me a glass of water?' she blurted out desperately.

'Uh, yeah.' He sounded a little surprised. 'Won't be a minute.'

He left, and Saffron sunk her head down on the dining table. What the hell was going on?

*   *   *

Clementine was deep in thought on the drive back to Fairoaks. Rex's words had worried her. 'Winging it' was what she thought he'd said. Winging it? The whole thing filled her with trepidation, especially when anyone with half a clue could see those two were attracted to each other. Mixing business with pleasure was never a good idea; especially when one let emotion and feelings cloud one's judgement.

She looked up at the blue sky and sighed. She did like that chap of Saffron's, and rather hoped they could work it out. But who could tell? Young people were so flighty when it came to romance these days.

As she turned into the lane to Fairoaks, Clementine saw Ambrose's muddy Land Rover parked haphazardly outside the house. Her heart sank a little: she wasn't in the mood for go-kart racing, or whatever his latest obsession was today.

But Ambrose wasn't in his car or by the front of the house, nor was he at the back door as she made her way round. Clementine frowned. Where could he be? Maybe he'd parked at her house and gone for a walk round the Meadows. It really wouldn't do: people flew round that corner at a ridiculous speed, and Ambrose had taken up half the road with his devil-may-care parking.

Inside, the house seemed even quieter than ever. Clementine switched the kitchen radio on. It was a local station with some ghastly advert, but even that was better than the silence she was starting to dread. She looked around her spotless kitchen, no crumbs left on the worktop by hungry mouths, no shoes kicked off carelessly by the back door.

Clementine started to prepare her afternoon tea with a vigour she did not really feel. One cup, one saucer, a small sliver of lemon drizzle cake. She'd already cut it before realizing she didn't really have an appetite.

She'd just sat down at the table with the latest issue of *Gardeners' World* when there was a rat-tat-tat at the back door, and Ambrose peered in at her. Clementine was actually rather pleased to see him. Maybe a little company would be nice after all.

She made her way over to the door. 'I was wondering where you'd got to . . .'

Clementine stopped mid-sentence. Ambrose had something in his arms and, as she looked down, two soft brown eyes met her gaze beseechingly.

Instantly, her heart melted.

'Oh, where did you find him?' she cried, taking the Labrador puppy's little face in her hands.

'One of the gardener's dogs had a litter,' Ambrose said, pulling the puppy's ears gently. 'Little stunner, isn't he?'

'He's just a darling,' she said, bending down. The puppy licked her right on the nose, making her laugh. 'Oh, sweetie.'

Ambrose held the puppy out. 'Here you go, he's yours.' The little warm bundle was promptly offloaded into her arms.

'I'm sorry?'

Ambrose grinned. 'I thought he'd be perfect for you.'

Clementine looked down at the puppy, which was now nibbling at one of her cardigan buttons. 'But, Ambrose, I can't possibly take him! I mean, it's very thoughtful of you but . . .'

'Course you can take him!' Ambrose looked back at the garden. 'All this good land going to waste, what you need is one of these little fellas.'

'But . . .' Clementine couldn't think of one single excuse. The wriggling bundle gazed up at her adoringly, and she knew it was over.

Ambrose's eyes twinkled. 'I'd say that dog's taken to you, Clementine.'

The bundle started wriggling even more. Clementine put the puppy down and he scampered off between her legs into the kitchen.

'Ambrose, I really don't know what to say! I'll pay you, of course.'

He waved a hand. 'Don't bother with any of that, it's enough if he gets a good home.' A look of kindness came over his face. 'They leave a bloody great hole when they've gone, don't they? I've lost a few great chums over the years.'

Clementine's famous English reserve was in danger of collapsing. 'Oh, thank you,' she said quietly.

Ambrose chortled. 'I don't know if you'll say that when you see what he's doing!'

She glanced back to see her best court shoes

being mangled. 'Oh dear,' she said faintly. She was rather out of practice with puppies.

'I'll leave you to get to know each other, then.'

Clementine called to her new companion. 'Here, boy! Oh dear, now get off them! Off!'

'I'll leave you to it.' Ambrose grinned.

Chapter 60

London

Excitement was growing at the centre about the show. When Harriet arrived on Wednesday she found Aunty Win in the kitchen, sewing what looked like a technicoloured bedspread. She held it up. 'What do you think?'

Harriet checked out the expert needlework. 'Fantastic!'

Win chuckled. 'I'm going to show this fashion lot Winsome Johnston can still pull the stops out.' She snapped off a bit of thread. 'Zachary not with you?'

Harriet frowned. 'No, I thought he'd be here.'

'He hasn't been in, as far as I know.' She leant back and called through the open door. 'Gray! You seen Zack?'

The volunteer popped his head in. 'No, but the rota says he's in. Maybe he's got his nights mixed up.'

Harriet felt a prickle of unease. Zack would never do that.

'He's probably had to go and do something.' Win patted Harriet's hand. 'Don't worry.' The tightening at the corner of her mouth suggested Win was more concerned than she was letting on.

*   *   *

When Zack still hadn't turned up by 9 p.m., Harriet *was* starting to get worried. He wasn't answering his mobile, and she'd already left two messages. She was just wondering whether to go round to his flat when her phone rang. *Zack mobile.* Sighing with relief, she hurried out into the foyer to answer it. 'Hello! I was starting to wonder where you were.'

His voice was low, and serious. 'I'm outside. Can you come out?'

Harriet looked through the glass doors into the main hall. Win was sitting on one of the chairs in there, watching her expectantly. 'Why don't you come in?'

'Just come out, Harriet, I'll explain then.'

Even in the dim light she could see the swollen bruising under Zack's left eye.

'Zack! What happened?' She peered at it anxiously. 'It looks so sore.'

He grimaced. 'It's not exactly pleasant.'

'What happened?'

His eyes slid sideways. 'Don't panic but I got jumped earlier.'

'Jumped? What do you mean?'

'Someone cycled up behind me when I was on my iPod and whacked me in the face.'

Someone on a bike. 'Do you think it was one of that gang?'

'I don't know.' He touched his face gingerly. 'They got me good though.'

'Oh, Zack, how horrible for you!' She took his hand and realized it was shaking. 'I know it's upsetting,' she said soothingly.

He snatched his hand away, making her jump. 'I'm not upset, I'm fucking angry!'

Harriet had never heard him swear before. Zack looked disgusted with himself. 'I didn't mean to shout.'

'It's all right. You've had a dreadful shock.'

He shook his head. 'I just wasn't expecting it.'

'Are you going to call the police?'

'There's no point.'

'Of course there is! Zack, this gang obviously have it in for you for some reason, maybe because you've stood up to them. Please, you can't play the hero all the time . . .'

'Harriet, no.' He gripped her arm. 'I don't want to worry Win or any of the others. Not with Fashion Cares coming up.'

'But . . .'

'No.' His voice brokered no discussion. 'I won't come in tonight, for obvious reasons. Tell Win I've got a headache, and I'll tell her I had a DIY accident when I see her.' He got some money out of his wallet. 'Make sure you get a cab back tonight, OK?'

She pushed it away. 'I've got money.'

He gripped her hands. 'Look, I know you don't think this is right.' Her silence spoke volumes. 'We're just so close to something good happening for us for once, I don't want a bunch of scumbags ruining it all.'

'I know about the knife,' she said quietly.

His face shifted. 'How did you . . . ?'

'I found it. By accident. I wasn't snooping.'

He sighed. 'Are you going to give me a hard time now?'

'Of course I'm not. I'm just worried about you, Zack. I don't think you should be keeping it at your house.'

A muscle flickered in his jaw. 'You don't understand, Harriet.'

'I do understand. I know why you're keeping it.'

He stared at her. 'You do?'

'Yes. You think you're safer with it, that it'll give you protection. For goodness' sake, Zack, that's what the police are there for!'

'Hey, I can look after myself, all right?' He hugged her, holding tight. 'I know you worry about me, but you really don't have to.' He tried to make a joke of it. 'I was brought up round here, remember? No one's going to pull one on me.'

'I know you can look after yourself.' She pressed her face against his chest. 'I just wish you'd hand that knife in.'

'If it makes you feel better, I will. Scouts' honour.'

She looked up at him. 'No more heroics?'

'No more heroics.' He touched her cheek. 'I love you.'

'I love you, too.'

Chapter 61

Churchminster

Saffron had just finished painting her toenails when the house phone started ringing. Hobbling down the stairs with cotton wool between her toes, she picked it up. 'Churchminster 364.'

'It's me, babe. Tom.'

'Oh, hi. How are you?'

'Actually, I'm at Bedlington station. Can you come and pick me up?'

'You're here?' She was confused. 'But it's Wednesday . . .'

'We've just finished the August issue and I've taken tomorrow morning off, I thought we could spend some time together.'

'Oh, right!'

'Can you come and get me, then?'

She felt panicked, like the rug had been pulled out from under her feet. Saffron had decided the only way to get through this thing, was by sticking her head in the sand. Because maybe, just maybe, it might sort itself out and go away.

Except that Tom was at Bedlington station, waiting. 'Great!' Her voice sounded unnatural, squeaky. 'I'll be there in fifteen minutes.'

*   *   *

He was sporting a new look when he climbed in the car.

'What's with the beard?' she asked.

Tom rubbed his new, hairier chin. 'I didn't shave for a few days, but then I kind of liked the look. What do you think?'

Personally Saffron thought he looked like a North Pole explorer. 'It's OK.'

'You don't like it?'

'I said, it's OK.'

'Right.' He leant back in the seat. 'How's the show going?'

'Things could be better. The VIP list still isn't looking very VIP.' She couldn't be bothered to tell him the new developments.

'You'll be OK, I have faith in you.'

Saffron didn't want to think about the show, because that meant thinking about Rex. 'You know what, Tom? I'm up to my ears with that bloody thing. Can we talk about something else?'

As they drove through Bedlington the conversation was stilted.

'That's new,' he commented, as they passed yet another freshly opened café. The market town was on a bit of a drive to smarten up, and every week it seemed a new deli or organic café was opening.

Saffron glanced at it. 'Yeah, I think it opened last week. Mum went there for lunch with a friend.'

'Did she have a nice meal?'

'I think so.'

The rest of the journey passed with barely a word spoken.

'Mum's out tonight, some painting talk,' Saffron said, as she let them in the front door. She wished Babs were here. She was suddenly terrified to be left alone with Tom.

They went into the kitchen. 'Drink?' she asked.

'Beer would be great.'

402

'Have you spoken to your brother recently?' She reached into the fridge and handed him a bottle.

'Thanks.' Tom popped the cap on the side of the table. 'We spoke the other night. He seems pretty tied up with the show.'

She busied herself pouring a glass of wine. 'Good catch-up?'

'You probably know more than me.'

She swung round. 'What do you mean?'

He gave her a look. 'I mean, with you guys working together so much.'

They fell into silence. Saffron watched Tom take a long swig of his beer, a study in casual indifference. She stood up. 'I thought we'd get a takeaway, hope that's OK with you. I've got a menu somewhere.'

His brown eyes looked into hers, troubled and searching. 'Forget the takeaway. I'm not hungry, anyway.'

She sat down again. 'Me, neither.'

'Oh, Saff.' He reached out and put his big hand over hers. 'What's going on with us?'

She shook her head dumbly. 'I don't know.'

He was searching for answers. 'Is it me? Is it something I've done?'

'No.' She sighed shakily. 'I don't know, I just *feel* different.'

He gripped her hand. 'I've been neglecting you.'

'Tom, you haven't.' Saffron rubbed at a water stain on the table, plucking up the courage to say it. 'Don't you think everything's gone wrong since we got engaged?'

He looked shocked. 'No, I don't think that. Do you?'

She shrugged miserably. 'I don't know. I don't

know anything any more.'

'Is this about Cassie?'

Suddenly, Cassie seemed like an age ago. 'I don't know. I guess I just felt like you didn't understand how I was feeling, you know. Like you expected me to simply smile and get on with things.'

'It just had so little relevance to me I thought you'd feel the same way. I got it wrong.'

She gave a half smile. 'S'all right. I cocked up with the awards ceremony, didn't I?'

'Saff, that's in the past, now.'

'I know . . .' She started rubbing furiously at the water stain.

'Look, you're just stressed at the moment. With the book and the show and everything. We'll go away somewhere after all this, have some proper time together.'

'Yeah, maybe.'

'You could look more excited.'

She knew she wasn't giving him anything back, but she couldn't help it.

'Saff, talk to me.'

She couldn't meet his gaze. 'I just don't know if we're doing the right thing. I mean, what if we're too young to get married?' She shook her head confusedly. 'I just feel like my life has completely changed and I don't know, Tom. It scares me.'

His face went pale. 'Saff, you're the person I want to spend the rest of my life with. You do know that, don't you?'

Her eyes filled with tears. She nodded.

His hand was holding hers so tight it hurt. 'Do you not feel the same any more?'

'I don't know,' she whispered.

He sat there, just staring at her. A moment later

he took his hand away and rubbed his face. 'How has this happened, Saff? I always thought we were stronger than this.'

A heavy silence settled over the room. Outside, Saffron could hear the wind brushing through the apple tree by the back door.

Tom spoke. 'What are we going to do?'

She shook her head, staring at the table. Tom put his hand on her chin and gently tilted it up. 'You've got enough on your plate with the show coming up. Let's leave it until after then to talk, OK? Maybe you'll feel different.'

'OK.' What if they were just putting off the inevitable?

'I do love you, Saff.'

'Oh, Tom.' She just couldn't say the words back. He dropped his head, looking like he'd been physically wounded.

His next question hit her like a sucker punch. 'Is there something going on between you and Rex?'

She felt the colour draining from her face. 'What?'

He looked up at her, his gaze steady. 'Is there something going on with you and my brother?'

'Of course not!'

'Have you got feelings for him, then?' She could see he was trying to stay rational. 'Look, I know what a great guy Rex is. People fall for him, Saffron.'

This was her chance. Come clean; tell Tom how she was feeling. She owed him that at least. But then again, what could she tell him? Nothing had actually happened between her and Rex. *Yeah, sorry, Tom, I want to call the engagement off because every time I look at your brother I feel like fireworks*

405

are going off inside me.

So she took the coward's way out, hating herself for it. 'I can't believe you're accusing me of that!'

'I'm not accusing you of anything.'

'Well, no, I don't,' she shot back. She felt trapped, her eyes flicking around the room for an escape route. 'God, Tom, this is so embarrassing.' She had an awful thought. 'Don't tell me you've asked Rex this as well?'

'I haven't said anything.' His eyes were on her, scrutinizing.

'Look, Tom, I know things haven't exactly been great recently. But it doesn't mean I'm jumping into bed with your brother.'

'OK, OK.' His shoulders relaxed. 'I believe you.' He held his arms out. 'Now can I have a hug, please?' Reluctantly she let him draw her in, feeling like the world's biggest traitor.

They slept on opposite sides of the bed that night. Not that Saffron did much sleeping, and from the sound of Tom's restless breathing he didn't, either. The six inches between them in bed suddenly seemed like a huge gulf.

There was little conversation as she drove him to the station early the next morning. As they pulled up in the car park, Tom turned to her. 'So I'll see you for the show? You know I've got that cover shoot next weekend?'

She tried to sound enthusiastic. 'Yeah, great.'

'I can cancel, pull a sickie if you want.'

'Won't Jeff go mad?'

'Probably.'

'No, babe, don't do that.' She gave a little smile. 'This is important for you.'

He gazed at her, trying to reach out. 'It's only

two weeks away, then we can have a nice time together, OK?'

She nodded, feeling sick inside. *Two weeks.* So much could happen between now and then.

Chapter 62

Clementine was taking the newest member of her family for a stroll to the village shop.

Buster, as she had named him, was making quite an impression on her daily routine. He'd already escaped twice, nearly given one of her hens a heart attack, and also chewed through the wire to the television. Clementine was only relieved he hadn't electrocuted himself. It wasn't as if she had any time to watch TV anyway, even though her beloved Wimbledon was on. Since Buster's arrival, it felt like she hadn't sat down once.

But no matter what he did, when those soulful brown eyes looked into hers, Clementine couldn't help but melt. Buster was the best present she could have wished for.

She reached the shop and tied him up outside, hoping he wouldn't find the time to chew through his lead. The puppy sat back on his haunches expectantly.

'You stay here, Buster, good boy.'

As she walked in, Brenda Briggs called out from behind the till, 'Cooee! Mrs S-F!'

Clementine's eyes widened. 'Good lord, Brenda, what on earth's happened?'

The shopkeeper's hair had been backcombed to within an inch of its life, while her blue and purple eyes looked like she'd walked into a lamppost. Brenda touched her face. 'Stacey's been using me as a model, to practise for the show. What do you think? I quite like it myself. It's nice to tart yourself up now and again.'

Clementine was rather stuck for words. The doorbell tinkled, and she turned to see the Jolly Boot's landlady, and mother of the aspiring make-up artist, walking towards her. Beryl Turner's hair had been brutally strong-armed into a lacquered beehive, while it looked like Clementine's great-granddaughter Rosie had been at her eyes with a marker pen. Beryl gave Clementine a sheepish grin. 'Afternoon, Clementine, Stacey's been trying out her Amy Winehouse look on me.' She turned her head carefully, as if the beehive might fall off. 'Have you got any fresh sage in, Brenda? We've had that bloody fox peeing in our vegetable patch, and Chef is throwing a fit. Says there'll be no food tonight if he doesn't get any herbs.'

'Coming right up.' Brenda bustled off. Churchminster's village store was a rather confused Aladdin's cave. One day there would be quails' eggs on the shelf next to a Vin Diesel DVD, the next the shop would be filled with absinthe and inflatable lilos. No one knew the rhyme or reason behind Brenda's ordering methods.

'Stace is ever so excited about the show,' Beryl said. 'Says it could be her big break! Well, what with all those famous people.'

'Has Saffron said she's definitely using her, then?' Clementine asked cautiously. She knew fashion was meant to be avant-garde, but this was taking things a little too far. Clementine sincerely hoped that it wouldn't lower the tone of the show.

'Stace has spoken to Saffron and that model chum of hers,' Brenda called. 'He's a good-looking fella, isn't he?' She came back with a pot of sage and plonked it down. 'Do you think they're having it off, or what?'

'Brenda!' Clementine was shocked. 'Saffron only lives next door!'

'She can't hear through walls, though, can she?' The shopkeeper leant on the counter. 'I mean, what's it all about? I know she's here writing her book, but you put two good-looking young 'uns together . . .'

Clementine wasn't going to fuel Brenda's gossip. She picked up her copy of the *Bedlington Bugle*. 'You've clearly been reading too many of your lurid romance novels again.'

'Before you go, Clementine.' Beryl Turner got her diary out of her handbag. 'What day shall I put you down for? It'll have to be when she's not at college.'

Clementine was confused. 'Sorry, my dear, I don't follow.'

'Your appointment with Stacey, of course! She's offered to give all us girls a free makeover before the show.'

'Bless 'er,' Brenda said. 'She's made me feel like a new woman. Now all I've got to do is find a new man to feel!' She cackled loudly.

Clementine started edging towards the door. 'I'm afraid I'm rather busy at the moment. Can I get back to you?'

'Course you can, love. Don't leave it too long, though, she'll get booked up!'

Let's hope so, thought Clementine, as she went out to untie Buster. If Stacey Turner got her hands on the models, the whole thing would be a complete disaster!

London

At *Soirée*'s offices in the West End, Harriet was filling up her bottle at the water cooler when Alexander Napier waltzed up. 'I must say I'm very excited about meeting your new beau at the show,' he said. Most of the *Soirée* team were coming to Fashion Cares.

'Don't try and flirt with him.' Harriet laughed.

'I'll do my best, darling, but you know what I'm like after a few glasses of bubbles. I'll try and mount anything.' He took a paper cup and filled it up. 'And how's our country author doing? She sounded a bit stressed last time we spoke.'

Harriet paused for a fraction of a second. 'She's good.'

Alexander didn't miss her hesitation. He raised an eyebrow. 'And our tasty Tom? I do miss looking at that lovely bum across the office.'

'Working hard, from what I hear.'

'Good, good.' Alexander took a sip of his water. 'How are the invites looking? I'll kill Saffron if she doesn't sit me next to Tom Ford.'

Harriet laughed. 'I don't think he's going!' She dropped her voice. 'Saffron's been having a few problems with the VIPs.'

'Well, I could have told her that from the start! They've picked the worst time to do it. Anyone who's anyone is away in the south of France.' Alexander checked his Philippe Patek diamond-encrusted watch. 'Who *is* going, then?'

'Well . . . can you keep a secret?'

'Of course!' he said, looking rather offended. Despite his gossipy manner, Alexander knew when to be discreet.

'They've got Bibi Brown.'

'Never! That's fabulous.' His Botoxed forehead attempted a frown. 'Why in heaven's name aren't they shouting it from the rooftops?'

'It's a long story, but Bibi's contracted to something else. It's taking longer than they thought.'

'Really? What is it?' Nothing normally happened in the fashion world without Alexander knowing about it.

'I have no idea. It's all hush-hush. Anyway, Bibi's being announced at the last minute.'

'How *mysterious*,' he said. 'Ooh, I wonder . . .'

His assistant Jemima was waving at him from the fashion desk. 'Al, I've got Alexa Chung's stylist on the line. It's about the shoot tomorrow.'

'Must fly, sweetie.' Alexander brushed something off Harriet's top. 'I'm going to look into this Bibi Brown thing, I smell a major exclusive.' And with that, he bounded off across the room.

Chapter 63

Churchminster

With only a week to go, Fashion Cares was bearing down on them with frightening speed. Rex had been busy choreographing the show and liaising with designers about the running order. They still hadn't seen Bibi Brown's clothes yet, but Rex was working the runway schedule round them. Even if they only had one outfit, Bibi was still going to open and close the show.

With all the meetings, castings and fittings, Rex had been to and from London constantly. He and Saffron had hardly seen each other, which she told herself was a good thing. She had her own stuff going on: she'd just sent the finished version of *Gloss* off to Pam Aston, and was nervously waiting to hear back. In the meanwhile she threw herself into the show, trying to drum up more interest. They'd sold a few more tickets, but things were still looking unnervingly B-list. At least she'd just got DJ Rev to do the music. That would add the all-important cool.

Even though it was all a massive headache, at least it was keeping her busy. Things were going from bad to worse with Tom. He was being patient and understanding, but it just made Saffron feel more confused than ever. It didn't help that Rex was in her thoughts constantly. Had things been about to go further in the dining room that day? She imagined Rex kissing her, his hands running over her body. She tormented and excited herself with visions of them lying together in his four-poster bed, his six-pack pressed against her stomach, the little gasp of pleasure as he entered her.

Her mum had tried to offer advice, but Saffron felt like she was going round and round in circles. Every time she thought about Rex, her mind would move to Tom. She tried to remember all their happy times—his kind, handsome face, the feelings she got when she looked at him—but it was becoming harder. It wasn't just his physical attributes that she was finding hard to remember. It was the *very essence* of him that was blurring further and becoming distant.

It was a stunning June day as she drove over to Byron Heights that afternoon. Saffron didn't notice any of it. She was too busy trying to quell the growing nerves in her stomach at the thought of seeing Rex again. At the entrance to Byron Heights she suddenly stopped the car. Her heart was racing so fast it hurt.

This was stupid. She was acting like some love-struck teenager, not a 26-year-old woman engaged to the love of her life. She had to get this stuff with Rex out of her head. People were attracted to each other all the time; it didn't have to mean anything. Except this thing was like a sickness, eating her up . . .

Get a grip. They had a show to put on together. Despite what she was feeling inside, Saffron had to stay professional. Taking a deep breath, she put the car into first gear and started off down the drive.

Rex answered the door almost immediately. Despite her best intentions Saffron felt her heart quicken. Even in a plain white T-shirt and faded blue jeans, he looked like a work of art: brown eyes more intense than ever, the perfect 'V' of his shoulder muscle just showing under the sleeves of his top. Saffron tightened her hold on her handbag strap. 'Have you got a minute?' she said.

'Come on in. I was about to call you, anyway.'

She followed him into the kitchen, looking anywhere but at the broad shoulders just inches from her, the smooth brown skin of his neck.

He swung round. 'Can I get you anything?'

'No, thanks.' The atmosphere in the room was heavy, expectant. Saffron put her bag down on the floor, and turned to face him. 'Rex, we need to talk.'

'There's something I need to talk to you about, too.'

She felt a funny thud in her stomach. 'You do?'

'Yeah. You first.'

'Oh, right.' She swallowed, trying to focus her mind. 'Rex, we need to confirm Bibi Brown. The show's only a week away, and I've got a whole load of names who haven't committed. Unless we have some sort of miracle, Bibi is the only person who can get them to. We need to put the word out, fast.'

His eyes were flat, dull. 'We haven't got her.'

Saffron didn't understand. 'I'm sorry?'

'We haven't got her, they pulled out.'

'What do you mean, they pulled out? They can't do this now!'

'I know.' Rex shrugged helplessly. 'She's not happy with the outfits, apparently, and hasn't got time to work on them. I've tried . . .'

Saffron snapped into work mode. 'I'm sorry, they

414

can't do this. You did get a written agreement, right? An email, anything?'

He looked stricken. 'I didn't know I had to.'

'Rex!' she wailed. 'You always get something in writing!'

He ran his hands through his hair. 'I've never done anything like this before, I just thought their word was enough.'

'I knew I should have taken this over,' she muttered.

'I am so, so sorry.'

He looked so upset she couldn't stay cross. 'Oh, Rex.'

He stood there, almost statue-like in his stillness. From nowhere he smashed a fist down on the kitchen worktop. 'Godammit!'

Saffron jumped, shocked by his reaction. Rage tightened his features, making him even more carved and sculpted. Saffron felt her breath catch again; Rex looked dangerous, beautiful. 'I am so fucking angry with myself!' he said. He started to pace up and down the kitchen.

She tried to reassure him. 'Rex, calm down. It's not that bad. Really . . .'

He stopped pacing and looked at her. 'Of course it is, Saff! This is a fucking disaster. We had the whole show planned round her.'

Saffron bit her lip. There was nothing she could say.

'I need some fresh air,' he said. A few seconds later the French doors were flung open and she watched his tall figure stride off down the garden.

Saffron was left alone in the kitchen, reeling from what had just happened. She didn't blame him really. Bang went their VIP list.

'Oh, shit.' She stared up at the ceiling unhappily. They'd lost their only hope. Without a headline designer, Fashion Cares was going to be a total washout.

Chapter 64

London

Harriet jumped off the bus with a spring in her step. It was a beautiful Saturday afternoon, and she'd just bought the most gorgeous dress from Liberty's for the show. It was an extravagance, but Fashion Cares was going to be worth it.

As she walked along, Harriet cast her mind back to that day in her flat in January, when she'd been hungover and unfulfilled. It seemed a lifetime away. Now she'd entered a new chapter with Zack, Win, and volunteering at the centre. It was a good feeling. For the first time Harriet felt like she actually belonged somewhere. And her father liked her boyfriend! She smiled to herself happily. Life couldn't get much better right now.

The centre looked uncharacteristically quiet, especially for a Saturday. Harriet went up and tried the doors. To her surprise they were locked. Nearby a young boy on his bike sat watching her. 'They closed it. There's been some trouble.'

'Trouble?'

The lad pointed to the road behind him. 'Police are up there, I think someone's hurt pretty bad.'

Zack lived that way. Harriet's heart flew into her mouth. 'Hurt? Is it Zack?'

The boy shrugged.

'You must know Zack, the one who's in charge here?' Her voice sounded high, funny.

He nodded. 'Yeah, that's what I heard, that man who runs this place.' Oblivious to the devastation he'd just delivered, the boy turned round and freewheeled off down the path.

Harriet had never run so fast. She flew down the road towards Zack's, a chill enveloping her whole body. *Someone's hurt pretty bad.* The boy's words were running in a merciless loop through her head. *He must have had a run-in with that gang again—had he been knifed?* 'I told you to call the police!' she cried, not caring if anyone saw or heard her.

She rounded the corner to Zack's block of flats expecting the worse, but the dead-end street was quiet and deserted. The police had to be parked somewhere else. Harriet flew across the road and started hammering on the door, her finger pressed down on the intercom. 'Zack! Are you there? Let me in!' Why was no one answering? 'Will someone let me in!' she screamed, banging on the door. Suddenly the intercom crackled into life, making her jump violently.

'What's that racket?' It was an elderly gentleman's voice, scared and angry.

'Please let me in,' she gasped. 'Zack's hurt, the police must be up there.'

'There's no police here.' Harriet recognized the voice as the little Indian man who lived next door to Zack and kept budgerigars.

'Someone told me Zack's been hurt . . .'

'Missy, he's not here. With walls this thin, I should know.' The intercom stopped, cutting her off.

Before she even realized what she was doing, Harriet was running back down the road. It was only a short way to Win's house, but her lungs felt like they were on fire. Gasping for breath, she turned right on to the street and stopped dead.

It was bedlam. Three police cars and an ambulance were parked outside Win's house, their lights flashing. Uniformed police officers hovered, talking into their radios while a crowd of people milled around. Their faces were white with shock. Harriet caught part of a sentence from one as she ran past. '. . . they found her just lying there on the floor . . .'

Dead? Her knees almost buckled but she carried on. In front of her, she could see Abby standing at the edge of the crowd, Kai in her arms. Tears were streaming down her face. Harriet ran over to her, heart thumping.

'Abby!'

Abby looked round in a daze. 'Harriet. I only just got here, Mum told me . . .'

It felt as if time had come to a standstill, as if everything was suddenly reduced to that moment. 'Is it true?' Harriet whispered.

Fresh tears spilt out of Abby's eyes. 'This is awful . . .'

Harriet stared at her numbly. She had to get to Zack, no matter what. But her legs felt heavy and leaden, unwilling to move. Snapshots of Zack skittered through her mind: the first time she'd seen him at the centre; the way his eyes crinkled when he laughed; when he'd told her he loved her . . . She let out a sob.

'Harriet!'

She looked towards the house. Like some kind of

beautiful, insane miracle Zack was there, pushing his way through the crowds. Harriet gaped, she just couldn't believe what she was seeing. 'Oh, thank God,' she wept, throwing her arms around him. 'I thought you'd been stabbed, I thought you were dead, Zack.'

His body was rigid. Harriet slowly pulled away, took in the sombre expressions, the ambulance and police cars.

'Oh no. Not . . .'

His eyes were vacant. 'It's Win, Harriet. Those bastards got her.'

No one seemed to know what had happened, except that Win had been found in a heap at the bottom of the stairs, with the place ransacked. It looked like there had been some kind of burglary, which Win had stumbled in on.

As Win was brought out on a stretcher, several of her neighbours started crying. 'Poor Win, what's she done to deserve this?' one of them sobbed. 'All she's ever done is good for this place.'

The ambulance rushed Win to hospital, sirens wailing. Zack went with her, so Harriet followed in a taxi. By the time she reached A & E Win had already been taken through.

Harriet found Zack pacing up and down the waiting room. She tried to talk to him, but he was in a world of his own, barely aware that she was there.

It seemed like an age before a nurse came out and called their names. They followed her through to a cubicle, where a surgeon was waiting to see them.

'It's not good news, I'm afraid,' he said. 'We've done a CT scan and found that Mrs Johnston has a

419

blood clot on her brain.'

Harriet's heart sank. She'd been hoping that somehow Win had just been knocked out and would be sitting up already, ordering everyone around.

'We're taking her down to theatre now,' the surgeon said. He looked at his notes. 'She's also got a broken wrist, which we'll deal with at some point. That's not an immediate concern.'

And a blood clot is. Harriet wondered if Zack realized the significance of the doctor's words. She placed a hand on his sleeve, but he didn't react. The surgeon turned to Harriet. 'Mrs Johnston's up in the neurosurgical unit. A nurse will be along to take you up to the relatives' room.'

It was a small, square place with wooden chairs and pictures on the wall. It was occupied already by another couple. Harriet smiled at the woman, who gave a feeble grin back.

They sat down, Zack still staring into space. The only hint of life in his face was a small muscle working in his jaw. She took his hand and squeezed it. 'Can I get you anything?' she asked. He shook his head, eyes still fixed ahead on nothing. Harriet left her hand on his, and sat upright in her chair. There was nothing else to do but wait.

*   *   *

Zack spoke once, at 2 a.m. Harriet had been dozing uncomfortably in her seat, and she didn't catch the words at first.

'What was that?' She sat up.

'It's my fault. They did it because of me.'

420

'Who, that gang?' Harriet massaged her stiff neck. 'Zack, you must tell the police about them when they arrive.' She looked at him. 'Are you sure it's them?'

'Of course it's them!' He turned on her, blue eyes suddenly ice-cold. 'They've been following me . . .'

'Following you? Why didn't you say anything?'

'You wouldn't understand . . .'

'Try me.'

Zack gave a dismissive shrug. 'They must have followed me one night and seen where she lived.' He dropped his head. 'I knew I should have done something earlier. I should've sorted it out.'

Harriet glanced at the other couple self-consciously and lowered her voice. 'Sorted what out?'

He didn't say anything.

'Zack!' He wouldn't look at her. 'When the police come in, tell them about your suspicions. If it is the gang, or someone from it, they'll find them.'

'Not if I find them first.'

She was frightened. A dark shadow seemed to have fallen over Zack, and she didn't know how to deal with it.

It was another hour before the surgeon came back to see them. He was still dressed in his scrubs and looked grim-faced. 'I'm afraid there have been some complications,' he said gently. 'We've operated on Mrs Johnston and removed the clot, but she's lost a lot of blood. With her age and weight, she is in a very serious condition.'

'Is she going to die?' Zack asked.

The surgeon met his gaze. 'We've just got to cross our fingers and hope for the best.'

421

'Is she?'

The other couple looked up at his raised voice, and Harriet put a placating hand on his arm. 'Zack.'

'It's all right,' the surgeon said, 'I'm not going to sugar-coat it, your aunt is gravely ill. I think it would be best if you went and saw her now.'

Aunty Win was in a private room at the end of the ward. Harriet's heart clenched when she saw her. Without the ubiquitous kaftan and turban she looked smaller, older. Her head had been shaved where they'd operated, a plaster covering the incision. A nurse was by her side, checking her blood pressure. She smiled kindly. 'I'll leave you to spend some time with her,' she said, silently slipping out of the room.

Harriet and Zack took a seat at either side of the bed. Harriet took one of Win's hands and held it. It was warm and floppy. When Harriet thought about the big, gregarious character Win was, she couldn't connect that with this silent, broken creature in front of her. Her eyes filled with tears. 'Oh, Aunty Win.'

Opposite her, Zack had his head bowed, both his hands over Win's right one. As she watched, a single solitary tear dropped down his nose on to the bed sheet.

There was a soft knock on the door and the nurse reappeared. 'The hospital chaplain is outside. He wondered if he could offer a few words to Mrs Johnston.'

Zack looked up, eyes red. 'Win would like that.'

The chaplain came in, and Harriet suddenly felt she was intruding. Zack needed this moment with Win alone. She stood up. 'I'll be outside if you need me.'

He didn't even seem to hear her.

Chapter 65

Harriet woke to find the nurse gently shaking her shoulder.

She had a second of blissful normality, before reality hit. Win. Instinctively she looked round. No Zack. She sat up uncertainly. Something was wrong, the nurse was grinning.

'Someone wants to see you.'

'Zack?'

The grin got wider. 'Mrs Johnston. She's woken up.'

Harriet's mouth dropped open. 'She's OK?'

'She's very weak, but there doesn't seem to be any lasting damage.' The nurse shook her head in disbelief. 'The surgeon says he's never seen a recovery like it.'

Harriet wanted to hug her. She couldn't believe it! Win had been on the brink of death just hours earlier.

'She's been asking for you.'

Harriet stood up and rubbed her eyes. 'Of course.'

In Win's room, a wonderful sight greeted her. Win's face was pale and drawn but it broke into a big smile. ' 'Arriet.' Her voice came out as a croak. 'How lovely to see you.'

The nurse followed Harriet in. 'How you feeling, Winsome?' She turned to Harriet. 'The police are here,' she said quietly. 'They want to talk to

Winsome about the burglary, but they'll have to wait.'

As the nurse slipped out again, Harriet sat down by the bed.

'What a nice lady,' Win said as Harriet sat down. 'And the surgeon, too. A lovely bedside manner—you don't see much of that these days.' She seemed back to her wonderful, irrepressible self already.

Harriet gripped her hand. 'Oh, Aunty Win! I'm so pleased you're OK.'

'I'm not letting some stupid boys get the better of me.' Win's voice was defiant, but Harriet could see the fear in the old lady's eyes.

'The police are outside, they want to question you about what happened. Can you remember anything?'

Win looked away. 'Bits . . .'

'Was it that gang?'

Win's eyes searched the room. 'Where is Zachary?'

'I thought maybe he'd gone down to the canteen . . .' Harriet trailed off. *Zack would never have left Win's side.* 'I'll go and find out.'

The nurse was behind the counter, putting something on the computer. She saw Harriet and smiled. 'How's the patient? None of us can believe what a fighter she is!'

Harriet smiled politely. 'Sorry to bother you, I was just wondering if you'd seen the man I was with? He's called Zack.'

The nurse frowned. 'Not for a good few hours. He left the ward in quite a state.'

'He left? Before Win woke up?'

'I think so, yes.'

'Oh dear,' Harriet said faintly. 'It's just that I'm

424

not sure if he knows about Win. About her pulling through, I mean.'

The nurse looked concerned. 'You can't have him walking round out there thinking Winsome has died.' She nodded down the corridor. 'It's forbidden to use mobiles in here, but there's payphones down the end.'

'Thanks.'

Harriet rushed back to the relatives' room to get her purse. She remembered the look on Zack's face last night, his threat to take matters into his own hands. She had to find him.

The payphone seemed tortuously slow, and there was an agonizing pause before she was connected. *'You have reached the voicemail of telephone number . . .'*

'Zack, it's me,' she said desperately. 'Aunty Win's OK! She's just come round, and the surgeon thinks she'll make a full recovery.' She clutched the phone. 'Win wants to see you, Zack, please don't do anything stupid . . .'

'I can't get hold of him,' she told Win, back in her room.

She may have been at half strength, but Win was still in full possession of her faculties. 'What's wrong, 'Arriet?'

'I might be making a mountain out of a molehill, but he said he was going to go after whoever did this to you.' Harriet's voice shook. 'Win, he doesn't know you're OK, and I'm worried.'

A shadow crossed Win's face. 'You must find him,' she croaked. 'Zack can't get into any more trouble . . .'

'Trouble?'

Win closed her eyes. 'He's got form.'

425

'Form?' Harriet was confused. 'I'm not sure what you mean.'

Win looked at her, her expression sorrowful. 'Zack's been in prison, 'Arriet.'

'Prison?'

Win looked pained. 'He can't be getting into more trouble now. He's got too much to lose.'

Harriet was reeling. 'Zack's been in prison? For what? When?'

'Oh 'Arriet, I shouldn't be the one telling you this. He was worried it would scare you off, but I told him everyone deserves a second chance. I told him you always saw the good in people . . .'

'Aunty Win, what was he in for?' The old lady looked away. 'Aunty Win!' Harriet forced herself to think of the worst possible scenario. 'He didn't, he didn't kill someone, did he?'

'He's never forgiven himself.' Win started to weep softly. 'Please, just find him before it's too late.'

Harriet didn't move, and Win reached across and took her hand. 'Please, 'Arriet, don't think badly of him. He's a good boy, and he really loves you.'

The old lady was labouring for breath. She shouldn't be going through this. Harriet forced a smile. 'Don't worry, Aunty Win, I'll find him.' She dropped a kiss on Win's forehead and walked out, her whole world suddenly upside down.

Chapter 66

Churchminster

Saffron was completely stunned. When she'd received the panicky phone call from Harriet, her first instinct had been to call Tom, but something had stopped her. This was nothing to do with him; it was for her and Rex to deal with. She went straight up to Byron Heights to break the news.

He was just as shocked. 'Is Win going to be OK?'

'I think so, but she's still in hospital. The doctors say she'll be there at least a week.'

They were standing in the hall, where Saffron had broken the news. 'Run the part about Zack past me again.

'Apparently he's gone on the run! After the people that did this to Win.' If it hadn't been so dreadful Saffron would have laughed. It was all just so unbelievable.

'And Harriet's worried because it turns out he's been in prison,' Rex said slowly. 'And he might do something stupid?'

'That was the gist of it. I can't believe it. Poor, poor H. He seemed such a nice bloke.'

Rex put his head in his hands. 'Jesus, Saff, the show is only five days away!'

'You don't have to tell me! If the press find out about this, we're fucked. Who's going to want to support a charity run by an ex-crim?'

Rex tried to look on the bright side. 'It might not be that bad. Whatever was he in for?'

'Harriet didn't go into details, but it sounded

pretty heavy.'

His broad shoulders slumped. 'Christ. And we've got no Win now, either.'

They looked at each other. For the time being, the sexual undercurrent had been replaced by raw despair.

'Oh shit,' Rex said. 'I think we're going to have to cancel the show.'

Chapter 67

London

Harriet blinked in the bright sunlight. Still in yesterday's clothes, she felt grubby and dishevelled, the metallic tang of fear and adrenalin coating her mouth.

Her phone started ringing in her bag. Zack! She scrabbled round for it, heart sinking when she saw it was work. They'd be wondering where she was. She couldn't answer it now; she'd send a text later.

'Watch it!' A cross-looking blonde woman in a suit banged into her. 'You can't just stand there in the middle of the pavement.'

Shooting Harriet a death stare, the woman hurried off. Harriet turned to walk away, but realized she had no idea where she was going. A cab had just dropped someone off at the hospital. Better to start with what she knew. She hailed it. 'The Gatsby Road Estate, please—as quickly as you can.'

As the cab made its way through the stop-start traffic, Harriet sat hunched up in the back. She still couldn't quite believe what had happened. How could Zack have kept something like that from her? He'd been in prison for murder! She felt physically sick at the thought that he'd taken someone's life. She stared out of the window, torturing herself with thoughts of stabbings, Zack beating someone to death in the street, even a shooting.

She squeezed her eyes shut, unable to reconcile such horrific violence with the gentle, loving man she had lain in bed beside, made love with. A spasm of nausea gripped her stomach, and she clasped her hand to her mouth, scared she might be sick. Her phone started ringing again. She snatched it off the seat beside her. It was Clanfield Hall's number.

'Harriet?'

'Hi, Daddy.' She had to try and act normal; there was no way she could tell him what was going on.

'Where are you? I just phoned your work, and they said they thought you must be sick.'

'I'm fine, honestly.'

'Are you in the car? Don't tell me you're pulling one of those sickies.' Her father sounded jovial. 'Honestly, you London socialites, out gadding about . . .'

Something in Harriet snapped. 'For Christ's sake, Daddy, I don't need this!' she shouted. The taxi driver's eyes flicked to the rear-view mirror.

Her father sounded stunned. Harriet had never so much as raised her voice to him in her entire life. 'Don't you take that tone with me! What the dickens is wrong with you, girl?'

Tears sprung into her eyes. 'Sorry, I can't talk now,' she said. She sobbed and cut him off.

429

She spent all day searching. Zack wasn't at the community centre, or his flat. Win's house was closed up and silent, police tape across the front door. Harriet walked every inch of the estate, and when she didn't find him there, she walked up and down Camden High Street, revisiting their usual haunts and asking after him. No one had seen him, or even a man matching his description.

She'd had several voicemails from a DS Cooper, asking her to call back, and a concerned Alexander had left a message saying the same policeman had been to the office, and was she alright? The situation was getting out of hand.

In desperation, she went to a snooker hall she thought Zack had mentioned once, but had no luck there, either. She'd just stepped outside, feeling more defeated than ever, when someone called after her. Harriet turned, then recoiled. With his weightlifter's build, tattoos and shaved head, the man walking towards her looked like trouble.

'I just heard you then. You after Zack?' He had a surprisingly soft voice.

'Y-yes.'

'Is this to do with Win?'

'You know her?' Harriet asked in surprise.

'I knew Zack, back in the day. He keeps a low profile these days, I don't see him much out.' The man looked grim. 'It's disgusting what happened to Win. If I was him I'd be doing the same.'

'Doing the same?' She felt terror and hope all at once. 'Do you know where he is?'

The man sighed. 'All I heard is that gang he's looking for are from Meadowfields. But you don't want to go up there, love, it makes Gatsby Road look like Disneyland.'

Harriet would deal with that later. She had a lead now, and that was all that mattered. 'Thank you,' she said.

The man shrugged. 'Like I said, I knew Zack.' He turned and went back inside.

Harriet returned to the main street. She looked left and right, suddenly overwhelmed by exhaustion and loneliness. She couldn't go home, not if the police were looking for her. Her fingers were dialling the number before she had even thought about it.

'Caro, it's me.' Her voice broke. 'Something terrible's happened.'

*   *   *

Just being in the comforting enclave of Montague Mews made Harriet feel a bit better. In-between tissues and cups of hot sugary tea, she recounted the last twelve hours. Caro sat with her arm round her on the sofa.

'What a dreadful thing to go through all by yourself!'

Harriet sniffed. 'I just can't let Win down, not after what she's been through. I have to find him.' She swallowed. 'The trouble is, part of me doesn't know if I want to. What if Zack really has killed someone? I don't know if I could ever get over something like that.'

'Oh, darling.' Caro looked helplessly at Benedict. He'd been standing by the window listening, but now he spoke for the first time.

'Well, one thing's for certain. You can't go down to this Meadowfields place by yourself. I'll take you there tomorrow, first thing.'

Harriet looked at her watch. 'I should be out there, looking . . .'

Caro put a hand on her arm. 'Benedict's right. It's too late to go out now, and you're exhausted. Let him drive you down there tomorrow.' She hesitated. 'Are you sure you don't want to ring the police back?'

'No! I can't speak to them yet, I promised Win I'd help him stay out of trouble.'

Caro and Benedict exchanged glances. 'OK,' Benedict said. 'But if we can't find him, we'll come back and then maybe call the police. Your information could put them on the right track.'

After what seemed like an age, Harriet nodded. 'I suppose it's the right thing to do.'

'You're staying here tonight,' Caro said firmly. 'I don't like the thought of you going back to your flat alone, and the spare bedroom is made up anyway.'

Harriet's eyes welled up. 'I'm sorry to have landed this on you both.'

'Nonsense, that's what we're here for,' Caro said. 'Come on, let's get you settled.'

Later, after Harriet had gone to bed, Caro came downstairs to find her husband staring out of the window. She went up to him and wrapped her arms round his muscular waist. 'For God's sake, be careful, Benedict. Don't get yourself in any dangerous situations.'

He turned, and put his arms around her. 'I have no intention of even getting out of the car. This is

432

more for Harriet's benefit than anything.'

'Do you really think Zack's *killed* someone?' They had all studiously avoided saying the word all evening.

'I don't know,' Benedict said.

Caro shivered. 'And we've had him in the house. He was playing with our children!'

'Let's give him the benefit of the doubt until Harriet speaks to him. Thinking like that isn't going to help anyone.'

'Poor darling Harriet. It's just an awful thing to discover about someone you love. That they have some kind of dreadful dark past.'

Benedict hugged her even tighter. Not that he would ever vocalize it but he had an extremely bad feeling about Meadowfields.

Chapter 68

Churchminster

It had been a hell of a day for Rex and Saffron. They'd spent it agonizing about whether to cancel the show or not, but with savage irony the press were going mad for the story. A major national newspaper called the *Daily Mercy* ran a double-page spread on Fashion Cares, and Saffron was getting increasing requests from radio stations wanting to do more interviews with Win. She'd even been door-stepped at home that morning by a reporter from the *Bedlington Bugle*, trying to get some quotes. Saffron had fobbed him off with a feeble excuse about Win being away.

Aside from that, Sue Sylvester was on the phone hourly to Rex, giving him updates on the caterers, the lighting people, and the time when the company assembling the catwalk planned to turn up. As Saffron fielded all the press interest, she realized she and Rex were mere cogs, now, in a massive juggernaut hurtling towards its destination. There was no way they could cancel.

One small positive had arisen from all the hoo-ha. Alexander Napier had managed to secure a funky new designer called Phillip Chan to open the show. By complete coincidence, he had some unseen pieces from his next year's spring/summer collection and was willing to donate them to Fashion Cares. Saffron didn't know what Alexander had said to get Chan, but she would be forever in his debt. Chan was no Bibi Brown, but at least they had *someone*.

It was near midnight by the time Saffron turned off her laptop. She'd never felt so tired in her life. When she checked her phone, she had two voicemails from Tom, the last one at 11 p.m. saying he had an early start tomorrow and was going to bed. It would be too late to call him now. She felt a pang when she realized they hadn't spoken all day. Was it one of relief? Or disappointment? Right now her brain was too tired even to guess.

Saffron slumped, her head on her arms. 'God, I am so knackered.'

Across the table Rex rubbed his eyes. 'Same.' His hair was ruffled, the white vest showcasing his extraordinary physique. He yawned, looking sleepy and cute. Dangerously cute. Aaargh . . .

'Got anything to drink?' she asked suddenly.

434

'Yeah, sure.' He stretched in his seat, muscles uncoiling. 'What do you fancy?'

'The hard stuff.'

'I think that can be arranged.'

As he went into the kitchen Saffron sat in her chair, waiting. Her heart had started to race again.

'Jack Daniels OK?' he yelled.

'Yup, fine!' she called back. Just then she caught sight of her reflection in the dark window opposite. Her body language was taut, expectant. She dropped her eyes as a feeling of shame flushed through her.

He came back with the bottle and two glasses. 'I'm over this room. Let's go through to the snug.'

The snug was a small, cosy room at the back of the house, with little else in it other than a giant plasma screen and two squashy sofas. Saffron sat down in one, and instead of going to the other, Rex came and sank down beside her. She watched as he poured out two hefty glugs. 'Here.'

They downed them in one, the fiery liquid making Saffron's eyes water. She stretched her legs out, tanned from afternoon walks in the country. 'I needed that.'

'I think we both needed it.' Rex refilled their glasses. Almost straightaway he chucked back half. They were drinking quickly, recklessly, and before long the bottle was almost empty.

At one point Rex got up to open the window. It was a hot balmy night, but it was nothing compared to the stifling tension in the room. He came and sat down again, his brown feet bare under the faded jeans.

'Tom OK?' he asked.

'He's your brother, you should know.'

Rex lifted his glass. 'Right.'

They sat there in silence, Saffron aware of the increasing rise and fall of her chest.

'Can I ask you something?' Rex said.

The question hung there in the air. 'Yep,' she said eventually.

'What's going on with you and Tom? You're not giving me anything, and Tom isn't, either.' Rex looked at her. 'I care about you guys, you know.'

'Do you?' she asked abruptly.

He looked surprised. 'Yeah, course.'

She exhaled heavily, as if it would somehow release all the confusion in her head. 'I'm not sure if I want to be engaged any more.'

He didn't sound very surprised. 'Why?'

Saffron stared into her glass unhappily. 'I just don't know if it's too *much*. Too soon. I mean, I love Tom.' At this her insides twisted. 'But what if we're rushing into this? I never imagined I'd get married, and even if I did I kind of thought it would be some crazy barefoot ceremony on a beach somewhere when I'm forty.'

'Hey, you don't need to convince me about all this marriage stuff.' He glanced at her. 'But I guess when you know, you know, right? If Tom's The One . . .'

His words hung in the air. Saffron swallowed. The words were stuck in her throat. 'I don't know if he is The One any more,' she said in a small voice. *Because if he is, why would my heart go a million miles an hour just sitting this close to you, his brother?*

She rolled the glass round in her hand, staring at the golden liquid. It had gone to her head, taking the edge off her tension. 'Tom asked me, you

436

know, if there was something going on with . . . us.'

He looked at her. 'What did you say?'

'I told him of course there wasn't.'

He nodded. 'Of course.'

A silence settled on the room. Saffron noticed her heart was starting to beat faster. She took a huge gulp of whisky, spilling a few drops down her chin in the process.

A car beeped somewhere in the distance. Saffron knew the right thing to do was to get up and head for home, but she felt paralysed. She noticed her already-short sundress had ridden up, exposing her thighs. She had just started to pull it down when Rex's hand closed over hers. He looked at her, brown eyes suddenly alive with lust. 'I'm sorry, Saff, I've been trying so hard, but I don't think I can stop myself.'

Suddenly his lips were on hers, soft yet masterful, his tongue slipping into her mouth.

Saffron half-heartedly pulled back, but his arms were around her, pulling her into him. Gripped by a wild uncontrollable passion, she started kissing him back, hands raking up and down his muscular back.

'We can't do this . . .' she gasped, drawing back.

'I know, I know,' he murmured. 'Oh, Saff.' As they started frantically kissing again she felt his hands moving up under her dress, finding the front of her lacy knickers. He groaned, feeling the warmth of her bush.

'I want to touch you so much.'

Saffron wanted him to, too, so much. She wanted him to fuck her. Dizzy with lust, they were at the point of no return.

Wordlessly he scooped her up in his arms, and

437

started towards the staircase. Saffron felt powerless to stop. Hands and kisses all over each other, she let him carry her upstairs to his bedroom.

Tom, I'm so sorry, she thought as Rex kicked the door shut behind them.

Chapter 69

London

After a sleepless night, Harriet came downstairs to find Caro already watching the television in the kitchen. The GMTV newsreader was reading the bulletin solemnly.

'A sickening attack has been launched on Winsome Johnston, the 76-year-old pensioner who has been hailed as the saving force behind the notorious Gatsby Road Estate in North London. Mrs Johnston was attacked at home last week by a masked gang who fled with a number of valuables, and she sustained life-threatening head injuries in the attack. She is now in intensive care at the Royal Free Hospital in Hampstead. This senseless act of violence could not have come at a worse time. The Gatsby Road Community Centre, which Win helps run, has been put up for a prestigious award . . .'

'Zack will see this,' Caro said reassuringly, 'and then he'll realize Win's OK. I'm sure of it.'

Harriet wasn't so certain. She'd been calling his mobile all night, and it was still switched off.

Benedict strode in, freshly shaved and showered. 'Ready?' he asked Harriet. She nodded numbly.

'Please be careful,' Caro repeated to her husband outside by the car, as he helped Harriet into the passenger side and shut the door. She lowered her voice. 'Darling, I've got a really bad feeling about this.' What would she tell Milo and Rosie if something happened to him?

Benedict kissed her on the forehead. 'Don't worry. I'll just drive Harriet round, and then bring her home and persuade her to contact the police. But we have to let her do this, she's adamant about keeping her promise to Win.'

Caro watched as the BMW bumped out of the little cobbled mews. All she could do was wait, and pray.

*   *   *

Since Harriet had been wearing the same clothes for forty-two hours, they were going to swing by her flat so she could have a quick freshen-up. It was going to be a beautiful summer's day, the sun already creeping up the cloudless sky. Soon London would be waking, going about its business as normal. It only made Harriet's situation feel even more terrible.

When she'd called the hospital last night Win had been asleep. The duty nurse had told Harriet Win was getting stronger by the hour. The police had been in to see her, but the nurse wasn't able to tell Harriet what had been said. She knew Win wouldn't have given away much though, holding back until Harriet found Zack.

It was still early, and bleary-eyed commuters huddled at bus stops. Benedict switched the radio on, and Harriet listened on tenterhooks for a news story involving a man fitting Zack's description, but there was nothing.

The traffic wasn't bad for once, and they were near her flat in no time at all. 'How are you doing?' Benedict asked.

She gave a small smile. 'I've been better, I suppose.'

As they pulled into her road she half expected to see a police car waiting for her, but she was in for a shock. Instead, her father was standing outside her flat, leaning against his mud-splattered Land Rover. As Benedict parked the BMW, Harriet undid her seatbelt and jumped out. 'Daddy?'

Her father looked relieved. 'There you are! I've been getting worried.'

'But what are you doing here?' Harriet didn't understand. It was so strange to see him here in his tweed coat and plus fours, against the urban backdrop.

'Come to see if you're all right, of course. You sounded in a right fix yesterday, and when I couldn't get hold of you I got anxious.'

Harriet hadn't been picking up his calls, and suddenly felt terrible that he'd driven all the way out to see her. 'I'm sorry, Daddy.'

'Don't be sorry.' Ambrose peered closely at her, and then went over to where Benedict was now stepping out of the car. 'Does someone want to tell me what's going on?'

'Oh, Daddy,' she said, and burst into tears.

'There, there. Come here.' She collapsed into his arms. 'Man trouble, is it?' he asked, stroking her hair.

'Something like that.' She sniffled.

Ambrose sighed. 'Dear oh dear,' he said. Harriet

440

had expected her father to demand to know exactly what was going on, but for once he wasn't full of his normal noise and bluster. She wiped the tears off her face and took a deep breath.

'Daddy, something has happened, and we've got to get to this scary council estate, Meadowfields. Zack could be there, and I'm worried he's about to confront some really bad people. I haven't got time to explain now, but please trust me.'

Ambrose looked at Benedict and back to Harriet. 'Well, we'd better get moving, then, hadn't we? Benedict, we can take my Land Rover, we don't want to be driving around in a BMW.'

Harriet could hardly believe her ears. 'You're coming?'

Ambrose crossed his arms. 'Of course I'm coming! What, do you think I'm letting my only child—and sole heiress to the Clanfield estate—go off on some mercy mission without me?'

*   *   *

Ten minutes later, once Harriet had changed and splashed cold water on her face, they were heading north towards the Meadowfields estate. Her father seemed to apply the same rules to London driving as he did in the country—there were no rules.

'Bloody traffic, doesn't it drive you mad?' he said, as he ran a red light, almost causing a car to crash into them from the left. The driver pressed down on his horn, but Ambrose carried on obliviously.

'Is Zack all right?' he said, looking in the rear-view mirror at Harriet.

'I don't know. I wish I did.'

441

'Careful, Sir Ambrose!' Benedict called out, as the Land Rover swung into a bus lane, just in front of a bendy bus. There was an outraged honking from behind them, and the driver shook his fist. Harriet closed her eyes; if they arrived at Meadowfields without being arrested themselves it would be a miracle.

As the houses and shops sped by, Harriet stared out of the window. She shouldn't have brought her father, not at his age. And Benedict had a wife and young kids to think about. *This is all wrong, we should have called the police*, she thought, before an image of Win's pleading face flashed into her mind.

Damn you, Zack! Harriet was suddenly angry. How could he just go AWOL like this, when there were people who loved and cared for him? Harriet thought he loved her. People in love didn't do this to each other.

Shoving her own feelings aside, Harriet thought about the centre: about lovely old Alf Stokes who battled on despite his heartache; about Bert who'd said the centre had saved him. What about Abby and Pete, who'd been given second chances? And all the others, who'd come to depend on the GRCC as a lifeline, something on their side for a change.

If Zack harmed anyone—or worse—he would go back to prison. The centre would surely be shut down, unless they could find someone to take his place. Zack had built that centre up all by himself, would he really let all that work go to waste? Two days earlier, she'd have said Zack lived for that centre. Now, she wasn't sure she knew him at all.

By the time they reached the Meadowfields estate, Ambrose had had a verbal spat with two white-van drivers and nearly mown down a cyclist he didn't see in the bike lane. Benedict had remained tactfully quiet for the journey, gripping on to the handle above his seat.

If the name Meadowfields conjured up an image of rolling pastures filled with wild grasses and flowers, the reality was somewhat different. Set off a busy main road, the estate was even bigger and more war-torn than the Gatsby Road. Like something out of *War of the Worlds*, six council blocks of grey granite loomed high over a sprawling mass of terrace houses. The Land Rover stopped at the entrance, and all three of them looked up.

'I don't like the look of this place,' Ambrose said. A heavy cloud blotted out the sun as he spoke, and Harriet shivered. It seemed like a bad omen.

Benedict looked back at Harriet. 'You still want to go in?' She nodded, trying to ignore the knot of nausea in her stomach. 'OK, let's do this,' he told Ambrose. 'Check your doors are locked.'

Ambrose shifted the car into first gear, and the Land Rover crossed the boundary into the estate. *We're in lawless territory now*, Harriet thought. A man was walking towards them, with a huge aggressive-looking pit bull on a lead. As he passed he stared insolently into the car, openly scoping the dashboard, as if looking for valuables. 'Nasty-looking brute,' Ambrose said. Harriet wasn't sure if he was talking about the man or the dog.

They followed the road into what seemed to be

the heart of the estate. Unlike the Gatsby Road, there were more people out and about here. They passed a group of girls all chewing gum or smoking. Even though they looked no more than fourteen, their flat, hostile faces made Harriet shiver. One of them stood irritably rocking a pram, while another, her hair scraped back into an unforgiving ponytail, made an aggressive gesture and spat at the Land Rover. A few of them smirked, while the others stared off, bored, into the distance, as if they'd seen it all before.

After fifteen minutes of driving round, they had gathered neither sight nor sound of Zack. *This is hopeless*, Harriet thought. He could be anywhere, what on earth had she thought they would gain by this? They could hardly get out of the car and start knocking on doors, the ones that weren't boarded-up, anyway.

Benedict caught Harriet's eye in the rear-view mirror. 'I think we should give up, have another think.' Until then, Harriet had held out a faint glimmer of hope. Now all she felt was despair. Ambrose grunted in agreement, and was just about to turn the car around when there was a sudden wailing behind them. Seconds later a stream of marked police cars flew past, their sirens flashing.

Harriet knew, just knew, it was something to do with Zack.

'Daddy, follow those police cars,' she cried. Her father sat still for a moment, as if stunned. 'Go!' she screamed.

Ambrose pushed his foot down on the accelerator. The Land Rover screeched forwards.

Chapter 70

As the last police car wailed past, they set off in hot pursuit. Ambrose screeched left, and then right, finally ending up in a wide, barren avenue with boarded-up houses either side. Half a dozen police cars were parked haphazardly round one. There was graffiti sprayed across the walls and an old mattress in the garden.

Harriet watched in horror as burly officers in riot gear walked up to the front door carrying a battering ram. Silently, they positioned themselves outside. Another officer standing well back gave a nod, and without warning they swung the ram against the door. It crumpled inwards like a piece of soggy cardboard. 'POLICE! POLICE!' they all shouted, and ran inside.

'Jesus Christ!' Benedict said. Harriet went to open her door.

'Don't you dare get out!' her father snapped. She cowered back in the seat.

A few minutes later the officers started to pull people out of the house. The suspects were handcuffed, all young and male, faces white and sullen. Harriet's heart skipped a beat as she recognized the thin, ratty face of the kid who had challenged Zack with a knife outside the centre. He was twisting and shouting in his handcuffs, and Harriet saw blood soaking the front of his T-shirt.

'Get your fucking hands off me! I know my rights.'

Harriet couldn't bear it any longer. Ignoring shouts from the two men, she unlocked her door and jumped out. She ran past the other police officers standing about, and headed straight towards the youth. 'Where's Zack?'

The pasty-faced hoodie stopped yelling and stared at her for a second. 'I know you.' His eyes narrowed. 'I stuck your boyfriend, what do you think about that?'

Cold fear gripped her. 'I don't understand.'

'What don't you understand, bitch? Stuck, stabbed, shanked—you getting it now?'

'You're lying,' she whispered.

Malicious triumph flashed through his face. 'Am I now?'

Suddenly, without warning he lunged at her, taking the police officers by surprise. He broke free of their grip and came at her, spitting and kicking. 'You're in it as well, you bitch!'

Harriet screamed, throwing her arms up to protect herself. But instead of an onslaught of pain, someone threw themselves in front of her.

'Don't you touch her!'

In total shock she looked up to see Zack with his hand round the kid's throat. 'If you come one inch closer—'

One of the officers ran up and pulled Zack off. 'Don't start now,' he told him.

'That's GBH!' the youth spat. 'He was fucking strangling me.'

'I think you've got more to worry about than that, sunshine,' said the other officer, leading him away. The hoodie turned and aimed one final defiant lob of spit at Zack. 'That was for Derrick!'

Harriet's legs were shaking violently. 'What's he talking about? Who's Derrick?'

Zack didn't answer. She saw blood pouring down

his arm from a cut on his shoulder. 'Oh my God, he did knife you!'

'It's just a nick,' he said. He looked exhausted and unshaven. As he stood there, Harriet could see the adrenalin draining out of him. A horrible feeling started to rise from the pit of her stomach.

'What have you done?'

He looked at her, ran his hand over his face.

'Why were you in there? *What are you involved in?*'

'Nothing!' he shouted. He took a deep breath. 'I'm not involved in anything, Harriet, I was the one who called the police.'

She couldn't believe it. 'What?'

He took a step towards her uncertainly. 'That's what I've been doing, tracking them down. I've been looking for them ever since Win...'

'Win's not dead!' Harriet exclaimed.

To her surprise he started laughing, a wild choking sound that gave way to a sob. 'I know. When I called the hospital and they told me ... I just couldn't believe it. She's going to be OK, Harriet!'

'So you knew?' she said slowly. 'You knew she wasn't dead and you just went off like that. You let me *think* ...' She just couldn't believe it. 'All this time I've been worried sick and you've been running round like some kind of vigilante!'

He reached out his good arm to touch her but she shook it off.

'I didn't want to involve you in something like that.'

'You should have let *me* be the judge of that, Zack!' she cried. 'I thought we were meant to be a team.'

447

He stared at her, eyes brilliant blue in the early morning light. 'You're right,' he said. 'I should have told you. But when I thought Win was . . .' he stopped. 'I just took off, I wasn't thinking straight. At that point I didn't know what I'd do if I found them.'

'Why didn't you tell me you were in prison?' she asked quietly.

She watched his face change. 'Did Win tell you?'

'Yes.'

He was perfectly still. 'What did she say?'

'Did you really kill someone?' Her voice was trembling.

Zack dropped his head. 'Believe me, Harriet, it will stay with me for the rest of my life . . .'

Her last hope gone, the confession brought out something unknown and primitive in Harriet. With no real control over her body, she swung her fist back and punched Zack squarely in the face.

Churchminster

One day to go, and Byron Heights was a mass of activity. The catwalk had been assembled in the ballroom, and by 8 a.m. the dress rehearsal was taking place. Genetically-blessed models, on loan from various agencies, were being directed by a harassed stage manager. Some of the designers stood in a huddle by the catwalk, watching. They'd moved in and now the back room of the house resembled something out of *Project Runway*, with sewing machines, fabric and rails of clothes everywhere.

As the music stopped, one young model came to

a halt, making the girls behind pile into her. The stage director groaned. 'How many more times! If the music stops, you don't. OK? So let's get moving.'

The place was utter bedlam, but Saffron was glad of the distraction. At least it put space between her and Rex. She could see him over the other side of the room, talking to someone. She looked at the sculpted face, the strong arms crossed over each other, and all she could feel was sick.

The morning after she'd woken in the unfamiliar bedroom, a whisky-induced hangover nagging at her head, Saffron had lain there in complete disbelief. It was as if she had woken from some kind of horrible dream. As she laid there, staring blankly at the ceiling, her phone beeped with a text message. She'd scrabbled round by the side of the bed and opened it. It had been a picture of their cactus on the kitchen mantelpiece. He'd grown a bizarre new appendage, which was stocking upwards like a huge phallus.

I think Leroy's been at the Viagra, Tom had written. *Mum is going to have to have some serious words when she gets home!*

Her instinct had been to laugh, but as the enormity of what had happened hit, Saffron had burst into tears. In that moment she realized just how much she still really did love him. How could she have treated him like that, thrown away what they had?

All around her was life and movement, but Saffron felt empty. The thought of telling Tom made her feel sick, but she owed him that. Their relationship would be over, irretrievably broken. Tom was a good man, the best she'd ever met. She

449

didn't deserve someone like him.

Her stomach lurched as she realized Rex was coming towards her. 'Hey,' he said cautiously.

'Hey.'

He bent down to drop a kiss on her cheek, but she turned away. He stood back, embarrassed. He folded his arms, before unfolding them again and looking round the room. 'Things seem to be going well.'

'Yeah.'

Rex cleared his throat. 'Saff, I feel as bad about this as you do.'

'No, you don't. Believe me.'

He sighed, and looked at the floor. 'I didn't want it to turn out like this. Your friendship means a lot.'

Friendship. What a load of bollocks. 'Are you going to tell him?' Rex said. 'Tom, I mean.'

After all those months of build-up, there was now nothing. All she could see now when she looked at Rex was a collection of lines and colours, a handsome, meaningless shell.

Her mouth twisted. 'Worried I'm going to drop you in it?'

'I wasn't saying that.' He rubbed his temples. 'It's just better if you stop and think, Saff, make sure it's the right thing to do?'

She was filled with contempt. For both of them. 'I think Tom knowing the truth is more important than us saving our own skin.'

'I didn't mean it like that!' He lowered his voice as someone walked past. 'Ah, shit. What a mess.'

Saffron laughed bitterly. 'You could say that.'

Chapter 71

London

As soon as she'd hit Zack, Harriet felt terrible. She'd never so much as killed a money spider in her entire life. 'I'm sorry,' she apologized, for about the tenth time.

Zack pressed the ice pack into his face. 'I deserved it,' he said, as one of the paramedics adjusted the bandage on his arm.

Ambrose poked his head into the back of the ambulance. 'Are you sure we can't offer you a lift back?'

Zack stood up. 'Thanks, Sir Ambrose, but we'll get a lift back with one of the police officers.' He looked at Harriet. 'I've got a lot of explaining to do.'

'Hmm, well.'

'I'll be fine, Daddy.' Harriet attempted a smile. 'I'll give you a call later.'

Ambrose nodded. Mercifully, he hadn't heard Zack admit he'd killed someone. He extended his hand to Zack. 'I want to thank you for saving my daughter.' He looked from one to the other, keenly. 'I'm not sure what's going on here, and I'm not sure I want to know, but it was damned good of you.'

Zack looked sheepish. 'Thank you, sir. I didn't really do anything.'

'Nonsense, man, take credit where it's due.' Ambrose patted his stomach. 'All this crime fighting makes a chap hungry. I think I'll stop by

451

my club on the way back for a full English.'

Harriet wanted to weep at the wonderful normality of him; she could always count on her father. And, she reflected, as she looked miserably out of the ambulance back door, men she could trust were rather short on the ground at the moment.

* * *

Once the paramedic had bandaged Zack's arm up, one of the officers dropped them back off at his flat. They walked up the stairs in silence. Inside, the place smelt still and stuffy, as if Zack hadn't been home for a while. He walked into the living room and opened the windows.

'Do you want a cup of tea? Only I'm not sure if the milk's still in date.'

She shook her head. 'I'm fine.'

Zack sighed. 'There's no point putting this off. You deserve an explanation. Please sit down.'

He remained at the window.

'Derrick Ebenezer was my partner in crime. Fighting, stolen cars, vandalism; we'd done it all by the age of seventeen.' He pulled down the neck of his T-shirt to expose the skull on his left pectoral. 'This was our gang tattoo. There were six of us, and they all looked up to Derrick and me. We pretty much ran the estate back then.' He smiled grimly. 'I thought I was bloody God. Stupid little boy I was.'

'Did Win know?'

Zack nodded. 'She tried to save me, but I was too far gone to care about anything, back then. God knows why she stuck by me.'

'How did you end up in prison?' Harriet couldn't believe they were having this conversation.

'I got caught doing a burglary, went into Feltham Young Offenders Institution for eighteen months. I had a lot of time to think in there. I'd always been angry, pissed off that I didn't have anything, that other kids had their nice little family set-ups, school, careers, futures. But then I had a reality check. Win.'

A wry smile crossed his face. 'I guess she had a captive audience for once. She came to visit me one day, and told me what I made of my life was my own responsibility, not someone else's fault. "You need to start being a man, Zachary," she said. I can still hear her voice now. That was when the penny dropped.'

'What did you do?'

'Retook my GCSEs inside and passed six, came out ready to start a better life. I was doing all right for a while. It was hard to distance myself from the boys—Derrick was still up to his old ways and he didn't like it—but I kept my head down and found a manager's job in a hardware shop. It was hard work, but I thrived on it. I turned that shop around, business was going well and everyone was pleased. The money wasn't great, but it was mine, you know? I'd earned it, not robbed it off someone else, or got it through dodgy means.'

Zack gave a short, dry laugh. 'Then Derrick came calling. He had this big job on, big enough to change all of our lives. I said no, but he was persistent. It was hard, we went way back. His family weren't exactly the von Trapps, but they'd been good to me. Fed me, let me doss in their house—even though they were bursting at the

453

seams already. Derrick started to play on my heartstrings, said he wanted to make a better life for his family, that he couldn't do it without me. Course, I couldn't help myself, could I? *Just one more time*, I told myself. I could do with the money; I'd be set up for life. I could take Win on a nice holiday, say thank you for everything she'd done for me.'

He still hadn't got on to the most important thing. The most terrible thought came into Harriet's mind. 'Zack, were you a hit man?'

He gave a shocked laugh. 'Jesus! No. It was an armed robbery, on a posh jeweller in the West End. I know it still wasn't right,' he added quickly, noticing the look on her face. 'All of us had a bad feeling about it. We tried to tell Derrick but he was having none of it, and being the fool I was, I let him win me over.'

His eyes glazed over, reliving the whole thing. 'I said from the start I didn't want to get involved with any of the heavy stuff, so I was the driver. All the way there my gut was telling me something, but the adrenalin took over. That's what it was about for me, Harriet, all the crimes I committed. I wasn't interested in what I stole, or hurting people. It was the adrenalin. It was such a buzz. It was the only thing that made me feel alive and happy.' He looked straight at her. 'I'm not trying to make excuses. I just want to tell you how it was, how I ended up in all this.'

She waited for him to carry on.

'Seven minutes, they said. Derrick had been there already and done a recce, so I waited, with the motor running. But as I sat there, there was this mum and her kid coming down the street towards me. This kid couldn't have been more than two years, beautiful little thing with a head full of blond curls. So there he was, coming along in his pushchair, and as he passed, this little kid looked straight at me, and his little face broke out into the biggest smile. He was so pure and innocent, and it made me feel sick. I thought if his mum knew what I was, what she was exposing her little boy to, then she'd drag him away screaming her head off. And as I sat there, it came to me: *I haven't done anything yet. There is still time to get out.* Then I thought of Win and the look on her face if anything happened to me.

'And all at once, I saw that I just had to get out.' His voice cracked. 'Suddenly my foot was on the accelerator, and I was pulling out, but what I didn't realize was that a bike courier was coming down the street behind me.'

His face was stricken. 'I didn't look, Harriet. I was so desperate to get away I just went, and this young bloke came flying into the side of me. I jumped out to try and help him, just as the boys came running round the corner with all hell breaking loose. We were just stupid amateurs— they'd bungled the whole thing—and the security guards were hot on their tail. It was seconds before the Old Bill were there, and we were in the back of a police van on the way to the station.'

'What happened to the courier?' Harriet was afraid to hear the answer.

'He died from head wounds in hospital,' Zack said, tonelessly. Andy Brooks. Young Australian kid, over here making some money for himself before going home. Dad called Ken, mum was Bree, younger sister called Susie. You know, Andy would have been thirty-two on the tenth of July, just a year younger than me. That date, it's part and parcel of me.'

The fact his mum had died in the same way didn't escape her. Harriet felt her eyes fill up. It was just too awful.

'My solicitor tried to get me to tell the court about my change of heart, to get their sympathy. But I didn't deserve any sympathy. I kept my trap shut and went down with all the others. Conspiracy to rob we all got—while I got death by dangerous driving added to my rap sheet. I was detained at HM Prison in Liverpool. We were all sent to different places around the country. I got seven years in all, served five for "good behaviour".' He smiled tightly. 'Ironic, isn't it?'

Liverpool. So that was why he'd behaved so oddly when she'd tried to talk about it. And she'd thought it had been because of an ex-girlfriend!

'What happened to Derrick?'

Zack shook his head. 'Died in prison, in a fight. It hit his family badly: Derrick had always been the man of the house. His mum and the other kids, they didn't want to stay round the Gatsby Road after that. By the time I got out, they'd moved on.' He looked at her. 'To an estate called Meadowfields.'

Meadowfields. It was all starting to make sense.

'The one who attacked Win, the one who tried to attack you, that was Derrick's brother, Flynn.' Zack sighed. 'He was just a little kid when I saw him last, running around the garden in his nappy.'

'But why did he attack Win? What's she got to do with anything?'

'Because she's close to me. I guess Flynn wanted

to hurt me, the way he thinks I hurt his family.'

'Zack, it wasn't your fault what happened to Derrick. You did the right thing.'

'I don't think that's how Flynn sees it. He's grown up in a life of poverty, his big brother dead, his mum tired and bitter because they missed out on their chance of making it.' He got up and went to the window. 'These kids, Harriet, they've got nothing. They feel completely done over by life, and they need to project their anger somewhere.'

'And so Flynn came to find you,' she said softly. Zack nodded. 'Do you remember that graffiti? EBZ? That was Derrick's tag. When I saw it I thought it must be some kind of mistake, a coincidence, but then Flynn turned up with his knife. I hadn't seen it for years, but I knew it as soon as I saw it. Derrick stole it during a burglary. We used it to start our gang, become "blood brothers". I still remember yelping when he cut my hand, we must have only been fourteen.' He shook his head. 'Jesus, we thought we were the mafia or something.'

'Is that why you didn't call the police? Because you didn't want Flynn going down the same route?'

'I thought if I could just get through to him . . .' Zack leant back on the windowsill. 'I went up to Meadowfields, but didn't get far. Flynn and his mates got me by the entrance. They cut me—and I got away and called the police.'

And now they were behind bars, just like Zack and his gang had been.

'What happened to the others?' she asked. 'The ones from your gang, I mean.'

'They've all stayed on the straight and narrow,

from what I hear. Most of them have moved away.'

'How can other people not know, Zack? People from the estate?' Had they all been laughing at her?

'I've been away a long time.' He looked down at his trainers. 'You can do a good job of making yourself invisible if you want to.'

Harriet sat on the sofa, trying to take it all in. Zack came over and crouched down in front of her. 'I'm sorry I didn't tell you. Win kept on at me, saying you were the kind of person who wouldn't judge me on my past. But I was scared of losing you.' He stopped. 'I still am.'

'Win's been so worried about you.'

'I promise, I won't put her through anything like this again.'

As she sat there, Harriet was overwhelmed by the most unbelievable exhaustion. It was as if she'd finally let go of the stress of the last forty-eight hours.

'What about you, Harriet?' He was tight with apprehension. 'Can you forgive me?'

She looked at him. Really *looked* at him, to try and find what she was searching for. Because, despite all that had happened, Harriet knew she loved him.

'Oh, Zack,' she said sadly.

Misreading her tone, the light faded out of his eyes. 'I do understand. If you don't want anything to do with me.'

Harriet's heart clenched at the thought of them being apart. 'But I do still want to be with you.'

He looked up. 'Really?'

'Really.' She touched his face. 'Just no more secrets, OK?'

He grinned, a flash of the old Zack back, and put his arms around her. 'You've got all of me now, part and parcel.'

Chapter 72

Churchminster

Something remarkable happened. Overnight, Win had become the most famous woman in the country. Somehow the press had got hold of every detail of the story and gone to town, recounting how the 'Saviour of Gatsby' had 'fought her way back from the brink of death' after 'knife-wielding hoodies' 'attacked her in her home'.

In the biggest national newspaper, the *Daily Mercy*, there was a front-page picture of Win sitting up in her hospital bed, looking weak but happy, while a senior politician stood by her side. He had waxed lyrical to the journalist about Win single-handedly 'mending Broken Britain'. The only fly in the ointment was a misquote from an unnamed source at the hospital, saying Win would be well enough to come to the show.

Back in Churchminster, by mid-afternoon the phone was ringing off the hook. Suddenly every A-lister worth their salt was clamouring for tickets. Saffron would rather have been anywhere but Byron Heights right then, but Rex had called her over for an emergency meeting to wade through all the requests. By teatime, they had a VIP list that read like an entry from *Who's Who*.

Saffron had just got off the phone with Simon

Cowell's agent, who had requested six tickets, one for himself and the others for his celebrity friends. She put them down on the list, after Elle Macpherson and Princess Eugenie. The whole thing was starting to feel surreal.

Across the dining room table Rex had been just as busy. As the only two people in the room, they'd been doing a good job of pretending the other one wasn't there all morning.

'Guess who that was,' he said.

Saffron lifted her eyes for a nanosecond, and went back to her list. 'I have no idea.'

'Bibi Brown's manager.'

That got her interest. 'What does he want?'

The triumph was clear in his voice. 'Apparently, Bibi has decided she can do something for us after all.'

'I suppose it's got nothing to do with the fact that half the fashion world are coming now?'

'Who cares. Saff, we got her!' It should have been their crowning moment, but Saffron couldn't have cared less. Rex's face fell. 'Did you hear me?'

'Yeah, that's great.'

'Great? It's insane!'

'What about Phillip Chan?'

'He can open the show. That's still a big deal. Bibi will dazzle us at the end.' He caught her expression. 'What?'

'You.' She threw her pen down. 'Acting like nothing has happened. Don't you have any kind of conscience?'

'Of course I do!' he said angrily. 'You think I don't feel terrible? Even without you projecting all your self-hatred on to me.'

'Now you just hold on a minute.' Her voice was

460

shaking.

He held his hand up. 'Where's that going to get us at the moment, huh? We're meant to be a team, Saff, and no matter what your feelings are towards me right now I need you to be *on* this!'

She stared at him defiantly. 'Fine.' As much as she hated to admit it, there was some truth to his words.

He sighed, anger gone. 'Can we please not fight? I haven't got the energy.'

For the next five minutes they worked in uncomfortable silence, until Saffron raised her head again. 'Rex?'

'Yeah?' He looked up from chewing his pen.

She tried to inject some normality back in her voice. 'I don't want to point out the obvious, but these people are coming because they think Win's going to be here. I spoke to Harriet, and that stuff about her being discharged is a load of bollocks. There's no way she's going to be well enough.'

It was almost as if he'd forgotten. 'Are you sure?'

'She's had a major head injury! Harriet says she'll be in hospital another week at least.'

Rex stared into space for a moment. 'So let people think she's coming.'

Saffron frowned. 'I don't get you.'

'Think about it! Win has become the poster girl for this show; we won't get people down without her. Let's just carry on with business as normal, then, on the night, I'll simply say very sadly that she wasn't well enough after all. We'll have everyone here by then, anyway.'

'Uh-oh, no way. We'd basically be lying to people.'

'No, we're just not correcting someone else's

461

mistake,' he said. There was something urgent in his eyes. 'Believe me, if we want to make this show a success, we need people to believe she's going to be there!'

'It's not fair, Rex, on the guests, on Win and Zack . . .'

'We're doing this *for* them! For the centre. All I want to do is make it the best show we can.'

It was like they were in free fall, with nothing to stop them. 'OK,' Saffron said unhappily. She was damned, anyway.

* * *

One more story made the news that day. Following a burglary and assault on a 76-year-old woman in North London, four youths aged between fifteen and seventeen had been charged and remanded in police custody. They were due to appear at Hendon Magistrates Court the following day. 'These suspects have been known to the police for some time, so naturally we are delighted with the result,' a police spokesperson said. 'Thanks to assistance from a diligent member of the public, we've removed four extremely nasty characters from the streets.'

JULY

Chapter 73

Like something out of a Mediterranean holiday brochure, the day of Fashion Cares finally arrived. By 7 a.m. the sun was already high in the wide expanse of sky, and weather forecasters were predicting it to be the hottest day of the year so far.

At Hardwick House Saffron was sitting at the kitchen table with a cup of tea after a fitful night's sleep. The French windows to the garden were open, and a pleasant breeze was creeping in. It was so quiet and tranquil; the calm before the storm.

Physically and emotionally drained, Saffron was running on pure adrenalin. In a few hours, she would have to pull off the biggest coup in the fashion calendar—and that was even before she tackled the tangled mess of her love life. She wondered what Tom was doing at this very moment. Was he thinking about her, too? Saffron cupped her mug tightly and looked out of the window.

'That was a big sigh.' Her mother had appeared in the doorway, dressed in a bobbly old dressing gown. 'You're up early, darling.'

'Lots to do.'

Babs came and sat down opposite her. 'Are you excited about later?'

'Actually, I think totally terrified would be more appropriate.'

'It's going to be wonderful, don't you worry.'

'Thanks, Mum.' Saffron looked round the kitchen. 'God, it's going to be weird not living here!'

Her mother's chin wobbled. 'Don't. I've got so used to having you.'

'I'll come back and see you lots, don't worry.'

'I know, darling. You're probably sick of me by now, anyway.'

'*Mum!* That's not true.'

Babs smiled fondly at her daughter. 'Is Tom coming?'

Out of nowhere Saffron's stomach dropped. 'Yeah, he's getting the train down later.'

Babs saw her face. 'Don't worry, darling, I'm sure once you see him you'll feel better. Things have a funny way of ironing themselves out.'

'It's too late for that,' Saffron muttered.

'What do you mean?' Babs said, looking slightly anxious.

Saffron was desperate to unburden herself, but she just couldn't do it. Her mother loved Tom. 'Nothing. I'd better go and get in the shower.'

*　　　*　　　*

The show didn't start until 5 p.m., but by the time Saffron arrived at 9 a.m. the place was already humming with activity. The silk, twelve-foot banner with its logo had been erected across the front gates. The words *Fashion Cares* ran across it and underneath, in smaller writing read *Style With Substance*. Saffron thought that was a nice touch.

All around people were rushing in and out carrying boxes, flowers and props. As she stood there watching, Saffron heard her phone beep. She pulled it out of her bag and looked at the text message. It was a number she didn't recognize.

466

'Hi, Saffron, I am so sorry I haven't got back to you! I've got a new phone and have only just got your message. For sure I'll be there, I think my manager is contacting you about tickets? Savannah x PS Is there a helipad?'

It was a moment of magic in the crapstorm that was her life right now. She stared at the phone in disbelief. 'Oh my God! We've got Savannah Sexton!'

She found Rex in the ballroom, talking to Sue Sylvester. As she walked up they were in the middle of a heated conversation, Sue talking at quite a volume compared to her usual whispered tones.

'All I'm saying, Rex, is that my last two invoices haven't been paid, and I'm getting a little concerned.'

'Sue, I've told you. There's obviously been some mistake at the bank. I'll get on to it as soon as I can.'

Saffron cleared her throat and they both looked round. 'Morning.'

'Saffron, hi.' Rex looked back at Sue. 'I promise you, it's my priority.'

'What was that about?' Saffron asked as Sue walked off.

Rex shrugged. 'A little admin glitch, nothing to worry about.' He stared after the little woman distractedly. 'How are you doing, anyway?'

'As well as you can after two hours' sleep.'

'You and me both.' As they tentatively smiled at each other, Saffron felt a sign of the first thaw. They had to put on a professional front today.

'I've got good news and bad news,' she told him.

'Hit me with it.'

'Don't you want to hear the good news first?' She paused, savouring the moment. 'Savannah Sexton is coming.'

'You're kidding me! That is fantastic.'

'Hold on, don't get too excited. We need to find her a helipad, of all things.'

'No worries, they can use the back field.' Rex pulled a face. 'Go on, then, hit me with the bad news.'

'We've had tons, and I mean literally *tons*, of press requests to interview Win today. What are we going to do?'

'I'll think of something.' His eyes travelled down to the dress bag she was carrying. 'That your outfit?'

'Uh, yeah.' She couldn't believe he was being so blasé about everything!

'What are you wearing?'

'Vintage Westwood, thought I'd better pay homage.' She hesitated. 'You?'

'Classic black suit, white shirt. I'm kind of channelling Tom Ford, with accents of Zac Posen thrown in.'

Saffron couldn't help but smile. 'Oh God, you're back in the lingo already!'

It was to be one of the few light-hearted moments that day.

*　　　*　　　*

The sun was scorching through the sunroof of the Golf as Harriet made her way to Clanfield Hall that afternoon. She hadn't wanted to leave London, and Zack and Win, but there was still a coachload of people going from the centre. Win had insisted. 'Who else is going to fly that flag for us, 'Arriet?' Harriet had left Win chiding one of the junior doctors about his appalling handwriting on her medical notes.

It was just past 3 p.m. when Harriet pulled up outside the Hall. She got out of the car and looked round. The estate looked glorious: vast lawns stretching as far as the eye could see, the flowerbeds her mother was so particular about, chests of colourful treasures in amongst the green. Harriet walked over to the huge fountain in the middle of the turning circle and dipped her hand in the water. She was just savouring the coolness when there was a loud banging from one of the upstairs windows. She looked up to see her father waving at her. She waved back. 'Hi, Daddy!' She went to get her suitcase out of the boot.

Moments later the door opened silently to reveal Hawkins, an island of unflappability. 'Miss Harriet, let me take your bags.'

'Thanks, Hawkins.' A figure popped up in the doorway behind him and Harriet felt her jaw drop. Hands on hips, her father drew himself up proudly. 'My new look, what do you think?'

Harriet took in the tight black trousers, the piano-key tie. She stared at the studded leather jacket, the black winkle-picker shoes. Ambrose did a slow turn, arms in the air, to reveal a *Rock Star* slogan across the back of the jacket. 'Got inspired watching that Wok Gan chap the other night. It's not just the ladies who can look ten years younger, you know.'

Without a word Hawkins took Harriet's bag and disappeared back into the house.

'Well . . .' Harriet looked her father up and down,

desperately trying to think of something positive to say. She was surprised at how snake-like her father's hips were. For some bizarre reason she couldn't fathom, Ambrose actually looked rather cool. 'You go, Daddy!'

Ambrose grinned, rooting around in one of his pockets. 'That reminds me, I bought you a present.' He brought out a skull and crossbones necklace on a long silver chain. 'Got it from the same website I bought my togs on. Here.'

As he handed the heavy trinket over, Harriet wondered just how her Boden wardrobe was possibly going to blend in with it.

*   *   *

At the show Stacey Turner had turned up with her Boots No. 7 kit, fully expecting to work. Saffron eventually took pity on her, and went to ask if any of the make-up teams needed some assistance. Antoine von Crapp, one of the industry's leading make-up artists, seized her offer gratefully. One of his team was ill, so Stacey was thrown straight in at the deep end. Saffron had heard from Clementine about Brenda and Beryl's Fright Night make-up, but didn't have time to worry, so she made her excuses and fled.

The backstage area was utter bedlam. One young designer was still on her sewing machine, frantically altering a bat-winged trouser suit.

Someone else was shouting about a model missing her train, while the ones who had made it were standing around looking bored and leggy. The little old ladies scurrying about with pins in their mouths might have looked out of place but they were the legendary dressers, the ones responsible for making sure the models were fit to step out on the runway.

Saffron had to admit, the clothes looked fantastic. Several of the designers might look like they were about to keel over from sleep deprivation, but they had really pulled the stops out. Each rail showed a different vision; from ethereal flowing garments with feathered headdresses (Julie Friend) to an amazing punk rock kid called Seth who had somehow managed to make a wedding dress made out of white PVC look totally stunning.

Saffron had just got changed and come out of the cloakroom when a familiar voice greeted her. '*Darling* dress!'

She turned round to see *Soirée*'s Alexander Napier, looking every inch the fashionista in a black suit and deep plunging vest. 'Al!' she shrieked, running over to hug him. 'Oh my God!'

'All seems well on the home front,' he commented.

'Honestly, hun, I can't thank you enough for all your help. We couldn't have done it without you.'

'Oh, I hardly did anything, just pointed Rex in the right direction. I must say he seems to have pulled it off.' Alexander touched her arm. 'Speaking of which, darling, there's something I need to talk to you about.'

Over Alexander's shoulder Saffron noticed quite a few models were starting to emerge with clown-like make-up, which looked suspiciously like Stacey's handiwork.

'Earth to Saffron?'

Another model appeared, looking like she'd

fallen face down on to one of Babs's wet canvasses. Saffron groaned. She knew that saying yes to Stacey had been a terrible idea!

'Al, I gotta fly.'

'But darling . . .'

'I'll come and find you later!'

Saffron half expected Stacey to be lying across a dressing table, having been stabbed to death by Antoine with a sharpened eye pencil. But to her astonishment a scene of great harmony greeted her.

The pair were studiously working side by side on a pair of models, the other girls waiting in line. Antoine looked up as she came in. 'But where did you find this girl, darling?' he said. 'I'm just so in love with her ironic reinterpretation of the classic eighties movement. We're sending all my girls out like it.'

Judging by the way Stacey was brutally scraping one wincing model's hair back into a Croydon facelift, Saffron suspected there was nothing ironic about it. In another corner a designer was having a hissy fit because a model's boobs were too big for his dress. 'If I'd have wanted Katie Price I'd have asked for her!' he screeched, trying to hoik the bodice up. 'Get me some thread, I'm literally going to have to stitch the poor cow in.'

Despite the frenzied activity Bibi Brown had yet to turn up. Saffron said a little prayer. *Don't let us down this time, or I'll kill you myself.*

*   *   *

By 4 p.m. the car park was crammed with sports cars and vintage Aston Martins, the odd Vespa

472

thrown in. A battered old bus with *Kemal's Coaches* across it was parked haphazardly across several parking spaces. Saffron thought it had to be the Gatsby Road lot as she saw a bunch of people huddled together, whispering excitedly to each other every time they saw a famous face. Saffron had already seen Kate Moss and Naomi Campbell air-kissing each other and quaffing champagne, while Alexa Chung and *Harry Potter* actress Emma Watson were moving easily through the glossy fashion pack.

Rex was working the crowd himself, moving from group to group shaking hands and air-kissing. Saffron, who'd just spent the last five minutes directing people to the cloakroom, found herself feeling a bit irritated. She'd hardly had time to get ready. With her hastily applied kohl and over-gelled hair she was now wondering if she resembled some kind of rabid parakeet.

She was just watching Boris Johnson, the Mayor of London, accidentally step on someone's dress, when she felt a hand on her arm. It was Harriet and Sir Ambrose, who seemed to have a new job as a Mick Jagger impersonator.

'H!' Saffron gave Harriet a huge hug. 'How *are* you?'

Her friend looked tired, but happy. 'Good, thanks, darling.'

Saffron stepped back and surveyed the baronet. 'Wow, Sir Ambrose, I'm loving your look!'

Ambrose looked chuffed to bits. 'Top drawer, isn't it?'

'Daddy's been getting quite a few compliments!' A champagne waiter stopped and offered them a glass. Saffron downed half of hers in one gulp,

473

trying to drown the butterflies in her stomach.

'I can't believe all the press here,' Harriet said. 'We drove past a big crowd of paparazzi at the gate.'

Saffron smiled weakly, feeling terrible she couldn't tell her they were there for Win.

Ambrose wandered off to look at an erotic painting on the wall.

'I just saw Rex, looking very dashing in his tux,' Harriet said. 'Oh, hello, Tom!'

Saffron's stomach dropped, as she turned round to see her fiancé standing behind them. The beard had gone, and he was wearing a white shirt and a grey linen suit that Saffron hadn't seen before. Her heart felt like it was about to leap out of her chest. He looked *gorgeous*.

'Hey, babe.' Tom smiled at Harriet. 'Long time, H.'

'Harriet! What the dickens do you think "a phallic rebirth" is?' Ambrose's voice cut through the crowd, making several people look round. Harriet smiled apologetically. 'See you in a minute, guys.'

Saffron and Tom were left standing there. Scrubbed up and smart, he was already attracting quite a few looks, with people making the connection between him and Rex. 'Don't I get a hug or anything?' he asked.

'Oh, of course,' Saffron said. Somewhat awkwardly she put her arms round him. Just the feel of his body reminded her of Rex's, and she pulled away, the guilt overpowering.

'Tom Boy!' Rex chose that exact second to walk up, and Saffron saw exactly the same expression in his face that she felt. Guilt. Rex gave his brother a big, jovial hug. 'Great to see you, bro.'

'You too, mate.'

Rex cast his eye over Tom's suit. 'Armani?'

Tom cast a smiley look at Saffron. 'Topman, actually.'

'I'm liking it.' Rex glanced at her. 'Hey. I've got someone I need to talk to, then I'll catch up with you in a bit, yeah?'

He glided off, back into the crowd. Saffron knew her face was flushing. To her immense relief she saw her mum fluttering around, like a moth trying to get out of a room. 'Mum! Over here.'

Babs swirled round. 'There you are, darling.' Her face lit up. 'Tom!'

'Can you excuse me for a moment?' Saffron said. 'I won't be long.' With that, she fled to the kitchen.

She leant over the sink, gulping down mouthfuls of water straight from the tap. She needed to get a grip; she couldn't even look Tom in the face. How could Rex act so glibly?

As she stood there trying to calm down, Saffron could hear raised voices coming from the walk-in pantry. She frowned. Who could that be? The kitchen, like upstairs, was strictly off-limits. Wiping her mouth, she walked over to tell whoever was doing drugs in there or having an illicit snog or God knows what, that this wasn't the place to do it.

But as she drew closer, Saffron stopped. She was sure one of the voices was Rex's. He seemed to be pleading, cajoling.

'Look, I wanted you to come to this to prove I am serious about making a fresh start. I want Reuben to know that I take my responsibilities seriously.'

'That's Mr Gold to you, sonny.' The other man's

475

voice was crisp, American. 'You lost your first-name privilege when you were caught leading his precious daughter astray.'

Saffron frowned. Reuben Gold? *The* Reuben Gold? The billionaire magnate whose daughter's wedding dress she'd been lusting after? But this didn't make sense . . .

'I didn't lead her astray.' Rex's voice was low, desperate. 'Summer is quite capable of doing that herself.'

'And you were the dumb-ass who got caught up in it.' The other man sounded scornful. 'If you two hadn't been so doped off your faces, Summer wouldn't have been caught on a DUI rap, and a thirty-million-dollar mansion wouldn't have gone up in flames. I don't need to tell you how *that* went down with Mr Gold.'

Saffron's head was whirling. What did Rex have to do with Reuben Gold? And his daughter, Summer? She held her breath, trying to hear more.

'As you know, Mr Gold is a very private man. Protective of his family, and even more protective of his business interests. The very reason he's a silent partner in Frontline is because he doesn't want all the attention that comes with such a high-profile brand. Too many people nosing around, asking questions. And you and his daughter nearly blew all that with that little shindig of yours!'

Oh my God. The pieces were starting to fit now. Reuben Gold owned Frontline clothing. Frontline, the clothing chain that Rex was the face of, or at least that he said he was before coming back to the UK on an extended holiday . . .

Rex spoke again. 'Look, Ari, this is the reason I

476

put on this show. To show Mr Gold that I am a professional, not this stupid party boy.'

Ari snorted. Or were you just crapping your Calvins that Mr Gold had put the kibosh on your contract, and you needed something to get back into his good books?'

Saffron's eyes widened. Rex had been dropped by Frontline? She was frozen to the spot.

She heard Rex sigh loudly. 'Look, I admit leaving wasn't the best thing to do. I wanted to give Reuben time to . . . cool off. When I planned this charity show, I thought it would be a great chance to redeem myself. To show Mr Gold he could trust me.'

'What about Paulina? Can she trust you? Reuben isn't happy with the way you've treated her. He counts her as family.'

'I loved Paulina. I told her nothing happened with Summer!' Rex lowered his voice. 'I'm gonna try and make it up to her, I promise.'

Ari grunted. 'Jesus Christ, you're pathetic.'

'Look, Ari, this show is going to be great. Mr Gold, Paulina, I'm going to prove myself to all of you.'

'We'll just have to wait and see, won't we? Mr Gold is a very private man, and he didn't like you upsetting the apple cart one little bit. But it just so happens, Rex, and it pains me to say this to your pretty little face, that you've been the most successful model Frontline has ever used. And as you know, Mr Gold is a very astute businessman. Even though he was far too busy to come to this hokey little set-up, I'm here acting in his capacity. And the message is if you can keep your act smartened up, then you might just keep your contract after all. *Comprende?'*

'Ari, I won't let you down.' Rex's voice was full of relief. 'Tell Mr Gold . . .'

'Tell him yourself, kid.' Ari coughed. 'I'm outta here, anything rural gives me a rash.' Saffron jumped back as a little man with a shiny bald head stepped out. He gave Saffron a distasteful look, as though she were the hired help, and scurried off, BlackBerry already clamped to his ear.

A few moments later Rex came out. He stopped dead when he saw Saffron. 'Did you . . . ?'

'Oh yes,' she said icily. 'Every word.'

Chapter 74

'You *used* me.'

Rex looked pained. 'It's not like that.'

'From what I heard, it's exactly like that!' Saffron was so angry she could hardly get the words out. 'All this time I've been busting a gut to help you, and all you've wanted to do is get back in Reuben Gold's good books!'

'Saff, please. Listen to me. I admit, in the beginning I was out for myself, but then I really started believing in this show. I started believing in us.'

'Don't give me that shit,' she said coldly.

'OK, wrong choice of words. But I honestly mean it when I said I wanted to be part of something good, make a difference. This whole thing has been life-changing for me.'

'So what?' she said sarcastically. 'You don't really want to save your arse and worm your way back in

Paulina's bed? You've done all this just for the *life-changing* experience?'

Suddenly, all the go slumped out of him. 'I'm broke, Saff.'

She stared at him. 'What do you mean you're broke? You must be worth millions!'

'It's all gone,' he said simply. 'I've blown it. Every last penny. This place.' He waved his arms round. 'I'm three months behind on the rent for it. Sue hasn't been paid. 'The show is my last chance.'

'You expect me to feel sorry for you?'

'No.'

Saffron shook her head. 'Jesus, Rex! I can't believe you shagged the boss's daughter.'

'Of course I didn't! Even I'm not that stupid. We just used to hang out, party. Reuben might think Summer is his perfect little angel, but believe me, she isn't.'

'Did you really burn his house down?' She couldn't help her horrified fascination.

'No! We'd been up all night partying pretty hard, and I eventually passed out. Next thing I know I'm being dragged out of the house by a fire crew and Summer has smashed Daddy's Lamborghini into a fire hydrant. Apparently she'd left some candles burning, and then decided it would be a good idea to go out and get some cigarettes. One caught fire and the whole place went up. Luckily no one else was there at the time, but Summer denied she'd done anything. Said I led her astray.' He gave a dry laugh. 'As if.'

'What about Paulina? You really think this is going to win her back?'

Rex looked shamefaced. 'I've been a fool, but I'm trying. I really love her, Saff . . .'

479

Her anger was starting to boil over again. She was furious at being misled, furious at herself for falling for his shit. 'You bastard. When I think about all the bloody hard work I've done for this show, for you . . .'

'It's not like that, honestly. I admit I was thinking of myself at the start, but as time went on, it started to really mean something to me.' He took a step towards her. 'You mean something to me.'

'Don't touch me!' she shouted. 'I can't believe how stupid I've been. I can't believe I let you inside my head. I can't believe I ever *thought* about you that way. I wish we'd never . . .'

'Wish you'd never what?'

They both whipped round. Tom was standing in the doorway, and the expression on his face scared her.

His voice was cold, deliberate. 'I said, you wish you'd never what?'

*   *   *

In the entrance hall outside Harriet was talking to the Toweys. 'Darling, I'm so pleased everything has worked out,' Caro said to Harriet, hoisting Rosie up higher into her arms. 'It's such a relief that Win's going to be all right.'

'I know, she's getting stronger by the day.' Harriet touched the skirt of Rosie's princess dress down, suddenly feeling rather overcome. 'I honestly don't know what I would have done without you guys.'

Benedict gave her a wink. 'That's what friends are for.'

'Benny-dict!' Milo was pulling on his stepfather's

480

hand, impatient to go off and explore the exotic surroundings.

'We'll go in a minute,' he placated him.

'There you are!' Clementine appeared in front of them, stately in a vintage Jaeger two-piece. 'Have you seen Rex and Saffron? Everyone is asking for them.' Her lips pursed disapprovingly. 'They can't just take off like this.'

'They'll be busy doing something,' Caro reassured her. She grinned. 'How exciting! They must be having the time of their lives, seeing it all come together.'

*   *   *

Click. Tom shut the door slowly behind him and the noise sounded deliberate, terrifying. He stood there, dark eyes black with anger. 'What have you done?' He was looking straight over Saffron's head at his brother.

'Bro, it's not like that.' Rex was trying to be calm, but Saffron could see a nerve pulsating in his neck.

As Tom moved towards them, Saffron shrank back. This wasn't her big, soft, bear-like Tom. Barely controlled rage made him seem ten feet tall, a frightening, unknown quantity.

'Tom.' Her voice came out as barely a whisper.

It was like he didn't even hear her. 'I can't believe you've done this again. You've slept with her, haven't you?'

'Bro, wait. *Listen* to me.'

'Again?' Saffron's fear turned to confusion. 'What do you mean . . .'

Her words were cut short as Tom lunged forward, knocking her out of the way. 'You

481

bastard!' As he made contact with Rex there was a loud thud, like two massive pieces of timber swinging into each other. The two brothers crashed into a pair of bar stools, sending them flying, and somehow Saffron found herself pushed to the ground.

All she could see were contorted faces, fists flying like pistons. 'Stop it!' she screamed.

Suddenly the kitchen door burst open and Benedict came running in, a child's cuddly toy in his hand. 'They're killing each other!' Saffron cried, as a water jug went flying.

Benedict leapt over the breakfast bar and with some difficulty managed to prise them apart. He shoved Rex away—'Stay there!'—whilst his arm went round Tom's neck. He pinned him back against the wall. 'Easy, fella.' Tom rested his head against the wall, his breathing short and laboured. Benedict glanced at Saffron. 'What the hell is going on?'

This couldn't be happening, it couldn't. She looked up at him tearfully. 'Could you give us a minute?'

As soon as Benedict left the room Tom was over, crouching beside her.

'I'm so sorry.' His voice trembled. 'I didn't mean to push you over, are you hurt?'

She pushed him away. 'What do you mean, Rex has done it again?'

Tom suddenly looked a thousand years old. 'Rex slept with Cassie.'

Saffron's mouth fell open. Rex hung his head, face as white as a sheet. 'You did what?' she asked.

'He slept with her,' Tom repeated. 'Didn't you, *mate*?' He said the last word mockingly. 'When he came down to visit me at uni. I came back from the bar and found them in bed together.' His eyes flashed. 'In my own bed.'

Saffron was struggling to take it all in. 'What, and you still got engaged to this girl? What the hell, Tom!'

'It was after I'd ended the engagement. We were still together as a couple.'

'I don't understand.' Saffron frantically thought back to the conversation they'd had, when she'd first found out about Cassie. 'You told me you finished it because you didn't want to marry her, not because Rex slept with her. You bloody awful liar, Tom!'

She saw him swallow. 'I didn't lie,' he said. 'I just didn't . . .'

She interrupted. 'How much longer did you go out for?'

'Three months.' When he saw her reaction, his face seemed to cave in. 'Look, we would have finished anyway! Me and Cassie didn't have a future together. Can't you understand why I want to forget about it? The fact that my own *brother* betrayed me like that?' He looked across at Rex, eyes burning. 'I would have given my life for you. It was the two of us against the world!'

'For Chrissakes, Tom, are you never going to forgive me?' Rex's voice was trembling. 'I even left the country to give you some space!' He shook his head. 'After Mum died . . .' he stopped, fighting off the tears. 'I was a stupid, dumb kid, in a bad place. Don't think I haven't regretted it every day since.'

'So much you did it again, eh?' Tom's voice was like steel.

'It wasn't like that!'

'I've heard those words before.'

Saffron was barely listening. 'Is that why you proposed? To warn Rex off? You only did it when he moved into the village!'

He hesitated a second too long. In that instant Saffron felt everything being ripped away from her. 'What is it with you two?' She stood up, shoving away Tom's hand as he tried to help. She looked at Tom, suddenly a stranger standing in front of her. 'I can't believe I've been beating myself up, when our engagement is one big fat lie!'

Pushing past him, Saffron ran out, slap bang into her literary agent, Pamela Aston.

'There you are, Saffron,' she exclaimed. 'I'd like to introduce you to Liz Astville, editor at Mayflower Publishing!'

Saffron was barely aware of the tall, dark-haired woman in her sharp suit. Liz smiled at her. 'Pam's sent me your manuscript, and I absolutely love it!'

Saffron glanced blindly at them. 'I'm so sorry . . . would you excuse me?' she choked. Walking, then running, she pushed her way through the jostling crowd and up the stairs.

*   *   *

It was here that Tom found her twenty minutes later, curled up on the four-poster in the end bedroom. He came and sat down beside her, the bed creaking under his weight.

'I proposed because I meant it, Saff.'

'But what about you and Cassie . . .'

'This was never about me and Cassie!' he said, suddenly fierce again. 'This was about me and Rex.

You're the love of my life, Saff, and always will be. Why can't you see that?'

Her eyes welled up. 'I've got something to tell you. About me and Rex.'

'He told me.'

She sat up, startled. 'He did?'

Tom sighed. 'About how you'd both been drunk and he tried it on with you. And you'd stopped it and walked out.'

He looked at her, as if willing her to agree with him. Saffron swallowed. So Rex had taken the wrap for her. Her confession was on the tip of her tongue. *It was now or never.*

'Tom, I . . .'

'What, Saff?'

She looked into his huge, sad eyes and couldn't do it. 'I did . . . I did have feelings for him,' she said instead. 'Or at least I thought I did.'

'I know.' She saw the pain in his face and hated herself. 'That's what Rex does, draws people into his world and sweeps them along. That's what he's been doing his whole life.'

'You must hate him.'

'He's not my favourite person right now.' Tom rubbed his eyes wearily. Rex isn't a bad guy. He did kind of lose it after Mum died and then when he and Cassie . . .' He sighed. 'He tried a few times, but I just shut him out. By the time I was ready to talk we'd drifted too far apart, and Rex was off on his ego trip.' He looked down. 'When he turned up here, I had mixed feelings. But it's been a long time. I wanted to give him the benefit of the doubt.' He gazed at her. 'I can't blame him for being attracted to you, Saff. You're one hell of a woman.'

485

'Oh Tom.' Her chin wobbled. 'I don't deserve you.'

'Hey, come here,' he whispered. He put his arms round her. 'Don't put it all on yourself. I've neglected you, Saff.'

She smiled through her tears. 'No, you haven't. I've been a moody old cow, only thinking about myself.'

'Let's call it "having a creative moment". You are a writer now, after all.' He paused. 'Rex told me. About Reuben Gold. I had a feeling something was up, anyway.'

She stared at the bedspread. 'What's he going to do?'

'He says he's going to fly back and face the music.' Tom managed a dry smile. 'He's had quite the wake-up call.'

'What will happen with you two?'

'It's going to be interesting,' he said reflectively. 'But we owe it to each other to try. I want my brother in my life.'

They sat there in silence for a few moments, before Tom laid his big hand over hers. 'Come back to me, Saff. Let's start again, right from this moment. We can't throw away what we have together.'

Her eyes blurred. *Tell him.*

He cupped her face in his hand. 'I love you,' he said simply. 'I always have. I don't want a life without you.'

Then and there, Saffron realized she didn't either. And how she'd nearly lost it. 'Oh, Tom,' she said, dissolving into fresh tears.

As they lay there in each other's arms, a strange whirring could be heard in the distance. It got louder and louder until it was directly overhead, an ear-splitting roar over Byron Heights.

Savannah Sexton had arrived.

Chapter 75

Long blonde hair teased into waves, and wearing a curve-lapping Valentino gown, Savannah made her appearance on the red carpet. The assembled press erupted like a pack of starving hyenas. 'Savannah, over here! Savannah, give us a smile, darlin'!' The Hollywood actress was the epitome of grace and spent a good five minutes posing and signing autographs.

As she was finally whisked away by her antsy-looking entourage she spotted Saffron. 'Saffron, hi!' she called out.

'Hey, Savannah!' Saffron was flattered and surprised she'd been remembered. Ignoring irritated looks from her people, Savannah came over and kissed Saffron on both cheeks. Up close she was even more exquisite: baby blue eyes and a peachy fresh complexion. 'Thank you so much for coming,' Saffron told her.

The actress smiled. 'It's the least I can do, it's such a good cause. And it's so good to be back in the country again!' And then she was gone, hustled away togo and spread some more of her sparkle elsewhere.

One of the photographers clocked Saffron's backstage pass round her neck. 'Where's Win, then?' he shouted rudely at her.

Two girls standing near Saffron overheard him.

'Oh my God, is she here?' one of them said. The rumour rippled through the crowd in seconds and the press pack's ears pricked up, ready for action.

'We want Win, we want Win!' someone started chanting.

'What's going on?' Rex had appeared by her side. He cast a quick, anxious look at Saffron.

She didn't want to be anywhere near him. 'I'll leave this in your capable hands,' she said sweetly and made her excuses.

*   *   *

The show was nearly about to start. The coveted front row was packed with A-listers and skinny fashionistas in head-to-toe black, posing behind huge bug-like sunglasses. Harriet had read the biogs on all the designers in the glossy brochure that had been left on her seat and was now trying to star-watch. *Goodness, was that Victoria Beckham?* Her father was sat next to her, shifting around in his seat. 'Damned trousers are about to cut my circulation off,' he grumbled. 'Wish I'd stuck to the plus fours.'

There had been much excitement amongst the Gatsby Road lot when one of the designers, a model down because she'd missed her flight back from Paris, had spotted Abby in the crowd and asked her to stand in. Now the 18-year-old was about to make her modelling debut in front of the world's biggest stars, and a line of photographers.

Harriet's phone, which had been lying on her lap, started buzzing. It was Zack. She picked it up quickly, ignoring a disapproving look from her father.

'Hello?' she whispered. 'I can't talk, the show's about to start.' She listened for a few moments and her eyes widened. 'Daddy, I'll be back in a minute.' With that, she jumped up from her seat and ran out.

* * *

With five minutes to go, the backstage area had taken on new levels of commotion. Someone was shrieking about stretching his dress with a too-hot steam iron, while Bibi Brown had just arrived in a blacked-out Hummer. Looking more like a fresh-faced school girl, she was now fussing over her star model, a stunning six-foot girl called Zuma who'd graced the front of British *Vogue* the previous month. Such was the secrecy of her collection that she'd been given her own dressing area, but one of the make-up girls had had a peek, and reported back that it was spectacular.

Saffron had left her mum and Tom to take her place backstage. As the models lined up like shimmering peacocks she couldn't get over how good the collections were. Forget some amateur show in the Cotswolds, these clothes were the stuff of avant-garde and couture, made for the pages of *ELLE* magazine. Out of the corner of her eye she could see Rex, waiting to get out and open the show. He was pulling at the collar of his shirt anxiously, eyes darting down to the prompt card he was carrying. Despite everything that had happened, Saffron felt for him. It was a terrifying prospect going out there. Taking a deep breath, she walked up and tapped him on the shoulder.

'Good luck.'

'What? Oh thanks.' His expression shifted when he saw who it was. 'Saff . . .'

She shook her head. 'Let's not get into that now. We've got a show to put on, remember?'

He sighed heavily. 'I'm sorry.'

'I know, Rex.'

He gave a ghost of a smile. 'I've walked out on more runways than I can remember. So why am I so nervous?'

'You'll be fine.' She managed a small smile. 'Go show 'em how it's done.'

He cast one final check over himself. 'Do I look OK?'

'You look fine,' she said. Next-door, DJ Rev was announcing his name.

'Here goes.' Taking a deep breath Rex fixed on a grin and stepped out.

Caro watched as Rex Sullivan took to the catwalk in a hail of lights and music. He bore no signs of the struggle that Benedict had broken up earlier, and she wondered briefly what that had all been about. As Rex strode confidently down the catwalk, Caro got a better look at him. He really was a handsome chap—the most extraordinary charisma—but she still preferred Tom. His loyal and loving manner reminded her of her own husband.

The microphone crackled into life. 'Ladies and gentlemen, I'd like to extend a warm welcome to you all. It's hugely exciting to have so many legendary names under one roof.' He looked round. 'As you know, Fashion Cares is more than just a catwalk show. It's haute couture with a heartbeat.' *Nice one, Rex,* Saffron thought from her place in the wings. 'We've got some amazing talent here tonight, as you're about to see.' He went on, 'And we're proud to be associated with the Gatsby Road Community Centre, the volunteer centre in North London which has become an inspiration.'

A cheer went up from the Camden coachload and Rex acknowledged it with a grin. 'The centre has become a lifeline for those less fortunate amongst us, and has given them a chance to realize that, yes, everyone can make something of themselves.' He stared into the crowd. 'No matter what their start in life.'

Saffron had to admit it. Rex knew how to work the crowd. If this didn't get Reuben Gold creaming his pants, nothing would.

His face became serious. 'But the Gatsby Road Community Centre, or GRCC as it is commonly known, can't carry on its good work without you. It desperately needs funds to keep going, to continue making a difference to people's lives. So I'm asking you, fabulous human beings with hearts of gold, to dig deep in your pockets after the show, and start bidding for those clothes!'

'Where's Win?' someone shouted.

Rex's smile faltered. 'I was just getting on to that, she's been delayed, and should be with us very soon.' A cheer went up, although Saffron could see several people from the GRCC exchanging puzzled glances. She groaned. What the hell had he said that for? It was only going to make things worse later on.

'Anyway, folks, we've got a show to get on with.' Rex looked at DJ Rev and the lighting guys, making sure they were ready. 'Get ready to dig in those pockets for the auction later folks, but in the meantime, I'm proud to announce the start of

491

Fashion Cares!'

The ballroom suddenly exploded with noise and light. They were off.

* * *

It may have taken months of blood, sweat and tears, but the show went by in a matter of minutes. Several of the designers had even taken their inspiration from the Gatsby Road Estate itself, with granite-coloured garments and heavy, graffiti necklaces made out of nickel. When Abby walked out, looking every inch the professional in a monochrome tight jumpsuit, the Gatsby Road lot went wild. DJ Rev pumped the bass right up, and the place literally started jumping. With the flashing kaleidoscope of lights, the whole thing felt like one big fantastic disco.

At the end, just when the atmosphere couldn't get any more electrifying, Bibi Brown's showcase started. With stunning separates and fabulous one-pieces, even the po-faced fashion cronies were wowed, scribbling in their notepads furiously. When Bibi sent Zuma storming down the runway in the final item, an iridescent dress with exquisite petal detailing and a long train flowing behind like a lake, the entire front row started squabbling over who would get their hands on it. Despite the traumas of the day, Saffron was practically hugging herself with glee.

There was one giant black cloud hanging over the horizon. The expected arrival of Win. Saffron had scribbled down a few apologetic notes to guide Rex what to say, but as he strode exuberantly out from the wings again, the shouts started up.

'Win, Win, Win!'

The noise became deafening. In a blind panic, Rex did an abrupt turn backstage again. 'What do I do?' he hissed to Saffron. 'They're going to go mental when they find out she's not coming!'

Now was not the time to say, 'I told you so.' As the chanting reached new levels, Saffron shrugged helplessly. 'You've got to get out there and tell them!'

Rex closed his eyes, steeling himself. Saffron watched as he muttered a prayer and walked out to face the braying crowd. It was a fate she wouldn't have wished on anyone.

The cheers and calls took a full minute to quieten down. 'Can we have some hush ...PLEASE!' The crowd looked at him expectantly. Rex took a deep breath. 'I'm afraid I have some bad news. We've just found out that ...'

'STOP!' From nowhere Harriet leapt out from behind the wings. Blinded by the lights, she looked over at Rex, and called out, 'Ladies and gentlemen, I'd like to introduce the Saviour of Gatsby, Winsome Johnston!'

As Win appeared in a wheelchair pushed by Zack, the audience leapt to their feet and started cheering madly. Win, still frail but beaming in a technicoloured kaftan and gold turban, started waving and blowing kisses like a member of royalty.

Backstage, Saffron was hugging Harriet. 'I just can't believe she made it!'

Harriet grinned. 'Win decided she didn't want to miss the show! I told Daddy and he said he'd pay for a private ambulance to get her here. Her surgeon had a blue fit, but eventually gave her the

493

go-ahead as long as one of the nurses came with her. "Exceptional circumstances," is what I think he called it. She's got to go straight back in afterwards. I nearly died when Zack rang me from the M4.'

Saffron peered out again, where Win was still parading up and down in front of the crowd. For once Rex was insignificant, and was watching the show in stunned delight.

She threw her arms round Harriet's neck again. 'Oh, H, we've only bloody pulled it off!'

Chapter 76

The bids flew in thick and fast. By the time the last item—a pair of puffball shorts made out of recycled car seats—had gone the show had raised nearly seventy thousand pounds. Win had been so overcome she'd burst into tears, and even Zack had had a little gleam in his eye.

With the booze now flowing, the Gatsby Road crew were happily mingling with the fashion pack and Gloucestershire's landed gentry. Antoine von Crappe had marched Sue Sylvester backstage to pluck her eyebrows and the retro-themed disco had kicked off, deafening everyone. Alf Stokes, with the energy of a man half his age, was twirling one of Clementine's bridge friends round the dance floor to a house version of 'Agadoo'. Saffron had been slapped on the back and congratulated so many times she thought her shoulder blades must be bruised.

It was just past 8 p.m. when Tom found her by

the bar. It was the first moment she'd had to herself. 'Where have you been?' She smiled.

'Talking to Rex.'

'Oh.' She looked at him uncertainly. 'Where is he? Everyone's asking for him.'

'Now, this you're not going to believe.'

'He's locked himself in the toilet?' she said, attempting a bit of humour.

'Try the M4, driving to catch a flight from Heathrow.'

'What?'

'He's just been summoned back to the States to see Reuben Gold.'

'Jesus, they don't hang around.'

They stood looking at each other, like two shy teenagers on their first date. 'Will we be all right?' he asked.

She took his hand. 'We'll always be OK, babe. I know that now.'

'Saffron!' Someone called her name and she turned to see Win being wheeled out by her nurse. 'They're making me go home now. How boring!'

Saffron could see how tired the old lady looked. She went over and bent down to kiss her on the cheek. 'Thank you, Win. We're just so unbelievably grateful you made it.'

Win chuckled. 'Happy endings all round.' She looked towards the front door to where Zack and Harriet were locked in a blissful embrace. 'Zachary! You going to put 'Arriet down and help me or what? And where's Brosie? He promised me a kiss goodbye.'

'She's amazing,' Tom said, as they watched Win disappear into a flash of camera bulbs.

Saffron squeezed his hand. 'So are you.'

By 10 p.m. the party was still kicking, with several of the guests looking more than worse for wear. Saffron had already seen the husband of a very famous singer disappear upstairs with one of the models. Needing a break from the noise, she made her way out through the house to the terrace where a few people were smoking. She saw her mother, in her Kermit-the-Frog green evening dress, standing at the end. She was gazing skywards with a rapt expression.

'Hey, Mum.' She went up to her. 'What are you doing out here by yourself?'

'Just looking at the sky. Isn't it heavenly?' The light had only just faded, leaving a trail of inky blue smudges amongst the patches of ochre.

'Sure is.' They didn't get sunsets like that in London. Saffron inhaled the fresh air. 'I really am going to miss this place.'

'And I'm going to miss *you*.' Her mum slipped her arm round her waist. 'Is everything all right now?' Babs had seen and heard enough that night to know something very heavy had gone down.

Saffron gazed over the fields. 'I think so.'

'It was a very hard situation, darling.'

'I know, me being here and Tom in London.'

Her mother looked at her perceptively. 'I mean with Rex,' she said gently.

'You knew?'

'It wasn't hard.' Babs smiled. 'Rex is a very charismatic man. But I always knew Tom was the one for you.'

'Mum, can I tell you something?' Despite her outward happiness, it had been consuming her all evening.

'Of course. What is it?'

496

Saffron swallowed. 'Tom doesn't know this, but something did happen with me and Rex. We didn't have sex,' she added hurriedly, 'but other stuff happened.' She was hardly going to go into details. 'We were up in his bedroom and I thought I wanted it, but then something just clicked in my head. I got up and pushed him off me . . .' She looked stricken. 'I just don't know what to do. Do I tell Tom? It was such a mistake, the biggest of my life.' Her voice broke. 'I just can't bear it, he thinks everything's OK again.'

Her mother reached to wipe a tear off Saffron's cheek. 'Darling, we all do things in life we regret.' She smiled sadly. 'That's how we learn what, or *who* really matters to us. You've got to ask yourself, is it worth telling Tom the truth? Because from what you told me, the truth is that you love him very much.'

'So you don't think I should say anything?'

'I think you should do whatever makes you happy, darling. And being with Tom makes you happy, doesn't it? Looking forward, building your beautiful life together.'

Who knew Babs could be so wise? Saffron felt really choked up again. 'Thanks, Mum.' She wiped her nose. 'You're right. It's about the future now, not the past.'

'My sentiments exactly. Why don't you go and find that handsome fiancé of yours.' She giggled. 'I'm very excited about welcoming such a big strong man into the family!'

'Oh yuck, don't talk like that!' They were back on familiar ground and it felt wonderful. Saffron hugged her mum. 'I'll see you later, then.'

Babs watched her beautiful, clever daughter walk

497

back down the terrace. Thoughtfully, she picked up her drink and was heading for the steps down into the garden when a sound made her stop. She leant over the balcony and when she saw the tall, shadowy figure she nearly dropped her glass. Tom was standing there with his back to her, staring out into the distance.

Babs jumped back quickly. He must have heard the whole conversation! Heart in mouth, she shrank back into the shadows as Tom appeared and made his way up the steps. She caught a glimpse of his jaw, eyes almost black in their density.

She had to warn Saffron. As soon as he'd gone inside Babs hurried after him, tripping on the hem of her dress as she went. As she ran into the ballroom she could see Saffron standing at the side of the dance floor talking to one of her friends from work. Helplessly, Babs watched as Tom cut through the crowds and made straight for her.

'Saffron,' she cried, but her voice was lost in the pounding music. It was too late . . .

Saffron was catching up on the gossip with Jemima, a fashion assistant, when she felt someone tap her shoulder. She turned and saw Tom. Her eyes lit up. 'I was wondering where you'd got to.'

As he stood there, Saffron thought he'd never looked more magnificent or handsome. Love burnt through every cell in her body.

'I went out for some fresh air.' His face creased up into a smile. 'Come on, babe, dance with me.'

THE END

498

Thanks to my editor Sarah Adams, you're the best out there and I'm very lucky. That's not forgetting all the great team at Transworld and my wondrous agent, Amanda Preston. Emma Messenger and Helen Rance for their ideal-readering and advice on police matters, and Lainey Sheridan-Young for letting me pick her brains about the world of fashion. All mistakes are my own. I should really also appease my old colleague at *heat*, Kay Ribeiro, for not only mistakenly implying she likes sex in lifts in *Naked Truths*, but then misspelling her name in *Wild Things*. The outrage. Kay, I hope this makes it up to you.

JO CARNEGIE'S FIVE ULTIMATE GIRLIE WEEKENDS, TRIED AND TESTED!

Fun with the girls
The Old Surgery, Tetbury
www.oldsurgery.stengard-green.com

Prince Charles' house is just down the road, but I know where I'd rather be staying. Built in the 1500s, The Old Surgery is a mixture of grand and cosy with open fireplaces, a vaulted dining hall and a high-walled garden, perfect for keeping those pesky Royals out. With only four (double) bedrooms you can hire the place out and live like ladies of the manor. Did I mention the personal chef and spa treatments?

Bonktastic break
The Residence in Bath
www.theresidencebath.co.uk

Sexy luxury is how to describe this converted Georgian town house, ten minutes walk from the city centre. White Company bed linen and champagne on tap, I pulled open a drawer to find an array of sex toys instead of the bog-standard Bible. If you do manage to make it out of bed, get yourself a Fake Bake or manicure at the swish new spa. They do treatments for Blokey as well.

Somewhere to take your mum
Millers64, Edinburgh
www.millers64.com

Mummikins will love this friendly boutique B&B, where you're greeted like old friends and revived with homemade shortbread. The place is stylishly done without losing any of the Victorian features and there's a lived-in library and garden. It's only got three bedrooms so book up in advance. You won't want to miss out on the legendary Millers64 Scottish breakfast.

Pure R&R
St Bride's Spa, Pembrokeshire, Wales
http://www.stbridesspahotel.com

Perched on a cliff top overlooking Carmarthen Bay, St Brides Hotel is a salute to nautical cool. The marine spa is an oasis of calm and you have to try the *piece de resistance*, an infinity pool that drops off the edge of the cliff. I'm always worried about starving in these places, but rest assured the Welsh like to eat. You would kill for the *moules mariniere*. Nice cutlery too.

Party house for a hen
The Hen House, Brighton
www.crown-gardens.co.uk/properties/the-hen-house

I'm still nursing the hangover and wolf mask from this one. For hen weekends you want

OTT and this four-floor chicken coop doesn't disappoint. Think Arabian Nights meets Monsoon interiors with its very own dance-floor in the basement. The HH sleeps up to twenty-four, but there are five bathrooms so you won't end up fighting over the mirrors. Brilliant central location.

Happy weekending!
Jo x